# Family Chorus

By the same author

*Sisters*
*Reprise*
*The Running Years*

# *Family Chorus*

## Claire Rayner

BOOK CLUB ASSOCIATES LONDON

This edition published 1984 by
Book Club Associates
by arrangement with Hutchinson Publishing Group

For Maggy,
who reads all my words twice over.
With gratitude

Printed in Great Britain by
Richard Clay (The Chaucer Press) Ltd
Bungay, Suffolk

# Prologue

Everyone was more concerned with death than with life the night that she was born. First the remote departure of the old queen, launching herself into oblivion from the marble and velvet splendours of the palace of Osborne in the Isle of Wight, and then the much more important death of Milly, sliding away wearily from her short existence in a stuffy back room of the dark little house in Sidney Street in the East End where she had lived with the clutter of children and neighbours who now surrounded her. They fussed over her or sat about uneasily getting in the way, depending on their genders, and paid no attention at all to the scrawny infant lying in the kitchen drawer where they had thrust her as Milly began to bleed so furiously. She was irrelevant as she lay there blinking at the hissing gaslight and opening and closing her minute bloodstained fists, and scowling at the world she had inherited; it was Milly who mattered, not the direct cause of her death.

And even after it was clear that nothing could be done for Milly, who lay dreadfully pallid and silent in a heap of feather bedding and pillows, they sat about and stared at each other and wondered what to do next; and no one thought about the baby, until she opened her small cavern of a mouth and shrieked her fury at her situation.

'Oh, Gawd,' Bessie said distractedly and stared at Fanny, who as the mother of a two-year-old must surely know what to do, but Fanny stared back at her, with handsome dark eyes opaque as pebbles, and said and did nothing. Busha too paid no attention, sitting with her arm placed with ostentatious protectiveness across Shmuel's shoulders. Bessie said again, 'Oh, Gawd,' as the baby wailed even more loudly, and went over to the kitchen drawer and stared down at her.

'Milk,' Fanny said contemptuously, as the noise increased and Shmuel looked up, peering through red-rimmed eyes at Bessie, who stared back at him helplessly and then at Fanny and said, 'Milk?'

'Oh, really, Bessie, don't be so stupid!' Fanny snapped,

and at last got to her feet and went to rummage in the corner cupboard. There was a bottle half full of milk there, and she took it out and then looked round at her husband on the far side of the small kitchen. 'Give me a bit of rag, Dave,' she commanded, 'an' a bit of thread. You can get some from the workshop – white rag –' she shouted after him as, obediently, he went clattering down the stairs. 'Clean white rag –'

Later they all sat and watched as she tied to the neck of the bottle the scrap of fabric that Dave had found and then pushed the makeshift teat into the infant's mouth, listening to the gulping and whimpering sounds she produced as she sucked the bulky rag and filled her small belly.

'Is that the right sort of milk for it?' Bessie said uneasily. 'Ain't it s'posed to be boiled and that?'

Fanny lifted one eyebrow and went back to sit beside Dave again. 'Won't make much difference either way,' she said. 'It's not goin' to do, is it? I mean, look at it – can't be as big as a plucked five-pound fowl and don't look much healthier –'

'Don't you be so sure.' Mother Charnick came into the kitchen from the bedroom, at last closing the door behind her on the sight of Milly dead in the big bed, the sight from which they had all been carefully averting their eyes. 'I've seen worse'n that one. It'll do, poor motherless nebbish – I wish you long life, Shmuel, Fanny, Benny, Joe, Bessie –' She went round meticulously shaking the hands of the chief mourners, carefully avoiding the stepchildren (for who knew better than Mother Charnick the right way to do things?) and at once, as though someone had fired a starting gun, the wailing began. Busha first, producing a wild sound that still somehow managed to sound controlled, and Mrs Feldman from the flat upstairs, and old Sophie from next door, tears streaking down their leathery cheeks as they rocked back and forth in the time-honoured fashion of mourners. Shmuel started then, his shoulders heaving painfully, and behind him the boys Benny and Joe looked at each other sideways, ashamed and embarrassed, not knowing what to do or say, and in the shadows in the corner the stepbrothers, Moishe and Issy, stood in matching embarrassment. Only Bessie sat silently, staring at the baby in the drawer, her face expressionless.

Fanny gave them five minutes after Mother Charnick had

6

gone, breathlessly heaving her huge bulk and her bag of unmentionable bits and pieces through the door (for as the local midwife she felt the need to carry many extraordinary instruments she would never dream of using, but which gave her a deal of authority and wisdom in her clients' eyes), and then nudged Dave sharply and stood up.

'Someone make a cup of tea for Poppa,' she said loudly. 'And a bissel somethin' to eat. You got to look after the living in such times. Bessie, make tea. Dave, go down the corner, get some platsels, she'll still be there, Mrs Cohen, and if she ain't, knock on the window, she should come down. In sad times people got to put themselves out. Benny, Joe, go round the shul, tell the rabbi we got to organize a lavoyah. When you got a death, you got to have a funeral. Moishe and Issy, you go too. Mrs Feldman and Sophie, thank you already for being such good neighbours –'

As usual everyone obeyed and noisily the room emptied, as the neighbours accepted their congé and went sniffing away. The boys also escaped gratefully, clattering down the lino-covered stairs to the street below as their older step-brothers followed them with alacrity, though more sedately, leaving only Shmuel and the women to share the stuffy overheated flat with dead Milly.

And the baby in the kitchen drawer.


On the day of Milly's funeral, all of Sidney Street turned out, and a good deal of Jubilee Street and Christian Street besides, as well as all the neighbouring tiny alleys and roads. It wasn't so much that Milly had been so popular, though she had fitted comfortably enough into this world of overworked women and their too numerous children and demanding men, as that people had an eye to the main chance and Dave Fox, Fanny's husband, was becoming a name to conjure with in this part of the East End. As new in his attitudes as the century, as pushy and hungry and determined as tomorrow was Dave, and Fanny was twice the man he was, as the neighbours well knew; so they turned out in strength for Fanny's mother's funeral and shivah, the ritual seven days of mourning.

Quite apart from anything else, it was a nice social occasion, though of course you shouldn't know of such

7

things, the death of a mother giving birth, nebbish, a terrible thing, but all the same – a break in the dull days, somewhere to go, a chance to gossip over a nice cup of tea after the prayers had been said, and a chance to see the Foxes' home. Dave and Fanny had a whole house to themselves in Arbour Square; none of your rubbish, Dave and his handsome Fanny, and their beautiful son Monty, c'naina horah, a lovely little boy two years old and walking everywhere already, and a lovely home. Nice to have the chance to peer about at the heavy mahogany furniture brought special from Shoolbred's in the Tottenham Court Road (who shopped in such posh goyisha places as that? For everyone else, Wickham's in the Mile End Road was good enough) and the two kinds of curtains at all the windows, Nottingham lace *and* velvet yet, and a kitchen with so many pots and pans it must take all day to clean them. Wonderful.

The funeral went well, as such things go, with everyone coming back to Fanny's house through the misty gloom of the late January afternoon to wipe their feet on the coconut matting at the doorway under Fanny's eagle eye, and then shuffle into her red-velvet-trimmed parlour to shake Shmuel's hand respectfully and then make the rounds of all the children. It caused a little gossip that the stepchildren didn't sit as mourners as well as Milly's own blood children, but Shmuel was a stickler for these things and had said firmly they shouldn't.

'Bad enough my Busha and Moishe and Issy lost their own mother, God rest her sweet soul, and had to say prayers for her – I don't want they should have to do it again, not even for Milly.'

He had managed to convince himself somehow that his older children had been of an age to pray when their mother had died, but of course they hadn't. Everyone knew the truth of it, everyone knew exactly how it had been, for Milly herself had told the story often enough; how she had been such a happy carefree girl in her parents' home in a village in Russia so tiny everyone had forgotten its name; how she had been a person of consequence then, the farrier's daughter, living a good life, spoiled by her parents and spending her days in her father's horse-scented stables and her mother's friend-filled kitchen. Until her only sister had died in the influenza epidemic, leaving behind Shmuel and four babies,

8

none of them even five years old yet.

'Fourteen years old she was,' Mrs Feldman reminded Sophie as they sat at Milly's funeral in London in 1901. 'Fourteen years old, nebbish, and had to marry and be a mother. Terrible, terrible the way it used to be in the stetl, the way they made the poor girl suffer so – but what could they do? Who better to be a mother to her dead sister's children but their own flesh and blood? It had to be – it was b'schert –' They nodded comfortably at each other and took another cup of tea from the ever full pot on the kitchen table.

And, indeed, suffer Milly had. She had learned to cook and sew and scrub for Shmuel and take care of his four clamorous children, and scrape a living for them all from the meagre earnings of his pedlar's tray and what her parents slipped her on the side, though heaven knew it had been little enough as times got so hard that they barely made their own living, and she had learned to cope with Shmuel's appetite for her body.

It wasn't an appetite for her at all, she had soon learned that; to Shmuel a woman was a woman, one was as good as another, and that this wife was Milly, the little sister of his dead Rivka, had mattered little to him. He had grieved only a short time for Rivka, and cleaved so joyously to Milly that by the time she was twenty-six she had not only her four stepchildren to worry over but four of her own – four who had lived, that is. There had been many more who had died at birth or soon after, and Milly had taught herself never to think about them. Just about the ones who lived. She had learned, too, not to think of the stepdaughter who had died, the one who had been the youngest when Rivka had left Milly the inheritance of a ready-made family. Only eight months old, and therefore the one Milly had loved best, that baby had followed her mother and her infant stepsisters and stepbrothers in the awful winter of 1890, leaving Milly, pregnant as usual, to harden her lips to a tight line and never think of her again, little Leah whom she had loved best.

It had got worse, if that were possible. The Cossacks had started their shouting and riding through the village square, and the peasants from the other side of the village near the church had jeered and set fire to the houses of the Jews, and the powers-that-were had turned their heads and seen

9

nothing and done nothing to protect them, and Milly had been very, very frightened. So, indeed, had been everyone; many were the people who were to sit at Milly's funeral in London who had themselves fled from the drumming hooves and burning houses and the wild shrieking people who had been their countrymen. Milly's experience hadn't been an unusual one. She, like thousands more, had stayed fearfully in the stetl while her man went off to seek a better place for them all, somewhere he could bring them where there would be gold lying in the streets for them to pick up, a place where they could sleep safe in their beds, free of the threat of death and disaster at every corner.

It hadn't worked out like that, of course. She had watched him go, comparing her fearfulness with his jauntiness, aware that she was pregnant yet again and sick with the fear of the death that could be to come rather than with hope for the life that she carried; she had soothed the seven children round her skirts and gone to work in the fields to earn enough to feed them till Shmuel should send for them, if he ever did.

But he had, and, hope stirring sluggishly in her, Milly had clutched the precious tickets in her hand and set off, her belly huge with baby and her head solid with terror. The baby had been born – and died – on the ship on the way, but she had coped with that, and with the strangeness of the new home in London, two crowded sour rooms above the sweat shop where Shmuel had a job as a presser, and tried to start a new life where there was no gold to be picked up in the streets but where they could indeed sleep safely in their beds.

So it had all started again, the eternal round of trying to get enough to feed them all, and tolerating Shmuel's constant demands for the comforts of her body and the inevitable pregnancies that followed. One after another they came, those babies, and one after the other they died, and Milly had grown thinner and quieter, and more and more exhausted, clinging to the old ways and the old language in the middle of this alien city that was now her home. She had never learned to speak English, relying on the children to deal with everything that needed a grasp of the ugly speech – for she always hated the sound of it – and limped wearily from day to day until at last she had managed to produce one live child, an English baby, one baby who breathed and cried and went on breathing instead of quietly dying, and died herself in doing so.

'Terrible thing, terrible,' Mrs Feldman sighed to Sophie. 'To leave such a baby as that. Terrible, you shouldn't ever know of such things. And who's to look after it, the poor little thing? Eh? Who's to look after it? Fanny?'

They both looked at Fanny, busily organizing the other women in her kitchen to make tea for all the visitors who had come to pay their respects to the grieving family, and then let their eyes slide sideways at each other, more eloquent in their silence than they could ever have been in words.

Fanny too was asking herself the same question. The baby, to her surprise – and perhaps, though she would have denied that hotly, a little to her chagrin – was still very much alive and making a great deal of noise. It cried often and fed voraciously, still sucking from the rag teat on the bottle full of raw cow's milk and seeming to be content on it – for an hour or so at a time, at any rate.

Obviously the question of the baby and who was to care for it was not going to be settled as easily as she had first thought. Someone was going to have to take on the responsibility, and, excellent manager though she was, and ideal person for the task though she might seem to be to onlookers – for hadn't she a splendid home of her own and a child of her own to prove her ability as a baby carer? – she had no intention of saddling herself with such a burden, even if that burden was her own sister. For one thing, there was something ridiculous about having a sister of that age; the last thing Fanny wanted was to be reminded of her own age at every turn, as surely she must be if she took the child into her home. A twenty-five-year age gap between them – ridiculous.

Anyway, Fanny had had enough of babies and feeds and nappies. She'd got Monty out of them at last, by dint of considerable effort, and she had no intention of getting involved in all *that* again. There would be no more children of her own to fret over – Fanny had quite made up her mind to that and was clever enough to know how to ensure that her decision was implemented – so why should she fret over Milly's? Milly had been a far from satisfactory mother for a woman as ambitious, as energetic, as Fanny felt herself to be; to take on her baby now would be to saddle herself with a burden she didn't deserve.

11

But someone would have to take over the child, and the sooner she, Fanny, gave thought to who that should be, the better. Because if she didn't plan it properly, it would all go wrong, and somehow they'd try to dump the infant on her and then she'd have the trouble of regaining her good name. Whatever happened, she wasn't going to take on the child permanently, but she wanted to be free of her in a way that left her still earning the respect of her neighbours.

She looked across the room at her young brothers, Benny and Joe, and then at her stepsister Busha, and thinned her lips a little thoughtfully and poured more tea. There should be time to have a quiet word with Dave about all this before the family started fussing about the wretched baby. In fact, she'd talk to him this very night, wouldn't even wait till the shivah was over. Getting on with things, that was the key to success; she'd learned that before she was fifteen, had learned the importance of thinking ahead, planning ahead – now she'd prove again just how essential it was.

She took a plate of biscuits to her stepsister Busha and smiled sweetly at her and asked solicitously after her baby Barbara and the boys Sidney and Melvin and actually seemed to listen to the answers for once, while upstairs in the front bedroom the baby lay in the cot that Fanny had magnanimously loaned, and stared with what seemed to be a fixed glare at the square of greyish pearliness that was the bedroom window, her hands again making those rhythmic opening and closing movements. She was an odd-looking baby, with her spiky dark hair and red face and thin scrawny arms and legs, but she was a very live one for all her puniness. After a while, as the sound of praying voices came up from the room below she opened her mouth and began to bawl.


'So the boys'll be no trouble to you, Poppa,' Dave said expansively. 'You'll have all the pleasure of them, such fine boys as they are, c'naina horah, and none of the tsurus. Boys can be a lot of trouble, hey? But for me they'll be no trouble.' He shot a conspiratorial look at Benny and winked at him. 'So, as I see it, it's the best way.'

'I dunno – dunno,' Shmuel muttered, and he moved in his chair as though he was trying to make himself even smaller than he was, and that was small enough in all conscience;

12

since Milly's death a week ago he had seemed to shrivel before their eyes, to have lost some part of his physical fabric. 'What does Fanny say?' He peered up at his daughter, blinking with little twitches of his papery cheeks. 'You think it's all right, Fanny?'

'Dave knows best, Poppa,' Fanny said and smiled at him. 'He's a fine son-in-law, believe me,' and she patted his shoulder. 'Good thing he's here to take care of us all, hey?' She lifted her chin and stared at Busha, who was sitting on Shmuel's other side, both her hands holding one of his tightly.

'So what do you want of my life, Fanny?' Busha said, and there was a wailing note in her voice. 'I should tell my Nathan he can't take his opportunities, he should tell his brother in New York, no he don't want to come? I got my Barbara and Sidney and Melvin to think of, ain't I? And I'll be looking after Moishe and Issy —'

'Oh, sure, they need a lot of looking after, such boychiks they are.' And Fanny smiled even more widely at her stepbrothers, burly and uncomfortable in their suits of heavy serge. 'Eh, Moishe?'

Moishe said nothing, just staring back at her, but then Moishe and Issy rarely had anything to say at home. Large and taciturn men, both close to thirty years old, they lived their secret lives in the sweaty greasy gymnasia of the back streets around Whitechapel in the winter, and at the race tracks in the summer, scraping an uneasy living in ways about which the family preferred not to know. Their announcement, a couple of days after Milly's funeral, that they were going to New York with their sister and brother-in-law had not unduly surprised anyone, though it had made Bessie look miserable and had made Shmuel weep; but then, everything made Shmuel weep now. He seemed to be regarding his Milly much more highly now than he had ever done when she had been alive. But Fanny's reaction to their decision had been to look pained and to murmur about her poor Poppa, and rejoice silently at how well her plans were being aided by the Good Lord.

Now she smiled again at Busha, a sweet, forgiving smile that made Busha's face redden. 'Listen, dolly, we shouldn't argue, we ain't going to see enough of each other in the future that we should argue now. Families is too important

13

they should argue. What's got to be has got to be! And we got to make the best plans for everyone now we lost our Momma, God rest her sweet soul.' She wiped away her tears with her lace-edged handkerchief – nothing but the best for Fanny's nose – and patted her father's shoulder again. 'So, Poppa, it's right the boys should come to us, Dave'll see to it they get a proper trade and behave themselves. Benny's all right, o' course, doin' well enough at Reuben Lazar's, but he'll do better with Dave. And as for Joe –' She frowned at Joe. 'A lobbus like that, he needs a firm hand, and you know how he gets away with murder with you –'

Joe scowled and Shmuel began to weep again, making no attempt to dry his eyes, just sitting slumped in his chair with the tears sliding down his nose, and Busha leaned over him and began to murmur at him, giving Fanny a sharp glare as she did so.

'It's no good being sentimental, Poppa,' Fanny said, and jerked her head at Dave. 'A boy needs a firm hand, he shouldn't run wild on the streets like some low life,' and she managed, by not looking at her stepbrothers, to make it exceedingly clear what she had in mind. 'And Dave, he'll look after the boys good. Me too. Without Momma to take care, who's goin' to deal with their meals and their clothes an' that? You got to see it makes sense –'

'So who looks after Poppa's meals and clothes and that?' Busha said, and once again murmured at Shmuel as his wailing got louder. 'Eh? It's all very well you worry about the boys, who takes care of Poppa?'

'So, Bessie, of course!' said Fanny. 'Don't be stupider'n you can help, Busha, already. Bessie. Who else?'

'So why can't she take care of the boys an' all?' Busha sounded triumphant. 'She looks after Poppa, she can look after the boys. You don't have to go takin' them away from Poppa, he needs his boys –'

'And they need a firm hand,' Fanny said. 'I told you, you got cloth ears all of a sudden, you don't hear? We don't want 'em running wild like – we don't want 'em around the streets. Momma, rest her soul, sometimes they listened to when she cried to 'em. But will they listen to Bessie? Anyway, she'll have the baby to look after an' all. She'll be busy enough –'

The room slid into silence and they sat still, and Bessie

lifted her chin and looked round at them all, a little dazed, for she had been sitting in a dream of her own as Fanny's ringing voice had gone on. And on. 'What did you say?' she said after a long moment. 'What did you say, Fanny?'

'Who better, Bessie? Eh? Who better than her own sister? You'll be just like Momma was, taking care of a baby her own Momma's died, such a tragedy. Just like Momma, you'll be.'

'Me look after her? How can I look after her? I got to go to work. Soon's this week's over, I got to go back to work.'

'No you don't, Bessie, doll!' Dave said expansively. 'You don't never need to work again at that lousy place. Five years you been slaving there and what's it got you? It's time you got a better life, time it was easier for you. We'll look after the gelt, see to it you got enough to pay your way. You stay at home, take care of Poppa and the baby, and be a mensch like the other women.' And he laughed fatly at his joke; to call the women menschen – the conceit pleased him and he nodded at Fanny, highly delighted with himself. And she in her turn smiled brilliantly at Bessie.

'You see, Bessela? We thought – Dave thought of everything. We take the boys, bring 'em into Dave's business, make a better opportunity for them, you give up the work and stay home with Poppa and the baby like a real little balabuster and we – Dave – we take care of the money. You won't want for nothing –'

Bessie felt it rising in her, that hateful cold wash of anger that she knew so well. For as long as she could remember it had been this way; Fanny making plans, Fanny getting the biggest slice of the cake and then giving her the leftovers with a wide generous gesture, Fanny getting everyone's attention and then, with a sweetness that made onlookers purr admiringly, bringing her misshapen plain sister forward to stand dumbly in her shadow where inevitably she would highlight Fanny's own superior charms. Now she was doing it again, getting all she wanted, a husband, a baby of her own, a home of her own, money to spend – and giving her, Bessie, the leftovers. As loudly as if she had trumpeted it to the whole of the East End, Fanny had said it. Bessie Ascher was no good to anyone. No man would ever come along to invite her to join him under the marriage canopy. No man would ever want her twisted little body, with its spine so

15

crooked after the tuberculosis of her childhood, her mousy head, her plain face with its long thin nose and sloping little eyes set too close together, and its slightly protruding teeth. No man would ever touch her flat little breasts or stroke her scrawny thighs. At the ripe age of twenty-one, there was no hope of Bessie Ascher ever having a real home of her own, so Fanny had given her the leftovers – her widowed father and her motherless sister. A secondhand man to take care of, a secondhand baby.

The furious words sizzled in her head, burned in her throat, made her tongue tremble behind her teeth, but they stayed there, held behind her closed lips as she sat and stared dumbly at Fanny's beautiful face, with its big round dark eyes and high colour and even white teeth, and Fanny smiled again, that sweet smile that had always made Bessie want to scream at her, and said, 'You see, Bessela? Dave thought of everybody. Everybody and specially you. You'll have the flat and the baby and Poppa, and the boys'll be out of the way with us – it'll be lovely, believe me. Not as lovely as if Momma had lived, God rest her soul –' she added hastily as Shmuel set up his thin weeping sound again. 'But lovely all the same. So what do you say, doll? Good, eh?'

Still Bessie said nothing, staring at Fanny with her eyes opaque with her effort to keep any expression out of them, and Fanny stared back, her own eyes beginning to glitter a little with irritation at her slowness, and then, as Fanny opened her mouth to speak, the sound that was becoming familiar began again: the high, bawling fury of the baby crying.

Bessie sat even more unmoving, if that were possible, still with her fixed stare at Fanny, and after a moment Busha clicked her tongue against her teeth and went to the bedroom and Shmuel sniffed dolorously as she left him and wept again.

Busha came back, the baby in its scrap of old blanket held against her shoulder, patting the child's back in a slightly distracted fashion, her face crumpled with distress. 'She won't stop,' Busha said. 'Mine always stop when I pick 'em up, but this one just goes on and on –'

'Oh, give it to me,' Fanny snapped, as Bessie made no move. 'What's the matter, you're forgetting already? Melvin's three and you're forgetting already how to deal with a baby?'

16

She took the child from Busha's arm and, with an expert twist of her elbow, set her against her own shoulder, crooning a sharp little sound into the tiny ear, and at once the baby began to bawl even more loudly, hiccupping a little with the effort. After a moment Bessie grinned, a feline little grin that showed her teeth.

'Monty's only two and you've forgotten as well, it seems,' she said. Fanny glared at her and after a moment thrust the bundle into Bessie's lap, and she, moving a little awkwardly, for she had little experience of handling babies, wrapped the blanket round her more securely and tucked her into the crook of her arm.

At once the baby stopped crying and looked up into Bessie's face with a sort of intentness, almost squinting as she blinked and then stared again, and then she hiccupped once more and, with the suddenness of the very young, closed her eyes and slept, leaving Bessie staring down at her with her own face expressionless.

This time it was Fanny who grinned. 'You see, Bessie?' she said, all her good temper returning. 'You see, dolly? She knows, the poor little baby, she knows who she wants. Believe me, Bessela, you got no choice. She's chosen you, she wants you to be her Momma. Who better to decide than the baby? So, what you going to call her? You're going to look after her, you should be the one to choose, eh, Poppa? Bessie can choose her name, hmm? You won't mind that—'

She's doing it again, Bessie thought. She's got her own way with what she wanted, and now she's giving me the crumbs. Choose the name — what difference would that make? She sat and looked down at the baby's face, with its crumpled forehead — for the baby seemed to be frowning all the time — and tried to hate it as much as she hated Fanny.

But it didn't happen. The more she stared at the scowling little face with its tightly closed eyes and sparse lashes, the more she wanted to. There was a satisfaction in looking at it, somehow, a sense of comfort. Staring at the small face framed in the old blanket was a pleasant thing to do and she thought, almost lazily, I must get her something better than that. A shawl, maybe, I could knit her a shawl — and then almost physically shook herself. No, I won't. I'm not going to do it. I'm not looking after her. Fanny can. I'm going back to work—

17

Back to work. Still with her eyes on the baby's face she saw the workshop, saw the banks of rattling sewing machines, the row of goose irons on the great hissing stove, the long scarred wooden bench where she sat with the rest of the felling hands in front of piles of heavy soap-stiffened cloth, and she could almost smell the reek of the steam as the coats were pushed through the big Hoffman pressers, the heaviness of hot machine oil as the treadles roared the day away, the thick ammoniacal stench that came creeping in from the old lavatory in the yard outside, and she felt the ache in her shoulders that filled her when she spent those ten hours every day bent over those interminable hems. Her shoulders didn't hurt now, not after a week of mourning for Momma here at home. The baby lay lightly in the crook of her elbow, warm against her thin chest, not at all heavy like a thick crombie overcoat of the sort she humped about day after day at the workshop—

I don't want to, she shouted inside her head. I don't want to take care of a baby. I want to live for me, for me, me, me! I want to work and learn and make it happen, the way I always said it would, the way it's got to. I can't always have Fanny's leftovers, can't stay here doing what she wants just because she wants it — I want to do what I want—

It's all nonsense, a small voice whispered deep inside herself, a voice full of cool reason. All nonsense — you, dancing — how can you dance? You with your back like a washboard and legs like sticks, how can you dance? You see them in the penny papers, the way they look, the dancers, the way they smile, the way they preen in their fluffy dresses. *That's* dancers, *that's* the way they look, not the way *you* look.

But here's this baby, another little voice joined in, here's this baby and Fanny saying you can stay out of the workshop for always and stay here and look after the baby and Poppa — go to the library, every day. Have time to read books when the baby's sleeping. Time to think about how you can make it better, make the dancing happen, time to—

'Alexandra,' she said loudly, so loudly that the baby opened her eyes sharply and her mouth opened too, as though she were about to cry, but then it closed again as she fixed her squinty gaze on Bessie's face above her. 'I'll call her Alexandra. After the new queen. Alexandra's a pretty name.'

18

'Bessie, for the love of – listen, Bessela, I said you should choose, but *Alexandra*? What sort of name is that for a Jewish baby? It's got to be a name for her mother, of course! Mabel perhaps, or Mary – Momma's Hebrew name was Miriam, so it's got to begin the same – you know that! Why not call her Miriam, even? But *Alexandra*?'

'If I choose, I choose,' Bessie said, and for the first time since Fanny had thrust the baby into her arms stopped looking at the small frowning face and stared at Fanny. 'You said I should choose, so I have. It's Alexandra.'

'Poppa, is that all right with you?' Fanny flicked her eyes away from Bessie's direct stare, visibly keeping control on her temper. 'She's your daughter – you say what she should be called.'

Shmuel had dozed off and now opened his eyes wide and looked at Bessie with his face blank. 'She's Bessie,' he said. 'Bessie–' He mumbled something under his breath and closed his eyes again, and Fanny looked at Dave with her brows lifted slightly and he looked back and made a small grimace.

'Fanny, it doesn't matter,' he said, and there was a warning note in his voice. 'Let Bessie call her what she likes, as long as she don't call her late for her dinner.' He tried to grin at his own joke, and then, at Fanny's stony glare, primmed his lips. 'Let's call it settled, eh? Bessie takes care of her and your father – and I tell you, it looks like he's going to need some looking after. He's taken it bad, poor old Poppa, taken it bad – and I see to it there's money in her purse every week, and shoin fertig – it's finished, it's arranged. The boys come to work for me, and Busha and the rest of them go to New York. Let's have an end to it already. I got work to do at home, got a business to run. I can't stand around here all day, much as I respect your Poppa, you understand. So can we go home already? It's settled, it's finished–'

And so it was. By the time her brothers had taken their few possessions to their other sister's house, and she had rigged up the trappings of baby things, the cot and the little scrubbed pine cupboard for clothes and the nappies and the bottles for feeds and the low chair for her to sit in while she gave her those feeds, Bessie felt as though she had been looking after a baby for ever. She learned to sit with a bottle held just so, so that the baby could get her milk without choking, learned how to boil the rubber teats that replaced the rag one that had started her on her life (Bessie had demanded the most expensive of items from Dave, implacable in her determination to have the best she could get for her baby out of Fanny), learned how to pin her into her heavy terry towelling nappies with the minimum of fuss.

By the time Alexandra was a month old, and had begun to look more like a normal baby girl and less like a ferocious old man, Bessie was beginning to realize that Fanny had, for once, given her something that would really give her pleasure. She may have arranged matters according to her own profit – and Bessie knew perfectly well that it had been Fanny's idea to annex her two younger brothers as extra workers for Dave's flourishing business as a market trader – but in so doing she had filled Bessie's life with something that it had always lacked. Someone who cared for her and needed her and relied on her. Someone who thought she was perfect just as she was, in spite of her ugly face and thin, dust-coloured hair and crooked back. The leftovers Fanny had given her this time promised to be the best gift that Bessie had ever had.

# 1

They were sitting in a row on the wall, eating the cherries they had stolen from the stall at the end of Jubilee Street market. Sammy of course had most, because he had planned the theft, and Barney was getting the second most, because he'd been the decoy while Sammy had filled his hat with the spoils, and the rest of them, Abe and Mossy and Rae, were enjoying the small shares that befitted immediate relatives of the lordly Sammy and Barney. Lexie had done well to get as many as four, and she sat there at the end of the row, bursting with pride at being part of so splendid a company, and rubbing the dark red skins of the cherries on her pinafore to burnish them to a rich glow. When they were bright enough she would hang them over her ears to be earrings and leave them there all afternoon, and not eat them till they were really warm from lying against her skin. A delicious prospect.

'What they do is lie on top of each other,' Sammy was saying, through a mouth so full that cherry juice dribbled down his chin. 'That's what they do. An' then, nine months after, pfft, out it comes, suckin' its thumb.'

'Out of where?' Rae asked and Sammy glared at her.

'None of yer business. This is what boys talks about. If you don't keep yer bleedin' mouth shut, you gotta go away, see? So shut up.'

'She don't have to,' Barney said, immediately aggressive. 'She can talk about anythin' she likes. She's my sister.'

'So? She's still a girl, ain't she? This ain't for girls to talk about.'

'Why not?' Rae was feeling argumentative. 'It's us they pffts out of, ain't it? Girls. So we c'n talk about it as much as you can.'

'It's dirty talk for girls,' Sammy said sententiously and spat the cherry stones at her. 'Barney orta know better'n to let his sister talk dirty.'

'She don't talk dirty!' Barney roared and began to wriggle from the wall, the better to get at Sammy at the other end.

21

'They come out of their bottoms,' Lexie said dreamily.

'Eh?' Sammy turned and stared at her, and Barney stopped wriggling and stayed on the wall, staring at her too. 'What'sat you say?'

'They come outa their bottoms. The front bit of their bottoms. You know, Rae – the bit where you – *you* know. Not out of girls, of course. Only out of ladies.'

'Blimey, she really does talk dirty, don't she?' Sammy said, almost admiringly, and made a face at Barney. 'She's a lot worse'n your sister.'

'They don't,' Mossy said suddenly, in his piping little voice that sounded as though he were about to burst into tears. 'They come outa their bellies – they splits open and they comes out o' their pippicks –'

'Who told you that? That's all a lotta –'

'My brother, he told me, Alf, he said they got brown lines down the middle o' their bellies and that's where they splits –'

'No they don't,' Lexie said and polished her cherries a little harder. They were getting wonderfully shiny. 'They comes out of their bottoms. Joe said, and Joe's a lot older than your Alf. Alf's only nine and Joe's ever so old. He's seventeen. Grown up.'

'My Momma says out of Mrs Charnik's bag,' Rae said loudly and wriggled off the wall, her black-stockinged legs in their over-sized boots scraping against the rough red bricks, which left marks on them. She straightened her pinafore with an air of condescension, very aware of its row of white broderie anglaise trimmings. Rae's mother was a dressmaker in a big way of business and could afford these special touches for her daughter. 'And my Momma knows more'n anybody about anything, don't she, Barney?'

'That's right,' Barney said and jumped off the wall himself. 'An' she said people mustn't talk like what you do, Lexie, so we ain't goin' to talk to you no more. Come on, Rae,' and he pushed his sister in the back to urge her along the street.

'Your Momma don't know as much as my Bessie knows –' Lexie shouted after them, stung. 'Bessie knows everything about anything anybody ever asked her. So you tell your Momma to ask Bessie where they come out – Bessie'll know.'

They were all off the wall now, except Lexie, and Sammy sniggered and hauled his smallest brother, Abe, on to his shoulders in a pick-a-back. 'Garn,' he said. 'From where does she know anythin'? Soppy old maid, that's what she is. No one'd ever want to get on top of her, old hunchback Bessie Ascher. Bessie Ascher, she's a hunchback, Bessie Ascher, she's a hunchback—' and he laughed and, with Mossy at his heels, went running off down the street, Abe bouncing on his brother's back and bawling as they went, leaving Lexie still on the top of the wall which suddenly seemed a very long way from the ground.

She looked down at the cherries in her hand and saw the way the juice was running over her fingers and on to her clean pinafore and tears tightened her throat and made her eyes feel as though needles were being pushed into them and she wasn't sure whether she was crying because of the loss of the cherries, because of her stained pinafore, because she was stuck on top of a wall and scared to get down, or whether it was because of the nasty things they'd all said about Bessie.

The trouble was, she got angry with Bessie, too, sometimes, wanted to shout at her and kick her, the way she went on about things like behaving right and talking right. That was the worst bit, Bessie going on about talking. Auntie Fanny and Uncle Dave never said anything about the way she talked, nor did Joe. Nor did Benny, but Bessie, she went on and on about it. 'Sit up straight, when you speak. . . . Don't talk with your mouth full. . . . Don't say "ain't".'

'Ain't, ain't, ain't—' she said loudly now and jumped, tumbling into the dust of the street and tearing her stockings and barking her knees painfully so that the crying, which she'd managed to stop, started itself off again, and she went limping home to Sidney Street, sniffing miserably and dodging the middle-aged women who tried to stop her with clucks of sympathy to find out what it was that was upsetting her.

The street was bustling in the late June sunshine as the women dragged their kitchen chairs out on to the doorsteps to sit fanning themselves and gossiping with each other as the heat of the afternoon began slowly to dissipate. The smaller children scuffled in the dust, squabbling and playing and squabbling again, and a couple of cats sunned themselves on upper windowsills. Lexie looked down towards Number Twenty-two, hoping that perhaps this time Bessie would be out with the other women, sitting on her doorstep, but of course she wasn't. Bessie never did ordinary things other people did.

She walked slowly along the road, past Mrs Fishman and Mrs Fleischer, heads together as usual as they sat and crocheted the vast pieces of putty-coloured networks they were interminably working with, past old Mrs Arbeiter, asleep in the sun with her head nodding over her vast folded arms, past the old men who stood outside Number Seventeen, the curls over their ears shaking and trembling as they nodded in vigorous discussion of some obscure piece of gibberish. The smells that were so much a part of her life slid into her nose: cats and dust and fried fish and garlic and human sweat and horse dung and hot cloth going through the pressing machines and oil and dirt; agreeable smells that began to make her feel better. It had been fun this afternoon at first, and then horrible because of the nasty things the others had said, but now it was getting better again. And maybe Bessie wouldn't be cross. Maybe Bessie'd be smiling –

She'd been busy all day, first humping her father around the bed as she gave him his weekly blanket bath and changed his bedding – a hateful job, for Shmuel was so heavy and so uncaring of anything she did and so unaware of what was happening to him; it hurt her that he had no modesty left, that he didn't care whether his nakedness was exposed to her gaze or not, didn't care whether she heard him fart, didn't care that he smelt and was so deep in his own private silent world that he probably didn't even know he didn't care. Then she'd cleaned his bedroom from top to bottom, scouring the floor, washing the windows, reaching into the corners for cobwebs and patches of mildew and finally making him his dinner and sitting feeding him with it.

That was the worst part of it all. Three times a day she had to do it, and three times a day she hated it, and hated him for making it necessary and hated herself for hating him. Pushing the mushed up food past his lax lips, catching the slobbering in her spoon, nagging him to swallow, to drink,

24

to eat, to *swallow* for God's sake – it was a purgatory every time she did it.

But then at last he'd been settled, snoring heavily in the clean scrubbed room, and she could turn her attention to the rest of her day's labours. To the living room and its over-stuffed, over-cluttered furniture. That was pleasant to do, because she could take some pride in that, if not a great deal. It was all very well for Dave and Fanny to keep sending her their furniture every time they bought something new and special from the West End – and these days they did that with ever-increasing frequency – but they made no allowance for the amount of space she had to put it in.

The room was barely twelve feet square, yet it contained two sofas, three armchairs and a large mahogany table with four matching chairs as well as all sorts of ornaments and pictures and vases of dried flowers; getting round it took time, and cleaning it took hours.

But still it had to be done, and grimly she did it. Never would anyone say her Lexie lived in anything but the cleanest of homes, the most tidy of establishments. Not for Lexie the casual squalor that was so integral a part of so many people's lives in these hot, sour streets. For Lexie it would be clean and pretty and good. Never mind that Lexie herself seemed to prefer the untidiness of other homes, actually enjoyed playing with the Levys next door, a place where you couldn't see the floor for the piles of magazines they had on it, and where the windows were in a perpetual state of fog, even on the clearest of days; as long as Bessie had any say in the matter Twenty-two Sidney Street would be the place Lexie deserved. Not as palatial as the Foxes' house at Arbour Square, perhaps, but all the same – and she settled to rubbing blacklead into the already shining range and then to cleaning the brass samovar her mother Milly had valued so much that she had carried it all the way from Russia, all those years ago.

Then there was the day's laundry. Lexie's pinafores, and Lexie's vests and knickers and dresses, and Lexie's stockings and handkerchiefs, as well as Shmuel's malodorous bedding and her own few bits and pieces. After that, while the washing dried on the clothes horse, ready to be ironed, the food to be prepared and cooked and set ready for Lexie's supper. A long hot hard day, and all through it, as her muscles ached with the efforts she was making and the sweat

25

stuck her hair to her scalp, the thoughts that kept her sane, the long rich imaginings of how it would be, one day. One day, when Lexie had her deserts, one day when everything would happen for her, one day when she would have silk underwear and pretty dresses and the sort of food that would make her face round out and become pretty, and her hair to curl as lusciously as the Levy child's next door.

Not that she was ever able, in these dreams of hers that filled her head as her arms pumped away, scrubbing, to see quite how it would happen. Sometimes she let herself see her sister Fanny and her husband run over by a brewer's dray as they went strutting down to the market at Petticoat Lane to make more money, and would see herself and Lexie getting Arbour Square and all it contained, but that never really offered any sort of satisfying dream, because, though imagining Dave and Fanny dead disturbed her not a whit, she couldn't bring herself to imagine the death of young Monty. Spoiled, noisy, whining child though he was, he was still a child. Only nine years old – how could she imagine him dead? But if she didn't, he would get Arbour Square and all its contents, so where was the point in making up hopeful dreams for Lexie of getting rid of Dave and Fanny? It just wouldn't work.

She had long ago given up any dreams involving herself. The days before Lexie when she had read her penny magazines about the dancers, had tried to see herself in those filmy ballet dresses, with her hair bound in a silver fillet and her ankles wrapped in pink satin ribbons as she danced, feather-light, in front of a vast and exceedingly expensive audience, seemed like another life now. That hadn't been Bessie who had had those stupid ideas. That had been someone else. A girl of twenty-one who had been too stupid to know what was possible and what wasn't. Now she was a balabuster, a careful housewife who was as near thirty as made no matter, a person with responsibilities, a senile old father, and a child.

A child. Now, sitting at her well-polished mahogany table, the smell of the fish she had fried earlier lingering appetizingly in the air, she heard the shuffle of Lexie's footsteps on the staircase below and lifted her chin in anticipation, and for a moment the fatigued, drawn face brightened and she looked almost pretty in her eagerness and in her pleasure. But the look faded as Lexie came dragging into the room and Bessie could see her.

'Lexie! For pity's sake, Lexie, what have you been *doing*? You look like a – you look like a ragamuffin! Have you no shame? You wanted to play, you said, wanted to play with the other children and I said, all right, you can play, only keep yourself clean. Didn't I? And now look at you! Just look!'

'Fell over,' Lexie mumbled.

'I can see! Did you hurt yourself?' Bessie was on her knees in front of Lexie, examining her torn black stockings and her stained pinafore. 'Is that blood? – oh, my God, is that – no – it's – where did you get that from?'

'Sammy Feld,' Lexie mumbled again, 'gave me some cherries. They got squashed.'

'And where did *he* get them from, hey? I've told you, Lexie, those are bad boys. You shouldn't play with such bad boys – they're dirty and they'll – they'll take liberties.'

'What's liberties?'

Bessie had started to undress her, peeling off the hot black stockings so that Lexie could scratch luxuriously, and then tugging off the offending pinafore. 'Where'd he get them from? ... Stand still,' Bessie said absently, beginning to unbutton the red serge dress the pinafore had covered. 'Liberties? They're – it's just that boys can't be trusted. They hurt little girls like you. Boys are dirty. Never you forget it, Lexie. Boys are bad for you – now come along. We'll wash you and then you can have your supper–'

'I'm not going to bed yet!' Lexie cried, alarmed. 'Am I? I don't want to go to bed! It's only five o'clock and I'm seven now. I don't have to go to bed at five o'clock! Let me put my dress on again–' And she tugged at Bessie's fingers, and tried to escape from her grasp.

It followed the usual pattern, Lexie protesting and Bessie first hectoring and then cajoling and finally giving in, and at last Lexie, clean and with her freshly washed hair lying in damp tendrils over her forehead, was once again dressed in her red serge dress, with a fresh pair of black stockings on her thin legs and her freshly polished boots back on her feet. Bessie sat her at the table and set her supper in front of her, the piece of fried plaice with the very tiny dab of chrane, the fiery beetroot-flavoured horseradish sauce that Lexie adored and which Bessie thought unsuitable for her, and a plate of bread and butter, and the next ritual started: persuading Lexie to eat.

A neat thin child with a natural tendency to be wiry, much as Bessie herself had been, she needed far less food than her sister thought she did and each mealtime was a battle as Bessie tried to fatten up the child to the peach-and-white plumpness she had so long yearned to have for herself, and Lexie, equally determinedly, refused to be stuffed like a Strasbourg goose. As usual Lexie won, and at last she scrambled down from the table and, as Bessie started washing the dishes in the little cubbyhole on the landing which was their kitchen, she started her wheedling.

'Just for a little while, Bessie. I'll come back as soon as the clock says seven o'clock, God's Honour I will, seven o'clock, soon's the clock says seven, I can tell the time proper for myself now—'

'Properly,' Bessie said automatically, her head down over the dishes she was rubbing with ferocious concentration. 'Properly.' It hurt her bitterly that Lexie so enjoyed going to see Fanny, hurt her deeply that the child seemed not to want to spend the long hot evenings here with her in Sidney Street. She often offered to sit and read a story to her, from one of her precious collection of special books, or to take her to the library to choose her own for Bessie to read to her, but it was no use. All Lexie ever wanted to do was to go to Arbour Square, to be with Joe and Benny.

At least, that was what Lexie always said. She adored her big brother Joe with all the passion that seven years old can display. In her eyes he was the handsomest, the funniest, the tallest, the nicest person in the world, and Bessie couldn't deny that her less than virtuous younger brother had developed into a personable young man. At eighteen he was turning the heads of a great many of the luscious black-ringletted brown-eyed girls who paraded along Whitechapel Road these hot summer evenings, and she could understand their partiality for him. Tall, with dark hair that waved sumptuously over a broad forehead and with particularly heavily lashed dark eyes that gave him a soulful look – as false as it was attractive – it was natural that girls should like him. But not little girls like Lexie, his own sister. So, Bessie told herself bleakly as Lexie went on and on with her nagging for

28

permission to go. It isn't Joe she loves. It's Fanny, hateful
Fanny. I wish she was dead. I wish she was in America like
Busha and the others. I hate her—

'All *right*,' she said at length, almost violently, as she hung
the tea towel over the stone windowsill to dry. 'All right, go,
if you want to. Cross the road carefully and come back not a
minute after seven—' And Lexie was gone, clattering down
the stairs in a scramble, terrified Bessie would change her
mind, and Bessie stood at the window and watched her go,
wanting to cry with the frustration of it. Always telling her
off, always fighting with her, instead of—

There was a wailing cry from the bedroom and she stared
down at the street just once more, watching the small red
figure running and hopping along, her damp hair bobbing on
her shoulders, and then she slammed the window shut and
went to see to Shmuel who was probably wet – or even
worse – again. It's something that Lexie's happy, she told
herself miserably, even if I'm not. And if she loves Fanny
more than me, what can I do? Just what I'm doing, looking
after her and loving her. Which is more than Fanny could
ever do.

A little contented by that thought, she picked up clean
sheets from the cupboard in the corner and went into the big
bedroom to take care of her father.

# 2

There was something new again at Arbour Square and Lexie
stood in breathless admiration in front of it, not knowing
what it was for, but greatly impressed by it. A curtain made
of brightly striped canvas hung in front of the door, with big
brass rings attaching it to a wooden rail above. It flapped
gently in the light breeze, showing that the door behind it
was open, and Lexie sighed with delight at the lovely way the
tantalizing glimpses of the inner hall were given to her, and
looked around to see if anyone else was about to see it. It
would be lovely if horrible Sammy or Barney were to walk
past to see the riches that lay within Number Seven Arbour
Square, behind the handsome curtain, and above all to see her

walk in, so nonchalantly, because wasn't she one of the family?

But there was no one there to watch her – just a few birds scratching desultorily in the dust and a couple of old people sitting beneath the sooty shrubs in the centre of the square behind the high railings, and she made a little grimace; that was the only thing she didn't think was as good about Arbour Square as it was about Sidney Street. In the Street everyone was outside as much as inside; they sat in their doorways, they ran in and out of each other's houses and there was always something to watch and someone to listen to; but here in the Square all was genteel silence. People remained inside their own houses, keeping themselves properly to themselves, and although Lexie quite understood that they preferred their houses inside, for if they were only half as beautiful as Auntie Fanny's house they were too beautiful to leave, all the same she regretted the lack of passers by. To be watched going into Auntie Fanny's was something that gave her great pleasure.

She pushed aside the heavy calico curtain, enjoying its roughness against her fingers, and stood in the hallway, cool and dim in the shadows thrown by the curtain, and took a deep breath of its familiar smells. None of the queasy mix of fried fish and heavy yellow soap and Poppa that was so much a part of home, but the faint scent of fresh coffee and cheesecake and wax furniture polish and dried lavender in big china bowls and, above all, fresh flowers. No one had fresh flowers in Sidney Street, unless someone was very ill, but Auntie Fanny always did, and also oranges in a silver bowl. That too was something you only had in Sidney Street if people were ill.

There was something else special about this house; the quietness. Auntie Fanny had the whole house, all to herself, just for her own family. No upstairs neighbours, no downstairs neighbours, just themselves. Not only did she and Uncle Dave have a private bedroom; so did Joe, and so did Benny, and so, incredibly, did Monty. Only nine years old and a room all of his own! This was even more rich than the polished furniture and the fresh flowers and the silver bowls. All that quiet space, all to themselves. To be Auntie Fanny and Uncle Dave – how magical! To be Monty, how incredible! And to be so close a relation as Lexie may not be quite as good, but still was very special, under the circumstances.

Lexie had never asked herself why it was that she addressed one of her sisters as Bessie, by her first name, and why the other, Fanny, had to be given the prefix Auntie, but there it was; so it had been ordained by Auntie Fanny and so it was. She accepted it, just as she tended to accept the way Auntie Fanny told everyone what they ought to do and then made sure they did it. She knew, because she'd heard so much talk about it, that Auntie Fanny and Uncle Dave were extremely clever and extremely successful. They had three stalls in Petticoat Lane as well as a neat shop in the Mile End Road with a big window and a grating over the front door that was locked with a padlock every night at nine o'clock. She knew that a great many people worked for them, and that often meant they didn't have to go out to their businesses if they felt like staying at home. She knew that the whole world revolved around Auntie Fanny – who of course was really the one who made it all work properly – and so she never questioned what Auntie Fanny said. That was the way Auntie Fanny was, and something Lexie would have to put up with. If she didn't, if she argued with her as much as she argued with Bessie, she knew what the result would be. She wouldn't be allowed to visit Arbour Square any more and she wouldn't be allowed to see Joe. And that would be unthinkable.

She hovered now at the foot of the stairs, her head cocked, listening. There was a murmur of voices coming from the parlour and she concentrated hard, trying to discover who it was, and then relaxed. Auntie Fanny going on and on as usual, and Uncle Dave grunting sometimes, also as usual. No sound of Joe or Benny; they must be upstairs, and moving softly she went up, tiptoeing on the strip of carpet that so elegantly covered the central few inches of each tread, biting her tongue for fear of being heard and called by that imperious voice from the parlour. It wasn't that she didn't want to see Auntie Fanny, so much as she did want to see Joe. And Auntie Fanny might stop her.

Joe was there, sprawled on his bed beside the window, and she stood in the doorway peeping round at him, just wanting to look at him for a little while before he saw her. He was wearing just a shirt and trousers, with his best red-and-blue

31

braces showing off the shirt's crisp whiteness very stylishly, and he was carefully combing his hair as he stared at his reflection in the small shaving mirror he kept on his windowsill. There was never a mirror very far away from where Joe was.

'It looks better with the curls,' she said after a moment, and he flicked his eyes sideways to stare at her, and then combed the curls out to make rows of neat waves. 'From where should you know?' he said. 'Are you Vesta Tilley, suddenly, you know everything there is to know about how men should look?'

She giggled and came slipping into the room to curl up at the foot of his bed, never taking her eyes from his face. 'I know what makes you look best,' she said. 'You look best in curls, I heard Rachel Abrahams say so.'

'You're a liar,' he said and looked at her again, and she stared back with her eyes wide and said nothing, and after a moment he made a face at her and began to comb the curls back into existence as she watched him unblinkingly.

'She know you're here?'

'No. I just came up. Where's Benny?'

'Out.'

'Oh.'

There was a short silence, broken only by the sound of Joe's comb moving through his crisp hair, and then she said carefully, 'You goin' out?'

'Mmm.'

'Oh.'

Another short silence and then she said, even more carefully, 'You goin' anywhere nice?'

'Might be.'

'Dancing?'

'P'raps.'

'Oh.'

She held out as long as she could, but it wasn't long. 'Goin' to meet anyone?'

'Haven't decided yet.' He set his head on one side and narrowed his eyes as he stared at the mirror. 'Might.'

'Go to the Paragon.' She said it then, letting it all come out in a rush. 'Go to the Paragon and take me, and don't bother with anyone else, just me and you, like last time. Eh, Joe? Please, Joe? Eh?' And she couldn't help reaching forward and

32

tugging at his shirt sleeve.

'No,' he said, and got off the bed and went over to the
wardrobe in the corner where his jacket waited ready on a
hanger, and began to brush it. 'Got better things to do than
go with a kid like you—'

'Please, Joe! I won't be no trouble, not a bit of trouble.
And I'll go to the lavvy before it starts and I won't say
nothing about anything, honestly, Joe! Please take me, like
last time!'

'I must have been out of my bleedin' mind last time,' he
said and shrugged on his jacket, carefully fastening just the
centre button of the three front ones. 'How'd I look?'

'Oh, Joe, you look wonderful, Joe! And I could look all
right too, if I took off my pinny and tied up my hair like
Rachel does and—'

'Bloody hell, kid! Seven years old and trying to look like
Rachel Abrahams? The Chief Rabbi'll be a pig farmer first.
Do me a favour, dolly, shut up already. I got better things to
do than take out kids. Go home to Bessie, you're gettin' to be
a nuisance.' He set his straw hat over one eye, carefully
perching it on his elegant curls.

She sat very still, staring at him, willing it to happen. It
wasn't difficult; all she had to do was think of her eyes, all big
and round, and imagine the great fat tears creeping up inside
them. It wasn't like real crying, which hurt like needles and
which, when it happened, made her face crumple up and
look funny. This was her own special crying, the sort that
made Bessie look so frightened and sometimes even made
Auntie Fanny relent over something after she had said no,
and which always, *always*, worked with Joe.

It did this time. He stood and looked at her uncertainly,
and saw the tears slide down her cheeks, after hovering
delicately on her lower lashes for a moment or so, saw the
way her lower lip shook and her cheeks flushed with distress,
and swore softly.

'Listen, I'll tell you what I'll do. I'll take you, buy your
seat, see you in, okay? But then I go on my own, right? You
go right home after, no hangin' around and no tellin' Bessie
where you've been, or I'll have her after me, and then you'll
be in it as much as I will. You understand?'

She was off the bed at once, tugging at her pinafore, but he
pulled on her arm roughly, and shook his head. 'You don't

have to go fancying up for me, believe me. If we're going, come on. Be quiet, for Gawd's sake –'

They went down the stairs as quietly as wraiths, listening at the way Fanny's voice was still coming from the parlour, and slid out through the curtained doorway just as her voice stopped and she came clattering out into the hall.

'Joe?' she called, and Lexie, running as fast as she could out of the door and towards the corner after Joe's lanky figure, already several yards in front of her, wanted to laugh out loud, and would have done if she hadn't been so breathless. To cheat Auntie Fanny and go to the Paragon with Joe, all on the same evening! It was wonderful!

All the way there, up Arbour Street on the far side of the Square, across Pattinson Street into Jamaica Street, past all the tight little houses and the street corner shops on into Hannibal Street and at last into Mile End Road, she was hard put to it to keep up with him because he walked so fast, his long legs and the malacca cane he carried twinkling along like clockwork, and he paid no attention at all to her at his heels. But she didn't mind. He was taking her, as he had on that one magic evening in April, to the Paragon. She was going to have a wonderful time, and Bessie couldn't stop her and tell her how vulgar it all was. Wonderful, wonderful, wonderful, wonderful –

It wasn't until they reached the edge of the pavement in Mile End Road that he slowed down and gave her a chance to catch her breath, and they stood there, waiting for a chance to get through the mêlée of vans and horses and buses and brewers' drays and even occasional cabs, and she crept as close beside him as she could, staring over the road to the heavenly, splendid, awe-inspiring place that awaited them.

'The Paragon Theatre of Varieties!' announced the great placard on the front of the building. 'Every day a matinee! Every day a tip-top show!' She shivered with delight as she picked out the words carefully, struggling a little over 'matinee' but not caring that she didn't quite understand. The whole place just looked so exciting that every aspect of it was perfect for her. The bright red and blue and green glass panels across the front, the huge pictures outside on the boards of Marie Lloyd and Vesta Tilley, George Robey and Harry Lauder, the even bigger pictures of jugglers and acrobats and conjurors, the decoration all over the front picked out in gold and red paint – it was all heaven on earth to Lexie. She could almost smell the scent that would greet them as they went into the vast red plush and gilt interior, of dust and oranges and Jeyes fluid and sticky chocolate and of course beer, and she felt almost sick with the excitement of it all.

They got over the road at last, and now Joe was not hurrying, but walking with a marked swagger, swinging his cane with an exaggerated air that Lexie admired greatly, and she scuttled along beside him, looking all around her for people staring at her beautiful Joe.

But very few were, because the attention of the many passers by, as well as the long lines of people queuing for the early doors, was fixed on the small square of pavement in front of the tightly closed entrance to the theatre. There a man with a barrel organ was standing, with a monkey capering over his one-legged instrument and over him with equal celerity, grinding out the tinkling tunes that had to struggle to be heard above the din of the passing traffic.

As Joe and Lexie joined the line for the sixpenny seats – 'It's all right, I'm flush this week,' he said in a lordly fashion as Lexie opened her eyes wide at his extravagance – the tune of the organ changed, became the lilting 'The Naughty Little Bird on Nellie's Hat', and she seized Joe's hand with great excitement and began to caper, much as the monkey was.

'I know that one – I know that one –' she cried at the top of her voice. 'It's the one Maidie Scott sang last time we was here – oh, Joe, do you remember? –' And she began to sing in her high young voice, 'For you don't know Nellie like I do, said the naughty little bird on Nellie's hat –'

'Go on, ducky, give us a turn!' The old woman standing in front of them in the line looked over her shoulder at them and then called as Lexie, looking alarmed, slid behind Joe's protective back, 'Garn, you don't 'ave to look like that – no one's goin' to eat yer, yer soppy little maid! Yer got a nice little voice, you 'ave. Go on, gi's a turn while we're waitin', and I'll give yer a penny –' And she plunged her hand down into the recesses of the many layers of rusty black fabric which wrapped her round and produced a penny. 'There y'are, ducks. Proves I mean it, don't it?'

Lexie stared up at the old woman, now leering at her with her mouth wide open to reveal a few stumps of blackened teeth, and shook her head vigorously, but suddenly Joe reached forwards and took the penny from the old woman's hand and gave Lexie a sharp little shove in the small of her back.

'Go on, then,' he hissed at her. 'What you waitin' for? Sing it, an' dance a bit – go on! Then you can have a bit o' pie in the interval –'

She thought about that for a moment. A bit of pie. He'd given her a piece last time she'd come, a strange confection of meat and onions and heavy pastry, as unlike Bessie's careful cooking as anything she could imagine, but she had liked its strange taste and laughed obediently when Joe had watched her and then roared a great guffaw and said, 'How's that for a bit of kosher nosh, eh, love? Oh, what Bessie'd say if she only knew!' and he'd laughed again.

She looked at him and at the penny in his hand and then at the old woman, now nodding encouragingly at her, with her mouth, glory be, closed in a grin and therefore less disagreeable to see, as the barrel organ again changed its tune and broke into the song she had heard Harry Champion sing last time she had come here with Joe. The words stirred in her memory and as Joe gave her another little shove, so that she found herself on the patch of pavement right beside the man with the barrel organ, she opened her mouth and let the words come by themselves.

> Any old iron, any old iron,
> Any, any, any old iron –
> You look sweet, you look a treat,
> You look dapper from your napper to your feet –

Someone from the queue for the fourpenny balcony shouted then, and it lifted her spirits for it was a cheerful friendly shout. 'Come on, ducks, show us what you're made of!' the voice roared, and then someone else shouted too, and she was suddenly filled with excitement, and twirled on her heels so that her red serge skirts and her white pinafore flew up and her black boots rattled on the paving stones.

The barrel organist grinned at her and nodded his head in time with his music and then began to speed it up and she twirled again, and this time others shouted out and now she began to dance. Not that she knew how to dance, not that

36

she had ever been told what dancing was; it was just something that happened as the tinny little tune, jerky and repetitive though it was, seemed to move into her thin black legs and make them move of their own volition.

She began to sing again, too, as she capered.

All in style,
Brand new tile,
With your father's old green tie on.
Oh, I wouldn't give you tuppence for your old watch
    and chain,
Old iron, old iron!

Now the queue was singing, too, and the organist, quick to see which side his bread was buttered on, rewound his organ so that it repeated the tune, and soon everyone was bellowing it lustily as Lexie went on with her leaping and twirling, now holding out her skirt on each side with a vague memory of having seen someone do that on the stage here at the Paragon last time Joe had brought her here, and tossing her head excitedly from side to side.

It seemed to go on for a very long time indeed, the singing and the excitement of the dancing, and her legs were hurting and her breath was hurting too, for it was becoming more and more difficult to breathe and sing and dance all at the same time, and she stopped and turned to find the comforting figure of Joe. But she couldn't see him and for a moment she panicked as the doors of the theatre began to open with a rattling sound so that the cheaper queues immediately stopped singing and began to surge forwards. She felt herself jostled as the man with the barrel organ pushed her aside to rush along the queue with his hat held out to collect his just dues and for a moment she was very frightened indeed, and felt the tears – the sort she hated – come pushing up behind her eyes. But then they died as she saw Joe at last.

He was standing a little way along the sixpenny queue, now shuffling its way into the theatre, beside a man in a very smart suit and with hair even curlier than Joe's, and with a straw hat set on one side of his head at an even more rakish angle than Joe's. Even to Lexie's Joe-bedazzled eyes, this man seemed to take from Joe some of his glory, and she moved nearer, reaching for Joe's hand as she did so, and stared up at

37

the stranger with her face in a scowl.

'All right, then,' Joe was saying as she came up to him. 'All right, Mr Lazar, if that's what you say. I'll give it a bit o' thought, discuss it with the child, like –' and his hand came down and pinched Lexie's arm so sharply that she whimpered, though the sound could hardly be heard in all the surrounding hubbub '– and we'll see what we can do. Saturday, you say. Tricky, a Saturday, o' course, but we'll see what we can do –' And the man in the rakish straw hat looked at Lexie and winked at her very solemnly and was suddenly gone as swiftly as he had appeared. And she was left staring at Joe as he scooped something out of his hat which he had been holding in his hand all the time.

'Joe, aren't we goin' in? We won't get in if you don't hurry – Joe?'

'We'll get in –' he said absently. He was counting the contents of his hat. 'Look at that!' he said after a moment. 'Bloody hell, will you look at that! Two and eleven, just for you jumpin' around and squawking. And then that chap –' He shook his head at her, his face blank with surprise. 'I tell you, doll, there's no shortage of idiots, is there?' And suddenly he laughed and bent and picked her up and swung her in the air above his head, and she shrieked with terrified delight and reached out to cling to him.

'Come on, doll. We'll go in and get you a basinful. You've really copped it tonight, ain't you? And we'll talk about what we're doin' on Saturday. We could be startin' something very funny here, something bloody funny –'

And he swung her round so that she was riding on him pick-a-back and marched along the line towards the box office.

# 3

'Bloody 'ell, 'oos idea was *that* one?' The man in the flat cap stared at the stage, squinting through the smoke that rose from the cigarette clamped between his teeth, and then shook his head lugubriously. 'Enough to make you cry, that is, if it don't make you laugh. I've 'eard of that there chutspah, but that's chutspah wiv brass trimmin's on it!'

'Poor creature,' the tall woman beside him said, and her voice was rich with sympathy. 'Some of these mothers – reelly they ought to be shet up in boxes, they treat their deah children so cruelly.' Her accent was so refined that the words sounded as though they had been squeezed through a laundry mangle. 'Thet child hes hed no training whatsoevah – and yet they set her on a stage and expect her to be able to perform. It is indeed an insult to the theatah.'

'Yeah, well, I don't know about an insult to the theatre – it's a bleedin' insult to me, as 'as to watch it. 'Oo brung the poor little cow in? D'jew know, Chalky?'

'Mr Lazar,' said Chalky, leaning on the ropes of the tableau curtains and watching the stage with the glazed stare of extreme boredom. 'Said as 'ow she was to go on around the middle, so's to be comfortable. One of the tribe, I dare say. Always is, ain't they?'

The tall woman beside them drew herself up and lifted her chin so that she looked like an affronted turkeycock. 'If you intend that remark to be an aspersion cast on the integrity of Mr Lazar, who is a Jewish *gentleman* of the highest respectability, and certainly *not* given to any – ah – acts of dubious – ah – practice, I must tell you that – '

'Oh, all right, Madame, all right. Give it a rest,' the man in the flat cap said. 'Meant no 'arm, for Chrissakes. Only said what everyone knows, which is that we all like to look after our own. I look after mine, you look after yours and Alex Lazar looks after 'is. Stands to reason – s'only natural. Thank Gawd, she's nearly done, poor little cow. Will you look at 'er. S'nuff to make yer cry into yer beer – '

'An' it's weak enough already,' said Chalky, and began to haul on the ropes to close the curtains as a thin splatter of applause, well laced with shouts and boos, came from the auditorium. The tall woman lifted her chin even higher and swept off towards the backstage area, leaving the two men to stare after her and grin at each other, as the small child in the white dress and black stockings came off the stage and pushed her way between them.

Her face was white and very stiff, and her eyes wide and dark in her pinched face. There was a thin film of sweat across her forehead and upper lip, and she wiped the back of one hand across her mouth tremulously as she reached the pool of light thrown into the wings by the off-stage floods.

'I'm – where's Joe?' she said, in a thin little voice, staring up at the man in the flat cap. 'Have you seen my brother Joe? I want Joe – '

But before he could answer her the orchestra on the other side of the wall of red curtains sprang into life again and Alex Lazar, resplendent in a tail coat and with a white tie carefully knotted beneath his exceedingly high white collar, swept past on to the stage, signalling to Chalky to raise the curtain as he did so. Obediently Chalky hauled on his ropes and the curtain swept up. Alex Lazar marched to the centre stage and held up his hands imperiously as though to still a roar of applause, which was in fact totally absent. The audience was producing a low growling muttering sound redolent of discontent rather than pleasure, and the man in the flat cap shook his head gloomily, and made a face at the child still standing at his feet.

'Got orf just in time, you did, ducks,' he said. ''N'other coupla minutes and they'd'v'ad yer guts for garters – '

'Ladees and gennelmen of Mile End!' Alex Lazar was bawling, as the orchestra settled down to a steady tumty, tumty, tumty, tum. 'Ladees and gennelmen of taste and judgement, as I must perforce call you! The next item in our show of our newest young talent is a very special one, one that'll make your hearts beat with the joy of new discovery, one that will make you sit up straight in your seats and cry, "Now, there is an *act*!" I do not deceive you, ladees and gennelmen, I do *not* deceive you! As I live and breathe, I, Alex Lazar, assure you that this next act is the one you've been waiting for – the one we've all been waiting for – the enchanting, the dainty, the delicious, the lovely Madame Gansella's gorgeous Girlies! And to add to your pleasure and delectation, her Bonny, Bouncing, Bee-utiful Boys! Ladees and gennelmen, I give you – Madame Ga-an-*sella*!'

The audience still muttered, but a little less noisily now as the tall woman who had disappeared backstage now reappeared, swathed in a vast purple garment that seemed to have no shape at all, but which shimmered very fetchingly in the lights, and swept on to the stage to bow magnificently to the audience and then across to the piano which was set on the far side. She sat herself down at it, and with wide sweeping movements that displayed a great deal of white arm embellished with glittering bracelets and rings produced a rippling arpeggio which would have sounded better had the piano been in tune. But she rode superbly over this, throwing her head back in appreciation of the sound, as though it had come from a perfect Bechstein, and created another arpeggio, this time nodding her head violently back towards the wings.

At once there was a rustle of sound and Chalky stepped back, pulling on Lexie's shoulder as he did so, and with a rush half a dozen children pushed past her, small girls in very fluffy pink dresses, which stopped at mid-calf to show ballet slippers fastened with wide pink ribbons, and with wreaths of pink daisies round their heads over cheeks which had been painted a matching bright pink. They also had blue-shadowed eyelids and pencilled brows, and Lexie stared at them with her own eyes wide as they bounced on to the stage, followed by a cluster of boys, all dressed in miniature versions of the white tie and tails that Alex Lazar was wearing.

The piano increased in speed as the children began to dance, with a great deal of swooping and swaying and a lot of noisy stamping from the boys, and Lexie for a moment forgot her desperate need for Joe and the urgent desire to get away with which she had been filled a few moments earlier, and crept closer to Chalky so that she could peer round his legs and watch. Each child wore a fixed grin and each snapped his or her head round sharply with each twirl, an effect which Lexie found fascinating, and she jerked her own head from side to side in unconscious rhythm with them. Chalky laughed above her head and said, 'If you'd done it that way when you was on, you'd 'a done better, ducks!' And she reddened and shrank away from him and felt again the rush of terror that had filled her earlier.

'Where's Joe?' she said and her face began to crumple as the tears suddenly leapt up inside her. 'I want Joe – ' And now her face was tight with misery and the tears were running down her cheeks.

'Oh, Gawd, 'ere we go – a right little bawler we got 'ere – now what do I – Oy! Mr Lazar! This is one o' yours, ain't it? Cryin' for its mother, it is – get it aht of 'ere, do me a favour already –'

'Oh dear, oh dear, what have we here? A little oyden pisher? Peeing with the eyes, yet? That'll never do! Come,

41

now, dolly – let's sort you out then – come on.' And Alex Lazar bent and picked her up and held her against his shoulder, and after a moment of holding herself rigid and pulling away from him she gave in and allowed herself to weep bitterly and luxuriously into the black barathea.

The sound from the stage – now a piping rendition of the highly sentimental Chirgwin song, 'The Blind Boy' – diminished as he bore her away, and she sniffed dolorously and wept more and then relaxed a little as the sound became even more distant. They had clearly left the stage behind and were walking along an echoing corridor and then into a big room with several people in it; she could hear conversation.

'Well, here she is!' he said with a booming sound to his voice that made Lexie stop sniffing and keep her head still for a moment. 'I'd have brought her sooner, only I had to get the Gansella lot on – she's a bit upset, poor little boobalah – ' And he jiggled her a little against his shoulder, at which Lexie lifted her head and tried to wriggle out of his arms. To be treated like a baby had stopped being comforting.

'Joe?' she said and looked around, squinting a little against the bright light after the comfortable darkness of Alex Lazar's shoulder 'Where's Joe?'

'Here.' Joe growled it, and she slid out of Alex's arms at last and stood beside her brother, holding on to his jacket hard, though he tried to flick it away from her grasping fingers.

'Not quite the ticket, eh?' he said and his voice sounded even to Lexie to be filled with a studied nonchalance. 'Not quite up to snuff this time?'

'You could say that,' Alex Lazar said a little sardonically, and then bent and patted Lexie on the head. 'Not her fault, though, no, nor mine either. Can't win 'em all, can we? It was just seeing her outside t'other night – she really had something. Lots of chein, you know what I mean? Style. Sweet little thing, dancing like a little – well, I dare say I got it wrong. Thought she'd had some training, you see, and I have to tell you, it's that that counts. Talent's all very well but you got to bolster it with a lot of real how's-your-father. The easier it looks, the more training in it, you see, and watching her I got the impression – well, there it is. Sorry you were troubled.'

'Well, we'll settle for the half dollar then and call it a day – '

Joe said, and suddenly Alex Lazar's voice lost its friendly note.

'Half a dollar? For a kid that can't so much as walk on a stage in time to the music, let alone dance? You must be joking!'

'You said half a dollar,' Joe said stubbornly. And his voice, though a little shaky with anxiety, came out strong and loud. 'A deal's a deal – '

'I'll say it is, boychik, I'll say it is. You told me as this child could dance, and I booked her for the talent show on the understanding that what you told me was the truth. If you reneged on the deal by giving me a bad artiste, there's no call for me to keep to it, is there? Let's not get nasty about this, eh? Let's be gennelmen and call it a day – '

'I never said that she was a trained dancer – ' Joe said hotly and at once Alex held up his hand and began to argue with him, and as she stood there between them, listening to the anger grow in the voices above her head, Lexie's tears started again. She felt dreadful, sick and frightened and very, very lonely. It was as though she weren't there at all with Joe, as though she were completely on her own, with a lot of strangers, and what was worse, strangers who fought over her the way she had seen cats in the street fight over a fish head. It was horrible – but it was something else as well. There were different feelings growing in her as she listened to the squabbling going on and on about whether or not the promised half crown had been earned and would be paid. They were not feelings she yet understood, but she was aware of them and the way they filled her with a sort of painful heat. It was a disagreeable sensation, and yet – and yet it wasn't, and she stood and listened and tried to understand.

More people came into the room, and for the first time she looked around, tried to see where she was, and discovered that it was indeed a big room, cluttered and noisy, with old chairs and sofas scattered about and a table in the corner where bottles and glasses made a cheerful huddle. The people there were much more interesting than the room itself, however: a conjuror in red plush tights with his face as painted as the women she sometimes saw in Commercial Road, and a man in a brightly checked suit and huge shoes with his face adorned with a great red grin and an even redder nose, stood talking earnestly with their heads together in one

43

corner, while women in dresses as frilly and pink as the children who had gone dancing on to the stage after her own ignominious departure and with heads covered in girlish curls but faces as lined as old Mrs Feldman's down the street, chattered busily in another. There were men with bald heads and moustaches wearing very neat black tail coats and white ties knotted as carefully as Alex Lazar's, over baggy old trousers and carpet slippers, sitting in a group drinking beer. There were men in overalls leaning against the wall smoking stubby little pipes and whispering together conspiratorially. It was all very confusing and alarming and also exciting.

But the most exciting were the people who had just come into the room – the children who had gone dancing past her on to the stage. She stared at them as they came pouring in, all chattering shrilly, and tried to think how old they were. Very old, she decided, for they were all a good deal taller than she was, and anyway they seemed to be very knowledgeable. One of them, a particularly tall boy with very smooth dark red hair cut in a fringe over his straight eyebrows, was helping himself to beer, as coolly as though it were a glass of water, and she stared at him open-mouthed, and then, when he caught her eye and winked, blushed crimson and looked away.

'Still heah, then, my deah? Not gone running away from our deah old theatah, after all?' It was Madame Gansella, sweating heavily under her thick make-up and seeming somehow less alarming than she had when Lexie had first seen her sweeping on to the stage.

'Just leaving,' Alex Lazar said firmly. 'All right, already, Have your half dollar. If you're so hard up you got to nag for it, take it already – ' and he began to fish in his trouser pocket.

'It's not for me, it's for the kid,' Joe said defensively and took it, but made no move to give it to Lexie. 'And anyway, a deal is a deal – '

'Don't start that again, for Gawd's sake. I told you, an untrained dancer I didn't take. It's a mistake, all right?'

Madame Gansella shook her head. 'I thought as much!' she said regally to the room at large. 'No training, you see! None of the polish that a little education at the right hands can provide! That was this deah child's problem. Lots of telent, I hev no doubt, but it needs nurturing, needs the care of a

44

teacher who has the inspiration to help a child partake of the joys of creative dancing –'

'Do me a favour, Poppy! I ain't the kid's mother! You can't get me to fork out the necessary. I saw the kid on the street with the barrel organ, thought she danced well enough – the queue were eatin' her up, I tell you – and I thought I'd found a good 'un. Got a bit of chein, you know? Not pretty but got something about her – a good 'un, I thought I'd found. And I hadn't! So this time Alex Lazar got it wrong – win a few, lose a few. But she's nothin' to do with me. You want a new pupil? Go talk to her brother here. He's the one reckons he's got her best concerns at heart –' and he threw a sharp little glance at Joe and went across the room to talk to one of the men from the orchestra, picking his way through the pink fluff that was the children sitting on the floor in the middle and squabbling over the plate of broken biscuits that one of the acrobats had good-naturedly given them to keep them happy till the second show of the day should start in an hour's time.

'So you're the deah child's brother, are you?' Madame Gansella said, and Lexie lifted her head to listen, fascinated by the odd mixture of rich tones and strangled vowel sounds. She'd never heard anyone talk in that particular drawling fashion in Sidney Street, nor even in Arbour Square.

'She has considerable potential, you know, considerable –' And Madame Gansella lingered over the word with some relish. 'Yes, indeed, young sir, con*side*rable potential. But she needs careful training, you understand. Careful teaching by an expert of sensitivity and integrity. One who can recognize the telent in a young performer, and bring it to flower by tenderly nurturing it –'

'Yeah, and that'll cost a bob or nine,' muttered a voice in Lexie's ear, and she turned her head sharply to see the boy with the smooth red hair standing close beside her. 'If not more,' he added and grinned at her. 'Want a biscuit? It's all garbage, of course, but it'll see you through to the next show.'

'Next show?' Lexie said, as the talk went on above her head between Joe and the vast purple shape of Madame Gansella. 'I'm not doing anything else here. I was awful. Joe told me to dance but he never told me how and I – I didn't know what to do. I was awful, wasn't I?'

45

He looked at her consideringly, his head bent to one side, and then he grinned. 'Yes,' he said. 'You were awful. But what's that got to do with anything? None of us is all that good. It's just that she —' and he jerked his head sideways, '— she knows how to make it look as though we're good. I'll grant her that. Silly old bitch.

Lexie's eyes widened at the bad word. 'How?'

He shrugged. 'I dunno. She just gives lessons and makes you count and shows you how. You don't have to be no good to do it. Just what she says. My Mum thinks she's the tops, goin' to make the family fortunes with me, my Mum, but I don't reckon. She just takes the money and nags us. And the old man.'

'Old man?'

'Her old man. Never mind about him. Boring old fart, he is.'

'You talk very rude,' she said reprovingly, and he laughed, so that his teeth showed very white against his painted face.

'Me, talk rude? You should hear some of 'em. Filthy! Daisy over there, and Baby Maisie — she's worse'n a Billingsgate porter! If you start lessons with the old bitch, you'll soon find out what talking rude's all about.'

She shook her head, alarmed. 'I'm not taking no lessons!' And she looked back over her shoulder at Joe and Madame Gansella, still in close colloquy. 'Bessie —' and then she stopped, suddenly, and stared at the boy again. 'What happens — taking lessons?'

He made a grimace. 'You work, that's what. She makes you practise all day, and then at night and on matinees we go and dance. All over the bloody shop. In a charabanc. It's a bit of a laugh sometimes —'

'What about school?'

Again he grinned, a sight she was beginning to enjoy seeing. 'Well, what about school?'

'Don't you have to go?'

'Sometimes. When they catches up with her. But most of the time nobody cares either way. S'long as you can read a bit it's all right. Got to be able to read because sometimes you have lines to say and if you can't read 'em to yourself, you got a problem. Can you read?'

She bridled. 'Of course I can. I'm seven — nearly eight! Well, seven and a half.'

'Ever so old,' he said, and laughed. 'I'm eleven and I can't, not properly. But she don't know. I get the others to tell me.'

'I'll read for you,' Lexie said, and went a little pink. 'I'm good at reading. I'm not good at sums, teacher says at Jubilee Street – that's where I go to school – she says I'm no good at sums, but I'm ever so good at reading. I could read when I was four – '

'Show off,' he said, but there was no rancour in his tone. 'Anyway, you can't read for me. We'll be off again next week. Over to Stoke Newington we are. Then to Stamford Hill and Finsbury Park. All over the place we go – '

'Can't I come with?'

'Only if you take lessons with her. The old bitch. Then you can – if you learn fast enough. She's lookin' for another girl, a little one like you. Jenny there, she's started to grow a chest, she has. Looks terrible, and the old B don't trust 'em, not once they've started their you-know-who's and get chests. Says they get themselves knocked up too easy. That's why she's going on at your brother there. She wants him to say you can have lessons so's she can put you on the line and get rid of Jenny 'cause you're so little.' He nodded sapiently. 'There's nothin' I don't know about what goes on in her business. It's the only way to get what I want, makin' sure I know what's goin' on.'

'Joe can't say if I can have lessons,' Lexie said, and frowned. 'Only Bessie can say that.'

'Yes?' the boy with the red hair said and moved away. He was beginning to get bored with her now; she knew that look, had seen it often enough on Barney and Sammy's faces. It was a look that big boys always got sooner or later when they talked to her. She never minded when the others did, though, because they were only Barney and Sammy, but now she did. She wanted this boy to be interested in her all the time and to talk to her all the time, and she turned her head towards Joe to listen to what he was saying. It was suddenly important to know.

'Nothin' to do with me, Missus. I told you, I'm just her brother. Thought it'd be a bit of a lark when Mr Lazar said bring her to the show – now I got other things to do. So never mind askin' me. It's got nothing to do with me –'

'Well, perhaps the family will care to consider the matter.' Madame Gansella dug into the dolly bag that hung on her wrist to fish out a piece of pasteboard. 'Mai card,' she said grandly, and put it into his hand. 'Ai can be reached at this address on most Sundays. If the femily are prepared to consider giving this little deah here her chance, and the opportunity to develop her undoubted gift with a teacher worthy of her telents, they may call upon me.' She bowed at Joe, smiled distantly at Lexie and patted her head, and went away across the room, making unerringly for the table where the bottles and glasses were.

Leaving Lexie to pick up the piece of card that Joe had stared at and then dropped on the floor before pushing her on her way towards the door and home and Bessie.

# 4

By nine o'clock Bessie was almost frantic. She had sat at the window until it was too dark to see out properly, and then had gone to stand at the street door to stare down the street, keeping one ear cocked for a call from Shmuel. The little squares of window along the street sprang into life one by one as householders lit their lamps and then, as the gaslighter made his slow erratic progress along the kerb, the grey street too became more visible, and she squinted towards the end of it as though that effort alone would be enough to make the small figure materialize.

But there was no sign of her, and distractedly she ran back upstairs and looked into Shmuel's room, where he lay staring up at the ceiling in his usual blank silence, and then ran down again. She had to go and find her, had to see what had happened, but Shmuel – what should she do about Shmuel? To leave him alone was unthinkable, and Mrs Feldman downstairs had gone to visit her newly delivered daughter and infant grandson, and Sophie from next door was playing her usual game of solo and would never agree to stop even for one hand just to oblige a neighbour. And Lexie wasn't home and it was dark and she'd promised faithfully after last week's trouble about coming home late that she'd come straight home from Fanny's – and Bessie began to weep, her face twisting into ugly little crevasses.

There was nothing she could do; yet she had to do something, and she ran upstairs again to look at Shmuel, lying in exactly the same position as she had left him, and then went down again, not taking her coat or her hat – she who was always so punctilious about dressing properly! – and went running down the street. She didn't lock the front door, feeling obscurely that this would be safer for Shmuel, alone and helpless in bed, though by the time she had reached the end of the street she wished she had, but it was too late to turn back. She had to find her Lexie, had to find her now – no time to waste –

When she reached Arbour Square she was wet with the sweat which had been drawn from her through fear as well as effort, for now she no longer attempted to control the terror that filled her. She saw vision after vision: Lexie run over by a horse and cart; Lexie crumpled and silent in a back room somewhere, destroyed by some murderer's hand; Lexie in the hands of the doctors at the London Hospital, struck down by some mysterious plague; and she was gasping with the sobs that filled her and her eyes were staring and fixed as she ran up to Fanny's front door and banged on it.

The first person she saw as the door opened was not Benny, who had his hand on the latch, but Lexie behind him in the hall, and she pushed Benny aside and ran in and fell on her knees in front of the child and tugged on her arm desperately, crying her name and repeating it over and over again.

'What's going on here? What on earth is all the row about?' Fanny's voice cut across the noise of Bessie's tears and the loud wails which Lexie had immediately started to produce, and she came out of her parlour with Dave close behind her as Joe came out of the kitchen with a cup in his hand and stopped short at the sight of the fuss.

'Where were you? Where *were* you?' Bessie cried. 'I waited and waited, and your supper was ready and I watched the street and – where were you? You promised me you'd come straight home at seven o'clock, it was nine o'clock already, and you still hadn't come, just like last week – where were you? What did you – '

'Bessie, be quiet! What's all this fuss? She's here, she's all right, what are you making such a drama about?'

'I thought she was hurt, thought she'd been – ' Bessie

shook her head and got awkwardly to her feet, and rubbed her eyes with one hand. 'I thought God knows what had happened – '

'But you knew she came over here!' Fanny said, and reached in her pocket and gave a handkerchief to Lexie. 'Stop that noise, Lexie! At once! Bessie, you're being ridiculous. She came here. Joe said he'd take the child out a while, what harm could she come to with us? You're not her only sister, you know. You're not the only one she can be with!'

Bessie stared at her, her face white beneath the tear stains. 'What did you say?'

'You heard me! You're making a ridiculous scene over nothing. Such a fuss when the child's with us!'

'I told her to come home at seven. It's time she was in bed, a child of her age!'

'So *I* said she could stay up, all right?' Fanny said coolly, and stared at her challengingly. 'So what are you going to do? Wash your hands of her? Send her here to live with me? She'd be company for Monty, why not, eh, Dave? She's my sister too. I can give her as good a home as you can – anyway, you've got Poppa to look after. I'll have her here, you can stop worrying and getting yourself so hysterical over where she is.'

'No!' Bessie shouted it, wanting to run across the hallway and hit out at that smooth handsome face and straight back, so different from her own, wanting to shriek her sense of injustice at the effrontery of Fanny's suggestion. Seven years of Lexie to be taken away, now that the long sleepless nights when the baby wouldn't sleep were over, when the struggle to teach her to be a well-behaved nice child who would have a better life than Bessie had ever thought possible for herself was at last beginning to show fruit? Seven years of dreaming and wanting and loving and worrying to be thrown away just like that because Fanny wanted someone for Monty to play with, because Fanny was at last beginning to see that Lexie could be an asset rather than a nuisance? She wanted to spit it all out, but all she managed was, 'No!' in a tight choked voice as she leaned over and pulled Lexie's arm again so that she was standing closer beside her. Again Lexie began to wail, tired and frightened now, and confused, and at once Fanny threw her hands in the air and turned to Dave and said loudly, 'You see! The child wants to come to me! She'd be

50

happier, better off without all this nonsense – '

'Do me a favour, Fanny!' Dave said disgustedly. 'Ain't I got enough problems with your brothers? Lay off already – ' And he went back into the parlour, slamming the door behind him.

'You see what you're doing? Upsetting Dave now with all your nonsense! Lexie, shut up! You see what you're doing, Bessie? I tell you, the way you are now, hysterical – you're not fit to look after her. You're upsetting Dave and he's a hard-working man, needs peace and quiet in his own home. A fine thing my own little sister can't come here but I have a great mishagass made! I won't have it – she'll come here – an end of it!'

Bessie bent and picked up Lexie awkwardly but firmly and held her close. Her own diminutive size and crooked back made the child look big in her arms, but she stood with her chin up and stared at Fanny very directly.

'You try and you'll see what happens. Seven years she's been mine, and so she stays. You try to take her away and I won't answer for anything that happens. You hear me? I'm telling you she stays with me.'

'So maybe she's got her own ideas,' Fanny said, and for the first time sounded a little uncertain, a rare note in that loud and self-confident voice. 'So maybe we'll ask her what she wants – '

'I want to go to bed!' Lexie said suddenly, and rubbed her face with both hands and then scrambled out of Bessie's arms to the floor. 'I want to go to bed – ' She ran to the front door and pulled it open, and Benny, who had stood silently watching all the fuss, stepped aside and let her.

'I know what she wants,' Bessie said, and her voice was flat and expressionless. 'She wants to stay with me. Good night.' She followed Lexie out into the street, and left them standing there, Joe still with the cup of water in his hand. Lexie seemed to have forgotten she'd asked for a drink.

'So don't stand there like a dummy,' Fanny snapped at him, as the door closed behind them. 'You've done enough harm for one night, shlapping the kid out that way, getting Bessie all stirred up! And if we get lumbered with her, it'll be your fault. Don't we do enough for you already, you have to make problems for Dave and me? Do we deserve it? I ask you, do we?'

'Listen, I didn't say she should come to live here!' Joe said, and his voice took on a faintly whining note. 'It was you said that – '

'So – I was provoked,' Fanny said. She turned and opened the parlour door and marched in. 'Dave, you'll have to do something about all this. I can't have Bessie making such a megillah all the time – '

'If anyone's making a megillah it's you,' Dave grunted. 'Shut up already, Fanny. The kid's not coming here. You know it, I know it. You were just talking the way you do sometimes, so shut up. I got an early start down in the Lane tomorrow and so have the boys, the last thing we want is you carrying on at us. It's over, forget it. She ain't coming here. Enough I got to keep them and have the house full of your brothers, I don't need no more aggravation – '

Bessie couldn't get it out of her mind. All the next day and the day after, and all through the week that followed, the spectre of it rose in front of her eyes. Fanny, swooping down on Sidney Street from Arbour Square to take Lexie up in her arms and spirit her away. Fanny loitering at the school gates, watching to steal her away, even Fanny coming in the night time to creep into her room and – it was ridiculous, but all the same she worried and fretted and was silent and grim as she moved through her daily work with Shmuel and the flat.

Lexie hardly seemed to notice any difference in her. She went to school as usual, came home as usual, but, not as usual, sat on the windowsill staring out at the street in the evenings with a book on her lap, instead of wanting always to rush out and play with the other children. She could think of nothing but the boy with the smooth dark red hair. Every time she thought of him there was an odd feeling inside her chest, a sort of tightness, and she liked the feeling and thought about him often, just to get the feeling again. But it got more and more difficult to conjure it up as the week wore on, and the memory of his face faded a little from her mind.

And that alarmed her, because she didn't want to forget him and she began to think about how she could see him again. No good going back to the Paragon Palace of Varieties, even though it wouldn't be too hard to get there on her own, without Joe. No good asking Joe to help her – and it was strange how now she thought about the red-haired boy all the time just as she used to think about Joe, without thinking less of Joe; very strange, that – because one of the few things Bessie had said to her since all the fuss that awful Saturday evening was that she wasn't to go to Arbour Square again, no matter what. And even though it usually was easy to get Bessie to do what she wanted, this time Lexie knew she meant it. She couldn't risk it. Joe was not accessible.

So what could she do? She thought and puzzled and imagined him walking down her street so that she could bump into him and then puzzled again, for she knew he wouldn't. She'd have to go and find him, that was the thing. But how? And where?

It was when Bessie was sorting out the laundry that she discovered how. Bessie was piling all her white pinafores in one heap with her white vests and knickers to be boiled in a bucket over the stove. She put her hands in all the pockets to check they were empty, and came out with the square of pasteboard Madame Gansella had given Joe.

'What's this?' Bessie said. 'Where'd you get this?'

Lexie thought for a moment of saying she didn't know, that she'd picked it up in the street, that a bird had brought it in its beak and put it in her pocket when she wasn't looking and then, almost without realizing what it was she was saying, or what memory it was that prompted her to say it, she said, 'She's a lady who says I could be a dancer. She wants to teach me.'

Bessie stood with the card in her hand, staring at her, her face once again fixed with that white blankness that meant she was thinking a great deal. Lexie knew that expression very well.

'I was dancing,' she said, suddenly knowing it was all right to tell her. 'A barrel organ. And this man came and said did I want to dance on the stage and I could on Saturday so I did and this lady said I could dance if I learned properly because of talent and she said she's always there on a Sunday because they're all over the place. That's where they are, all the children, all over the place – '

Her voice dwindled away and she sat there on the windowsill, staring at Bessie who had sat down hard, and was looking at the card in her hand. 'Madame Gansella,' it read. 'Specialist in Terpsichorean Art. Children a speciality.

Rates moderate. Personal callers at 17 Cephas Street, adjacent Paragon Palace of Varieties.'

'You were dancing in the street and a man came and said – gevalt!' Bessie almost whispered it, and then she looked up and said more loudly and with a note of urgency, 'This man – who was he? What did he say? What did he do? Did he interfere with you?'

'Interfere with me? He was nice. He cuddled me when I cried,' Lexie said. 'Bessie, can I learn how to dance in a pink dress? She said I could. She told Joe I had talent – '

Bessie, who had gone a sick yellow colour, caught her breath. 'Joe? You were with Joe? He knows what all this is you're talking about?'

'Oh, yes, Joe was there all the time. He said I could do it. He said it'd all start something very funny, and it did. That lady, Bessie, she said I could dance. Can I be a dancer, Bessie? I want to be. I saw them all dance at the Paragon and I want to do it – '

She sat very straight on the windowsill, staring at Bessie. The odd feeling had come back, the one she had felt there at the Paragon on Saturday night. A feeling of heat and excitement, a sort of wanting very deep inside her, and she jumped down and stood very stiffly in front of Bessie.

'I've got to,' she said. 'I've got to dance like that. They kept twirling their heads, like this – ' and she twirled and jerked her head sharply forwards as she did so, in perfect imitation of the children she had watched on stage, fixing her face in a wide grin as she did it. 'I didn't do it right, and they all shouted at me, the people watching, but I *could* do it right. I know I could, if I was to have lessons like she said. Lessons to dance – ' And she twirled again, snapping her head round, grinning ferociously, and seeing clearly in her mind's eye the smooth red head of the boy at the Paragon.

Bessie said nothing, sitting there at the table with the laundry piled on it and the pasteboard slip in her hand, staring at Lexie, but inside she was all emotion, all excitement, all terror. Lexie, wanting to dance? Lexie seeing herself in pink dresses? It was strange and painful and yet exhilarating to sit there and watch her own secret dream shimmer and change, watch the small figure who had been herself, dancing inside her mind, change and shift and become not Bessie but Lexie. Lexie plumper and with her hair in curls, in pink

54

drifting dresses and ballet shoes with satin ribbons –

She shook her head weakly and said, 'I – you never wanted to dance before. Why all of a sudden you want to dance? All of a sudden you want lessons? Such mishegasses to get into your head –'

Lexie stopped twirling and looked at her with eyes that were round and very bright, and after a moment she said, 'I want to learn to dance. Auntie Fanny'd let me dance if I lived with her. She'd let that lady teach me to dance if I lived in her house. I want to dance – '

There was a heavy little silence and then Bessie said, 'It's got nothing to do with Fanny if you dance, it's up to me, not her. It's me that decides.'

'Oh, Bessie, please!' Lexie said and threw herself into Bessie's lap, and after one startled moment Bessie put her arms round her. It wasn't one of Lexie's more usual actions to be so affectionate. Usually she allowed herself to be picked up and hugged only when she was tired or upset, but to throw herself into an embrace like this – Bessie's arms tightened round her.

'I don't know, boobalah,' she said after a moment. 'It'll be expensive. That woman – she don't get cards printed like that for tuppence ha'penny, you know. She'll want money –'

'Ask Uncle Dave and Auntie Fanny,' Lexie said at once. 'They'll give it to us, like they always do. Eh? Tell them no more furniture, just money for the lady to teach me to dance.'

Bessie shook her head, with a sudden fierce little gesture. 'No,' she said sharply. 'It's nothing to do with Fanny and Dave. And if you say a word to them that'll be the end of it. No dancing lessons. You hear me?'

'I hear you.' Lexie lifted a radiant face to her. 'Oh, yes, Bessie. If I can have dancing lessons I'll never say a word to *anyone*.'

Except, a little voice deep inside her whispered, except the boy with the smooth dark red hair.

# 5

'One *and* two *and* three *and* four,' the voice brayed again above the thump of the piano. 'One *and* two *and* three *and* four,' and the dust spurted up from the bare floorboards and made her nose sting again and her eyes hurt, and she wasn't quite sure whether it was the dust or the way her feet and ankles ached that made her eyes run, too. Obediently she repeated the steps as the counting started again, but now she stumbled and nearly bumped into Maisie, who dug a sharp elbow into her arm, and Madame shouted, 'Lexie, what are you, for heaven's sake? A dancer or an elephant?' And the others – especially Maisie – tittered and Lexie's eyes got wetter still. If she wasn't careful she'd start crying properly and that would be dreadful.

Doggedly she went on repeating the sequence of steps in her head; ball change, heel down, toe down, ankle flick, tap, kick; ball change, heel down, toe down, ankle flick, tap, kick; ball change, heel down – right foot, left foot, right foot again. She wanted Bessie suddenly, wanted to be sitting at the table at home in Sidney Street while Bessie nagged her to eat something, instead of here in a cold bare room in Cephas Street with feet and ankles that ached so dreadfully that they felt as big as Joe's boots.

That was the trouble, of course. After all the fuss she'd made to get here, after all the worrying and counting of money that Bessie had done, after all the promises never to try to talk to Auntie Fanny or Uncle Dave and Joe and Benny about the dancing – or about anything else at all, in fact – how could she not go on with these horrible lessons? The fuss would be dreadful and anyway there would be nowhere to go except home to Sidney Street, and without Arbour Square to escape to sometimes that would be even worse than what was going on now.

So she went on with it as the counting continued; ball change, heel down, toe down, ankle flick, tap, kick and realized, startled, that she'd been doing it without thinking for the last minute or so and suddenly felt better as the

56

thumping tinny piano and Madame's voice rang in her ears; perhaps she could learn it all, after all. And soon it would be time to rest a bit and then she could sit and talk to Alf and that would be lovely, and she turned her head to see him in the line behind her and at once Madame's voice bawled, 'Keep your eyes to the front, Lexie! And smile, will you, *smile* – you must never stop smiling. You've got to look as though you're enjoying it, or no one else will – '

Across the bare room the door opened and the line faltered as the dancers looked up to see who had arrived, eager for anything to break the tyranny of practice, and Madame swore and banged her hands down hard in a discord and shouted, 'What the hell do *you* want, for God's sake? Haven't I told you I don't want to be disturbed when we're – '

'Lovely woman, lovely, ain't she? What a way to treat a husband, I ask you, eh?' The newcomer winked at the children, now standing awkwardly, waiting to be told what to do, and then grinned at Madame Gansella. 'I know the rules, ducks, but there's times to break 'em, and this is one,' and he walked across to whisper in her ear, and she sat and listened, and as she did her eyes swivelled to Lexie and narrowed.

'All right, I'll come down. Children, rest time! I have business to deal with. Lenny, keep an eye on them – ' and she swept out and went clattering down the stairs as the children collapsed on to the floor and began to chatter to each other.

Lexie turned at once towards Alf, but it was too late; he was already in close colloquy with two of the other boys and she'd learned the painful way that this meant she wasn't to interrupt. He could be friendly and lovely when he wanted to be, the way he'd been the night she'd first talked to him at the Paragon, but he could also be cruelly unkind if he was in that sort of mood, producing stinging words that made her face flame. Now she drew her knees up and hugged them and miserably watched him and the other boys with their heads together and said nothing.

'So, dolly, how's it going? Enjoying your lessons, eh?'

She looked up and after a moment nodded. He made her feel uneasy, with his sleek shiny black hair that always looked wet and his tightly waisted striped jacket and his red flower buttonhole. He smelled of violets very strongly, and tobacco even more strongly, and most strongly of all of something else that was like beer but not quite, which she didn't like at all, especially now as he came and squatted on his haunches before her, the cloth of his black and white striped trousers straining over his crotch and thick thighs, and breathed into her face.

'Yes, Mr Gansella, thank you very much,' she said politely and scrambled to her feet, so that he had to as well, and that helped, for now he was well above her and she couldn't smell his heavy breath.

'Ganz, dolly, Ganz is good enough for me. I don't need no fancy Italian-type names to make my business work, thank you very much – '

'Yes, Mr Ganz,' she said, wondering for a brief moment what his business was. He seemed to be around the house in Cephas Street all the time, never seemed to go to the Lane like Uncle Dave and the boys did, never seemed to sit with his head in books writing down numbers, the way Auntie Fanny did. He wasn't always dressed as fancy as he was this morning though, because she'd seen him unshaven and dressing gowned with the sleek black hair hanging lankly over his unshaven face when she'd arrived some days, even when it was as late as nearly dinner time. But still he was always there and doing little more than reading newspapers. Not that it really mattered much to her; the ways of grown-ups were strange, whatever they did.

'So, lessons goin' all right, are they?'

'Yes, thank you,' she said again, and wanted to move away but felt she couldn't because he was staring at her so closely.

'And does your – Uncle Dave like your dancing?'

She looked at him, startled. 'Uncle Dave? Do you know my Uncle Dave?'

He laughed fatly at that. 'Who doesn't know your Uncle Dave? Warm fella, very warm fella! Halfway and a bit more to a fortune, he is! Charming man, o' course, and your lovely Auntie Fanny. Lovely people. So tell me, is she your father's sister, or your mother's?'

Lexie frowned, puzzled. 'She's my sister,' she said and Mr Ganz's eyebrows shot up.

'I thought she was your aunt! Well, well! Even closer, hmm? Sister – very nice to have such a rich sister! So she's the one financing your classes, hey?'

'Pardon?'

58

'Pays for your lessons, hmm?'

She shook her head. 'No, Bessie does. She says Auntie Fanny mustn't know I'm doing lessons. It's a secret!' She reddened suddenly and looked at him doubtfully. 'I shouldn't have told you.'

He laughed and patted her head, and she bobbed it slightly for his hand was heavy. 'Then you haven't. I won't tell no one. But tell me – why should it be a secret?'

'Don't know,' she muttered, and tried to move away from him. She was liking him less and less.

'Wouldn't approve, maybe? Your Auntie Fanny, got a proper idea of what's what? Wouldn't want her little niece – sister – goin' around with a lot of vulgar dancers?'

'Don't know,' she said again, and then relaxed as the door opened and Madame came back, a faint frown on her face.

He turned and looked at her, thrusting his hands into his trouser pockets so that the heavy gold chain across his belly showed clearly between the edges of his jacket.

'So I can go now, thank you very much?' he said with heavy sarcasm. 'You don't need no nursemaid no more?'

'Yes – thanks – ' she said abstractedly and Lexie looked at her, surprised. She sounded quite different again. Lexie had grown used to the way Madame Gansella had one voice for talking to people at the theatre – it was the same one she used for talking to Bessie and the other children's mothers – and a different, much more ordinary one for talking – actually shouting – to the children when they had their lessons, but this was a third one. It was quieter and even more ordinary than her shouting one, and she sounded much the same as the women who sat and gossiped in Sidney Street doorways on summer evenings.

'You're wasting your time with that one,' he said as he reached the door and shot a sharp little glance at Lexie. 'Dave Fox don't even know she's having lessons from you. So you can forget your fancy notions, eh? *He* ain't going to invest in no Juvenile Jollities. Even though he's the brother-in-law – '

'Brother-in-law?' Madame said, and now she was no longer abstracted. 'I thought – well, it doesn't matter, anyway. Go on, Len. I'm busy. Go away.' And Mr Ganz, after one more sharp little grin at Lexie, went away. Madame Gansella went back to the piano and continued the lesson as though there had been no interruption. But she didn't shout

59

out at Lexie any more, even though she made a lot of mistakes now because she was so mixed up by the odd things that Mr Ganz had said.

'Right, children, that's enough! Downstairs with you! Change quietly, and wait for your mothers in the hall – no pushing and no shouting – no, Lexie, not you. Just wait a minute, dearie, will you?'

Lexie stood very still, feeling fear climbing up inside her. Madame had never called her dearie, not in all the weeks she'd been coming to these lessons. Maybe she was angry with her? Maybe she was going to tell her to go away and never come back? And suddenly the feeling she'd had before, the wanting-to-go-away-and-never-have-lessons-again feeling, exploded and came down in a little shower of eager hotness inside her, quite different now; she *did* want to dance, she did, she did, and no one was going to stop her. No one at all –

'Please, don't make me – ' she began, but Madame rode right over her words and, incredibly, bent down and picked her up and held her close, and Lexie was too amazed to resist her. She just sat there in the circle of that big arm, with Madame Gansella's face so close to her she could see the fine hairs on her upper lip all caked with powder, and said nothing.

'Dearie, I have some sad news for you. I hope you'll be a brave little girlie and keep a stiff upper lip. It's tragic sometimes in life, and we all have to learn to live with it.'

Lexie watched her upper lip, fascinated at the way the lines in between the powder-caked hairs came and went with each word.

'Your poor dear Poppa has passed away. He suffered a lot, Miss Ascher told me, and it was all very peaceful. Really it's blessed release, isn't it?' she said. 'You do understand, dearie, don't you?'

'Yes, Madame,' Lexie said, and then after a moment shook her head. 'No, Madame.'

Madame looked irritated for a moment and then tried again. 'Your Poppa, dearie. He's been ill?'

'Oh, yes,' Lexie said cheerfully. 'Poppa's always ill. He lies in bed all day and Bessie has to give him his dinner on a spoon.' She didn't tell Madame about the wet and dirty beds. That was something you didn't tell strangers.

60

Madame brightened. 'Well, dear, you won't be too surprised then to know he's passed away. Gone to sleep, you know.'

'He's always asleep,' Lexie said.

Madame's lips tightened. 'He's dead, dearie. Died this morning.'

'Oh!' Lexie said and then stared at Madame's face, looking at her eyes now instead of that fascinating upper lip. 'Oh. Poppa dead?'

'Yes, dear,' Madame Gansella said, and set her on her feet again and then stood brushing down her dress. 'I'm afraid so. And Miss Ascher says it's best you don't go home till the shivah's over. You're staying here with me a week. It's better. So go downstairs now, and change, but don't put on your coat and hat, of course, and I'll think of something for you to do this afternoon while I take a class of the big ones. Perhaps you can watch – yes, that'll be nice for you. You can watch the big ones. And then, when it's all over, Miss Ascher will come and take you home –'

She looked down at the child again for a moment before opening the door and shushing her out. 'Oh, and yes – I wish you long life,' she said and Lexie stared at her uncomprehendingly and then went slowly downstairs.

'I don't know what's got into her, and that's a fact. And I'll tell you something else. I think she's gone meshuggah. She's a crazy woman,' Fanny said loudly and she sat down firmly at the table and folded her arms over her lace-fronted bosom. Always well dressed at the best of times, she had, in the last few years, become a very fashionable lady indeed, buying the most expensive materials for her dressmaker, Sadie Copperman, to make up into elaborate ensembles of tight-waisted high-necked blouses and sweeping skirts with myriad tucks and trimmings, all surmounted by the most intricate of hairdressing modes with curls and fringes and swirls. She wore a good deal of jewellery too, but today was wearing only jet – if rather too much of it – in deference to her status as a mourner.

'Ah, so she's got a little maggot in her head!' Dave said. 'Listen, Fanny, they've all gone now – bad enough we have to sit here every day as it is. Do me a favour, let's go home, eh? It's hot in here – ' And he fanned his shining face with his homburg hat (for he too liked to dress fashionably) and glowered at Bessie, who was sitting silently on the low chair that was obligatory for mourners.

She was the only one still so ensconced, for now the last of the visitors who had come to offer cakes and condolences in the traditional way had departed. Joe and Benny had gone to sit at the open window, where what little air there was from the fetid street outside was to be found on this hot August night.

'Do me a favour, Bessie,' Dave said after the pause had become painfully long. 'Tell us where she is already! Believe me, no one's goin' to take the kid away from you. You think Fanny wants more problems than she's already got with our little lobbus? That Monty'll be the death of us yet, believe me! It's just she wants to know where the child is! We all do – it's only natural!'

Bessie lifted her chin and stared at him. 'You mean it?' She'd been silent so long that her voice was husky. 'You don't want to take her away from me?'

'Of course not!' Dave said heartily. 'It's just that – '

'I don't make no promises,' Fanny said loudly. 'She's my baby sister, bless her, I should let go just like that? What do you take me for, Dave? I make no promises!'

'Phtt!' Dave made a noise so filled with disgust that even the lugubrious Benny grinned. 'What's the matter with you, Fanny? Of course the child's staying with Bessie! I got no intention we should take her away – and when I got no intention, then *you* got no intention. So shut up already. Listen, Bessie – the kid's all right?'

'She's all right,' Bessie said, and her voice was flat and toneless.

'Then shoin fertig – I'm happy. It's done, forget it. I'm going home. Fanny, Joe, Benny, home.' And he got to his feet and set his hat on his head with great attention to its angle. 'Bessie, I'm sorry it's all turned out this way. A family argument no one enjoys and me least of all. I'm a man of peace but my Fannela, bless her, she's a strong-minded woman, what can you do? As soon as you can, as soon as you've thought about it, do me a favour, you should come and see us, tell Fanny you're friends again, bring Lexie to see her, so she feels happy in her mind the child's all right, there'll be no more problems. I promise you. Me, Dave Fox, I promise you. And what I promise gets done. I didn't get to my stage of business with three stalls and a shop and seven people working for me and another opening next month, please God, breaking promises. But you be a sensible girl, bring the child to see us, it'll be all over and forgotten.'

Fanny too had got to her feet and was smoothing her kid gloves on to her hands. 'But I tell you this, Dave,' she said and her voice tinkled with frost. 'Until she brings that child to see me, not a penny does she get from us. You hear me? The money stops. Poppa's dead and I got no responsibility no more. She wants to be a gunsa macher, keep the child to herself? So let her! She can see how it is to live without our money to keep her warm on a cold night. She can go back to work in the sweat shops if anyone'll have her after all this time. What experience has she got? None that'll be any good – and see what sort of living she can earn. Believe me, she'll come soon enough asking my pardon for her stupidity and her wickedness when she's tried it a few weeks. All these years we've kept her in luxury, a real lady, nothing to do but sit around here all day on our furniture, in a place we pay the rent, and she behaves like this! You hear me, Dave? Not a penny! Come on – ' And she swept out of the flat, her heels slapping purposefully down the stairs, and the boys followed her, after a sheepish glance at Bessie sitting silent and very still in her low chair.

'Well, there it is, Bessie, I did my best,' Dave said. 'You should stop being a foolish woman! Because you know how it is – Fanny says no money, then no money it's got to be. She's my book-keeper, you know that, and she knows every penny we spend to the last ha'penny. For my part, you can have it and welcome, but even for you, Bessie, I don't have fights with Fanny. So come see us soon, bring Lexie, it'll all be sorted out – I wish you long life,' and he too went clattering down the stairs, leaving Bessie alone in her flat, contemplating a future without any money, with no means of support, and the dreaded task of finding some sort of job that would keep her and Lexie fed. And not only that, but Lexie's lessons paid for.

Because no matter what happened, Bessie promised herself, Lexie was going to go on dancing.

# 6

'So what are you askin' me for?' Alex Lazar said. 'I mean, I remember the kid, lovely child, lovely! Thought she had a bit more talent than she – well, you understand. It's like I said, I thought I'd do her a good turn and as it turned out – well, you win a few, lose a few, you know how it is.'

'Yes,' she said, and clutched her bag on her lap a little more tightly. He was a frightening man, this Alex Lazar with his expensive clothes and his tightly crinkled hair and his cigar-scented breath, sitting staring at her across a cluttered desk in the back room at the Paragon Palace of Varieties. It wasn't that he was being anything but polite and nice to her; indeed, he'd been so polite and nice she'd been speechless at first, with his handshakings and careful offers of chairs to sit on; not treatment to which she was at all used. It was just that he seemed so busy, so important, with the telephone on his desk, and its urgent ringing noise that kept interrupting them, and people bustling in and out all the time. She wanted to get up and run, and then she remembered Lexie's eager face when she chattered about her dancing lessons, and Fanny's tight closed one when she had talked of taking Lexie away – and took a deep breath.

'I thought – you'd seen my Lexie dance, saw what she could do, how lovely she is. I thought perhaps you'd see a way, could suggest a way, maybe find how she could go on having lessons. I started them, you see, with Madame Gansella, and she says she's learning and all, but now my father's died, I got to get a job and I can't yet and – there's no money for her lessons, and my sister Fanny says –' And suddenly, to her own horror, her voice disappeared, drowned in the tide of tears that rose in her.

Alex stared at her, his face almost comic in its expression of embarrassed distress, and after a moment he leaned forwards and patted her hand a little awkwardly. 'There, m'dear, no need to fuss, now, is there? We'll sort this out, some way or another. Let me understand, now. Your sister – Fanny, you said? What about her?'

She rubbed her nose with her big handkerchief, grateful for his prompting. 'Her and her husband, Dave, you know. Dave Fox – do you know them? Everyone does–'

He leaned back in his chair again and stared at her, his head on one side and his eyes suddenly very bright above the cigar clamped firmly between his teeth. 'Dave and Fanny Fox? Oh yes. I know them. Know 'em well. Your sister, is she? Well, well, who'd 'a' thought it? Dave Fox's sister-in-law, asking me for favours.'

She reddened painfully. 'No, not favours. Advice more. Well, maybe a favour – I mean, I thought you could ask Madame Gansella to go on with the classes, wait for the money for the lessons till I got a job. It's the slack time, you see, so there aren't many jobs around, and me, I'm not experienced no more. Been at home looking after Poppa all these years, and Lexie of course and – anyway, I thought if you asked Madame to wait a bit, she would for you more than she would for me. I'd pay it back, every penny, of course. I just need time, you see, and I'm scared to go and tell her so, to tell you the truth, in case she says no and I got to take Lexie away. If I do that Fanny'll take her away from me – or so she says, though Dave doesn't seem to – well, anyway, that's what I thought–'

He was grinning now, a self-satisfied little grin, as he looked down at the chewed end of his cigar, and she faltered and stopped, staring at him with her forehead creased.

'So, tell me, why should you come and ask *me* to talk to Madame Gansella for you? Why not someone else?'

She frowned. 'Lexie told me – it was you told Joe she had talent. It was you said she was pretty and – she told me everything that happened here that Saturday. Did she get it wrong?'

'No, she didn't get it wrong.' He looked up at her and grinned even more widely. 'It was like she said. I did see her dancing for the queue and I thought she had real chein – not exactly beauty, you know–' And he slowed, picking his words carefully, remembering the odd child with her dark straight hair in a thick curtain round her face and her huge eyes and her pointed little chin. Attractive, yes, pretty, never – but he couldn't imagine saying as much to this devoted sister of hers. 'Not exactly a beauty, but something much better. A real personality, you know? She certainly wasn't quite as clever as I'd thought she was – and that takes personality. To fool Alex Lazar – believe me, that takes a *lot* of personality, a *lot* of talent. She's one little nosh, that Lexie of yours. And she's Dave Fox's sister-in-law, hmm? And he wants her to live with him and she doesn't want to? Have I got it right?'

'Sort of,' Bessie said carefully, trying to identify the source of his sudden good humour and scared of spoiling it. Keep him this way and maybe she'd get the help she'd come to ask about. 'It's not exactly Dave that wants her, I think. It's Fanny. She'd do anything to spite me–' And again she reddened, her nose showing the colour most clearly in her pinched, anxious face.

After a moment of staring hard at her Alex nodded. 'Tell me, Miss Ascher – you got any special – um – you get on good with your sister Fanny?'

'No,' she said after a moment, and could not help but say it. To speak ill of your own relations was bad. In these closed and narrow streets people spoke as well as they could of their own. However many fights you might have inside the family, you didn't go shouting your mouth off outside; that was the unwritten rule of the quarter. But she couldn't manage to keep to it, seeing Fanny's self-satisfied face in her mind's eye, hearing Fanny's loud, self-assured voice in her mind's ear, feeling Fanny's self-centred anger still burning in her belly. 'No!' She said it more loudly now, defiantly, and at once his grin spread even wider. He looked young suddenly, like a wicked child, and she found herself producing a watery grimace in return.

'Well, I'll tell you something. I'm not crazy about Dave Fox neither. He tried to do me dirty – me, Alex Lazar, been doin' business around here since I was a boychik, fourteen, fifteen I was when I started. A boychik fresh from the haim, the old country, and never done no one dirty. Good businessman I may be, got my eye on the main chance and do the best for myself, but I don't do no one dirty. If they're fools, don't know how to do business, that's different. It's their fault. But I don't do no one down deliberate, you understand me? But Dave Fox, he cheated me. He sold me goods I saw, agreed a deal, and then he does the switch act, and there ain't no way I can prove it. Nasty it was, nasty. I tell you, I haven't spoken to the mumser from that day to this, and it's – oh, it's got to be five, six years now. And here you are, telling me that you want my help to stop him and his shprauncy madam of a wife gettin' something they want! Rich, ain't it? I tell you, the Talmud's right. Everything comes to him who waits. And if it ain't in the Talmud, it ought to be–' and he laughed, his eyes crinkling even more, and she laughed too, uncertainly at first but then with a real note of humour in her thin voice. He was so fatly pleased with himself, sitting there with one hand on each plump knee and his cigar held fast between his teeth at a sharp angle, that it was impossible not to share his delight.

'So, let's get it clear. All you're asking is I should hold the old – Madame Gansella – off for her money? Dolly, I can do better'n that–'

She shook her head vigorously. 'I don't want anything else than that, Mr Lazar,' she said a little sharply. 'It's me that's going to pay for everything for Lexie. No one else, only me. She's always goin' to know it was her sister Bessie as did it all, no one else. Just hold her off till I get a job, get the money, that's all – I don't want you paying for her, if that was what you were thinking.'

He nodded abstractedly. 'Yeah, sure. Yeah. I see–' And then he leaned back in his chair and took the cigar out of his mouth and blew a cloud of smoke in her general direction. It smelled good and she relaxed a little, beginning to allow real hope to move in her.

'Tell me, Miss Ascher – can I call you Bessie? Ta, I'm a friendly type, you know, can't be doin' with airs and graces. So tell me, Bessie, what sort of job you looking for?'

The little flame of pleasure that had lifted in her flickered and died and she shrugged her shoulders. 'Whatever I can get,' she said, and her voice sounded as flat as she felt. 'I used to work with Isaac Ritter, the trouser maker over at Adelina Grove, you know? – till my mother died and then – well, not since then. Seven years it's been. I was a felling hand, and I dare say I'll learn again, soon enough. When the slack season's over and I can get in somewhere. And I will.' And her voice sparked a little. 'I will, you'll see, and then I'll pay her back, every penny, you'll see. You can trust me, I won't let you down. You ask her for me, I really won't.'

'You any good with figures?' he said abruptly.

She stared. 'Figures? What kind of figures?'

67

'One, two, three, fourpence ha'penny and a farthing over, those kind of figures,' he said tartly, and again the ready colour tipped her nose.

'I used to be good at arithmetic when I was a kid. Went to school till I was twelve, used to come top in arithmetic often. I can count, if that's what's worrying you. I won't forget what I owe her.'

He shook his head irritably. 'I'm not talking about Madame and her lessons. That's the least of it right now. I'm talking about a job for you. If you can keep books straight, organize things.'

She lifted her chin at him, her eyes brightening suddenly. 'I can do that. I've been looking after Poppa and Lexie and me on tuppence all these years. Fanny and Dave go on about how much they gave me, but I'll tell you, it was a struggle. If anyone understands about making money stretch, I do. And if that's the sort of organizing you mean, I can do it.'

He nodded, never taking his eyes from her. 'And do you know what's clean and what's dirty in a kitchen—'

She laughed aloud at that. 'Me, clean, in a kitchen?' And she laughed again, and he nodded, this time in satisfaction.

'I'll give you a try,' he said. 'Listen, I've got a couple of tea shops. Nice little places. One in Whitechapel Road down near the Yiddish theatre. Used to have a coffee stall there, I did, only now I got a tea shop. And then last year I started another in Mare Street, over at Hackney, and last month—' And he seemed to swell a little with importance as he said it. 'Last month I opened a third. Tottenham Court Road,' and he said it with an air of such enormous casualness that she wanted to laugh. He wasn't all that different from the street corner boasters, the great Mr Alex Lazar, after all. Except that he really had the things he boasted about, unlike the street corner variety.

'That's very smart,' she said. 'I went up the West End once. New Year's Eve, it was. Poppa took me. Before Momma got ill, when he was all right—'

'It's the smartest damn' tea shop you ever saw,' he said, and laughed and slapped his knees with each hand in an excess of delight that was very appealing. 'Marble everywhere, more glass'n the Crystal Palace ever had – a real class place. And I can't get the right person to keep an eye on it, manage it, you know? Keep the books straight – nothing

68

fancy, just daily accounts of how much comes in, how much goes out, the takings, all that. Keep an eye on the waitresses, they don't cheat me, you know how it is. I got to have pretty girls as waitresses – all class places has pretty girls – but round the back, in the office, what I need is a bit of commonsense and someone I can rely on. I reckon I do you a favour with Madame Gansella for your Lexie, you turn into someone I can rely on, right? I'd hoped my own niece'd do the job for me but–' His face clouded then. 'You know my brother Nathan Lazar? The letter writer? His daughter Hannah, my niece, lovely girl, exceptionally well educated – ex-*cept*-tionally – lives in Eaton Square in Belgravia you know, with Mrs Mary Damont, very high-class lady – no? Well, never mind. Anyway, she don't seem able to take on the job, which is a pity. So I got to look around. And I got a hunch you could be right. I don't make no promises, mind you, but if you're good at it, play your cards right, this could turn out good for you.'

He paused and looked at her, his eyebrows slightly raised. 'What do you say?'

She sat there turning her bag between her hands, her eyes down, staring at the rusty black of her dress, and the broken though carefully polished shoes beneath its hem. She, Bessie Ascher, a manageress in a fancy West End tea shop? It was crazy. She'd never worked in such a place, never imagined anything so glorious could ever be possible. She remembered that one night in the West End of London all those years ago, before she'd had the tuberculosis that had twisted her spine and left her with her crooked shoulder and her ugliness, remembered dancing along the pavements beside Poppa, past the wonderful shops with their crystal and their bright lights and their cornucopias of beautiful objects and dresses and shoes and glittering jewellery in them. She remembered the white-painted front of the tea shop they had passed and how she and Poppa had stood outside on the dark pavement, staring in at the waitresses gliding about in their black dresses and beautiful lacy pinafores and caps with trays of cakes and lovely silver teapots and real china cups on them. She could almost remember the smell of tea and whipped cream and jam and warmth that had come wafting out of the doors as they swung to and fro to let in the wonderfully dressed people who were the tea shop's unbelievably fortunate customers, could almost recall the way the hot sweet tea and raisin-filled bun Poppa had bought for her at a coffee stall had tasted, afterwards, when he had seen her eager face as she had watched the tea shop and told her he couldn't afford that, but that there was somewhere else they could eat—

She lifted her head now to look at Alex Lazar and shook her head. 'Me?' she said. 'How could I go to a place like that? Not me.' And she picked, almost unconsciously, at her rusty black skirt.

He grinned again, the same cheerful grimace she was beginning to feel she'd known all her life. 'Listen, doll, I ain't stupid, you know! 'Course you'd have to have proper clothes. I buy the uniforms for my waitresses, so I buy office clothes for you! I got my own little business in the Lane for that sort of thing – no sweat. This I can fix easy. Part of the job. Pay you twenty-five bob a week and there you are – you don't have to worry.'

'Twenty-five—' She couldn't finish the sentence. She, who had been keeping herself and Lexie and Poppa on just fifteen shillings a week, to have so much. That would be enough not only for Lexie's lessons but for new clothes for her as well – her face twisted as she stared at him.

'But—' she began and then swallowed and tried again. 'Me in a West End tea shop! I can't imagine it.'

'In the office, you understand,' he said reassuringly. 'I told you, I got all the pretty girls I want servin' in the place. Pretty girls you can get anywhere, but a good Yiddisher kopf is somethin' else. So you'll try?'

'Yes,' she said, and tried not to care about the pretty girl she wasn't. It shouldn't hurt any more, not after so many years of being as she was, but it still did. A little. Especially somehow, with Alex Lazar—

She stood up, and bobbed her head at him a little awkwardly. 'There's just one thing. My – Fanny and Dave. You won't say nothing to them?'

'Are you mad? I told you! I got it in for that fella, and if I can do him down by doin' you good it makes me feel marvellous! I ain't the vindictive type, you understand, Bessie. Me, I'm an easy-goin' fella. Like to do business sharp, I grant you, but never nasty. That's why I couldn't do nothin' to Dave Fox when he did me. But now – this is different! I make life easy for you, I make it tricky for Fanny

70

and Dave Fox – I like it, I like it! So listen, I'll go see your Madame Gansella, if you like, but let me advise you. Let me give you a sub against the job. I got an instinct about people, and you're goin' to be all right, I reckon. I won't lose if I advance you a bob or two for the old B. And it don't do to let that one think she's doin' you any favours. She's a bit of a villain, in her own way. No, don't look like that! She teaches the kids fine, but when it comes to money she looks after number one, first, second and third. With Lenny Ganz for a husband, believe me, she's got to. Better she doesn't know you're a bit strapped for the ready. I'll see to it she's paid, all right? Good. Now, go already, doll. I got work to do. Come here tomorrow, about half past two, I'll take you up to the Lane, get you the uniform and that, and after we'll go see the tea shop. I reckon we're in business together, eh? And Dave Fox'll never know –'

And he laughed and slapped his knees again as Bessie, more than a little bemused, went out. She could hear him laughing all the way down the stairs.

# 7

'MADAME POPPY GANSELLA'S JUVENILE JOL-LITIES!' screamed the poster, in huge scarlet letters. 'THE SHOW OF THE SEASON! THE WONDER OF THE AGE! *DO NOT MISS THIS*!!!' and then in a different type face, but still as urgently, 'EVERY CHILD AN ARTISTE – EVERY ARTISTE A CHILD!' And finally in neat squared letters the name of every one of them. Baby Myrtle Levy. Little Doris Finer. Wee Lily Lassman. Sweet Maisie Kupfer. Young Joel Josephs. Master Sidney Soutar. David and Daniel the Tannenbaum Twins. And right at the bottom, in a line of its own, Lovely Alexandra Ascher and Darling Ambrose Asquith, a Symphony in Dance.

'Doesn't it look lovely, Alf?' she said, tucking her hand under his elbow and squeezing his arm, and he tightened his biceps against her grip so that her hand was caught warmly against his body. It felt lovely there and she held on tightly, aware of his touch all down her side and hoping he wouldn't notice how unevenly she was breathing, as the faint clouds of water vapour appeared in the bitter November air from her slightly parted lips.

'I'd like it better if they'd used a different size of lettering for us,' he said judiciously. 'I mean, we're the stars of the show, aren't we? We ought to get the best billing.'

'We have,' she said. 'I mean, right at the bottom, on a line by ourselves. And your name looks deevy. Ambrose Asquith! I mean, it's a bit of a change from Alfie Abrahams. Very posh—'

'Yours is too!' he said. 'Mine's no different—'

'But mine's real—' and she giggled. 'I think you were very clever to have thought of it. Much better to choose a new one than to get stuck with the one you've always had. Alfie, shall we—'

'If I'm going to be called it on the bills I might as well use it,' he said. 'I don't answer to Alfie any more. If you say it I shall pretend you don't exist. Like this—' He pulled away from her and moved towards the billboard and leaned against it, one leg crossed over the other so that the toe tip of his highly polished shoe rested on the pavement with the trouser leg slightly lifted to display his cream-coloured spats, while his rabbit fur-collared overcoat fell open negligently to display his blindingly white shirt and sleekly cut suit. He looked magnificent and a good deal older than his seventeen years, and was well aware of it as he stared into the middle distance over her head with an air of deeply casual unawareness of anyone else around him. His hair, still showing that deep red tinge in spite of the heavy application of oil he had used to sleek it down, gleamed in the dull morning light. She sighed with pleasure as she looked at him, and then giggled again.

'That pigeon's going to dollop on you,' she said conversationally, and at once he ducked awkwardly, looking fearfully above his head. She skipped a few steps towards him, pointing her finger at him and crowing until he too had to join in.

'Bleedin' posh you are, talking that way!' he said, and made a mock punching movement at her. 'Ladies – real ones – never talk about things like that.'

'And thank God I'm no lady, this is no lady, officer, this is my partner – listen – Alf – Ambrose, all right, all right,

Ambrose – let's go and have some tea and toast somewhere. I'm flush this week. I'll stand you.'

He shook his head. 'Can't. Got to go and get some gear for the old B. She's got some shoes on order at Gamba's. Gave me a tanner for my bus fare for once, mean old cow. I'd better go.'

'I'll come with,' she said and again tucked her arm into his elbow and sparkled up at him. She was wearing one of the newest of deep-brimmed hats, surmounted with a pair of glossy blackbirds' wings sweeping high into the air, and the heavy fringe of her exceedingly fashionably bobbed hair shone blackly beneath them with an equal gleam. She had chosen the hat very carefully this morning, hoping she would be out with him, and had spent half an hour deliberating over which of her new outfits to wear. The Russian tunic in crimson felt to be worn over the black hobbled skirt? Or the coat with the even more closely hobbled skirt in dark brown to be worn under a matching frock trimmed with braid? She had settled at last for the deep blue suit with the cutaway fronts and the big rabbit fur muff with the almost-ermine tails.

It dangled now from one gloved hand, the tails trailing elegantly against her black-stockinged legs, and she felt she looked almost as superb as Alfie. It had been a battle to persuade Bessie to let her have such fashionable clothes; if Bessie had had her way, Lexie would still be wearing short white frocks and have her hair down her back, as befitted people of her age – not quite thirteen. But Lexie had been determined to look as much like her idol, Irene Castle, as possible. Every picture of her published in the penny papers she cut out and thrust under Bessie's nose; every piece of gossip about 'those great American dancers, Irene and Vernon Castle' that she could cull from the columns she brought home, and in the end Bessie had relented, as she always did these days, now that Lexie had learned the trick of getting her own way. And today she was exultant to have got it over her clothes. Only in an outfit as splendid as this could she possibly walk along the street beside someone as elegant and smart as Alfie. No, Ambrose, drat it; it would take a little time to get used to his change of name.

'You'll have to pay for yourself then,' he said as he turned away from the billboard outside the Empire Theatre and

73

began to walk along towards the bus stop at the end of Mare Street. 'I'm skint—'

'You always are,' she said joyously, and fell into step beside him. He hadn't said no, he hadn't said no! It was never easy to judge his mood; all morning as she had dressed in her small room at the back of the flat in Victoria Park Road, overlooking the sooty laurels and shabby grass of the park, she had hoped and planned and hoped again, going through all the rituals she used to comfort herself, like setting all the things on her dressing table in perfect alignment, and counting backwards from a hundred without making a mistake as she brushed her hair. And it had worked. Here she was now walking along Mare Street with him, going up to the West End. Wonderful!

It hadn't been so wonderful dealing with Bessie, though. She'd been awful for weeks now, ever since Madame G. had said they were going on a real tour, outside London and not just around the local Empires and Hippodromes doing cod talent shows. They were going to be the real thing, at last, now that it was properly legal. All the years of pretending they were amateurs because children under twelve couldn't work professionally for the hours the show needed, the way they'd had to when she started *Juvenile Jollities* five years ago, had been a bit boring, compared with what was to come, and Lexie had been bursting with the excitement of it when she had come home to tell Bessie all about it, early in September.

'Leeds, Madame G. says! And Glasgow and Liverpool — and, oh I don't know — Cardiff, and all over the place. Trains and sometimes we'll have to have our own charabanc to go across country and she's got great big new skips and everything. I'm going to be a topliner, she says, with Alfie, and he's going to have a new name, to make it look good on the bills, and I'm going to have all my name and not Lexie any more and she says I've got to have new costumes and she'll tell you where to go for them and everything—'

'Oh yes?' Bessie had said, as she slapped Lexie's dinner on the table in front of her. 'And who's going to pay for these new costumes, tell me that?'

Lexie had stared at her, startled. 'What's the matter, Bessie? Don't you want me to go? It's a marvellous opportunity! I'll get seen all over the country! And I'm going to have three speciality numbers and I'm going to sing and everything! What are you looking so miserable about?'

'On the road,' Bessie said after a moment. 'It sounds awful. Racketing about – we'd be better finding you a new teacher –'

And then the fight had started; Bessie getting more and more mulish, as she always did when they had an argument, and Lexie getting more and more determined to do it her way. At first she hadn't been all that excited about leaving London, not after listening to the Tannenbaum twins talking knowledgeably about it, for they had had experience, been on the road for years, they said loftily, long before they joined Madame G.'s soppy company. They'd made it all sound very dreary, with cold digs, if you were lucky enough to get digs at all and didn't have to sleep in the chara or on the trains, and nowhere to go when you weren't working and people getting on each other's nerves all the time; but then Alfie had lifted his head and said shortly that they were talking rubbish – that he was going to have a marvellous time, so shut up. And at once she had known that she too would have a marvellous time. On the Road. It sounded wonderful and she visualized herself tramping along busy roads side by side with Alfie as people watched and admired them go by. It was lovely.

And now here was Bessie making a fuss, going on about who would look after her and who would do her laundry and see to it she got enough to eat, and slept properly, and at once Lexie had flared back at her, 'I can manage! I manage now when you're at your damned tea shop late, don't I? I'm not helpless, you know!' And then Bessie had gone white and quiet the way she always did when Lexie said anything about the time she had to spend in the flat on her own while Bessie was working at Alex Lazar's office, and then had started to cry so that her nose went red and her eyes got puffy, and Lexie hated that. It meant she had to go and hug her and make a fuss of her and wheedle her happy again and that was miserable. But it was her own fault; she knew the right way to get what she wanted; she'd learned, painfully, not to be too direct, not to say straight out what it was she was after, but this time she'd been so excited, she'd done it wrong. Her own fault, she told herself as she hugged the sniffing Bessie, her own fault.

In the early days of living here in Victoria Park Road, in a really nice flat with a bedroom for each of them as well as a living room and a kitchen and only one other family sharing the bathroom, she had had a different way of controlling Bessie when she got difficult. She just had to cry and, if that didn't work, say she wanted to go to live at Auntie Fanny's, and at once Bessie would come round. But that had been before the night that Alex Lazar had been there, and taught her better.

There had been a fight that night too, over Madame G. She had told Bessie that Lexie needed more rehearsal time and said she should let her stay away from school even more than she did – and heaven knew she missed enough one way and another – for after all her real future lay in the theatre, but Bessie had for once put down her foot firmly.

'No,' she'd said, when Lexie pleaded with her because she found school boring anyway. 'No. You've got to be properly educated as well as a dancer. Not enough, just to dance. Look at me, if you want to see why. Here I am, running Mr Lazar's office and all because I was good at arithmetic at school –'

'I hate school, I hate arithmetic, I hate everything,' Lexie had screamed at her. 'I'll stay away from school even if you send me. I'll run away, I won't do nothing even if I'm there – and I'll tell Auntie Fanny you won't let me do more rehearsals and she'll let me –'

She had paid no attention to Alex Lazar sitting at the table in the middle of the living room with a pile of ledgers and some cash in front of him. He did that frequently, when he had some special reason not to want the people around the tea shop to know what he was doing. Bessie he could trust, of course; working in her place was like working in his own, only better, because she was there to sort things out for him if he needed her. So he often came to Victoria Park Road to do the figures with Bessie, and on this day when Lexie had come bursting in she had just nodded at him the way she usually did, just accepting him as part of the furniture and then forgetting he was there, launching into her fight with Bessie over rehearsal time with all the energy she had.

But he had not done as *he* usually did, and got on with his own affairs. He had lifted his face from his ledgers and stared at her as she stood there in the middle of the room, her fists clenched with passion and her face white as she went on and on at Bessie, and after a moment he had got to his feet and gone over to stand beside her, looking down at her.

After a moment she had faltered and stopped, staring up at him and then at Bessie sitting pale and tense at the table, and then back at him again.

'Listen, dolly, I don't go in for interfering in what ain't my business. I got enough business of my own to keep me busy. But I don't reckon to sit here and listen to you going on at your sister this way, not when she's done so much for you. Here's you, nine years old and —'

'I'm ten!' she had flared at him. 'I'm ten! I'm old enough to know what I want and —'

'You're old enough to get your tochus tanned, young lady!' he'd roared then and Bessie had jumped up, protesting, but he'd shaken his head at her. 'No you don't, Bessie. Listen, you're a great office manageress. Getting you to do my books was the best thing I ever did, but bring up a child! — you shouldn't know from herring, you're so terrible! You ought to meet my sister-in-law Minnie, you want to know how to bring up a child! One word out of place and they go flying, her lot — and this one here could do with a bit of the same!'

'No, Mr Lazar, please —' Bessie said. 'Don't shout at her. I can't stand it if you shout at her.'

'So what are you going to do? Let *her* shout at *you* for fear I should shout at *her*? Pfui! You're a crazy woman, you know that, to let the kid behave this way! It ain't good for her — you ought to know better —'

And then Lexie had blinked, because after a moment Bessie had said amazingly, 'I know,' and then sat down and stared miserably at Lexie. 'I know. But what can I do, Mr Lazar? She knows how to upset me. What can I do?'

'I'll tell you what you do, Bessie,' Alex Lazar had said, going back to the table and sitting down. 'You call this little madam's bluff, that's what you do. So you want to back to your Auntie Fanny? Get her to spoil you? So, go already. Here — I'll give you your bus fare —' he had reached into his pocket and pulled out a sixpence and set it down on the red plush tablecloth in front of him.

'Mr Lazar!' Bessie had cried, but he had shaken his head at her. 'Go already, dolly,' he'd said genially to Lexie. 'You've still got your coat on, still got your hat on, here's the money

– go to your Auntie Fanny. See if she'll pay for your dancing lessons, work all the hours God gives to take care of you the way Bessie does. See if she'll get her Dave to invest his money in your dancing school the way I do – I do it to please your sister Bessie, and you might as well know it. But I don't do it no more if you go to Fanny, of course. She can take over the business with Madame G. and her debts. If she won't, o' course, no more Madame G. dancing school. Still, that won't worry us, will it, Bessie? We'll have no worries. You'll be at Fanny and Dave's –'

Lexie had stood stock still in the middle of the room, staring at him, and then as what he was saying slid into her mind properly the tears started, choking hot tears, and a sick feeling of misery. Until now it had been so easy getting her own way; all she had to do was say she was going to leave and Bessie would crumble. But now Bessie sat there beside Alex Lazar looking at her with her face quite blank and no sign of any of the usual confusion that Lexie could read like a book and which always meant she had succeeded. She had just sat and looked at her, and after a long moment Lexie had turned round and gone to her bedroom to take off her coat and sit on her bed and cry. There was nothing else she could do.

He had come to sit on her bed beside her before he left, and for a moment she'd wanted to shout at him and hit out at him and hurt him, but he was a very big man, so much bigger than Bessie, so all she could do was thrust out her lower lip and sit and stare at the floor and say and do nothing.

'Listen, dolly,' he'd said amiably. 'I'm talking to you for your own good. You're a clever little girl and one of these days you'll be a clever big girl. If you listen to me. You got a lot of personality, a lot of drive, but you ain't going to get what you want in this world being noisy, you understand me? Making threats you don't mean never gets you nowhere. If you're going to make people do things your way you got to box clever. I showed you tonight what you can't do. I like your sister Bessie. She's a good woman, a gutena shumah, and I don't like to see her unhappy. So I pulled your teeth out so you can't nip her no more. But let me tell you, for the future – you want to get people to do things your way? Don't shout. Box clever.'

And he had got up and walked over to the door and she

had lifted her chin and watched him go and then said, almost without thinking, 'How?'

'How what?'

'Do what you said. Box clever.'

'Ah,' he'd said and grinned at her. 'That'd be tellin'. It's something everyone has to work out for themselves. You'll find out how to get what you want, a kid looking like you do. Not beautiful, that's you, but you've got more chein than a barrel–load of monkeys. Use it, and that'll be boxing clever. Get what you want the quiet way, not the screaming way–'

'I want to dance more instead of going to school,' she said. 'How do I do that?'

'You think,' he'd said promptly. 'You don't go screaming and nagging, you *think*. You smile and you say yes and then you think about what you can manage. Maybe you get ill a bit at school, hmm? Have to go early? Maybe you got to go get more exercise to feel better? Little things like that.'

'They'll ask Bessie,' she'd said, but she was interested now, excited, too. She didn't hate him any more as she had before. Now she felt his approval, his interest in her, and she warmed to it. 'If I tell lies, they'll ask Bessie and then they'll get more mad at me. So will Bessie.'

'Bessie, mad at you?' he'd said and laughed. 'That'll be the day. Anyway, who said anything about telling lies? I never tell lies. I just make things happen the way I want them to happen. I tell myself – this is how I want it to be, so this is how it ought to be and so this is how it *is* – so when you think that way, and you know it's true because you believe it, then everyone else does. You understand?'

She stared at him, not moving, and he grinned again. 'You will,' he said. 'One of these days you will. You want a lot? Then you got to work out first what it is you want, and believe it and then make it happen. That's all there is to it. You'll find out.' And he had gone, closing the bedroom door behind him with a quiet snap, leaving her sitting on her bed staring after him.

It had taken a good deal of time for her to understand what he'd been telling her, but eventually she began to, dimly, as she saw how much easier it was to coax Bessie to let her do what she wanted instead of trying to force her. It was so easy she was amazed she'd ever been a shouter. All she had to do was make a plan inside her head for what she wanted to happen. She wanted to spend the day at Madame Gansella's house so that she could be there all the time that Alfie was there? Then all she had to do was imagine herself there, see it happening, see reasons for her being there, and then just explain them to Bessie – Madame Gansella had seemed to say that if she had extra practice time she might be able to have her own solo speciality number. And that was something she wanted, as much as Bessie wanted it too, she told Bessie, so it was worth putting up with all the extra work, even though it had to be Sunday, the only day they could usually be together. And Bessie had listened and been unhappy but hadn't been able to argue back the way she would have if Lexie had shouted and nagged, instead of doing it Alex Lazar's way and being reasonable and convinced about the good sense of what she was saying.

And it had worked in the other direction too, making even Madama Gansella do things Lexie's way. The story about practising to be in a speciality number of her own became so entrenched in her own mind that somehow she managed to transfer the dream to Madame G.'s mind, and when she had spent five consecutive Sundays working extra at Madame G.'s house, in the hot dusty attic that was labelled rather grandiosely the Dance Studio, Madame G. actually did give her a lead dance of her very own, with Alfie as her partner.

She had thought about trying the trick with other things too. Like being a singer. That had been much more difficult; she had always had a true enough voice, could hit the notes easily enough, but it was a small voice without much power behind it. Until she had started to see herself inside her own head as a singer, saw herself being offered extra singing lessons, and Bessie paying for them – and somehow she managed it. She talked a little of her dream, just enough to prime Bessie and to interest Madame G. and made sure that both of them heard her practising scales all on her own – and above all kept on with the wanting, the determination to do it, lying in bed night after night thinking about it, and hoping and planning and hoping it. And one day Madame G. told Bessie she thought Lexie should have some singing lessons – and now she sang in the show. Not incredibly well, not all that powerfully, but well enough to be heard and with a sweetness of tone the audience seemed to like, for they applauded her a great deal. And she had chalked that on her private scoreboard as another success for what she now thought of as Alex Lazar's way.

And now, today, it had worked again. As soon as she had overheard Madame G. arranging with Alfie to go to the Empire Theatre in Mare Street this morning to make sure the bills had been put up properly, she had decided to spend the day with him. Five years of being with him most days at dance lessons, or sharing the phoney 'amateur talent' shows with him around North and East London, had done nothing to alter her admiration for him. He was still the most exciting person she could imagine being with, still the person she most wanted to impress, still the person she had in her mind's eye when she went down the Lane to choose new clothes. Would Alfie like this or that or the other? Did it make her look old enough for him? Grown-up enough to be interesting? After all, he was seventeen now, a grown man, really. Not quite thirteen was very young compared with seventeen, but if she thought herself old she would be. And she had thought herself old and so made Bessie let her buy the sort of clothes she wanted, and this morning had thought herself out with Alfie all day, and so made Bessie agree. Not easy, for when it came to Alfie, Bessie was funny. Jealous a little, Lexie thought. But that couldn't be helped. Lexie wanted to be with him and that was that.

So she had coaxed and planned and hoped and wanted and now here she was, exactly where she had intended to be. Arm in arm with Alfie, the new Ambrose, walking down Mare Street on her way to the West End to spend the day with him. Not that he knew it was going to take all day, of course. But Lexie did, and that was what mattered. She was already forming the images in her mind, already seeing them both at the shoe shop and then having their dinners in a tea shop and then going to Oxford Street to look at the big stores. If she tried very hard indeed, she could make it all happen, just as she made everything else happen.

# 8

The shop was small and dark and crowded and smelled wonderful: new cloth from the boxes of shoes that lined the walls and the racks of ribbons that adorned the counter, and rosin, and cigar smoke, and patchouli drifting in waves from the voluble woman standing at the counter and chattering in very fast Italian with the man standing behind it and smoking the cigar, and charcoal braziers and hot chestnuts from the street outside, and sauces rich with herbs cooking in neighbouring restaurant kitchens. Lexie lifted her nose to it and took a deep breath and wanted to hug herself with excitement.

The voluble woman took her package and went bustling out on a tidal wave of scent, and her place at the counter was taken by a lugubrious woman with a very pale face and dark eyes who greeted the man with the cigar in tones so deep and sad that she might have been announcing the end of the world. Ambrose caught Lexie's eye and winked, and she wanted to giggle. But she managed not to, and the pale woman launched herself into a great cascade of French, with which, to Lexie's admiration, the man behind the counter seemed to have no difficulty, and the rest of the shop's customers settled down to wait as patiently as they might for their turn.

Not, Lexie decided, that it was at all difficult to wait patiently here. She had enjoyed the walk in the grey rain-threatening morning, making their way to Gamba's shop through the tangle of Soho streets from the bus stop in Oxford Street at which they had alighted, loving the bustle and strangeness of it all. Heaven knew the East End was busy enough, and full of strange and interesting people, but this was a different sort of bustle, a different sort of strangeness. In the East End the bustle was born of desperation, of poverty and hunger and fear, but here it was different. Here in Soho people were sure of themselves, rushed about for pleasure rather than in anxiety, seemed to know they were going to be as well fed tomorrow as they were today, seemed to have no fear of displaying their foreignness. They chattered loudly in their French and Italian and Spanish and German, unlike the East End where people whose native tongues were Russian and Polish and Latvian stood with their heads close together and almost whispered as they talked, not wanting others to hear them, afraid they would be jeered at and despised.

Maybe, Lexie had thought, as she and Ambrose picked their way over the tangle of rubbish dropped by the stallholders in Berwick Street market, maybe it's all right to be a foreigner as long as you're not a Jew as well. But the thought went away as swiftly as it had come, and she stared at the stalls piled high with exotic fruits and vegetables that glowed like jewels beneath the dull rainy sky, and at the stallholders in their wide-brimmed hats and leather trousers, and thought how much better a market it was than boring old Petticoat Lane, where the stallholders were all people she'd known all her life. There they only sat and plucked chickens in clouds of feathers, or sat with bagels threaded on long poles, crying their wares or haggling over heaps of secondhand clothes, but here was excitement and new sights and smells and she loved every bit of it.

'Isn't it *romantic*, Ambrose?' she'd said, hugging his arm close to her. 'Isn't it all wonderful? I hate the East End. One day we'll both be stars in a show over there – ' and she had jerked her head in the direction of Shaftesbury Avenue and its great glossy theatres, ' – and we'll never have to go to the horrible East End again – '

He looked down at her and made a face. 'It's not that different here to the East End, ducky, and never you think it. They're all robbers and thieves wherever you go.'

'Not everywhere!' she had said, and sounded genuinely shocked. 'Not here in the West End! People here have real class – I'm going to be here one day, you see if I don't. It's going to happen – I've made up my mind to it – ' And for a moment she'd actually considered telling him her secret, about her special way of making things happen, and then just in time bit her tongue. It wouldn't work if she told people. Even Ambrose, who wasn't really people, but Ambrose, the important one. It had to stay inside her head, her private way of getting what she wanted and had to have.

It was still early, not quite eleven, and she'd tried her way again, just to prove to herself it worked. Tea and toast, she'd thought. Imagined it, all hot and dripping with butter, the scent of tea, a marble-topped table, with Ambrose sitting on the other side of it and smiling at her, and as they'd left Berwick Street behind them and crossed into Wardour Street had closed her eyes just for a moment to concentrate on the image. Just as he had said, 'We've lots of time. There's a tea shop over there – what about that nosh you said you'd stand me?' and her eyes had flown open and she'd cried, 'Oh, yes! Let's.' And almost danced across the street to the little Italian café Ambrose had seen, the tails on her muff swinging with her delight. It worked, it always worked!

Now, standing in Mr Gamba's delicious-smelling little shop in Dean Street, waiting for their turn to talk to the many-tongued Mr Gamba who was still chattering to the pale lady over a pair of cream satin slippers, she began to weave more images in her head. She wasn't quite sure what she wanted to happen this afternoon: perhaps a visit to the shops in Oxford Street, strolling between the counters in the huge emporia, gazing at silks and satins and glass and silver and clocks and carpets and curtains, pretending to be setting up a home with Ambrose? Or would it be more fun to go to a matinée at the Alhambra in Leicester Square? To do that they'd need rather a lot of money and she hadn't all that much, not now that she'd paid for her bus fare and the tea and toast for them both. Could she imagine Ambrose saying in a lordly fashion, 'Come on, Lexie. I'll take you to the theatre'?

She closed her eyes to make the pictures come in her head and with it the wanting feeling inside – the hungry needing that was so much a part of the imagining – but it didn't really work, somehow. There were things she could imagine, and some things she couldn't, and Ambrose suggesting things was one of the difficult ones. Maybe she could persuade him to lend her some money and then suggest they go to the matinée and she'd pay – now, that was one that might work –

The shop door tinkled as it opened, and the bell above it was sent swinging wildly on its spring. She opened her eyes to see the customer before them busily explaining to Mr Gamba what he wanted – this time speaking in loud German – and a newcomer waiting alongside them.

The man who had come in was tall and thin, wearing a

coat with the heaviest fur collar Lexie could ever remember seeing, and a bowler hat with the curliest of brims. His clothes, unlike Lexie's and Ambrose's, looked expensive – really good – and she felt a little stab of anger at the way his splendour dimmed theirs and felt her face stiffen as it always did when she was angry. He had very dark eyes and a luxuriant moustache that looked silky in the gleaming electric light that shone over the counter, and as she looked at him she saw him smile, but not at her. He'd caught Ambrose's eye and she flicked her own glance at Ambrose to see he was smiling too.

'Lovely morning!' the man said to Ambrose.

'Lovely, yes.' He sounded a little odd, Lexie thought, and she glanced at him again. He seemed a little pink, and she was puzzled. Did he know this man? And if so why didn't he say, 'This is Lexie', the way you're supposed to when you meet people who don't know each other, and you know them both?

'Nice to see you again,' the man said, and still didn't look at Lexie.

'Er – yes,' Ambrose said. 'Er – I mean, I don't remember seeing you before anywhere – '

'Oh, dear, am I so unremarkable?' the man said, and laughed, an easy, soft laugh that sounded as though he practised it. 'You're in the business, surely? Like me? I'm in *Hello Ragtime*, you know. At the Hippodrome. Where are you working?'

'We're in Madame Gansella's *Juvenile Jollities*. We're the stars of it,' Lexie said loudly, and the man with the moustache looked at her and raised his eyebrows slightly.

'Really? Madame – yes, very nice, I'm sure. The important thing is that you're working, isn't it? I've been in *Hello Ragtime* for almost a year now – we're having a marvellous run. Caught the show, have you?' And he looked again at Ambrose, his eyes smiling.

'No, not really,' Ambrose said, and grinned suddenly. 'Hardly likely to, either. We're not exactly West End performers, are we?'

'Well, give it time,' the man said, and laughed again, that soft little sound. Ambrose seemed to copy it as he laughed too, and Lexie felt chilled and more angry than ever. It was as though she weren't there and she said, again loudly, 'We're going on the road with our show. Starting soon, we are. London first and then we're going to all sorts of places. Leeds and Manchester and all sorts – '

'Yes,' said the man, never taking his eyes from Ambrose. 'As I say, great to be working. Number one tour, is it?'

Ambrose went a little more pink. 'Not that sort of tour,' he mumbled. 'We're – it's not like your sort of show, I mean. We're going to the music halls and that. Start of the second half we are – run about thirty, forty minutes – '

'Ah, I see!' the man said. 'Not legit stage at all – really, with your looks you could do better than that. And I dare say you're a pretty dancer, hmm? Certainly got the build for it,' and his eyes slid down Ambrose to his long legs.

'So, who is next please?' The last customer had gone and Mr Gamba was standing behind his counter with an impatient air. Ambrose said to the man with the moustache, 'Oh! Yes – excuse me – got to pick up a parcel – ' and hurried across to the counter.

'For Madame Gansella,' he said. 'You've got some things ready for her, she said, the girls' shoes she ordered last week – here's the docket – ' And Mr Gamba nodded and went away to the bowels of his shop, leaving the three of them waiting.

At once the man in the moustache started his chatter again, wandering over to the counter to stand lounging beside Ambrose in such a way that Lexie couldn't stand there too, not without pushing in in an obvious sort of way, and she didn't think Ambrose would like that, for he was certainly showing every sign of being interested in the tall man's conversation. She stood and watched them, glowering now, as he went on and on about how boring it was being in a long run and how the other chaps in the chorus could be really nasty sometimes when a fellow did well and attracted a bit of attention from the management, and she felt the pinch of coldness inside her grow and spread and tried to think again about how they would spend the afternoon when they had collected their parcel and were able to escape into the street.

But somehow the images wouldn't form in her mind, try as she might. All she could see were the two male backs standing in front of the counter, talking at each other about nonsensical things that didn't matter. Who cared about the backstage gossip from the Hippodrome? She and Ambrose

86

didn't. Why did this horrible man keep on and on about it?

'Miss!' Mr Gamba had come back bearing several pairs of white satin ballet shoes in his hands. 'Miss, are you one of the dancers these shoes is meant for?'

'Mmm? Oh, yes,' she said. 'Madame Gansella measured all of us last week and sent the order in – '

'I think this is the one for this docket – *think* it is, but I'm not certain. So, we must check, yes? Yes. I have here the shoes with the names. You should come, please, miss, check the names with me against the docket, we see we have the right shoes, maybe you try yours on, we find them and this makes certain we have the right order, yes? Yes. Come on – back here, we try on. You should excuse us, chentlemen, we have business to do. It's a good thing he brings you with to collect the order, hmm? If he doesn't, maybe we got problems. As it is, maybe we don't.' And he bustled her away into a dusty back room and sat her down so that they could go through the order.

All the time, checking the shoes against the measurements on the docket, trying on her own – which fitted perfectly and confirmed that this was the right order – she strained her ears, trying to pick words out of the faint murmur of voices coming from the front of the shop. What were they talking about, Ambrose and that man? Why did it make her feel so horrible that they were talking at all? Just some silly man with nothing better to do than chatter about himself to anyone who'd listen – but she couldn't rid herself of the sense of irritation that filled her, and as soon as Mr Gamba let her go she hurried back into the shop.

As she reached it the bell on the shop door tinkled again, and someone else came in, a harassed woman with three noisy children in tow, and it was impossible to say anything to Ambrose in the resulting hubbub. Mr Gamba packed up the shoes and gave the parcel to Ambrose with a flourish, and then turned to the moustached man, who smiled at Ambrose once more as they made their way to the door, past the children who were now running about and shouting in a very distracted manner, and then put one hand out towards Ambrose.

'Nice talking to you,' he murmured, and Ambrose nodded. Lexie, glad to be escaping, managed to smile too, and then they were out in the street and it was as though someone had lit a little fire inside her to melt away the coldness, she felt so much better.

'I didn't like that bloke,' she said as she tried to tuck her hand into his arm again, but he was holding the parcel of shoes in the crook of his elbow on that side, so she couldn't. 'Nasty pushy type – '

'Oh, I don't know,' Ambrose said, and her belly tightened into a little knot. She hated that tone of voice; it meant he'd gone off into one of his brown studies, and almost desperately she said, 'Let's go back to Oxford Street, shall we, Ambrose? Maybe they've started putting up some of the Christmas stuff in the shops. It's lovely when they do that, isn't it? We could go and have a look and – '

'No,' he said shortly. 'That's boring. Might as well go back now as do that.'

'Well, let's go to a matinée then. At – at the Alhambra. I haven't got all my money with me, but I could get it when I got home. If you've got the cash now, I'll stand the tickets, only you'll have to lend it to me till we get back – ' She sounded a bit feverish now, and she knew that was the wrong way to do it. This isn't boxing clever, this is being like I used to be, all nagging and getting upset –

'I don't – ' he began, and then there was a call from behind them. He turned and looked back, and she did too. The man with the moustache was standing outside Mr Gamba's shop, and as they looked he lifted one arm in an imperious beckon. Ambrose stared at him and then said uncertainly, 'I think he's calling us – '

'Don't take any notice,' she said loudly, but she knew it was too late. He'd pushed the parcel of shoes into her hands and said in a tight little voice, 'Won't be a sec. Just see what the fella wants – ' and had gone loping back up Dean Street towards Gamba's.

She wanted to run after him, but didn't. It was as though she could hear Alex Lazar's voice inside her head calling out to her, 'Box clever!' and she stood and watched, the parcel of shoes tucked behind her muff, and tried to be relaxed and comfortable, even though the cold feeling had come back inside her.

Ambrose came back after a while, walking towards her with a casual swagger that he sometimes used on stage when they were doing one of the cakewalk sort of performances.

He managed to smile, but it wasn't a friendly grin of the sort she knew meant good things were going to happen. It was quite different, tight-lipped and private, as though he were laughing inside his head at a joke only he knew.

'Listen, Lexie, got a bit of a problem. This chap – good fella really – reckons I could do better than being with a daft kids' show like the old B's and so do I, come to that. And – '

'He's got a nerve! What's it got to do with him? It's none of his bloody business!' she flared, and at once his face went mulish and she could have hit herself for being so stupid.

'You sound like a Billingsgate tail, swearing like that! Why shouldn't someone take an interest in me? He's a dancer, knows about dancing – '

'Fat lot he knows about your dancing! He's never seen you!'

'He knows personality when he sees it!' Ambrose snapped. 'And that's almost as important as dancing talent. You should know, ducky. You haven't exactly got the greatest share of talent there is, have you?'

'You – you mumser!' she shouted, unconcerned at the curious stare of passers by. 'You stinkin' lousy – '

'Like I said, a Billingsgate tail!' Ambrose said, and grinned, a vicious little grimace that made the tears sting her eyes. 'Anyway, I don't know why I'm bothering to talk to you about him. He's none of your business. He's my mate, not yours, and he's given me a ticket to his matinée. He'd only got one, he said, or he'd have given you one too. Mind you, the mood you're in you wouldn't have deserved it anyway – '

'I wouldn't go to his stinking show if it was – '

'Yeah, well, that's as may be. Anyway, you don't get the chance, do you? You take the shoes back to the old B. I'm staying here to go to the Hippodrome to see *Hello Ragtime*. Hard luck on you, ducky!' He patted her on the shoulder and bent and kissed her cheek with a little flourish, then turned and went back to the man still waiting outside Gamba's, marching away down the street with the same swagger he'd used before but now greatly exaggerated. And Lexie stood in the middle of Dean Street, in her grown-up fashionable clothes, clutching a parcel of new ballet shoes, with tears filling her eyes so that she could hardly see. It had started to rain at last, and the rain and her tears fell down her cheeks together, equally unheeded.

# 9

All the way back to the East End in the bus, and then in a tram, she continued to weep, trying not to, but quite unable to prevent the tears from collecting in her eyes and running down her cheeks. Not that anyone seemed to notice: the bored bus conductor took her fare money and pinged her ticket without looking in her face, and her fellow passengers sat and clutched their parcels and chattered at each other or gazed ahead in dull silence, locked in their private worlds. So she was able to sit and stare blindly out at the passing grey streets and their sluggish burdens of vans and horses and pedestrians and lumbering drays, and let the tears run and not care.

The drizzle thickened, becoming heavy relentless rain as she changed from bus to tram at Aldgate, and she stood at the stop waiting, not really caring that the water coursed down her skirt and dripped off the brim of her hat down her neck, feeling that the weather matched her feelings and it was right that it should be so. By the time she reached Cephas Street her clothes were sopping and bedraggled as the cheap fabric lost its dressing and the feathers on her brave little hat sagged and drooped.

She fiddled through the letter box for the string hidden behind and drew out the key, not bothering to knock. Madame G. always complained bitterly at being expected to open the door, and Lenny Ganz never paid any attention if anyone did knock, so the key was kept in its well publicized hiding place and the school's pupils came and went at will.

She put the sodden parcel of shoes down on the table just inside the front door and stood uncertainly for a moment. The house was silent; none of the usual thumping and clatter came from the attics where the dancing classes were carried on, and she was puzzled for a moment. Then she remembered drearily that they'd all been given a day off, even the little ones. Madame G. had private business to attend to, she'd said yesterday, and as long as Ambrose checked the posters at the theatre and collected the shoes their time was their own; so the house was empty, as dull and dismal as she felt, and she sniffed dolorously, finding some melancholy pleasure in the sound in the stuffy little hall with its walls lined with posters of past shows and Madame G.'s productions.

''Oo's 'at?' The voice made her jump, so certain had she been that the house was empty, and she stood still as the sounds came from the front room; a heavy chair pushed back, footsteps shuffling across a carpet, and then he appeared at the doorway and stood peering at her in the dim light.

''Oo's 'at?' he mumbled again and then as he saw her, and came further out into the hall, grinning a little. 'Well, if it ain't the little Ascher. What ho and all that, nice to see you –'

'Hello, Mr Ganz,' she said dully. 'I brought the shoes. There they are. Tell Madame Gansella I'm sorry they're wet, only it's raining.' She turned to go, but as she fumbled with the front door he came shuffling across the hall to catch her arm.

'No need to rush off like that,' he said. 'No need in the world, lovey! Come and have a – here, you're soaked to the skin!'

She looked down at her sleeve, on which he'd set one hand. 'I said, it's raining.'

'Pissing down, more like – sorry, sorry! Got to watch my language with you young 'ns around, eh? Don't tell the old B, will you?' And he shook her arm roguishly. 'Oh, I know what you call her! I know you all call her the old B. That's what you call her and that's what she is. You're not wrong, you bright young sparks, you. A right old B, that she is! Still, we won't say nothing to her, will we? No.' And he leered at her in the half light and shook her arm again. 'Come and get dry.'

'You've been drinking,' she said disgustedly and stared at his face, unshaven and puffy-eyed in the dark hallway, and drew back from his breath which was heavy with gin. 'You're drunk!'

'Drinking I wouldn't deny. On a day like this, all alone and nothing to do, what else is there but a little something to keep the draught off? But drunk? Never on your life. No one can ever say Lenny Ganz gets drunk. Happy, yes. Comfortable, yes. Cheerful, yes. But drunk? Not on your Nelly

Kelly. And if you ever says so, you'll – '

'I'll what?' and she drew away even further.

'Stop being my friend,' he said after a moment. He grinned at her, and at last let go of her arm and leaned against the wall. 'And I am your friend, you know. Who is it covers up for you all when the old B gets her dander up, eh? Who calms her down when she starts coming it a bit too brown? Eh? Me or the man next door?'

She was ashamed for a moment. She didn't like him much, but it was true that he often did calm Madame Gansella down when she hit one of her noisier moods, and started shouting at them all, and it was he who was able to make her stop working them when they were so exhausted they could hardly put one foot in front of the other, and she said awkwardly, 'Well, anyway, you *have* been drinking.'

'Of course I have! Any sensible fella would, day like this. No one in but me, rain coming down fit to bust, so there's no joy poppin' out for a quick one, and anyway there's no dogs today so no need to get a bet on. So here I sit, all on my tod, lonely and having a nip by the fire. Come and have one.'

'No thanks,' she said and began to fumble with the door again.

'Suit yourself. It'd be a lot better'n going out into that,' he said, for now the door was open and she could see out into Cephas Street where the rain was coming down more heavily than ever and the gutters were running furiously as the few passers by went scurrying along, heads down under streaming umbrellas. It was cold, and she shivered involuntarily as a gust of the icy wind whipped round her ankles, wrapping her wet skirt around them. Her feet were frozen, she realized, as she moved her toes in the thin sogginess of her shoes; they'd looked lovely when they were new, these shoes, but now – and she wanted to cry again.

'Might as well sit by the fire till the worst of it's over,' he said, and turned and went back to the front room, pulling the dressing gown in which he was wrapped round him as he went. She stared after him and then at the rain, and after a moment closed the front door and followed him.

It was wonderfully warm, for the fire was piled high, higher than it ever was at home in Victoria Park Road. Even though Bessie was earning good money working for Alex Lazar, she still had to count her pennies carefully, what with the rent and food and bus fares to work and the cost of Lexie's lessons and her insatiable appetite for new clothes and constant need for costumes and new dancing shoes, and big fires were a luxury they just couldn't have. So the sight of this one, with the coals piled in a great crimson mountain and the flames leaping merrily from its peak to reflect in the glossy mahogany sideboard and the mirror over the mantle-shelf and the horsehair-stuffed leatherette sofa, and sending its shadows dancing on the ceiling, was very comforting.

She shivered again and he grinned at her from the fireside chair into which he had settled himself and said, 'Well, stand there if you like it better. For my part, if I was in those daft shoes o' yours I'd take 'em off and come over and get me feet dry.'

She stood for only one more uncertain moment and then came over to the fire, pulling off her hat and looking at it mournfully; it was a wreck, for the gloss that had seemed so much a part of the blackbirds' feathers had washed off in grimy runnels to reveal ordinary pigeons' feathers under-neath, and not very sturdy ones at that, for they had collapsed entirely under the onslaught of the rain, and the hat's brim was drooping and misshapen. After a moment she dropped it on the floor and looked at her muff instead, but that too looked thin and meagre now it was wet, none of the richness it had seemed to have at the start of the day having survived the relentless London downpour. She dropped that on the floor too, and began to peel off her jacket. The rain had gone through to the white blouse beneath, making the colour run and leaving ugly stains on the thin fabric, and the lace fronts were twisted and sagging as well. She stared down at herself and again the tears filled her eyes.

'Here, you're really soaked through, aren't you? You'll catch your death like that. Why didn't you take shelter, you soppy kid? Look at you!' He sounded genuinely concerned as he got to his feet again, came over to her, and picked up the wet clothes from the floor. 'Here, I'll go and get the clothes horse from the kitchen and we can set it all to dry. Better take your skirt and that off and all – no, don't be so daft! You're not shy of me, are you? Known you since you was a nipper, for Gawd's sake. Nothing to be shy about with Lenny, do me a favour! I'll get you something to put on if you're going to make a fuss about it – '

He came back from the kitchen with the clothes horse and with one of his own dressing gowns over one arm. 'Here you are, kid. Get those rags off and put this on. Come on, it won't bite you! I'll take this stuff out to the kitchen and put it round the range there. It'll get in the way here.'

He went away and she could hear him whistling as he pottered about in the kitchen, and after a moment she did as she was told and took off the blouse and her skirt and put on the dressing gown. Her chemise and drawers were wet too, and as blue-stained as her blouse, but she couldn't take them off – they'd have to dry on her just as her black stockings would. She crept nearer to the fire and crouched on the rug in front of it, and for the first time since she had left Ambrose in Dean Street some of the misery in her abated. Not much, but enough to make her feel grateful for the small physical pleasure of being warm again.

He came back with a kettle in one hand and a cup in the other and set the kettle on the fire, balancing it carefully on the coals, and almost at once it began to whistle softly.

'Thought it was nearly on the boil!' he said with satisfaction. 'Give it a minute and we'll have as nice a toddy as anyone could order between here and the Ritz down Piccadilly.' He crouched beside her on the rug, fished under his armchair, and brought out another cup and a bottle of gin, half empty. 'And here's the rest of the necessary,' he said, digging triumphantly into his pocket and pulling out a lemon, a small bag of sugar lumps, a knife and a teaspoon.

'Soon have you as right as ninepence,' he said. 'Right as ninepence you'll be,' and he began slicing lemon into the cups and adding sugar as the kettle began to whistle more purposefully.

'Right, now,' he said after a moment. 'Drop of the necessary and – '

'I don't like gin,' she said quickly as he unscrewed the bottle, and he looked at her with his head set on one side. He looked better now, for he'd combed his hair while he was in the kitchen, and he looked perkier and brighter-eyed, too.

'Bet you've never had it!'

'No,' she said. 'Of course not. Bessie'd never – '

'Then how do you know?'

'Know what?'

'That you don't like it.'

'I mean I've never had it,' she said and giggled suddenly, for he was looking at her so drolly, with his head on one side and his eyes so bright despite their puffiness, that she couldn't help it.

'Then don't say you don't like it,' he said, pouring some into the cup and a good deal more into his own. 'I've only put in a teaspoon, see? See how you like the taste, and it'll warm you up a treat. Time you tried, anyway. Your age – not a baby any more, are you? Got to grow up some time, no matter what your sister says. They're all the same, these women. Try to stop likely kids like you growing up, having a bit of fun for themselves. You drink up, lovey. I've put lots of sugar in – ' And he poured some boiling water into the confection and set the cup down in front of her.

She looked down at it, steaming there on the rag rug. The scent of the sugar and the lemon drifted to her nose as the steam curled lazily from it, and she suddenly thought how long it had been since that tea and toast in Wardour Street. She shivered again, for now the warmth was creeping into her slowly and she was more aware than she had been of her ice-cold feet. He laughed and said, 'Go on, soppy! It won't bite you! Time you tried. A young woman your age – ' And she thought confusedly of Bessie and the way she would fuss if she knew, and of Ambrose walking away and leaving her in Dean Street, and without realizing she had done it she had reached out and picked up the cup and sipped at its contents.

It tasted lovely, sour and sweet and above all hot, with a herby pungency underlying the taste that was new to her tongue, but not disagreeably so, for she had smelled the juniper reek of gin all her life as she had walked past the myriad street corner pubs of the East End and the shouting raucous customers who came out of them to go reeling down the gutters singing and laughing and smelling as this steaming cupful tasted. She had never particularly liked the smell, but now that she could taste it as well it was rather pleasant. She sipped again, and the warmth from it spread gently from her throat down to her chest and then to her belly and moved outwards, wafting gentle fronds of sensation as it went. She grinned at him and sipped again.

He got to his feet and went to sit in his armchair again, watching her as she sat there on the rug, her knees curled up and her arms resting on them as she held the cup to her lips and sipped steadily.

'Like it, then?' he said after a while. She looked up at him, her thick black hair swinging round her face as she turned and smiled, and he frowned suddenly. The light was failing outside the streaming windows as the rain went relentlessly on and on, and here in the front room of the small house there was just the flickering light of the fire and in it her eyes looked even more huge and slightly slanted than they were, and even darker. Her lashes shadowed her face startlingly and when she smiled, as she did now, the planes of her cheeks shifted and gave her a sculptured look. She'd never seemed pretty to his eyes, not like Maisie Kupfer with her fluffy red-gold hair and staring baby blue eyes, but now she looked more than pretty. She looked exciting, and not at all like the child he had known for so long.

'Have a drop more,' he said after a moment, and his voice sounded a little thicker, but she paid no attention. She was feeling better than she would have thought possible: comfortable and languorous and above all warm. She wriggled her shoulders inside the silkiness of the over-large dressing gown and it slipped a little: she knew it showed the shoulder of her stained chemise and didn't care; she didn't care about anything at all, she decided, not even horrible Ambrose leaving her in the street, and when Lenny Ganz came and crouched beside her on the rug again to make another cup of toddy for her – this time with rather more gin than the first one had contained – she watched him dreamily and said nothing, just picking up the cup to resume her steady sipping as soon as it was ready.

He didn't go back to his chair now, but stayed there squatting beside her, and after a while he shifted a little so that he was not squatting but sitting beside her, also with his knees drawn up and his cup held in both hands, as they both sat and stared at the fire.

After a while he put his cup down and held his hands out to the flames. 'Dry now, are you?' he said in a conversational tone. 'Got rid of all that damp?' and he moved one hand to drop it lightly on her leg. 'Those stockings dry, are they?'

'Mmm?' she said. 'Stockings? Don't know,' and looked down at her legs and at his hand resting on the shin of one of them. It was odd how the movement of her head made her feel. It set the room dancing a little as well as the firelight; the

96

light danced and the room danced, and as she looked at her leg it seemed to move too and she giggled. 'Dancing!' she said.

'Lovely legs for dancing,' he said at once, and his voice was still thick. 'Lovely. Always said you was one of the best we had. Anyone can dance, but you've got something else. Style, that's what you got. Style and personality, and lovely legs. Anyone ever told you that?'

'No,' she said, and moved her head sharply again, lifting it to look at him, wanting to make the room dance some more.

'Well, you have,' he said, and suddenly leaned forwards and kissed her mouth. They were so close together on the hearth-rug that he hardly had to move at all to reach her.

'Good,' she said, and then frowned a little. It was very odd how she felt. Her head was dancing all the time now and she wasn't as sure as she had been that it was a dancing she really liked. And Mr Ganz was being –

He leaned closer still and put an arm round her, and at first she pulled away, but that made the movement in her head increase. She stopped and that meant she leaned against him, because they were so close, and he felt the yielding in her and caught his breath sharply. He moved awkwardly on the hearth-rug, widening his legs to accommodate his sudden excitement and discomfort, and for a moment pulled away from her himself.

'Here,' he said and his voice now was very thick indeed. 'Here, what the hell am I – here, this won't do. I got to be mad or really pissed – am I pissed, lovey?'

'Don't know,' she said, and giggled softly 'I'll tell the old B you swore at me, you go on talking like that.'

'I wouldn't swear at you,' he said. 'Nice little girl like you. You wouldn't never tell the old B nothing about me, would you? She's an old B to me as well as to you lot, you know. Tight with her money, tight with her – tight with everything. Not like you, eh?' His arm closed more firmly round her as his moment of caution vanished, and he rested his cheek on top of her head. 'Nice little girl like you. You got to have someone to look after you, you have. Talented little girl, got a big future, you have – lovely little girl; got lovely legs – dancing legs – ' And his hand again reached down to touch her shin. 'Got to dry those lovely legs, haven't we?'

She looked up at him, pulling away so that she could see

into his face, difficult though it was, for the room was darker now and the flickering firelight made everything she looked at seem to jump and dazzle. All she could see was a faint whiteness and the slash of his mouth and she said earnestly, 'Am I a good dancer, Mr Ganz? Am I? Really?'

'You're the best, lovey, the best there is. Got a lot of talent – and I should know. Watched 'em come and go, come and go, and more gone than stayed – got a lot of talent.' Suddenly his face loomed larger in her eyes as he bent forwards and kissed her again, his parted lips, hot and rather moist, pressing hard on hers and trying to force her lips apart too. She shook her head against that almost irritably, wanting to make him talk more.

'Am I really good? Can I be a really top dancer? A real star, in a show like *Hello Ragtime?*'

'Eh?' He blinked in the dimness, peering at her, disconcerted. '*Hello Ragtime?* What about *Hello Ragtime?*'

'Could I be a star in that?' she said again, louder this time, for her voice was beginning to sound a long way away in her own ears and she was afraid he couldn't hear her. 'Could I get into a show like that?'

'Of course you could, lovey, if you wanted to. Course you could – ' Again he bent forwards, his arm tightening even more around her while his other hand gripped her leg more firmly, moving upwards towards her knee.

'How?' she said, and tried to push him away, for the funny feeling in her head was changing now. She felt less dancing than she had, more muzzy, and she wanted to shake her head to get rid of the muzziness, but she couldn't because he was holding her so tightly.

But he couldn't be pushed away and she began to feel breathless as his weight leaned on her more and more, and she was being pushed so that she was lying on the rug on her back and he was on top of her and the hand that had been on her leg had slipped up to her thigh and was pulling on it, the fingers digging in deeply so that they hurt, and she tried to call out to tell him to stop it, he was hurting her, but somehow the more she moved the more excited he became.

Her legs had to give way now because his fingers hurt so much, and she tried to move, tried to bend her knees upwards, but she couldn't because he was too heavy for her, and she opened her mouth to yell at him but she couldn't do that either, for his weight was completely on top of her now and her face was buried in his dressing gown.

The muzziness had gone from her head now, and the dancing feeling. She felt sick as the heaviness on her pressed down harder and harder and he was pulling at her chemise and her drawers and now for the first time she was very frightened. To have her drawers torn – Bessie would go mad, Bessie would shout and cry. This was what Bessie had tried to talk about sometimes, getting all hot and red and never managing to explain properly. This was boys taking liberties, only it was a man. Liberties was what Bessie had called it and Lexie had never known what liberties meant before, but now she did as his fingers went scrabbling deeper between her legs, painfully, and she opened her mouth and tried to bite him, but got only a mouthful of dressing gown.

She could feel his body against her now, not just hot and heavy but painfully hard as well, pushing against her legs, and she had a sudden image of Ambrose swaggering down the street towards the man with the moustache and she fought even harder, even though that seemed to make Lenny Ganz more excited, more breathless. Then at last she managed to turn her head and get her mouth open properly and took a breath, ready to scream, when above her head, many miles above her head it seemed, she heard it, and at first she was more frightened that she might come into the room and see it all than grateful it had stopped as abruptly as it had begun.

Because suddenly he was gone, rolling off her, leaving her breathless on the rug, her drawers twisted around her bottom and her stockings torn, hearing Madame G. in the hallway outside, stamping her wet feet on the mat and calling, 'Lenny?' in a loud, imperious voice.

# 10

She was sitting on the rug with her hands held out to the fire when they came into the room, and she looked over her shoulder at Madame Gansella and smiled at her, a thin anxious smile, but in the dim light it looked normal enough.

99

'I got ever so wet,' she said. 'It's spoiled all my clothes. Did you get wet, Madame?'

'Why did *you* bring the shoes?' Madame demanded, staring at her, frowning. 'I sent Alfie – Ambrose.'

'He said I could go with him,' Lexie said, and wriggled her bare toes in front of the fire, staring down at them so that her bobbed hair swung forwards and hid her face. It was easier to talk naturally when she couldn't be seen. 'Good thing I did, really. He had to go off somewhere after we got them, so he said I could bring them back. And they got wet. Are they all right?'

'Hmmph. They'll do. More by luck than judgement,' Madame said. She pulled her own wet coat off and came over to the fire.

'Well, it was better to open the parcel right away to see if they were all right, wasn't it?' Lenny said and leaned against the door, carefully not looking at Lexie. 'I'd have looked sooner, only I was getting this stupid kid sorted out. You should have seen her. Looked like a drowned rat, it did. We'd 'a' had her sister after us like Gawdelpus if we'd let her go home in that state.'

'I'm sure,' Madame said and then, abruptly, 'What did he do, Lexie?'

'Who?' Lexie said, feeling her face going red and not knowing what to do about it. She'd moved quickly as soon as Lenny had gone out to meet Madame in the hall, had pulled her clothes straight and dragged off her torn stockings and hidden the gin bottle under the chair again as fast as she could, knowing instinctively it was the right thing to do, the only thing to do, and now here she was asking questions –

'Ambrose, who else?' Madame snapped. 'You said he had to go somewhere. Where did he go? What did he do?'

'Oh, yes,' she said and considered for a moment. Tell her? Make a fuss for Ambrose? Cover up, box clever for Ambrose? She saw the image again, saw him walking away with her with that swaggering walk along Dean Street to the man with the moustache –

'He met someone who said he could do better than be in your shows,' she said clearly. 'Fella from *Hello Ragtime* at the Hippodrome. He gave him a ticket for the matinée but there wasn't one for me. So I had to bring the shoes home, and I got wet.'

'Christ, I'll kill that little bastard,' Madame Gansella said and Lexie looked up, startled at the viciousness in her tone. 'What's he trying to do? Get me in real shtooch? For Christ's sake, Lenny, didn't you talk to him last time? I told you to tell him I won't have it! He'll get me in real trouble, the bloody little pansy–' She stood up and turned back to the fire, then caught sight of Lexie staring at her and tried to smile. 'Nothing to worry about, dearie. It's just that – you know how it is, I don't like you children going off with strangers.'

'The man said he'd seen Ambrose before,' Lexie said, remembering. 'He said, "Nice to see you again." But Ambrose didn't reckon he'd seen him before, he said.'

'It's the sort of thing they always say,' Madame said, and began to unpin her hair, letting its heavy swathes fall down her back to dry. She looked younger and yet tired that way, and Lexie looked at her and just for a moment wished she'd said nothing about Ambrose and the man with the moustache.

'It'll be all right, won't it?' she said now. 'I mean, Ambrose, he's all right. He's grown-up. Seventeen–'

'Not grown-up enough for that,' Madame said.

'For what?' Lexie scrambled to her feet, carefully pulling the dressing gown round her as she did so, not looking at Lenny Ganz.

'Never you mind, dearie. Just remember, people shouldn't talk to strangers and certainly not go off with them. Even to matinées. Lenny – when he gets back, tell him. It's a bad example for the younger ones, tell him. Tell him – oh, anything you like. Only it's got to stop. You understand? He won't listen to me, but maybe you'll be able to get him to see–'

'Yeah, sure,' Lenny said and opened the door. 'See if your things are dry, shall I, Lexie? Time you were going home. Your sister'll be home soon, wondering where you are–'

'If I only had more boys, Can't get my hands on boys, that's the trouble. They don't fancy dancing enough – and I've got to have boys for the show. Tell him, Lenny. He'll listen to you, knows he's got to learn to be trusted to take care of himself properly, stupid little – you hear me? As soon as he gets back, whenever that may be. Tell him.'

Lenny said nothing but went out to the kitchen and

101

brought back Lexie's clothes, still damp, but she didn't care about that. He gave them to her, still not looking at her, and she took them without a word and said to Madame Gansella, 'Can I go upstairs to get dressed, please, Madame?'

'Hmm? Oh yes. You could do it here, if you like. It'll be warmer –'

'I'd rather go upstairs,' Lexie said, and Madame nodded tiredly and stretched her neck, rubbing at the back of it with her fists.

'Well, at least *you'll* be no trouble to me. Nice modest kid like you. All right, dearie. You go and get dressed, and thanks for bringing the shoes. I'll sort out Ambrose tomorrow. And when you're dressed, Lenny'll see you to the bus home. Take the umbrella, Lenny. It's still coming down cats and dogs. Tell your sister I'm sorry you got so wet – I dare say your things'll be all right when they're pressed –' She sat down in the chair at the fire, rested her head on the back of it and closed her eyes.

He said nothing all the way, walking punctiliously on the outside of the pavement, holding the umbrella carefully over her head, and not seeming to mind how splashed he was as horses clopped by and cabs thundered through the streaming gutters. Not until they got to the end of the road and the bus stop for the Mare Street bus that would take her back to Victoria Park Road did he say anything, and then it was as though the words were being squeezed out of him.

'That was a funny game we got to playing there, eh, Lexie?'

'Game?' she said. 'I didn't know it was a game.' Don't nag, don't get excited, box clever, she thought suddenly, feeling icy cold, very much in control. Listen to him, don't shout out now.

He reddened and the hand holding the umbrella shook a little, sending a shower of drops scattering over his own head. 'You know what I mean, lovey. I just got a bit soppy there, that's all. Not my fault. You're getting a big girl, you know, and you're quite a – not my fault, you know.'

'It wasn't mine,' she began hotly, and then stopped. Box clever, don't nag – remember, don't argue with people.

''Course not, lovey, 'course not. You was great, really you

102

was. I mean, getting it all tidy and then sitting there as though–' He shook his head in admiration, peering down at her in the darkness. 'If you'd been twice your age you couldn't 'a' been cooler. Some actress you are, I tell you. Some actress.'

'Yes?' she said, pleased, and then shook her head. 'I don't feel well.' Nausea was stirring inside, deep in her belly. 'Don't feel well.'

'Got a cold coming, that's what it is. Caught in the rain, caught a cold. Tell your sister you got a cold coming. She'll dose you. Oh, yes and – here–' He reached in his pocket and pulled out a small paper bag which he held out to her. 'Have one of these.'

'What are they?'

'Cachoux. Breath sweeteners.'

'Oh,' she said and after a moment took one. It was sweet and sickly, tasting of violets, and she felt more nauseated than ever.

'Anyway, we won't say anything about this afternoon to anyone, hmm?' he said, and the wheedling tone in his voice made her feel less sick for a moment. To have an adult talk to her like that! It was the way she had used to talk to Bessie sometimes. That tone was as familiar as her own voice, and she smiled at him suddenly. He looked at her anxiously and then smiled back, eagerly, his unshaven face drawn in the dimness of the gaslit street.

'I dare say not,' she said in as cold a voice as she could muster, for her stomach was making itself more and more felt and her mouth was dry. 'As long as everything else goes all right–' And she didn't really know what she meant by that, just that it seemed the right thing to say.

'Yes,' he said doubtfully, staring at her, and then, as the bus came lumbering along, its lamps glooming heavily at them through the steady drizzle, said, 'Will you be all right now, get home all right?'

'Yes,' she said, and held out her hand to stop the bus. 'I'll be all right. And don't worry, I won't say nothing to anybody. Not unless I've got to–' The bus stopped and she got on. The conductor shouted, 'Hold very tight there please!' and rang the bell, and she stood on the platform looking at him as the bus lumbered away. He looked very small standing there on the pavement, diminishing with the increasing distance, and she watched him until he was out of sight. How strange that she had ever found him frightening, she thought. How very strange. And then, as the bus lurched, she closed her eyes. She was going to be very, very sick. Soon.


'So what do I do, Mr Lazar? Tell her no? If I do that she – well, you know how she is. She gets upset. And she says it's a chance, a real chance – oh, I don't know. I just hate thinking of her like that, running around the country like some sort of –'

'Not exactly running around, Bessie. You've never seen what it's like, these shows. I have – any number of them. They work hard. Rehearsing on the stage in the mornings, getting the show right, then sleeping to get over the performances' late nights – and then sitting around in cold trains and charas – there's no time for any hanky panky, if that's what's worrying you –' He leaned back in his chair and took a deep and rather noisy pull at his coffee cup, and then bit with huge relish into an onion platsel, so that the cream cheese and smoked salmon with which it was lavishly filled bulged out to leave his mouth ringed with it like a greedy baby's. He wiped the back of his hand over his lips and then nodded at her, his jaws working busily. 'Believe me, you're worrying for nothing,' he said as soon as he could get the words out. 'Poppy Gansella, she don't let nothing happen in her shows might spoil the takings. She watches her kids like a hawk, so you don't have to worry. The kid wants a career in the business? She could go further and fare worse. What else do you want for her? She should work in the sweat shops? Come and be a waitress for me?'

'She could do worse than that, that's for sure,' Bessie said and smiled at him suddenly, and it lifted her face into unusually pleasant lines. Generally she looked anxious and abstracted as she busied herself about her day's work. He nodded back at her now, liking to see her pleased. 'It's the best thing I ever did.'

'Well, not exactly a waitress, are you? Good right hand to me, that's what you are. Hasn't done me any harm having you here, and that's the truth of it. Best thing I ever did, taking you. Even if my Hannah had been interested in the job, I'd have been in stooch now, without you. She's got better things to do than work for me, hmm?'

She smiled, well aware of how much delight he took in his widowed niece and her child. 'How is she?' she said politely, and at once he launched into an account of the charm and intelligence and the altogether superior qualities over all other three-year-olds that his great-niece enjoyed, and the marvellous courage and dressmaking skills and wit and general wonderfulness of his niece, as she knew he would. Bessie settled to thinking her own thoughts, letting him rattle on as she chewed mechanically through the early lunch they were sharing over her desk behind the Tottenham Court Road tea shop.

Outside brooms and buckets clattered as the cleaners got the restaurant ready for the lunchtime customers who would soon descend on them from the offices and shops around, and the smell of roasting beef and boiling vegetables came drifting from the kitchens. It was usually her favourite time of day, this, when her desk was clear and the books for the previous day straight. Soon she would have to go and inspect the waitresses, to make sure each of them was scrubbed and pin-neat in her black frock and lace-trimmed apron, that each had her hair neatly tucked out of sight behind the matching lace-trimmed headband with its black velvet ribbon threaded through it, that fingernails were clean and tables laid just so, and the mirrors and chrome all shining invitingly. But now was her own time.

It should have been an even more agreeable time with Mr Lazar dropping in on one of his rare visits to check the books and compliment her – as he always did, for they were kept with impeccable care – and gossip a little. But Lexie had spoiled all that. Worrying about Lexie spoiled so much these days, she thought for a moment, and felt an unexpected stab of anger at her. The child she had loved and protected and worked for so hard seemed to have died, to have run away, to be replaced by a totally different and much less lovable person. The new Lexie was not only taller and a different shape, with a long narrow waist and sleek hips and a hint of a roundness over her chest – only a hint, for she had a boyish look rather than a luscious one – but a sharper, more determined person and a much more self-assured one.

But she didn't ask or plead prettily or coax as she had been

105

used to and which Bessie had so enjoyed, even when she knew she was being manipulated. She just said quietly that she was doing this or that, seeming quite unaware of Bessie's dislike of some of her proposals. Her clothes, her discreet use of make-up even when she wasn't on the stage, her determination to have her lovely thick black hair bobbed in that ugly modern fashion – all of these things she just did and smiled calmly at Bessie, whatever she said, and showed no interest in her feelings.

No wonder I have to worry about her, Bessie thought now, pushing away her plate of sandwiches as Alex at last stopped talking about his precious Hannah and Mary Bee. No wonder. I wish she'd leave me in peace – and then hated herself for the thought, for who else was there for her to love? Who else was there for her to worry about? And she looked across her neat desk at Alex Lazar, now swallowing the last of his coffee with obvious relish, and thought – I wish I could look after you – and at once suppressed it. She had realized long ago, within a year of starting work with him, that that was a ridiculous dream. It wasn't only that she was plain and misshapen, bad enough as that was; it was just that he was so absorbed in his work, so satisfied with bustling about his many different businesses that he had no time for more than the occasional night with one of the prettier and sillier waitresses. Certainly he wasn't interested in his chief clerk in the way she had become interested in him – no, that was not to be thought of.

'So I should let her go?' she said after an interval. He looked at her and sighed, then pushed his plate to one side and leaned forwards on the table, his arms folded in front of him.

'Dolly, will you ever understand what you got there in that kid? You got a tiger by the tail, that's what you got. A real tiger. She's ambitious, that one. She's so ambitious, it don't matter what anyone does.'

'Ambitious? I suppose so. But what good'll it do her? So she goes on the road, gets this chance to be top of the bill and all that. What good'll it do her if she never has any fun, the way a kid should? Always working – what sort of ambition is that?'

He grinned then. 'My sort, doll, my sort. I'm cut out o' the same piece o' cloth, I am. That's how I know what your

106

Lexie is. Know better than she does.' He stopped then and stared at her, his eyes glazing a little. 'That's the thing about it, you know. It takes years to find out what you're really like. Here am I, old man–'

'No, not old!' she protested at once, but he waved a hand at her.

'Old enough, old enough. Forty-five. It's only now I know what makes me tick – or some of what makes me tick. I'm not sure I've found it all out yet. Your Lexie, she don't know yet, neither. She's got a long way to go and a lot to find out. And nothing you say, or I say, or anyone else says, is going to stop her. She's on her way, that one. She's hungry, you see. Hungry for everything and anything – it's all meat to her. Work and attention and making things go her way. Oh, she'll do well, she will. And if you want to go on having any part of her life, Bessie, you'll stop trying to pull the other way. You'll lose all the way down the line if you do. She'll just cut the rope you're pulling on and leave you flat on your back in the mud–'

'You make her sound so hard! So cruel – but she isn't! She's just a kid, that's all! She doesn't know what she wants, and she needs someone to look after her, to guide her–'

He sighed and shook his head. 'Haven't you listened to a word I've said? I told you – she's *ambitious*. Hungry. She won't take guidance from you or anyone else. She'll do it her way – and I'll tell you something else. She'll make everyone around her do it her way, too. So lay off. Say yes to the things you can't say no to, and then maybe on the little things she'll give in and let you have your own way once in a while. Let her go on her tours, let her work at the business all the hours God gives, and then maybe when she needs a bit of a rest and looks like she won't take one, you'll be able to persuade her to take a holiday, and maybe she'll listen. And you'll stay close, that's the thing. But you try to make her live her life your way, and she'll be gone. Just like that–' And he blew in the air and made a comical face at her. 'Just like that.'

'I wish I didn't love her so much,' she said, almost to herself as he got to his feet, and went to peer through the curtain shrouding the glass door of the office at the restaurant outside, now sparkling clean, and tables laid ready for the day's business. 'I really do.' She got up and went over to the

107

door too, to see the waitresses already lining up outside ready for her sharp-eyed inspection. 'It's just that – well, she's all I've got.'

'I know how you feel,' he said. 'It's like me and my niece. You love someone, you love 'em and there's nothing you can do about it, for all it's a nuisance, gets in the way of business and all. You just have to love 'em and run when they need you. But sometimes you have to stand back and let 'em live their own way and not come running. I had to do it when my poor Hannah lost her husband, three years ago, you know? Now, she's fine, running her own nice little business. You've got to do the same for your Lexie. Stand back, let her suffer her own pain, go through her own mistakes. It's the only way.'

'I suppose so,' she said drearily, and she nodded, putting her hand on the doorknob. But he stopped her, his own hand on her shoulder, and she was very aware of the warmth of it and of the fact that it was her twisted shoulder he was touching. He seemed unaware of that, though, and she didn't know whether that made her feel better about it or worse.

'Listen, Bessie, your sister Fanny, your brothers – you ever see them?'

She shook her head. 'No. Not since – all that fuss. No, I don't. I was always afraid they'd try to take her away, you see and–' She shook her head, startled to find suddenly that tears were very near the surface of her voice.

He made a little face. 'I was wrong, maybe. Shouldn't have encouraged you to keep your distance that way, moving house an' all–' He grinned then, disarming in his honesty. 'Tell you the truth, Bessie, it gave me such pleasure to do that mumser Dave Fox in the eye, I couldn't resist it. But I shouldn't have included you in my private fights, hmm? Anyway, all these years – it's water under the bridge – you should forget old quarrels, hey? Families, for all they drive you meshuggah, they're all you've got when you come down to it. These people you get stuck with may be a lot of trouble to you, drive you mad the way the people you choose as friends never do, but when it comes down to it, family's family. Go see Fanny already, Bessie. You need your own people–'

'But, Lexie – they might still want to–'

'Ah, phooey to that! I don't suppose they ever would have

taken her anyway. They were just having a go at you. That's families, ain't it? Anyway, it don't make no never mind any more. There's no one in the world'll make your Lexie do anything she don't want to. I've told you. She's hungry, she's ambitious, she'll do what she wants. She's not much more'n a kid in some ways, but in most of the ones that matter she's a mensch, a person, a real grown-up person. You don't have to be afraid no more for her. Go see your sister, Bessie. Whatever else she is, she's still your sister.'

# 11

'Aim sure Ai don't hev to tell you brave boys how proud we all are to be heah with you all this evening—' Madame Gansella trumpeted, her face gleaming with sweat and her hair curling in wild tendrils round her forehead. 'Today of all days — to be privileged to be amongst you, who hev made so many sacrifices for us, heah on the Home Front — Ai assure you we are all speechless with admiration for you—'

'I wish she bloody well was,' Sid whispered into Lexie's ear. She nudged him with a sharp little elbow and he squeaked with pain, while Madame Gansella threw a furious glare into the wings and then sailed on triumphantly, lifting her arms to the audience to show the swathes of her purple gown. It was beginning to show signs of its age, that purple thing, Lexie thought; thank God for footlights — they hid a multitude of sins in their glare.

'And now, as we stend heah in the light at the end of the interminable tunnel—' ('There she goes again,' whispered Sid, and this time Lexie giggled too) '— we give up our heartfelt thanks to you, to all of you, and to those of your Dear Old Pals who made the great, the supreme sacrifice, for all of us!' She bent her head for a moment and then, after the most scant of pauses, lifted it and went on even more loudly, if that were possible. 'We offer you our own humble little contribution to the war effort — an effort we must all now pray, on this great Armistice Day, will soon be ended for all time. Not our little show, of course, but your great sacrifices—' And aware that she had made some sort of error, she hurried on, 'Ai give you, all of you, our offering to you from us as a small measure of thenks for all you hev done – Ladies and Gentlemen – *Babies – on – Parade!*'

'We're on –' Sid said. Fixing his face into its practised stage grin he jerked his head at the people behind him and off they went, batons twirling and heads tossing, marching to the thumping of the slightly tinny piano to the centre stage. Lexie watched them as step followed familiar step, the flashing knees of the girls beneath their khaki satin skirts, displaying their khaki satin knickers, and the boys in their mock officers' uniforms, all of the highest rank, kicking and stamping as they held their wooden rifles at the present. It's all so tired, she thought, as tired as I am, as tired as she is – and she looked at Madame Gansella, now standing on the opposite prompt side watching them, her face heavy in its fatigue now that she was no longer smiling.

Thank God it's over, Lexie thought as her cue came and she went marching on to take her place centre stage as befitted the star of the number. Thank God it's all over, I can go back to London, leave this lousy show, get a real shop – left right, kick, change, this is a lousy routine, time step, kick, change – a lousy boring routine. I'm tired, tired, tired–

In the wings Madame Gansella's face had lost its heavy look, the sagging flesh around her mouth lifting as she watched Lexie approvingly, saw her long legs looking even longer in those khaki stockings, the thick dark hair gleaming in the lights, and the provocative little grin that tilted the corners of that narrow mouth to match the slant of her eyes. Already the audience was reacting as they always did when Lexie came on; sitting up straighter, leaning forwards a little, actually watching rather than just letting it all go on in front of their eyes, and Madame Gansella smiled a sharp little grin now as she caught the pianist's eye and he beamed and nodded at her. She'd told him her top-of-the-bill was a real goer, but he hadn't believed her, thought she was covering up when she'd told him Lexie didn't rehearse, didn't need to, not for this number. He'd grumbled, said they always rehearsed every concert party that came into the hospital, but she'd ridden over him, told him Lexie was different, and now there he was, nodding away and grinning like a great monkey. Bloody men, always grinning for the wrong reasons. It wasn't Lexie's dancing, that was for sure – and she

110

winced as Lexie missed a step and then relaxed as she slipped in another, recovered the beat and went on as though nothing had happened; bloody men, they know nothing about dancing. All they see when they look at her is sex. And her only twelve years old.

Supposed to be only twelve years old, she reminded herself as the number moved into its climax, with the boys picking Lexie up, tossing her from one to the other as though she were no more than a bag of feathers – and indeed she was skinny enough to be no heavier – *supposed* to be. She told everyone who booked *Babies on Parade* that it was the wartime version of her famous *Juvenile Jollities* show, 'Every Child an Artiste, Every Artiste a Child', and assured them loftily that no performer was over twelve. She'd got away with it with Sid, stunted little ass that he was, and the others were none of them over fifteen, but Lexie had been more of a worry to her. She'd watched her all through the war years as tour followed tour and audience after audience fell for her, terrified that she'd suddenly shoot up the way kids often did, terrified she'd grow a great pair of breasts and vast hips, but thank God she hadn't. At almost eighteen she still had the same slender boyishness she'd had four years ago. Her face had sharpened a little, lost its baby smoothness, and her legs had become even more shapely, but the rest of her was much the same. Thank God, she thought again as the number came to its usual riotous end, with the audience roaring its approval. Thank God – and she hurried on stage as the curtain swished into place to push the collection bags into the girls' hands – the biggest to Lexie as usual – and hurry them on their way to the real business of the evening.

Considering the fact they were all patients deemed too ill to leave the hospital to go into Keighley to celebrate Armistice Night in whatever fashion that dour Yorkshire town thought fit, they were generous. As Lexie moved from bathchair to bathchair, her eyes wide and her mouth pouting a little, a look that encouraged them to believe she was only twelve, she felt the silver weigh down her bag more and more heavily and knew Madame G. would be cheerful tonight. There'd be a good supper for them all, and maybe, this time, I'll be able to get some money out of her, mean bitch.

The old B, she thought suddenly, and remembered

Ambrose, who'd named her that in the first place. No one ever called Madame G. the old B any more, not since he'd left the show. I wonder how he is? she thought now, and then, dodging with a skilful sideways slip of her hips as she passed the bed of a man who clearly didn't care whether she was twelve or twenty, so long as he got his hands on her, pushed the memory of Ambrose away. Probably in the army now. Probably dead like so many others, after this past four years—

Later, lying in bed in the attic the hospital had set aside for the use of the travelling shows that came to entertain the patients, she thought of him again, wondering why she should have thought about Ambrose after all this time, and then remembered the man in the bathchair set in the shadows, the one with the bandage over his face, who had held a shilling out towards her, his head lifted as he tried to see her through the small aperture left in his bandage over his right eye. He'd had the same dark red hair above the bandage that Ambrose had, that was it. And I'm tired and it's been a funny day, what with the war being over and all—

She rolled over on her belly and pushed her face into her pillow, trying to make sleep come by staring deep into the blackness behind her closed lids. She often did that, making great circles of light appear as she stared, followed by glittering dancing kaleidoscopes of colour, but tonight it wouldn't happen. Tonight she couldn't sleep as easily as that, and after a while she rolled over again and sat up and stared round the attic.

There in the corner she could just see the curtain that Madame G. had rigged up for herself, as she always did when she had to share a room with the girls of the company – which was depressingly often – and around her the four humped shapes that were the other girls. Stupid creatures, every one of them country lumps, not like the lively London girls who had been part of the show when it had first become *Babies on Parade*, the khaki equivalent of the show that had toured the country all through early 1914. These had been recruited wherever Madame G. could find them after the others had gone rushing back to London when the news had come that August day that there was a war on. Bessie had written frantically, trying to make Lexie go back too, but she'd decided not to. What would there be to do in London if she did go back? she'd asked herself. There wouldn't be another show, and there wouldn't be anywhere worthwhile to work. Even a lousy show like this one, with country bumpkins who could barely hop, let alone dance, would be better than sweating it out in London.

So, in spite of Bessie's entreaties, she'd stayed on the road, constantly writing to Bessie that she was too busy to make visits to London, too tired to get there, too involved in her war work, everything except that she couldn't afford it, for Bessie, she knew, would have sent her the fare money. It was all she could do in her letters to keep Bessie from visiting *her*; she'd written vaguely of mixed-up dates, of not knowing where *Babies on Parade* was going next, of not being able to ensure Bessie would have somewhere to sleep – anything to keep her at arm's length. Why she had to do that, Lexie was never quite sure – she just knew it was important to her to be detached, to keep contacts with her young years and her young life – and therefore Bessie – as remote as she could. It was as though she was only a real person, her own person, away from the East End and from Bessie.

So, she stayed on the road, helping Madame G. teach the newcomers, helping run the whole thing, and getting more and more involved with it all as she became less and less involved with home.

But not involved enough to get any money out of it. Sitting now, leaning against the attic window, staring out at the hoarfrost-shrouded countryside which looked for all the world like a newspaper photograph in its stark monochrome, she brooded on that. She, Lexie, had been the one to think of the idea of sending the cast out among the audience to take a silver collection after the performances, instead of trying to get themselves paid by the organizers at the hospitals and theatres where they played. She'd been the one who'd devised the way they'd get round quickly to get all they could out of the audience while it was still excited and elevated by the show, and yet Madame G. had managed to hold on to the lot.

She paid for their food and shelter, she'd told Lexie grandly, sorted out the costumes, arranged the transport – of course the money was used wisely, and for the company! But sometimes Lexie would see her with Lenny, whispering with their heads together, and she knew with a bitter certainty that

113

it was about money, that they were making a profit, that they were feeding their own pockets, that there should be more for the company, and most especially for Lexie, than they admitted. Even Lenny Ganz tightened up and refused to speak of the matter when she confronted him. Even threatening to tell Madame G. of what had happened that rainy afternoon four years ago didn't have any effect on him.

'Tell her,' he'd said. 'After all this time you think she'd believe you? It's not as though you've ever let me get within a bloody six foot of you ever since. If you had, maybe you'd have something to complain about, but as it is, ducky, you ain't got nothing on me. Go tell her what you bleedin' well like. It won't get you nothing.'

Silly, I was, she thought now, staring dreamily out at the silver and black and grey beyond the steamed windows, and thinking of Lenny Ganz asleep now in the adjoining attic, with the boys. If I'd known then what I know now I would have—

What? jeered a little voice inside her head. What would you have done? What could you have done? Made rows over him? Not worth it, stupid little geezer – and anyway, it would have upset Madame G. –

She thought a while about Madame G. Over ten years it had been now that she'd been dancing for her. Over ten years – for ever really. She'd not liked her much, not from the start, but there was something about her that made her feel – what? Impatient yet concerned. Irritated but protective. That's it. She didn't like her, thought her stupid with her special voices for special situations and airs and graces, but all the same there was something about her that demanded Lexie's care. So she gave it, and that was why she'd never told her about Lenny's 'game' with her all that time ago.

And she grinned now in the half light of the frostlit Yorkshire night at how naïve she'd been. She'd known when it had happened it was something that shouldn't have happened, that Lenny wouldn't want his wife to know about it, but not really known why. That knowledge had come slowly, during the touring years, listening to stage hands guffawing and gossiping with each other, listening to the girls in the company who were older than she was, sharing confidences. Then she'd found out what it was all about.

And hated it. She'd stood in front of a mirror in a scruffy

114

little hotel somewhere north of Birmingham, and looked at her own body, strong and springy and as full of movement as a newly wound clock, and had turned and twisted, staring at her narrow hips and flat belly and the small breasts that perched on her chest front so absurdly, and hated the idea of anyone else ever having any share of it. It's my body, she had thought, gazing at herself and liking what she saw. My body, my bones, my muscles, my dancing. No one else shall ever do to it the things men do to women's bodies. It's mine and I shall keep it —

And then she had thought of Bessie, alone and lonely in London, writing those reams of letters to her, following her around the country with great fat envelopes, never offering a word of complaint about the scrappiness of Lexie's own answers, and her sometimes transparent excuses for keeping herself apart, but somehow managing to plead in every line for more from her, and she had shivered. Is that what happened to people who didn't do with their bodies what the girls talked and giggled about, what the men guffawed about? And she had been filled with a huge and sudden anger at the accident that had made her a girl instead of a boy. If she'd been a boy she'd have been able to dance harder, leap higher, twirl on her points longer —

I'll be all right, whatever I am, because I'm me, she thought now, and shivered as the chill of the night bit more deeply through her thin nightdress. I'll do fine. I've got to get out of this lousy show and back to London and find a proper shop. She ran back across the bare boards to burrow under the thin blankets, and curled up as small as she could to conserve her body heat. I'll find a London show to get a shop in. Chorus if I must, but with all my experience I ought to be able to do better than that. A speciality spot, maybe, a featured performer, that's what I'll be — almost a star —

Sleep began to creep towards her and she curled up even more tightly and let her mind wander, let it choose its own images for her to live instead of directing it as she usually did. And as drowsiness slid even closer she saw herself, a small figure in the middle of a dark stage, dancing and leaping and drifting bubble-light, and she heard the roar of an excited audience. It was a sound she'd heard in reality often enough, but never as loudly or as enthusiastically as she heard it now in her mind, and she knew that this was because it was a West

End audience that was watching her, admiring her, truly appreciating her for the artist she was, not a lot of glittery-eyed men watching her and not caring about dancing at all—

The images shifted, shimmered, split and doubled, and there she was, not dancing alone as she had been, but with a partner, a tall partner with dark red hair, and, half asleep though she was, she frowned and didn't like it. A star on my own, that's what I'll be. On my own. I don't want anyone sharing it. No one at all. And she concentrated and made the image of the tall boy disappear. It was a good thing to manage to do, that, and she fell further towards sleep, enjoying her own power.

Tomorrow, back to London, she told herself as the last vestiges of consciousness shredded and disappeared. Tomorrow I'm going back to London – Madame G. can do what she likes with her show. I'm going home to Bessie. I can do better than this, if Bessie'll help me. And she will, even though I've been away all these years.

She will.

# 12

'So, when are we going to have a simcha, Lexie, hmm? When? A big girl like you – eighteen already, time you were thinking of it – '

Lexie stared at her, her face blank, hiding her confusion and the undertow of irritation as best she could. She had known that Bessie had made up the family rift at the beginning of the war; she'd written and told her so, page after page of gossip about how Auntie Fanny was doing this and that and how much money she and Uncle Dave were making and how the boys had managed to get themselves into reserved jobs so that they didn't have to join the army and how well Monty was getting on at college learning to be an accountant, but she hadn't expected to find them all there as a welcoming committee on the day she got home for the first time after being away so long.

But there they all were: Fanny, somewhat stouter than Lexie remembered her, but dressed exceedingly fashionably

116

in a green silk chemise dress daringly midcalf in length and with her hair bobbed as short as Lexie's own, and Dave stouter still, but otherwise unchanged, and Benny as quiet as he had always been, and Monty grown into unrecognizable adulthood, all staring at her with a curiosity that made her want to scream at them with anger.

The only one she might have been pleased to see, her once much loved brother Joe, was the only absentee, and she was too put out at the mass descent by them all on the Victoria Park Road flat to show any interest by asking after him, and no one offered an explanation. She could only look at them all from behind the barrier of her expressionless face and feel anger; they had no right to be there getting in the way when she wanted to talk to Bessie, had plans to make, things to sort out – she caught Bessie's eye on the other side of the room, and tried to contain her irritation even more firmly. Bessie was so patently excited to have her home, so pleased and happy, that Lexie had been startled.

For her own part, coming back to London had meant the hope of a new job with a better company, meant being rid of the Gansella show, rid of Lenny, Sid and the country bumpkin dancers, and being with Bessie again had not figured large in her anticipation; she hadn't thought of what it might mean to Bessie, and it had been disconcerting to be greeted so lovingly and with such towering excitement. Disconcerting, but a little agreeable too. She had remembered Bessie's care as being cloying, too controlling, boring, and that was why she had needed to stay away, but now it felt like a warm blanket and she rather relished it.

Or did until she had realized that Bessie needed to share her excitement and had asked the whole family to come and visit, on her very first day home, and now she sat in the crowded living room of the familiar old flat with all of them sitting round the table and staring at her over the coffee cups.

'Simcha?' she said now, lifting her chin. 'What do you mean, Fanny?' That was the first thing that was to change, she told herself. No more of that childish Auntie and Uncle stuff.

Fanny shook her head in mock roguishness. 'Oy, oy, don't tell me you've spent so much time shlapping around with the goyim that you've forgotten all about who you are! A simcha! A wedding, my dear. To stand under the chuppah, to be a kallah, a bride – it's a great mitzvah. The Talmud says it, you know. Eighteen. It's the time for marriage – '

'She's been doing war work, Fanny,' Bessie said, and Lexie could hear the anxiety in her voice. 'You can't expect her to have as much Yiddishkeit as if she'd stayed at home here with me – '

Fanny shook her head. 'War work? So, do me a favour, Bessie! This dancing around with a cheap show is by you war work? War work is doing something for the *war*, like me and Dave! We've been making uniforms for soldiers since it started. By me this is war work.'

'And by me it's making a good living,' Dave said, relighting his cigar which had gone out for the fifth time in a quarter of an hour. 'Which God 'elp us is likely to change now the Armistice is here. Still, there'll be other things to do – so lay off already, Fanny. The kid's been home five minutes, you're nagging already – '

'Well, you know how I feel! She shouldn't have gone on such a mishaguss! My mother, rest her dear soul in peace, must be whirling in her grave like a dervish. She was always so careful of us all, so anxious we should be good well-behaved Jewish girls – '

'Lexie's a very good – ' Bessie began, but Lexie's voice cut across crisply.

'I've no intention of getting married, Fanny. I've got much better things to do,' and she reached for the coffee pot and poured another cup for herself and for Bessie, pointedly ignoring everyone else. 'Since you ask, though, I don't see it's any business of yours.'

'Hoity toity!' Fanny said and laughed, but she shot a sharp glance at Dave all the same, almost daring him to let Lexie get away with her rudeness, but he ignored her.

'Sure you have, doll,' he said, and wheezed a little as his cigar went out yet again and he had to lean back to reach for his matches from his pocket, hard to get into as his clothes strained over his broad buttocks. 'You've grown up lovely, lovely. Not exactly grown *up*, mind you. I swear you're still as big as a ha'penny – but grown up, you know what I mean? Very nice, very nice indeed. These soldiers you been dancing for, they must have just eaten you up – '

'Oh, yes,' Lexie said composedly. 'I'm very good.'

Fanny lifted her eyebrows. 'Self-praise is a poor recommendation,' she said tartly. 'If you're so good what are you doing shlapping round with such a lousy little show like that? I remember your Madame Gansella – Poppy Ganz like I remember her, mind you, not this goyisha Gansella stuff – I used to see some of her things, charity evenings, you know? Went to a couple, I remember, 1911 – or was it 1912? Anyway, I remember I bought the best seats and gave double the price, it was such a good cause, the Jewish Hospital appeal – and it was a lousy show, lousy.'

'Oh, I agree,' Lexie said calmly, sipping her coffee and staring very coolly over the rim of her cup at Fanny. 'A lousy show. But *I'm* very good. You'll find out, one of these days. If you're lucky enough to get to see me work on stage, that is.'

'Oh,' Fanny said, nonplussed, and blinked at her, and across the room Bessie grinned suddenly and caught Lexie's eye and she smiled too, and for a moment a bubble of understanding hung in the air between them.

'And now, if you'll forgive me, I've got a lot to do. Unpacking, you know. I'm sure you'll excuse me. Give my best to Joe, Benny. I dare say he had better things to do than come running round here, hmm? Yes. Well, so long, everyone – ' And calmly she walked to the door and went out, leaving them staring after her.

'Well!' Fanny exploded after a moment. 'Such rudeness! Such chutspah to talk to us like that! I told you, Bessie, letting her go away like that – it was the ruin of her. Didn't I tell you? I knew as soon as I heard what she was doing it was going to ruin her! Oy, what Momma would say!'

'She'd be pleased she's happy,' Bessie said, and got to her feet and began to collect the coffee cups. 'Because she is – and it's true. She's very good. You'll see. As for rude – times have changed, Fanny! The young ones, they don't kowtow no more, not like we used to. I was scared to say boo to a goose, I was – never let anyone know what I felt or what I wanted – and much good did it do me to be so quiet! Better to be like Lexie, stand up for yourself – eh, Benny?'

Benny reddened and bobbed his head and Dave looked at him sideways and shook his head in resignation. 'Listen, the day Benny's got anything to say for himself, the sky'll fall in. Come on, Fanny. I've got things to do if you ain't. Tara, Bessie. Come round the weekend for supper, bring Lexie, hmm? I like the way she's turned out. Yes I do, Fanny. Don't go glaring at me that way. She's a mensch, that one. Won't let no one push her around. Not even you.' And he laughed fatly. 'No, not even you, and good luck to her.'


'I'm sorry Fanny was so stupid,' Bessie said later as she ironed Lexie's newly unpacked clothes ready to put them in the wardrobe. 'I shouldn't have said to come round, I suppose – but I wanted them to see you as soon as you got home and – '

'That's all right,' Lexie said, and peered into the mirror that was resting against the teapot. 'I remember Fanny was always like that. Doesn't bother me – ' And she went on plucking out the excess hair that grew between her thick straight brows.

'Bothered her, though,' Bessie said, and gave a little crack of laughter. 'I wish you'd seen her face after you went out – a real picture it was! I wish I'd 'a' stood up to her like that when I was younger – mind you, if I had, I wouldn't have had you, would I?'

Lexie lifted her head and stared at her. 'What do you mean?'

Bessie went a patchy red and bent her head to concentrate on the movement of her iron over the cloth. 'It doesn't matter. I shouldn't have said it. I'm sorry – forget it – '

'Said what? Come on, Bessie. You can say it, whatever it is. What do you mean, if you'd have stood up to her, you wouldn't have had me?'

There was a little silence and then Bessie said awkwardly, 'When Momma died. It was difficult, you a new baby and all – no one knew what to do, and – well, it was Fanny said the boys'd go to her and I'd have you. I didn't really – well, at the time, I thought – looking after Poppa and you – I was twenty, where did I know how things'd turn out? As it is, it's the best thing that ever happened to me, not standing up to Fanny.' And she threw a scared little look at Lexie and then bent her head to her ironing again.

There was another little silence as Lexie sat and looked at her. She's almost forty, she thought. Almost forty and what sort of life has she had? Nothing really. And she tried to see her as though she wasn't just familiar old Bessie who had always been there in the background of her life, but as a separate person, her own person, just as Lexie was her own person. She looks a little better than she used to, Lexie thought, noting the neat suit with the sailor collar, and the silk blouse under it. And she does try to make the best of herself, plain as she is, and her hair's nice done that way – for Bessie had pulled the front hair down over her ears a little to make it look as though it were fashionably bobbed, though she hadn't been brave enough to go the whole way, and had pinned the rest of it back in a thick bun. She wore a bandeau round her forehead made of cloth that matched her suit and she looked neat and sensible and agreeable, Lexie thought. Abruptly she said, 'You ought to wear a bit of powder, you know. And some rouge. I'll show you how.'

Bessie stared at her and then laughed and her face lifted, her eyes crinkling, and Lexie said again. 'No, really. It'd suit you. You could look really nice.'

'Me, with stuff on my face? Never! What'd Mr Lazar say?'

'What does it matter what he says? He doesn't own you.'

'No, I know, but still – he is my boss and anyway – the waitresses – they'd think it gave them permission, wouldn't they?'

'Well, don't wear it at work then. Just when you go out – '

'But I never go anywhere but work,' Bessie said, going on with the ironing. Lexie sat and looked at her and felt guilt rising, and with it anger at Bessie for creating it.

The anger subsided slowly but it left the guilt still hovering over her and after a moment she said, 'Bessie – I'm sorry.'

Bessie didn't lift her head from her ironing. 'What for, Lexie? Telling me to wear make-up? No harm in that.'

'For not being here all this time. For being away.'

Bessie raised her eyes for a moment to give her another of those scared little looks. 'Well, you had to, didn't you? The war and all – '

'Yes, of course. The war and all,' Lexie said and tried again, reaching deep inside herself for the truth she wanted to share with Bessie, and not certain she really understood herself what it was. 'I mean, about wanting what I want so very much – that's why I stayed away really. Because of all the wanting – '.

'I know,' Bessie said and turned over the frock she was ironing. 'Mr Lazar said – I mean, I know.'

'Mr Lazar said? What did he say?'

'He said – ' Again there was that note of timidity in Bessie's voice. 'He said you were hungry. That that was why you had to do what you do – '

Lexie stared at her and then laughed, a soft little snort of a sound. 'Too sharp for his own good, that one. Yes, I suppose so. I do want a lot. It's more than just wanting. It's hard to explain really. It's just that there's a way it's got to be for me. *Got* to be. And I don't intend to be mean to you or anything, but sometimes, when it's something to do with a show, when it's work, you understand, I sort of forget about everything. You and everything. I get this feeling inside and it's though there aren't any other feelings and never were. A hot sort of feeling – '

She bobbed her head back to the mirror and began plucking again at her eyebrows, feeling a wash of embarrassment that was as painful as it was unexpected. Had she explained? Probably not. How could she, when she didn't really understand it all herself? There was just that welling up of need in her, that urgent hotness that meant she could think of nothing except work, nothing except what she was doing. It was a bit like dancing in a spotlight, she thought then, when the light seemed to form great walls round her and she couldn't see anything but the brightness, feeling it holding her hot and urgent and yet safe inside its sharp edges, and she looked again at Bessie, at the iron moving so smoothly under her hand, and she knew she hadn't explained, and probably never could.

There was a silence between them for while, broken only by the faint hiss of the iron and the crackle of the fire under the other iron on the range, and then Lexie said abruptly, 'I'm not going back to the show – Madame Gansella's. She doesn't know yet.'

Bessie slapped the iron down on the table and lifted her head to look at her and again the guilt rose in Lexie, for her face was radiant with delight. 'You mean you're staying home? Staying with me? Oh, Lexie, that's – '

'I don't know,' Lexie said brusquely, and once more turned back to the mirror. 'Depends.'

'Oh! What on?'

'What sort of job I can get. I want to find a shop with a decent show somewhere. West End. I'll stay in London if I can,' and she tried to make it sound casual, as though getting a place in a West End show was the most natural thing in the world.

And Bessie accepted it that way. 'Which show?'

'I don't know, really,' Lexie said, still with that studied air of nonchalance. 'Whatever I can get.' She lifted her head then and leaned back in her chair. 'What's on?'

'Eh?' Bessie stared at her and then grinned again, once more lifting her face into a transient charm. 'What's on? In the West End, you mean? Don't be ridiculous! From where should I know?' And she went back to her ironing, moving rhythmically and seeming to find pleasure in her activity, as though touching Lexie's clothes was the same as touching her.

'Don't you ever go to shows, Bessie? Don't you go out anywhere?'

Bessie shook her head. 'No time. The war, you know – so many of the girls had to go and do munitions and be in hospitals and that, we've been short-staffed. I've had to help out at the tables in the busy times and that means doing my own work in the office in the evenings. So I don't get home much before ten – or I didn't. It might be different now. Now the war's over – oh, Lexie, isn't it marvellous? It's all over and none of the family got hurt or anything – though the Zeppelins got one of Dave's warehouses – and now it's all going to be all right again.'

'Is it? I hope so,' Lexie said and stood up. 'Listen, Bessie, tomorrow I'm starting to sort things out. Going round the agents.'

'Agents?'

'Mmm. Try to get myself a job – but I thought I'd like to see some of the things that are on now. Will you come with me?'

'To shows?' Bessie went pink with delight. 'Really? You want me? I'd like that – if I can get away – '

'You see you do,' Lexie said, and smiled at her. Again there was a fragment of closeness there between them, a pleasure in each other's company, and Lexie was grateful for it; the earlier feelings of guilt about Bessie had been very disagreeable and she had other things to cope with, other things to think about, than Bessie and her problems.

They went to the theatre every night for a week, with Bessie getting more and more excited and interested in all she saw. There was *Tails Up* at the Comedy Theatre, put on by the French revue king André Charlot , and a riproaring Cochran show at the newly opened London Pavilion. There was the long-running *Maid of the Mountains* at Daly's with Josie Collins a dream in the lead part, a performance which left Lexie wide-eyed with envy and hope for her own future, even though her daily trudge around the agents' offices was proving totally fruitless. They saw a Védrenne show at the Royalty and voted it dull, and a magic show of Maskelyne's at St George's Hall, which entranced Bessie and bored Lexie hugely, for there was no dancing in it. By the end of the week Bessie was exhausted, though delighted with it all, and Lexie was a great deal more thoughtful than she had been. It clearly wasn't going to be as easy as she'd imagined to get that London job on which she'd set her heart. Perhaps it was just as well she'd told Madame Gansella she was just going on holiday rather than that she was leaving the show. Even something as third-rate as *Babies on Parade* was better than no job at all.

On the Saturday night they ended their theatre-going marathon at the Shaftesbury Theatre, seeing *Arlette*, a George Grossmith musical with enough dancing to please them both and enough scene changes and effects to captivate Bessie in particular, for she found the trickery of the stage especially fascinating, and constantly whispered to Lexie for detailed explanations of how this effect worked, and how that quick change of costume had been engineered. Afterwards they went out to supper.

That had been Bessie's plan, and she had announced it importantly during the second interval, and after a moment of demur Lexie had agreed. At the beginning of the week she had been angry when Bessie had insisted on paying for their tickets for the shows they saw, feeling she was being babied again. However she had agreed when Bessie had pointed out so reasonably that she had been earning a lot from Mr Lazar, who paid her most punctiliously for the extra work she had been doing, and that she had so little time to spend it that it was a pleasure to find some activity that would let her enjoy being extravagant. By Saturday night Lexie no longer felt any discomfort at all when Bessie delved into her bag and paid for everything. Anyway, Lexie had so little cash after her years with Madame G. that she had small choice in the matter. And after Bessie had paid for so many stalls in so many theatres, what was a supper, after all?

But it wasn't just an ordinary supper for which Bessie was paying, as Lexie found. They walked down Shaftesbury Avenue towards Piccadilly Circus, pushing their way through the strolling crowds out in force despite the chill of the winter night, and still liberally sprinkled with the khaki and dark blue of uniforms and not a few men in hospital blues, even though the war was over. The people around them were determinedly cheerful and all set on making the most of a night out Up West, and Lexie's own spirits lifted a little as she caught the infection from the good-natured crowds who jostled and laughed their way along the brilliantly lit street with them, passing the bright shops and the theatres and the restaurants spilling their glitter out on to the grey November pavements.

When Bessie turned into the Trocadero at Piccadilly Circus Lexie stopped short. 'Here?' she said. 'No, really, Bessie, this is too much! You don't have to spend this sort of money! We can find a tea shop somewhere, have a poached egg or something – that'll do perfectly well for me – '

But Bessie shook her head with an air of barely contained mystery, and took her arm and urged her inside. There was little Lexie could do to stop her, for Bessie was clearly very determined and very excited, with patches of high colour in her cheeks and her eyes glittering a little in the reflections from the silver and crystal inside the big restaurant.

'We are expected,' Bessie said rather grandly to the tall flunkey who greeted them, and she showed him a piece of pasteboard which she had taken from her handbag. At once the man bowed, a little less imperious now and indeed somewhat obsequious, and turned and led them across the floor, threading a way between the tables as Bessie and Lexie followed. Lexie was suddenly aware of her rather simple blue frock and coat and wished she'd worn a proper hat tonight instead of the squashy beret she had on. It had seemed so fashionable and right earlier when she'd put it on, very dashing and Pearl Whiteish, and she'd been pleased with her appearance, but now in a room full of men in evening dress and women much bejewelled and coiffed, some with diamond-studded fillets round their brows and feathers in their headbands, she felt positively dowdy. Oddly enough, Bessie didn't look particularly out of place in her severely cut suit and deep-crowned hat with the tall feather, and Lexie thought again how much Bessie seemed to have changed over the past four years.

The tall flunkey stopped and said something to the occupant of a table at the edge of the dance floor, and Lexie craned to see who it was, but she couldn't, for he had a bulk as imposing as his manner. Then the man bowed and stood back to show them to their seats, and revealed Alex Lazar sitting there with another man, both of whom stood up and bowed as the women sat down.

'Lexie, it's a pleasure to see you! After all this time you still look lovely – delicious, in fact. I love your hat, my dear – so smart and yet casual. Lovely!' He beamed at her and then at the man on his left. 'You know Bessie, Peter, of course, but you haven't met her little sister, I think. The dancer I told you about. Shake hands with Peter Hyman, Lexie. He's an old friend and colleague and he's André Charlot's dance director. Thought you two ought to know each other. Waiter! We'll have a bottle of champagne. I'm in the mood for it tonight – '

# 13

'What did you say?' Lexie said it very loudly and the buzz of noise in the room stopped as if someone had thrown a switch. Every head turned and every pair of eyes stared at her.

'What did you say?' she said again, and took a few steps forward, so that she was right inside the room instead of just in the doorway. Ahead of her the rows of lights around the mirrors glittered, reflecting from the sequins on the costumes, and showing every squalid detail of the cluttered sticks of make-up and dirty powder puffs on the tables so brightly that she wanted to blink, but she didn't. It was important to hold her gaze, to show no sign of any weakness. That mattered. It mattered a lot.

'Mabel Leary, it was you who said it, I think. So repeat it. I'm a *what*, did you say?'

'Oh, leave it alone, Lexie,' someone muttered, and one or two of the girls tried little giggles, but Lexie, wearing little more than a chiffon scarf and a headdress made of feathers, stood as straight and still as ever, staring fixedly at the tall girl in the middle of the room.

The girl shrugged and lifted her eyebrows. 'Eavesdroppers never hear good of themselves,' she said in her nasal little voice, and gave an inane giggle. 'Anyway, it's true. So there's no call to stand there looking like that, stupid cat.'

Lexie took a deep breath and was across the room so fast that she hardly realized she'd moved until her hand made stinging contact with that sneering face. At once there was uproar as the girl broke into a loud wail. The others rushed to comfort her while a short fat woman came pushing her way through the hubbub from the back of the room.

'What's bloody goin' on 'ere, then?' she bawled, pushing the girls aside as though they were inanimate objects. 'I've told you I won't 'ave no fightin' in my dressin' rooms, and if this don't stop right now I'll 'ave Mr Charlot in 'ere and the 'ole bleedin' lot of yer'll be out on yer arses and serves yer bloody right – Mabel, shut that bleedin' row. You – Lexie. What's goin' on?'

'Ask *her*,' Lexie said contemptuously, and turned away to the mirror and started to take off her headdress as though nothing had happened. 'Ask her, if you can get her to stop whining long enough to get a word in edgeways. Ask her what she said and then see how you feel about telling Mr Charlot.'

'Well, it's true. She *is* a sheenie and she *is* canoodling with that other bloody sheenie, and they *do* stick together. An' if you want to tell Mr Charlot that, Ethel, then you go ahead and do it. And see where it gets you. They're all the bloody same, these sheenies. Stick together like flies in a bleedin' jampot.'

Ethel turned her head and looked at Lexie, and for a moment Lexie saw it there too, deep in her eyes. The flicker of a sneer, the same sort of look that was on the others' faces, and she felt again the desolation of aloneness, a desolation that had been increasing with every week that passed until now, in midsummer with the thermometer outside cons-

127

tantly in the eighties, she seemed to feel cold all the time.

In all the years with Madame Gansella she had never had reason to think about the fact that she was Jewish. In the early days, when the show had been *Juvenile Jollities*, they had all been as she was, from the same narrow streets, with the same sort of families, the same voices, the same tones, and the same likes and dislikes in food and drink and chatter. All Jews together. And even after the others had gone home to London at the start of the war and Madame G. had had to recruit local dancers, there had been no problems. People from country towns, as the newcomers were, had seen the established members of the company and Madame Gansella and Lenny Ganz themselves as exotic simply because they were Londoners, with a rich metropolitan gloss that made them shine in their eyes. The fact that they were East End Jewish Londoners had meant nothing to them.

So Lexie had never in all her life met the sort of barely disguised and off-hand scorn she had met here at the Vaudeville. At first, when it had started, she'd paid no attention; it had been, she told herself, the business of being new. She could remember how she herself had behaved to the newcomers to Madame G.'s; cool, haughty, often disdainful. It was part of the fun of being there first. In time, of course, she had admitted the new people to the camaraderie of being one of the crowd, unremarked and unremarkable, and she had assumed the same would happen to her after André Charlot had given her a place in the back row of the chorus when Alex Lazar and Peter Hyman had arranged for him to see her. But now she had been with the company over six months; they were into their second show together, yet still the girls of the chorus treated her as an outsider, and a very much unwanted one.

Slowly it had grown on her that it wasn't just her newness, that it went much deeper than that, and she had wondered for a while if it was because of Ambrose. When she had seen him again and realized he was part of the company, she had shrieked her delight and hurled herself at him in a fashion that had made it very clear she knew him extremely well – and after all, she had told herself, he *is* the best-looking boy on the line. Maybe they're jealous of me, she had thought, sitting at her table in the communal dressing room putting on her make-up, while everyone around her chattered to each other and ignored her. Maybe they are – I'll give them something to be jealous of.

And she had tried very hard to do just that, ignoring the girls, spending all the time she could in the theatre with Ambrose and the other boys, chattering to him with bright and brittle gaiety whenever any of the girls were around to hear her, larding her conversation with 'dahlings' and 'sweeties' and being altogether as familiar and flirty with him as she had known how to be. But she had realized fairly soon that this was a stupid game to play, on two scores.

First it annoyed Ambrose, who after the first moment of surprised recognition had shown no great wish to be close to her or to treat her as his childhood sweetheart – a role in which she had cast herself – concentrating all he could on his work. He never stopped practising, whether with the rest of the boys in the chorus or on his own, and never stopped exercising when he wasn't dancing. He had grown into a very remarkable-looking young man; the dark red hair of his boyhood was still there, and the deep amber-coloured eyes, but now he had filled out and had a sleek muscularity added to the slenderness of his boyhood that made him very beautiful indeed to look at. He was clearly highly contented with himself and determined to use every atom of energy he had on improving his dancing technique and taking care of that perfect body and marvellous face. So Lexie's attentions pleased him no more now than they had when she'd been a child.

Flirting with him had been pointless on a second score – it didn't upset the girls at all, and made no difference whatever in their attitude towards her. The men they were interested in were the stage door denizens, the top-hatted and evening-caped vapid young men with money to jingle in their pockets and a burning ambition to be seen at Romano's or the Trocadero with a chorus girl – any chorus girl – hanging on their arms. So it wasn't Ambrose who had anything to do with their scorn of Lexie.

It had been some time before she had realized that Peter Hyman's attention to her might be upsetting them. It had seemed to her absurd that he had been interested in her at all, except as a dancer. He was such a short fat little man (though in spite of his unlikely appearance he was delicate on his feet and had an unerring sense of timing that made him an ideal dance director, for all he looked so ridiculous when he went cavorting about the rehearsal room showing them what he wanted) that she could not take him seriously.

She had never imagined for a moment that he could have any interest in her other than as a member of the chorus. He had given her a place in the line, to be sure, but not as a favour, not even to oblige his old pal Alex Lazar; all he had done for him was agree to audition his little friend. To get her place Lexie had had to be a good dancer. She had known that, and known too that she had no reason to be specially grateful to Peter Hyman. To Alex perhaps, but to Peter definitely not. So, when he had asked her to have dinner with him or lunch or any other meal, she had been first amazed and then amused, and had consistently refused. But the girls had noticed the way he watched her as they worked, had seen the way he was always hovering in the wings as the back line left the stage, and drawn their own conclusions.

But even that wouldn't have been enough to explain their enmity; dance directors, after all, were notorious for their attempt to use a chorus line as their own private harem. She had been in the business long enough to know that, even though she had spent most of that time with one show that was little more than an amateur shambles compared with a really professional one like an André Charlot revue; but as long as the object of such a man's interest wasn't promoted beyond her level of ability none of the other girls in a chorus really minded. But these girls clearly did mind about her, even though Lexie remained firmly in the back line, well out of any share of the real limelight. It had taken a long time for the full reason for their hostility to seep through to her, and when it had she had first been amazed, and then puzzled, and then hugely, impotently, angry.

Impotent until tonight. Until this evening she had heard no direct comments she could seize on to bring their attitude out into the open, had had to suffer silently the helpless fury of hearing just snatches of words, seeing sidelong glances and listening to their giggles rise and then subside as she came into the room. Until tonight, when at last Mabel Leary started whining in that high nasal tone that she affected about the bloody little sheeny of a dance director who had fined her just because she'd torn a shoe ribbon and his bloody sheeny favourite, Ascher – and at last she could get hold of it all,

130

could force them to stare her in the face and say it.

Now, standing in the middle of the dressing room with the other girls ranged in front of her, and with Ethel, who was supposed only to be their dresser but who in fact ran the dressing room like a sergeant-major, she had said it and she felt better, as though she had been sitting in a bath of ice-cold water for a very long time and had at last got out of it. Warmth was filling her from her belly outwards and it felt good. She stood there with her head up and stared back at them with her eyes glittering.

'You're moanin' because she called you a sheeny?' Ethel said. 'Well, so what if she did? Eh? So bleedin' what? You are, aren't you? She's Irish and she wouldn't go shouting off her mouth and hittin' you if you told her so, would you, Mabel?'

'No,' Mabel said, sniffing, and made her mouth tremble delicately. ''Course I wouldn't. Like you said, it's true, Ethel. An' she hit me for talkin' the truth.'

'It is not true that I'm having any sort of – that I have anything more to do with Peter Hyman than any of you,' Lexie said, staring at her and feeling the warmth that had been so agreeable getting less agreeable. 'That's a rotten lie –'

'Well, I can't say as I blame you for mindin' anyone sayin' that,' Ethel allowed with great magnanimity. ''Ooky-nosed fat little bugger like that – 'oo'd ever fancy 'im? Tell 'er yer sorry for that, Mabel. Come on. Right now. This minute. Say you're sorry –'

Mabel opened her mouth to protest but Lexie was too fast for her. 'I don't want her damned apologies,' she said. 'What I want is –'

Behind her the door opened again and a head came round. One of the boys from the dressing room next door called plaintively, 'Has anyone here got any cloth glue? My damned trousers for the matador number won't hold no matter what I do – Ethel? Girls? Can you help? Ambrose said – oh, here he is – Ambrose, you *did* say they had some glue in here that'd hold my poor old bags, didn't you? One more performance in these and I swear to you they'll have me up on an indecent exposure charge –'

'Come on in, then,' Ethel said, and shoved Lexie aside as she went lumbering to the door. 'I'll fix the bleeders for yer – give 'em 'ere –'

131

'Ambrose!' Lexie called loudly, running towards him and taking his arm. 'Ambrose, you've got to do something about this – they're calling me horrible names just because –'

'What?' He had come in behind the other man, a willowy-dark-haired fellow with his hair plastered close to his head with very heavily scented brilliantine, who was now staring at Lexie with his head on one side and his lips a little pursed. Ambrose frowned sharply. 'What is it?'

It was as though she were a small child again, and he the lordly big boy who had alternately rejected her and been kind. She felt better and held his arm even more tightly.

'They're calling me sheeny, Ambrose – it's horrible. They've been hateful all along just because I'm Jewish. Tell them that –'

'Tell them what?' Ambrose said loudly. 'That they ought to be young ladies and never say anything you don't like? Pigs'll fly first.' The girls behind her giggled and Ethel gave a sudden croak of heavy laughter as she pushed her way back to her domain at the back of the dressing room with the trousers in her hand.

'I'm told that when we go to America they'll call us Limeys or some such,' Ambrose said, his voice still loud, and he stared at her with his eyebrows raised. 'And if we ever go to Australia they'll call us something else odd, I dare say. Cobbers, isn't it? Really, my dear, what does it matter? You're making a great fuss about nothing.'

'But you –' she began and then stopped, for his eyes seemed to have brightened sharply as he stared at her, and as though he had said it aloud she heard the warning.

'I mean,' he said easily, grinning at the other man beside him, 'I mean, if I were Jewish I'd ignore it too. It's only a word, after all.' He pushed past her, and with the other boy at his heels went through the clutter of girls standing behind her until he reached Ethel, whom he began to tease with a string of heavily flirtatious jokes that made Ethel giggle as coyly as a twelve-year-old. Lexie, standing by the door, was left staring after him and feeling very cold indeed.

She waited for Ambrose long after the others had trooped out of the stage door and down the alleyway in a haze of patchouli and Parma violet on their way to lobster suppers.

She stood pressed against the wall outside so that she was in the shadow and no one could see her. She wondered after a while whether she'd missed him and was about to turn and go home to Bessie when she heard the clatter of footsteps on the stairs inside and his voice shouting something to someone. At once she stepped out into the patch of light thrown on to the cobbles from the stage door keeper's cubbyhole as he appeared, blinking, in the doorway.

'Ambrose,' she said breathlessly, 'I must talk to you –' She took his arm and pulled him back into the shadows. 'Ambrose, I've been waiting for you. For heaven's sake, what did you mean when you said –'

The words slid out of her mind as she stood there very close to him. He was hot, so hot she could feel the warmth of his body through his shirt, for his jacket was left negligently open to display the cream silk of the shirt and the carefully casually knotted cravat tucked into the open collar. He smelled as good as he looked, a mixture of expensive eau de cologne, soap and Turkish cigarettes. She slid her hands up the silk and round his neck, clasping her fingers together so that he couldn't help but bend his head to bring it close to hers.

Her eyes were fully used to the dimness by now and she could see his face very clearly; could see the gleam of his eyes, the thickness of his lashes, the shape of his mouth, and suddenly she found herself lifting on her toes to pull his head down more urgently, even though there was resistance in him. She put her mouth on his and hung on, feeling a rush of sensation that was unlike anything she'd ever felt before, even when, long ago, she had lain in bed on cold nights remembering him, missing him and weeping for him. But now he was here, real and solid, and kissing him was the most marvellous experience she had ever had – better than the first time she'd been lifted in a dance, better than the first time she'd managed to get up on her points, better even than her first solo, better than anything –

She let her lips open, let her tongue push against his, but he was trying to speak, pulling back from her, and she couldn't hold his head down any longer. Unwillingly she let go. Cool air moved between them and the sensation in her belly flickered and subsided.

'Listen, you –' he began in a harsh whisper. 'Listen, Lexie.'

133

Now he sounded all reasonableness, relaxed and friendly, almost the Ambrose she had known all those years ago. She grinned up at him in the dim light and said softly, 'Yes?'

'This sheeny business – don't be a fool, ducks. Make a fuss about a thing like that, and you're in real trouble. These people – they make you sick, but you don't want to take any notice of 'em. It's not worth it. Do it my way, lovey, and keep your mouth shut. What's it got to do with anyone who you are or what you are or where you come from? Just keep your mouth shut –'

She shook her head, not believing him. 'What do you mean, keep your mouth shut? Let 'em say what they like about you and not care?'

'No, donkey.' He tried to make it sound jocular but it sounded merely strained. 'Just don't let 'em know things about you that'll give 'em handles to use against you and names to call you. I don't, and I won't. What you do is your affair. You can say what you like about yourself, if you must, but I'll thank you to say nothing about me. That's my way and it suits me. I tell people I come from the Cromwell Road area if they ask me, and that's all about it. And I don't want you making trouble for me saying anything else. Do you understand me?'

She still kept her arms round his neck, and she didn't let go. But the warmth that had been there had dissipated. She felt bleak and alone again. Almost experimentally she pulled his head down again and kissed him, and at once the sensation came back, the rich glow in her belly, the lifting of excitement and she was, somewhere deep in her mind, relieved, for she had feared that it wouldn't come back and a small voice whispered in her head, 'What does it matter anyway, Jewish or not? He's right – he's right – kiss me, Ambrose. Kiss me as I'm kissing you – what does it matter? None of it matters but you – Ambrose –'

But he was pulling away from her now. He tugged her hands away from behind his head and shoved her away so that her shoulders scraped painfully against the brick wall behind her.

'Stop *that*, for Christ's sake,' he snapped as the tall young man with the brilliantined hair came out of the door behind them. 'That's the last thing that'll get you anywhere –'

'Ambrose?' the tall young man called, and at once Ambrose stepped forward into the patch of light, pulling his cravat into place as he did so. The other stared at him, head on one side, and Ambrose said loudly, 'My dear – women! Like bitches on heat, some of 'em. For pity's sake get me *out* of here! If I stay another moment the poor wretch'll have my bags from me. Don't *ever* leave me alone again for so long –'

He tucked his hand into the other's elbow and they went off down the alley, leaving Lexie leaning against the wall staring after them, feeling the roughness of the brick behind her through the thin cotton of her frock.

# 14

All the way home in the bus and then on the tram she brooded on the girls and their jibes, going over the evening's episode in her head again and again, inventing conversations in which her own comments were so blistering, so pithy and so brilliant that all of them, especially Ethel, were rendered totally speechless. She heard the rolling phrases she hadn't used, heard the neat barbs that had not come from her lips, then started it all over again, experiencing their scorn and then humiliating them twice as much as they had humiliated her. Doing that helped her not to think about Ambrose and his behaviour, and it was important not to think about that.

But long before she reached Clapton Pond, where she had to change buses, she had to let go of the fantasy about putting the chorus in their place; she couldn't sustain her anger at a high enough pitch, and she began to think instead about her general situation. She'd been thinking about that anyway, before this evening, getting more and more restless about it, and now, fed by her anger, her restlessness increased, became actually physical so that, instead of sitting still in her seat, staring out of the window into the blue summer night as the bus went on its swaying bumpy way, she fidgeted, moving from one buttock to another, twisting her gloves between her fingers, tapping her feet on the floor.

Six months, she told herself. Six months since I came back to London and where am I? I've been in over two hundred performances of this damned revue, and if I've actually been seen by that many people it's a lot. Back row of the chorus, hidden under stupid great heaps of feathers and sequins – who could notice me even if they wanted to? And why should they want to, doing those dreary routines and those boring steps? She thought of Peter Hyman and his skilful but unadventurous choreography, and made a sharp little tutting sound of disgust that made her neighbour on the bus look at her curiously. What hope did she have of getting anywhere like this? Six months – I ought to have my own flat by now, instead of living with Bessie. I ought to have enough to take taxis everywhere, and be riding home in style after the show instead of sitting on this horrible bus full of old men reeking of shag tobacco, unwashed clothes and grease. I ought to be hearing applause for myself, not having to stand there listening to them stamping and shouting at Delysia mopping and mowing in her stupid Parisienne fashion (although Lexie had to admit in her deepest heart that the girl *was* good). I ought to be almost there by now, almost at the top. I haven't time to waste, no time to waste, to waste, to *waste*–

She knew the flat was empty even before she'd climbed the stairs from the front door. There was a dead feeling to it. She let herself into the living room and looked round at its neat polished perfection, at the flowers that Bessie always kept on the centre table, and was suddenly hugely angry. How dare she not be there when she wanted to talk to her? How dare she just go and leave a note? The fact that usually she was profoundly irritated by Bessie's eagerness to sit and wait up for her after the show, and that often she went straight to her bedroom, refusing the supper that Bessie had always carefully prepared, she preferred to push aside. Bessie wasn't here tonight and she should have been–

'So sorry – had to go to Fanny's,' the note read. 'Dave's aunt ill – plate of sandwiches in the meat safe on the kitchen windowsill – hope to be home soon – sorry not in when you get home – Bessie.' Lexie stared round at the silent room and smelled the hot stuffiness of it and the slightly cloying scent of wax polish and almost without thinking she turned and went out, slamming the door behind her. To be alone tonight – no. She couldn't cope with that.

It wasn't until she had nearly reached Manor House, at the gateway to Finsbury Park, where Dave and Fanny had moved as soon as their wartime earnings had made them rich enough to do so, that she thought, 'They won't be there – perhaps I'll have to just turn round and go back.' Black depression settled on her and she half rose from her seat on the bus to get off. But she'd come this far, so she might as well go the rest of the way.

The surge of relief she felt when she peered up at the block of flats on the corner and saw the light burning in the window of Number Seven lifted her spirits greatly. She went at a skip up the stairs scented with the familiar mixture of Jeyes fluid and soap – for this was a superior block that had a porter who kept it clean – and knocked cheerfully on the door, not caring who she might disturb, even though it was now past eleven-thirty, and most well-ordered London citizens were safely in bed.

Dave answered the door. He stood for a moment, peering out at her in the dark hallway and then, as he saw who it was, split his face with a grin.

'Well, if you ain't a sight for the sorest eyes! Come in, doll, come in, take the weight off your feet and tell me how you are!' He shepherded her into the flat with much delighted crowing, puffing at his inevitable cigar, and she let herself be bustled along, comforted by his patent delight in her presence.

The flat breathed warmth and opulence at her from its lustrous chandeliers to its thick Turkey carpets and overstuffed chintz-covered furniture. Much as she disliked her sister Fanny and her pretensions, her vulgarity and the constant display of her wealth, she liked her flat. It had all the qualities she wanted in a place of her own, and when she wove daydreams about how her future life would be, she saw it in a flat much like this one, with its big square rooms, long hallway and the tile-lined bathroom with the big gas geyser that spewed out vast torrents of hot water. Now, as she reached the sitting room, and saw the cosiness of the sofa with its nearby standard lamp throwing a pool of warm glow on to it, she pulled off her hat and sank into its wide embrace with a deep sigh of satisfaction.

Dave stood at the door and grinned, his mouth wide on each side of his cigar. 'Oy, dolly, you look oysgermatert, you poor little nebbish –'

She laughed up at him, amused as she always was by his Yiddishness. Fanny might irritate her profoundly, but not

137

Dave. There was an engaging friendliness about him that was very disarming.

'I look what?'

'Oysgermatert! Worn out! Exhausted! Don't you know nothin'?'

'I don't know much Yiddish,' she said, resting her head on the back of the sofa. 'But if that's the Yiddish for the way I'm feeling I'll try to remember it. I'm oysterwhateveritis.' She yawned suddenly and shook her head so that her thick bobbed hair swung round her face and then settled back into its neat shape.

He stared at her for a moment. 'You need a little drink, maybe? I was having one myself, with Fanny being out and all. She fusses, a fella has a drop o' schnapps, you know how it is. But I got some here —'

She remembered then and was embarrassed for a moment. 'I'm sorry — I should have said. You have someone ill in your family?'

He shrugged and went over to the sideboard between the two wide windows to pour her a drink. 'Listen, doll, she's an alter kucker, a real oldie, my aunt, must be nearly eighty, the time comes for everyone, it's come for her. But Fanny says we got to show willin', you know how it is, so when my cousin sends a message I should come and I got business to look after she says all right, Benny should drive her, she'll go over to the East End, do the right thing.'

'Bessie went with her?'

'Bessie's a right gutene shuma — oy, I got to explain that, too? She's a good soul, too good for her *own* good. Anyone wants anything, Bessie's there to do it. I don't have to tell you, hmm?'

'No,' Lexie said non-committally. She took the glass he put into her hand and sat and stared into it.

He looked at her thoughtfully and after a moment said cheerfully, 'So, there it is! I'm here all on my tod, and that glad to see you I could sing you a song.'

'Good,' she said, and drank deeply. Then, leaning back in the sofa again, she stared up at him. 'Dave, what do you do when people call you a sheeny?'

He laughed and sat down beside her, stretching his legs out widely. He was wearing carpet slippers, his shirt sleeves were rolled up to the elbows and his braces were off his shoulders,

138

dangling over his hips. He looked relaxed and comfortable in a way he rarely did when he came visiting at Victoria Park Road with Fanny.

'What do I do? As long as they don't throw nothing, and it don't cost me no money, I much care! I chalk it up as another one against the lousy goyim and pay no attention. I should drey mein kopf over ignorant slobs that call me names? That'll be the day, an' I don't think!'

'It's not always that easy,' she said, and drank again.

'Maybe you been lucky,' he said and shot her a shrewd little glance. 'Fanny goes on and on about how you never learned to be a good Yiddisher girl, always traipsin' around with those farpotshket shows, but maybe you done better than us, at that. You don't learn to be Yiddish, you don't get people callin' you names, because they don't know you ain't the same as them. Assimilation they call it, and for my part it's no bad thing. Too late for me, but for you young ones – young Monty, he's as English as a fella can be, with his spats and his topper and his fancy accent. His mother could die, the way he won't go to shul, won't live like a good Jew should, got his own place and all, but for my part it's no bad thing. He don't get people calling him names often neither. So when they do it feels worse, I suppose. You can't win every game, though, can you? Who called you sheeny, doll?'

'The girls in the show.' She wriggled in her seat with the memory of it. Dave leaned closer, put his arm round her shoulder in an avuncular fashion and squeezed her.

'That little bunch o' shicksers? You worry they called you names? I saw them – when we came to that ferstinkeneh show – a right mess of little yoikelters on their way they are –'

She gave a little crack of laughter. 'You're as bad as they are, Dave! They call me sheeny, so you call them shicksers and yoikelters –'

He nodded, highly satisfied. 'You see how good Yiddish can be? They can only insult you in one language – me, I can insult them in two – and Yiddish has some great words for insults. Believe me.'

He hugged her close again. Lexie turned her head and laughed up at him, grateful for his cheerfulness and his comforting presence. He was right – it didn't really matter. She wouldn't worry about it. They were just stupid –

139

shicksers. She drank again, aware that the brandy was reaching her shoulders and her face; her muscles felt tingly and it was an agreeable sensation.

'I'm going to leave the show anyway,' she said abruptly. 'That's what I'm going to do. I'm going to do better than back row of that mess –'

'Attagirl! That's the way to show 'em. You can do better than any of 'em, you can! You go out there and get in a better show and you won't never have to worry what they call you –'

'It's not as easy as that,' she said, and felt gloomy again. 'You can't just walk up to a producer and say, "Give me the lead in your new show, I'm the best dancer in town," can you?'

'Why not?' he said. He got to his feet and was pouring second drinks for both of them, and he came back and sat down beside her again, a little closer this time so that she could feel the heat of his body through her thin frock. 'It's the way I do business! I see an opening, and I say to the guv'nor, "Here," I say, "I got somethin' good for you. It'll cost you this and that, but it fetches you that and this," and usually the fella says, "Yeah, okay, you got a deal." Why not you? You go to a man puttin' on a show, you say, "Here, I do this dance an' I sing that song and the people'll want to come and see me, so how about you put me in your show?"'

She laughed, amused at his naïvety. 'It doesn't work that way, Dave. A show has a book, a story line, and its own songs and dances. You can't just bring in your own. You're talking about cabaret acts, people doing their own little show –' She stopped, sat up a little straighter, and turned to stare at him. 'What did I just say?'

He blinked and looked puzzled. 'Eh? You said I was talking about cabaret acts – or somethin'.'

She laughed then, put her hand on his shoulder and almost shook it. 'I did, didn't I? I said cabaret acts! My God, I did. Of course, that's what I want to do! My own act, my own choreography, my own music – that'd show them. My God, but that'd show them –'

He emptied his glass and set it down on the small table beside him and then beamed at her. 'Sure, doll, that'd show 'em! I told you, it's good business to tell people what you got and make 'em buy it your way! The schmutter business, the

140

dancin' around and singin' business, what's the difference? It's all business! So, old Dave ain't so bad, eh? He's got good ideas for you, eh? Soon they'll all be talkin' about you, all over London, and it'll be old Dave set you on the right track –'

But her face had clouded as she sat back in her corner again. 'It's not going to be that easy. I need to get a good act together. Get some good songs, a pianist, a dancing partner maybe –'

'So go get! That's good business too. You got to speculate to accumulate. You heard that said often enough, surely! Speculate to accumulate,' and he nodded owlishly at her, clearly pleased with the phrase, even though he was now having to concentrate on speaking it clearly.

'It takes money,' she said, leaning wearily back into her seat again. 'A lot, to start a thing like that. I'd need time to get it together, to rehearse. Have to buy the songs, costumes –'

'You need money?' Suddenly the slurriness of his speech was gone and his eyes sharpened a little. 'That's no problem –'

'Bessie'd find it, I suppose. She's earning enough, she says, and she doesn't spend a lot. And I know she'd want to. But –' She wriggled in her seat again, but with irritation this time. 'Oh, I don't know – it'd be something else from her. She does too much as it is.' And wants too much back, a small voice whispered deep in her secret mind. Wants loving and caring and company, and looks at you with those big eyes and says nothing, but wants and wants and wants –

'There's Mr Lazar,' she said after a moment. 'He got me the introduction to Peter Hyman that got me this job. Maybe if I put it to him –'

'You don't go getting no help from that mumser!' Dave said with a sudden violence in his tone. She stared at him, puzzled for a moment, then remembered and grinned.

'Oh, yes! I'd forgotten. You two don't get on, do you? Had a row, Bessie said, but not what it was about. What *was* it about, Dave?'

He shook his head and bit hard on the stump of his cigar, then irritably pulled it out of his mouth and ground it out in the ashtray beside him.

'Never mind that,' he grunted. 'It's none of your never mind. I got my own reasons for not liking Alex Lazar. Listen to him, you'd think everyone else in business was a crook. You got to be clever sometimes, I don't deny, and I'm clever, I promise you that. But that don't give the likes of Alex Lazar permission to go telling *me* what's right and wrong. A cholera on him! Listen, doll, you need money to do whatever it is you want to do? Okay, you got it, Dave Fox'll see to it. You don't need no one else but me.' He stopped then as she sat up and stared at him, her face alight with excitement. 'Mind you, you don't have to say nothin' to Fanny about it. She's a good girl, but she's got different ideas to me. I got a lot of irons in the fire these days she don't know nothin' about and I want to keep it that way. This can be one of them —'

'Oh, Dave!' she said, and threw her arms round his neck and kissed him hard. 'Oh, Dave, thank you! I won't say a word to anyone! I know just what I'm going to do! I'm going to get Madame G. I knew that show'd fold once I left it, and anyway, with the war over who wants a show called *Babies on Parade*? She's looking for a shop, I know she is, and I'll take her on and she can play the piano for me and be a dresser and generally look after things. I know that'd work — I can make her do whatever I like, I always could — and then I'll look for some good material and really get an act right and find an agent and everything —'

She still had her arms around his neck and he was staring at her. Suddenly he leaned forwards and kissed her, but not in the way he had in the past, not the kiss on cheek or forehead that had been part of her growing up years. This was the same sort of kiss she had given Ambrose just a couple of hours ago, and as Dave's mouth became more urgent on hers she felt the control she'd been exercising over her memory of that ten minutes in the dark alley outside the stage door slip and then crumble. Ambrose had been there in her arms and she'd kissed him with all the feeling she had in her and he'd pulled away. And then when that other man had come he had talked about bitches on heat, and now here was Dave kissing her and the feelings weren't the same. It wasn't Ambrose and it should be —

Another memory came surging back; herself in a rain-stained chemise and drawers and wet black stockings, sitting in front of a hot fire in Cephas Street with Lenny Ganz. She had been crying inside because of Ambrose that time, too;

he'd left her alone with a parcel of shoes to go off with a young man in a fur-collared overcoat, just as tonight he'd left her to go off with a tall young man with brilliantined hair. She thrust the memories, now inextricably entwined with each other, deep into her mind and refused to think about what was happening.

'I'll look after you, doll.' Dave was holding her closer now, whispering thickly into her ear, and she could smell the mixture of cigar smoke and brandy that hung around him like a cloud. But it wasn't unpleasant. He felt warm and strong, and it was Dave, someone she'd known all her life, and what did it matter anyway? Ambrose had called her a bitch on heat and maybe she was, after all, for there was a sensation inside her that was growing and rising and it was pleasant, even if it wasn't the same as she had felt with Ambrose. What did it matter anyway, and if it made Dave feel good—

If Fanny knew, what would she do? whispered that wicked little voice again in her ears as he kissed her again and his hands began to move across her body. If Fanny knew? If Bessie knew? And Alex Lazar who had been the one to send her to that lousy show where girls called her sheeny and Ambrose called her a bitch? They'd all be so angry and so noisy, there'd be tears and trouble and I'd be the one that had started it all. And I'm going to have my own act and he's going to give it to me, and why not? It's all so *stupid* anyway.

And all through the rest of it, as he pulled her dress away from her small breasts, and nuzzled at them, as his heavy legs pushed hers apart and he fumbled at her belly and her groin, trying to find his way, that was all she could think. It's all so *stupid*, so really stupid, that I don't know why they all make such a fuss about it and the girls giggle about it and leave me out of their giggling when I know how daft it is—

And painful. Dreadfully, agonizingly painful. Then she was crying and not thinking about how stupid it was at all, as Dave, grunting and sweating, eyes closed and his face set in a grimace, rose and fell rhythmically above her, ignoring her cries of pain, and went on and on and on hurting her.

# 15

'You must be crazy!' Ambrose said. 'D'you really think I'd give up a sure part in an André Charlot revue to act as second string to you? Crazy!'

'Not so crazy,' she said equably. 'Not when you think it through. What's so special about the part you've got at the Vaudeville? Front row of the chorus – I grant you it's the front row, but where do you go from there? Take over the lead? When will that be? Tomorrow or the day after, d'you think?'

He flushed. 'So, what's wrong with chorus? It's a steady job, and it's a class show –'

'But you're not class in it. You need a decent solo spot for that, and I'm offering you one. I've already got someone sorting out cabaret bookings for me – good ones. Café Royal, Ambassador's, Miramar Club –' She spoke the names casually, praying he'd take her word for it and not ask for proof. He did, swallowing it whole. 'And I'm offering you the chance to ride on my back. Of course, if you want to stay chorus with that lot, that's up to you –' She stood up and began to draw on her gloves. Lexie was looking particularly splendid today and she knew it, in a knee-length picture frock of emerald silk, with tiers of frills falling down the skirts, ending just below her knees to display silk-clad legs and small kid shoes, the whole ensemble surmounted by a very fetching cavalier hat well trimmed with matching ribbons. She stood there in the middle of the restaurant knowing she was being stared at, and waited until he did as she knew he would. He capitulated.

'All right. You could be on to something at that, I suppose. And I've been getting a bit bored –'

'Oh?' She lifted her eyebrows at that. 'Young Alan gone off you, has he? Found himself a new playmate?'

He went scarlet. 'For Christ sake, I told you – lay off that! D'you want to get me hung? I only said I'd see you today because you promised you wouldn't say anything about that –'

'I've changed my mind. I don't see why I shouldn't talk about anything I like. And I will.' She had sat down again and was leaning back in her chair, staring at him over the rim of her cocktail glass. 'And talking about you and your jolly little pals can be a useful thing to do. Stops you making a nuisance of yourself, doesn't it?'

He looked at her, nonplussed, and then shrugged. 'I don't know what you're talking about.'

'Yes you do. I'm telling you that unless you behave sensibly and do as you're told, then I chatter in all the wrong places. People who do what you and your Alan do can get into nasty trouble. Can't they?'

'My God, but you can be a bitch,' he said, and it was almost admiring. 'You really don't care what you do to get your own way, do you?'

'No,' she said. 'I don't care.' I do, I do, the little voice inside her head whispered. I care about you. And I'll change you, I will, but we've got to be together for me to change you, and this is the only way.

'The routines'll have to be good,' he said.

'Of course they will. The best there are. I've got Madame G. to play for me for rehearsal and –'

'Her? The old B?' He laughed then, his amber eyes crinkling. 'The old B and the young one. I like it. It's got class.'

'Yes. A lot of class.' She laughed too. 'But it'll be different now. I'm in charge. I call the tune. It's my money backing me, and what I say goes. She'll be a different old B to the one she was when we were kids, I promise you.'

'How come you've got this sort of money you're talking about? If you're going to pay me four quid a week and pay her and buy costumes and songs and all the rest of it and keep yourself till we start – it can't be tuppence ha'penny.'

'It isn't,' she said. 'And it's my business where it comes from.'

He grinned. 'Boyfriend?'

'Maybe.'

'That's better. It'll keep you out of my pants.'

'You're vulgar, you know that? You talk like a street arab. If you're going to work with me you'll have to learn how to do better than that.' Ambrose held his hands up in mock alarm, but there was a hint of real anxiety behind his gesture.

'All right, all right. I meant no harm! I'm just making a point. I'm not interested in hanky panky and soppy games, that's the thing. I'm a serious dancer and I want to work. That's *all*. And if you've got the money to launch a good act and you want me, it makes sense. You're not marvellous as a dancer, but you've got a lot of –'

'Yes, I know. A lot of style. Anyway, you don't have to be Pavlova to make it now. You'll see – the next ten years it's all going to change. What with films and all – it's different styles they'll want. They'll want mine. You'll see –'

'Yes,' he said and beckoned to the waiter across the big restaurant. 'Yes, I rather think I will. Well here's to us, hmm? What are we calling ourselves?'

'Ourselves?' she said. 'There's no ourselves about it. There's just me and my company. The billing'll be Alexandra Asher. That's all. Just Alexandra Asher. A new act, a new spelling – a modern one. It's my act, and everyone's going to know it.'


With Ambrose finally settled, she felt she could breathe again. It had been a difficult and yet exciting time of bustle and planning and more bustle, and it had taken a good deal of concentrated effort, not least because of the need to be so circumspect and put on a show of normality while going so determinedly about her own affairs. No one must know what she was doing until she was ready to do it, especially not Bessie who would fuss and get very anxious if she were told Lexie was to leave the Vaudeville Theatre. Much of the work she did by leaving Victoria Park Road early after Bessie had gone to work, instead of sleeping late as she usually did, and going to Dave's office in his cluttered building at the corner of Petticoat Lane to use his telephone and sort out money with him.

He had tried at first to pull away from the plan, not so much because he wanted to save his money but because of his fear and shame about what had happened between them, but she wouldn't have that. The following day she had gone to the theatre as usual and danced as usual, even though she could feel the ghost of his invasion of her body still lingering as a disagreeable aching, and that evening had tried to call him on the telephone from the theatre. But Fanny had answered it and Lexie had hung up without speaking. She had no intention of talking to Fanny any more than she had to, so she told herself she would just have to call again and hope to get him when Fanny was out. She did, eventually, but it took a week of persistence.

She'd told him she wanted to talk to him at once, and though he'd hedged and humphed into the mouthpiece she'd been coolly persistent and at last he told her to come to his office the next lunchtime.

'I'll give you a bit o' lunch, we can sort it out then,' he'd grunted and she'd said demurely, 'Thank you Dave,' and gone to meet him wearing the simplest clothes she could find in her wardrobe. In a little sailor suit with black stockings and shoes and a round boater hat of the sort that schoolchildren wore she looked a good deal younger than her eighteen years, and that was how she wanted to look.

By the time that lunch was over she had him precisely where she wanted him: almost reassured that he could trust her to say nothing about what happened, almost sure that it could happen again if he really wanted it to, definitely sure that he wanted to spend the money she needed on her new act. She sat there across the restaurant table from him, as sweet and as biddable as any ten-year-old, smiling and nodding at everything he said as she ate salt beef and potato latkes, and he relaxed before her eyes, seemed to blossom into a new Dave, one who regarded himself as a bit of a dog, a lively chap, and one well able to keep even a wife as redoubtable as Fanny in her place – which was to be totally unaware of this situation.

By the time lunch was over she had a neat wad of five-pound notes tucked into her handbag, and the address of his bank where she would be able to draw up to five hundred pounds. A princely sum, she told herself gleefully, as with a childlike innocence she bent over and kissed his cheek – which made him smirk at the other customers in the restaurant – and more than enough to get it right.

It had to *be* right, and it had taken considerable effort to ensure the rightness of her backstage arrangements. For all Madame G.'s lack of spectacular success as a producer of shows she had, as Lexie well knew, a great deal of organizational ability and Lexie wanted her as dresser and general manager. She knew better than most just how much time and effort went into making certain the right clothes were in the right place at the right time, and since she already had the germ of an idea for her act, an idea that involved several quick changes of costume, Madame G. was a must. Lexie didn't consider the possibility that she wanted the older woman because she had been her first introduction to the theatre, that she needed the security of a familiar face and familiar ways to shore up her shaky young self-confidence, because she didn't want to consider it. But somewhere deep inside she knew that was a part of it.

Tracking down Madame G. had not been difficult, for Lexie knew she had come back to London when her show had folded and had wearily set about starting all over again. When Lexie came to see her at her old house in Cephas Street she was teaching a class of rather lumpy ten-year-olds the basic time steps, and when Lexie had walked into the familiar dusty room, wearing the best of her new Spanish-style outfits with the heavy fringed shawl over it and a dashing tricorne hat, Madame G. had jumped to her feet, knocking over the piano stool in her excitement, and wrapped her in great hugs of delight. She had apparently forgotten that Lexie had ruined her show by calmly walking out of it the day after the Armistice.

At first she had demurred, putting on a great show of being unable to accept Lexie's offer of work and saying that her pupils – her classes – her responsibilities – were too onerous, but that soon crumbled. She was struggling to make a living, and it was obvious that it was getting harder, not easier.

'He's left, you know,' she said to Lexie, her eyes bright and challenging. 'Said there was nothing to come back for when the show died. Went off with that Elsie Shorter – the tall fair one, you remember? I thought there was something going on with those two, and I wasn't wrong.'

'I'm sorry,' Lexie had said, and just for a moment wanted to tell her of her own experiences with Lenny Ganz. But she just leaned forward and patted her hand. 'So you'll join me? Take the risk?'

Madame G. had nodded and hugged her, wiped her eyes, blown her nose and begun to talk rather grandly, in her best stage voice, of what she could and would do for the new act that was taking shape. Lexie had listened and smiled to herself and walked away from Cephas Street with a jaunty little swagger, feeling more exhilarated than she would have thought possible. That imposing figure of a woman who had once been so alarming, that woman who had run her life for so many years, now to be her employee! Oh, it was marvellous, wonderful, exactly as it should be, and she marched into Mile End Road in a state of such high glittering excitement that passers by actually turned to stare after her as she went hurrying to the bus stop.

Then there had been the business of trailing along Archer Street round the agents' offices, listening to music at the publishers' in Charing Cross Road and at last finding a handful of songs she could use – a couple of plaintive ones and a couple of little bouncy tunes that made small demands on her voice but which she could deliver with style and vivacity in her odd husky tones; and then the blissful hours spent at the costume designers in Newman Street – weeks and weeks of sheer delight. It had made the evenings of dancing at the Vaudeville and the grim silence from the rest of the chorus bearable, and she went round always with a faint smile on her lips that infuriated them all hugely.

Not that she cared. She had better things to look forward to than dancing in the back row of this stupid little revue, she told herself happily, and the rest of the company were puzzled by her and not a little repelled. There was something very odd indeed, they told each other, about someone as quiet and composed and long-distance as Alexandra Asher was. Very odd. 'Still waters run deep,' they said to each other darkly. 'More to this one than meets the eye – you'll see –'

Bessie too noticed and worried and watched and worried again, but she couldn't find out what had happened to change Lexie. That she had changed was undoubted, and that she was up to some business of her own even more certain. She came home at night at her usual time – Bessie knew that because she was there; but she also knew that she left much earlier than she needed to every morning. Mrs Bernstein downstairs, the eyes and ears of the whole road, let alone the house, had told her that. Bessie had tried asking Lexie where she was going, but Lexie had at once closed up like a trap, her eyes developing that opaque look that Bessie so hated and which Lexie always displayed when she felt she was being pushed in any way. So Bessie had had to bite her tongue and just watch and wonder and worry.

149

It must be something good, Bessie had told herself, as she sat at her desk at Alex Lazar's office. It has to be. She looks so beautiful, so blooming, so healthy and excited. It has to be something good. Maybe she's in love? Maybe she's meeting a man somewhere and –

But Bessie didn't want to think about that. It would be natural enough, heaven knew, but to Bessie that would be a disaster. Lexie in love would mean Lexie going away to someone else, and she had little enough of her as it was. No, it couldn't be love, it mustn't be love. What could it be? Bessie continued to do her book-keeping as punctiliously as ever, watched the waitresses with her usual eagle-eyed thoroughness, put in the orders for supplies, checked the tills for the tea shops, reported back to Alex as usual and watched and wondered and fretted.

Lexie had known that, of course. She was as aware of Bessie's reactions, fears and hopes as Bessie was aware of hers. That was one of the things that made life so complicated, and one of the reasons she was so anxious to get this act right. If it was right, and she got the bookings, she could then look for her own flat. A small one, with a bathroom she could have all to herself, instead of sharing it with Bessie and Mrs Bernstein downstairs, and a bedroom that would be big and quiet and very, very elegant, not filled with the frippery bits and pieces Bessie kept putting in hers, the pink satin cushions, the lacy counterpane and the heavily draped windows – all that ferocious daintiness that irritated her almost as much as Bessie did. She yearned for a room that would be spare and severe and darkly coloured with black satin sheets – and Lexie would scheme and plan and scurry about her preparations, keeping her own counsel well hidden behind that triangular smile that hovered over her lips most of the time these days.

Now at last it was all ready. Ambrose, after a good deal of goading, had agreed to listen to her. She had known from the start that he was the partner she needed. He could dance, really dance, much better than she could, and she needed his skill to show off her own abilities.

She had no illusions about her dancing; she knew it to be little more than competent, but she also knew what she did have. Her gift was a personality and a style that was unique. No one else had her odd looks, with her square bobbed hair

150

and slanted eyes and small physique. No one else could sing as she did in that strange little voice that was both husky and childlike. No one else could contain the ambition to succeed that filled her, and that would make her act the best of its kind ever seen.

But someone else could provide the best frame for the picture she wanted to show, and that someone else had to be Ambrose. He had made it clear to her in the most painful way possible that he preferred other company to her, but that his private tastes had to be his own – though she did hope in the deeper recess of her soul, where all her most important thoughts were stored, that in time she could get him to reverse that choice – and she knew she had to accept that at present. But it wasn't Ambrose as a person she wanted, she told herself firmly. It was Ambrose as a dancer, as a foil for herself, as the best accessory she could possibly have for her costumes and her style.

And now she had him. She sat there opposite him in Romano's restaurant drinking gin and wanting to shout her success at everyone who would listen. She was on her way. She, Alexandra Asher, really was on her way. Her own act, her own choreography, her own partner, her own every-thing. She was about to burst on the London scene with a glitter that would leave them all dazzled and breathless with the glory of her. It was going to be the best thing that ever happened to anyone, all that was going to happen to Lexie. The year 1919 was dissolving into autumn and the new and wonderful world of 1920 was on the horizon. It was hers and no one else's. She raised her glass to Ambrose and grinned at him. Taken aback at her sudden change of mood he grinned too, and for a moment they were locked together in a bubble of memory, children again, learning to dance.

# 16

'I hear they really are desperately in love,' the woman at the table behind said in a piercing whisper, as Ambrose went into the whirling section of the 'Princess in the Park' number, twisting Lexie round his head apparently as effortlessly as though she were a swansdown powder puff, though his muscles bulged beneath the silk of his jacket. 'So sweetly pretty and dainty – I'm going on to the party at Grosvenor Square afterwards, you know – Margery swears to me they'll be there – too divine – '

Bessie let a smile curl her lips and looked sideways at Alex, but he was unaware of anything but the small square of glass floor in the centre of the darkened restaurant with its softly glowing submerged lighting throwing the dancers into high relief, and she smiled even more widely. He liked the act, he *liked* it; and though she had been certain he would, it was still wonderful to see him sitting beside her so entranced by them. She could have hugged herself with pleasure. To see Lexie looking so wonderful, and to see Alex so pleased with her – there was little more that Bessie could ask for from an evening.

The act had moved on now, and Lexie was sitting on the white grand piano at the edge of the stage, her slender silken legs crossed to show her knees, her head thrown back to display her long throat and the exceedingly low-cut bodice of her cream silk frock. For a moment Bessie frowned to see her looking so wanton and then made herself relax. It was just a costume, just a stage costume and didn't mean anything, she told herself firmly. Just a costume –

Lexie had begun to sing, a silly lilting song about a girl picking cherries in someone else's garden, and at once Bessie forgot what she was wearing, entranced as ever by that hoarse little voice with the plaintive note in it that was so much Lexie's trademark.

The audience loved it too, some of them humming along with her, and even the waiters were standing still and listening, which was rare at the Café de Paris. They saw the best acts that came into town, because this was the place every cabaret artiste wanted to play; they clamoured for a booking as much as would-be diners clamoured for a reservation, and it took a very special act indeed to impress the cynical sophisticates who served at tables here. But this was a special act, and again Bessie swelled with pride as she listened to the applause that greeted her Lexie, now standing in the centre of the small stage, very still and straight, not bowing but accepting her ovation as her just due. She was wonderful, the best act there could be, and she, Bessie, was part of it. Because wasn't she Lexie's own sister, the person who had brought her up and loved her and looked after her?

Used to look after her, she corrected herself bleakly. She leaned back in her chair, her pleasure in the performance evaporating. She'd never get used to it, never – had tried from the first to persuade Lexie she didn't have to live alone as she did, but there, Lexie had as always insisted on her own way. It hadn't been so bad for the first three years, when her flat had been at Manor House, in the same block as Fanny and Dave; Bessie had been amazed that Lexie was making enough money to pay such a high rent – fifteen shillings a week, it was, a dreadful amount – but Lexie had said she could afford it and so she had, and the fact that Dave and Fanny were nearby to keep an eye on her, Bessie had told herself in those first years, had helped.

But now all that was changed. The day Lexie had told Bessie she was moving into a flat in Mulberry Walk, in Chelsea, Bessie had only just managed to control her tears. Lexie so far away, in so alien a part of London – it sounded so raffish, so unprotected, so *dangerous* that her belly had tied itself into a knot, and she had told Alex of her fears as soon as she could, hoping he'd be able to think of a way to stop Lexie from being so foolish.

He'd sat as he always did, with his head on one side and his knees spread wide to accommodate his steadily burgeoning belly, his heavily ringed hands firmly set on each knee and his cigar stuck between his teeth at a jaunty angle. He had listened carefully, then made a face and shaken his head.

'I know how you feel, Bessie,' he'd said. 'Funny people round there, very funny. M'niece has lived there for years, you know, years and years – but do you think she knows any of her neighbours? Hardly a one – and the way that girl's suffered, I tell you, she needed good neighbours.' He had launched himself into an account of his beloved Hannah's problems and Bessie had listened as patiently as she could, wanting desperately to bring him back to her own worries but not able to do so until he stopped to take a breath.

'The thing is, it's so expensive.' She'd let the words come out as carefully as she could, not wanting it to sound as though she were criticizing Lexie but needing his reassurance too much not to explain what it was that was distressing her. 'I mean, five pounds a week, she said, for the rent! For a place

153

with a bedroom and a living room and a kitchen and a bathroom, that's all. I've got *two* bedrooms at Victoria Park Road and it costs me just seven and six a week and – '

He had laughed fatly, the ash from his cigar shaken over his waistcoat by his mirth. 'Victoria Park Road – you should forgive me, Bessie – is a slum compared with Mulberry Walk in Chelsea. Respectable, you understand, but a slum. In Hackney you could get the whole Park and a few roads besides thrown in for a fiver! Listen, five pounds – it's not so much for such an address. A good address, you see – it costs money. You got to pay for it – '

'Yes, but who's paying for it, that's the thing,' Bessie said, and then went scarlet. 'Oh, that sounds so awful. I didn't mean it, really I didn't – '

He had stared at her and taken his cigar out of his mouth for the first time. 'Yes you did,' he said slowly. 'That's just what you meant. You got reason to believe that she ain't a nice girl no more?'

'I don't know,' she had said miserably, and then the tears had started. 'I just don't know! Can she be making enough money out of that act to pay that sort of rent? She's got to find the costumes and the music and then there's Ambrose and Poppy – they get paid as well. She can't be making that much money. Can she?'

'You've asked her?'

'Of course I've tried, but you know how Lexie is – ' Her voice had trailed away.

'Yes. I know how Lexie is. She bullies you, that's how she is. She crooks her finger, Bessie comes running. She doesn't crook her finger, Bessie sits home and cries. She smiles, Bessie smiles. She don't smile – pah!' And the soft little sound was full of affectionate anger. 'I tell you, Bessie, after all these years you still make me so mad I could throw you out o' the office, only no one else could do the job you do for me! I told you, you shouldn't let her get away with it – '

'What can you do when young people insist on going their own way? What can you do if you love them, except follow them?'

'You make 'em toe the line, that's what,' Alex had said grimly. 'My Hannah, she's havin' the same sort o' trouble with her girl – a bit younger than your Lexie, I'll grant you, ten years younger, but it's all the same. Hannah dances when her Mary Bee pipes a tune, and so do you for Lexie – for God's sake, Bessie, tell the girl what's worrying you! Ask her who's payin' the rent – it's the only way you'll feel right.'

But she'd shaken her head and gone on fretting. All the time she was helping Lexie move out of the Manor House flat and into Mulberry Walk, all the time she had hung curtains and filled cupboards, she had tried not to count the cost of the new furniture delivered from Maple's in the Tottenham Court Road, the best of everything in chrome chairs and Chinese-style laquered furniture and crushed velvet drapes and Lalique glass ornaments, but she had not succeeded. Lexie had paid for everything so cheerfully, writing cheques as casually as though they were made of confetti, that her anxiety had deepened, and now at the first night of the new act with all the new material at the Café de Paris her fears came back with a rush. She'd have to find out, somehow, how she was doing it. She didn't want to know, but she had to.

After the show was over, and the dance band had taken its place on the miniscule stage and the glass floor was crammed with foxtrotting couples sweating in the crush, Lexie came out to sit with them. Again Bessie felt a stab of pleasure as the woman at the table behind them fluttered and exclaimed at being so close to the star of the cabaret, but Lexie ignored her with great aplomb and sat down beside Alex, smiling at him brilliantly as she slipped into her chair. She had changed from her flimsy costume but what she was wearing now was almost as revealing and Bessie literally bit her tongue. If she wanted to wear little more than a scrap of silk and chiffon and show her knees, why should Bessie distress herself? It wasn't as though she didn't look wonderful. She did, with that thick square-cut fringe of hers over her slanting eyes and her thin but seductive little body. She looked wonderful, and that, Bessie tried to convince herself, was what mattered.

'Ambrose'll be here soon,' Lexie said. 'It takes him twice as long to change as it does me. I told him if he's not here by two I'll go to the Bag o' Nails on my own. I'm not going to miss the best party of the year while he curls his toenails or whatever it is he spends so long at. Dearest Alex – it's divine to see you! I did so hope you'd catch the act – ' She smiled at Alex Lazar with a practised sparkle and he smiled back, beaming and contented to be in her company.

155

'Bessie told me that Fanny and Dave couldn't come, last minute, so naturally here I am!'

She shook her head at him, and laughed. 'One of these days you'll have to tell me what it is with you two. Always slanging each other – '

'Hey? What's that? He's been saying things to you about me?' Alex said and his forehead creased sharply. 'If that man's been – '

'No, no,' she said, leaning back in her chair to catch a waiter's eye. 'Of course he hasn't. It's just that once ages ago he said the sort of things you say – that you don't get on. Nothing more. Bessie, do you like the new act? What did you think of the "Princess in the Park" number?'

'Lovely,' Bessie said, and then, hating herself for the words that came out, knowing what the effect would be, went on, 'What's this about the Bag o' Nails? I thought you were going to a party at someone's house in Grosvenor Square and then – '

At once Lexie's face hardened and she flicked a look at Bessie that made her sit back in her chair, her cheeks hot. 'Ah, here's a waiter at last. What's that you two have there? Oh, I need better than that – make it a pink gin, Joe, will you? And quickly, because I can't stay here long. I'm due somewhere else. As soon as that wretch Ambrose gets out I'll be gone. Send someone round to tell him to hurry, Joe, will you?' She smiled at the waiter with the same trained sparkle she had shown for Alex, and Bessie said no more. She knew when she was defeated.

But Alex did not. 'So, Lexie, what's this about the Bag o' Nails? It's not a nice place, that – '

'No, thank God! I wouldn't be going there if it was, would I? I want a little fun after a day slaving over a hot act – why not come too, Alex? You'd love it. Lots of fun there – they've got the most divine jazz band you ever heard, I promise you. It's not one of these milk and water imitations but a bit of real New Orleans stuff. And the best cocktails in town – '

'I've got work to do tomorrow, young lady,' Alex said, reaching over to pay the waiter who had brought her pink gin. 'And so has your sister. We'll be on our way. Ambrose is taking you, you say? Hmm. Well, I suppose as long as there's someone there to take care of you – '

'My dearest old owl, I hardly need taking care of, you know!' Lexie's tone was still a bantering one but there was an edge beneath it that made Bessie feel a stir of anxiety in her belly. Don't let her make a scene, she said inside her head. Don't let's have a scene, please. Not with Alex. Not here.

'Yes you do,' Alex said unperturbed. 'Any girl as pretty as you needs to be looked after. The way I look after your sister. She's a whole three weeks older'n you, but I still like to look after her.' He grinned at Bessie and the danger subsided as Lexie laughed, drank her gin and watched them both over the rim of her glass, her eyes amused.

'You two ought to have an affair, you know,' she said and lifted her brows at Bessie. 'Do you both the world of good. Or are you already? Maybe I've been too busy lately to notice – '

'Lexie!' Bessie gasped, but Alex just laughed.

'Wouldn't you like to know! But want'll have to be your master, Miss, because we ain't tellin'! Eh, Bessie?' She smiled at him as best she could, picked up her own neglected glass and pretended to drink. She didn't know what hurt more: Lexie's awareness that what she had said was absurd, or Alex's chuckling sharing of the joke. Why should it be funny to think of Bessie having an affair? Why should Alex laugh at the idea so cruelly? And then her commonsense took over and she managed to laugh too, for it was funny, after all. She, Bessie Ascher, having love affairs like ordinary people? A lunatic idea, ridiculous, hilarious. And she did her best to laugh.

'Did Dave and Fanny say why they couldn't come?' Lexie asked casually, but Bessie's ears sharpened. Lexie's voice was almost too casual, her interest in the answer to her question too obvious.

'He's probably too busy screwing some poor fella out of his life savings somewhere,' Alex grunted, and lit another cigar. Bessie shook her head at him in mild reproof and turned to take her wrap from the back of her chair.

'Fanny said she wasn't well,' she said. 'I spoke to her this morning. She told me she felt terrible. You know how Fanny is, always got something wrong with her these days. I told her she should see a doctor, but she wouldn't. Said they make more trouble than they save, but I don't know – anyway she's not well and Benny's in Scotland, seeing after some deal or other Dave's doing there, and with Joe in America who else could stay in with her but Dave? So he couldn't come either. He said to tell you good luck and mazeltov – '

'Good,' Lexie said, and sounded abstracted now. 'Good. I mean, thanks for the message. I just wondered – oh, at last! Here's the answer to every girl's prayers, and I don't think.'

Ambrose had come across the big restaurant, stopping at table after table to chatter and giggle, but now had reached them, and at once Lexie stood up.

'I was all set to go on my own,' she said crisply and picked up her own wrap, a fragment of satin and feathers that looked as though it would blow away in the least breath of wind. 'Goodnight, Alex, Bessie. See you soon – '

'When?' Bessie said it without thinking, and Lexie looked back at her over her shoulder, her eyes bright yet somehow empty.

'Oh, dearest one, I can't say! I'll phone you, I dare say. At the office if the boss doesn't mind! Goodbye, Alex – lovely to see you. Thanks for the gin – too divine – ' And she went, not looking to see whether Ambrose was following her.

'And if I don't go I'll have my boss after me!' Ambrose said, twinkling at them both. 'Enjoyed the act, I hope? Full of great new stuff, isn't it? Did you see those twirls of mine, Bessie? How about that, then, hmm? I tell you, I topped myself with those – oh, all *right*! She's getting mad, got to go – 'night all!' And he was gone too, leaving them both sitting and staring after them.


She's a lot more ill than they know, Lexie thought, staring out of the cab window at a rain-washed Piccadilly and its clotted crawling traffic. A lot more. And suppose it gets worse, then what? Dave on his own – he won't care then who knows, and anyway he may want – oh, damn. I wish I'd never started it. I wish he'd go away. I wish Fanny wasn't ill – and she blinked at her own reflection in the wet window. Fanny, who'd always seemed too remote and rather alarming when she was a child and had become a boring and irritating irrelevance in her life in her older years, now seemed to shift in her mind, to take on a new and protective role, like Bessie's. While Fanny was there, behind Dave, he couldn't be a nuisance. He could go on as he'd been this past five years, devoted to Lexie, signing her bills, providing what she needed, and getting nothing back but vague promises and teasing and occasional dinners and dancing in the sort of restaurant where no one knew him and those who recognized her cared nothing about with whom she might be spending her time. But if Fanny were no longer there, then what? He'd start wanting more. And if he didn't get it, then maybe the spring would dry up and the drought would start – she thought of the way her costs were spiralling now, even with his name on the rent book at Mulberry Walk, and shivered slightly in her flimsy wrap.

'Cold, ducky?' Ambrose said. He put his arm round her shoulders and hugged her. 'Never mind. Soon be there – I say, it went like a dream, didn't it, tonight? Did you *hear* the way they shouted? At the Café de Paris, yet! They *never* shout there – but they shouted for us – oh, I reckon we're on to a goody with this stuff. So does Poppy, you know. She said so, and she should know. She's sat and listened to enough managements' conversations to have all the nous anyone ever needed. She says we're on to a winner – '

'Yes,' Lexie said with none of his excitement in her voice. 'We're on to a winner. We've got a month at the Café and then they want us at the Mirabeau, and then we can go back to the Café with a couple of new numbers. We're all right – '

'Great,' he said. 'Isn't it great?' He hugged her again and she felt the tightness return in her chest and was furious with herself for allowing it, but could do nothing to stop it even though she knew she was a fool to feel so. She had realized within a year of their starting the act that she had been barking up any number of wrong trees as far as Ambrose was concerned. Nothing she did or could ever do would change him; he had his Alan and his Clive and his Douglas and now that stupid American, Irving, and she felt her throat tighten when she thought of Irving and the way Ambrose was when he was around. There was nothing she could do about it: Ambrose felt for Irving what she felt for him. Or had, she told herself now as she patted his hand and smiled the cheerful smile she always used for him, and said nothing. What would be the good of saying anything? They were great friends, colleagues, partners, everything but what she wanted them to be. Settle for that.

And I'm not missing all that much, she told herself as at last the cab reached the middle of Piccadilly and could turn left into Half Moon Street on its way to the Bag o' Nails nightclub. It's only a lot of stupid tumbling about and messy groping and who cares anyway? Such a fuss about so little. She thought of the last time someone had got a crush on her and had begged her to accept him as a lover, and shook her head in the darkness. That had been so *boring* and you couldn't say anything worse than that. To be bored – it was like being dead. And sex was boring. Men were boring. There was just work and getting money to make everything come out the way she wanted it and getting the act to bigger and better venues and making more money. That's all. And having a partner who dances like Ambrose is more important than having any number of stupid lovers – and again she patted his hand as it held her upper arm, and he grinned at her and said, 'Attagirl,' with vague good humour as at last the cab drew up at the dark doorway with its discreet brass plate that read, 'Bag o' Nails. Members only.'

# 17

For the first half hour or so it was fine. The place was full of people she knew well enough to talk to but not so well that she was irritated by the company. There were strangers who had caught the act at the Café and were filled with extravagant praise, there were lots of cocktails, and the jazz was good.

But then the clock turned past two, and the crowd thickened, became noisier and more frantic in its chatter and dancing, and as Ambrose was whisked away by that damned Irving, gloom settled on her again. She thought for a while of going home, but that would be dreary. She was still keyed up from the excitement of the performance, needed time to come down, to loosen up and begin to yawn. Nothing was worse than going home too soon, to sit in the flat, listen to the distant noise of traffic from the King's Road, and lie awake and awake and awake.

She sat at a table in the corner, her back to the wall, watching them all, surrounded by people who gabbled and exclaimed and shrieked with laughter, and yet it was

160

curiously peaceful. She could lean her head back against the yellow velvet upholstery and stare round and see without making any real effort to be part of it. She could be there, and yet remote from it. The light immediately above her head threw an agreeable warmth on to her neck and she liked that, for it was a cold night and even here in this crowded basement she could feel the chill of the rainy October dark that filled the streets outside, seeping through the walls and into her fragile bones. So she sat and let her own thoughts fill her, giving up the impossible task of keeping her mind a blank. It would be wonderful she told herself dreamily, if she could. But it just wasn't possible –

I shouldn't have started it. Shouldn't have let him do it. Should have seen it'd lead to all sorts of problems. But at the time it had seemed so reasonable, so sensible. Dave had money and wanted to spend it on her, and all she had to do was flirt with him a little. She had told him that she wouldn't ever let anything happen again, that once had been too often because, after all, Fanny – she had let her sister's name hang in the air between them and watched him wriggle and suffer and had said nothing more. She hadn't needed to. And it had seemed right, somehow, to let Dave suffer so. He'd used her, she'd told herself, that evening when I was so miserable and needed someone to comfort me. He *used* me, just as though I wasn't a real person, just someone who happened to be there. He didn't care about me at all. Why should I care now about him? Why should it worry me that he's so agitated that whenever I come into his office he gets all hot and uncomfortable – and now sitting at the Bag o' Nails on a cold October night in 1926 she remembered the way Dave had changed, how confused in her company he had become, how eager to please her, how abject when he didn't, and her lips curved a little – not with pleasure, but with a small triumph. All those long tired years with Madame G. thumping out all those awful dances with all those awful kids had to be paid for, somehow, and Dave had done some of the paying. Why not? she thought now, why not? Other people have used me, so I'll use him –

But it's not fair, that wretched small voice that came to plague her sometimes whispered inside her head. Not fair. He didn't hurt you all that much. He only used your body, not you, and what does that matter? It's only sex. He didn't

161

hurt *you*. Fanny did, sometimes, stupid Fanny, she did with the things she said and did, she hurt you, but it's not fair to treat Dave so just because of her — and anyway she's ill now, she's dying.

She's not dying! Lexie thought then, and lifted her glass and drank some more. She's not! People don't die that easily. She's just being Fanny wanting her own way, getting it any way she can—

Like you. Just like you, her little sister—

Shut up, she told the little voice. She drank again and held out her glass when someone else at the table leaned forward with a bottle of champagne held unsteadily in his hand. Shut up. You aren't the same as them, you aren't like Bessie who yearns after you all the time and nags you with her eyes, and you aren't like Fanny who pushes people around and wants her own way, and — you're just you, Lexie, Alexandra Asher, a star. You are a star, you are, you are, you've made it—

No, you haven't, said the little voice contemptuously. Of course you haven't. Top-line cabaret spot you may be in, but it's only once so far, isn't it? You've got to do more than that. You can't just settle for that, not if you want to stop Dave paying for you. Not if you want to be a real star, living at the top, right up in the butter, on your own money, on money you've danced for, not bullied for—

I'm not a bully. Am I? Not a bully—

If you're not, why are you worrying? jeered the little voice. If you're not, why does the idea come into your head? Of course you are! You bully Bessie because she infuriates you with all that damned love, and you bully Dave because he can't keep his eyes off you and aches to put his hands on you and you despise him for it, and you bully Ambrose because he doesn't ever want to put his hands on you, not the way you want him to, and you despise him for that, and—

'Shut *up*,' she whispered, letting her lips move. Leaning back on the yellow upholstery, she gazed at the scene before her, refusing to let the little voice have any effect on her. She stared at the expanse of yellow walls, the glittering black and chrome tables and the long bar so lavishly lined with mirrors that everyone on the dance floor could be seen reflected over and over again in each squared off segment, stared at the sweating grinning band on its floodlit podium, stared at the scurrying tired waiters and thought — this is fun. I'm

162

supposed to be having fun.

But it wasn't easy.


He had been sitting there for half an hour before he'd noticed her, trying to think of a way he could persuade David to leave, and totally failing to come up with an answer, which was a rare experience for him. Usually, he thought wryly, I've got an answer to everything. But not this time. Wretched David, wretched man! I'm in court in the morning, dammit – I'll be a wet rag–

But then he'd seen her across the room and he'd stopped thinking about David Damont at all. She was in the opposite corner to his own, sitting right against the wall, just as he was, under one of those stupid lights that had been made in the shape of exotic flowers, all curled glass petals and twisted stamens, and it splashed her head with such a glow of gold that suddenly he stopped thinking the lights were stupid and decided they were rather cleverly designed, after all. The light made her hair gleam as though it was burnished ebony and beneath its heavy fringe she had eyes which slanted but still managed to be wide and very dark. Her skin, even from this distance, looked rich and matt like thick very pale cream, and her neck and shoulders, visible above the scrap of a dress she was wearing, had a birdlike fragility about them that was very appealing.

He wondered for a while who she was, worrying at that thought like a dog at a particularly small bone. It didn't matter, and yet it did, especially because he felt obscurely that he knew her. But the trouble was that the longer he stared at her the harder it was to decide whether he had known her before or was learning her face so rapidly that it seemed he had known it for ever. That was something that happened sometimes, he told himself sententiously. You look at something because you like it and then convince yourself it's always been part of your life.

The girl in the corner moved sharply, lifting her chin, and that made his spirits lift too, in the most stupid fashion, and he raised his eyebrows at himself and deliberately looked away. Ridiculous, staring at a girl in a nightclub as though he were a ten-year-old at a funfair seeing a bearded lady for the first time! Not that this girl was bearded or anything but delectable to look at. But it was absurd to stare—

But he was staring again, without realizing he was doing it. Now she was leaning back against the yellow walls, her hair shining even more richly against the garish colour – with her eyes closed. He could see now that there were fine shadows beneath those strange eyes, violet smudges that spoke of fatigue, and he wanted to go over to her and tell her not to sit there like that, that it was time to go home and get some rest—

The music swooped, changed, and left the ragtimes and jazz rhythms behind to start on a particularly frantic rhumba. The people at the table she was sitting at got up, obscuring her from his view, and he watched, wanting to know with sudden urgency who she was with. Some vapid capering idiot, no doubt, with no more wit than a flea—

The couples formed, left the table behind them with much giggling from the girls and slapping of each other's shoulders among the men, and then he could see that she was not one of a couple at all, but was still sitting there. Her eyes were open now, but she was still leaning back, glancing vaguely round the room much as he had been himself. She looked at him then, and he shrank back against the wall, suddenly embarrassed. Then, as her gaze passed him by without paying any attention to him, he realized how stupid he had been. She couldn't know he'd been staring at her, after all—

Someone came pushing across the crowded dance floor and made his way purposefully through the tables, going unerringly to the corner one and he watched, no longer caring whether anyone noticed he was staring. A tall redhaired young man, very lissom – damned lounge lizard, the watcher thought, and then grinned at his own prejudice. It was clear he knew the girl very well, for he slid into the seat beside her with an easy intimacy and at once started talking eagerly to her. She sat and listened, her head bent slightly sideways so that she could hear above all the noise the band and the dancers were making, and still the man in the opposite corner watched, swirling his brandy in its big glass, amused at his own interest in the little cameo scene being played out there.

Cameo scene, he thought. Of course! Cameo scene. She's an actress of some sort. Must be. I must have seen her in something. Now, I wonder what? I know I've seen that odd

164

little face somewhere before. Not pretty, but damned interesting –

The lissom young man had her hand in his and was pulling it. She got to her feet, moving in a way that was, it seemed to the watcher, unwilling or at least uncertain. She was saying something and shaking her head, but the young man was urging her. Suddenly she seemed to droop a little, shrugged her shoulders and went with him.

But they didn't go to the dance floor as the watcher had expected them to. Instead they flanked it, coming round to his side of the big glittering room. He watched them come close, leaning back lazily against his own section of yellow wall, using all the experience he had to make himself seem relaxed and unaware, nothing but another merrymaker sitting at a nightclub table –

They passed within a few feet of him, and he could hear their voices clearly, even above the hubbub.

'Don't be so stuffy, Lexie!' the young man was saying. 'It's only a giggle, after all! And they say it feels marvellous –' and then they were past, and he was staring after them, his forehead creasing.

He didn't know why the idea came into his head, why he should be suspicious, for after all David had never said anything to make him think it might be among his problems, but all the same, David being David –

He got to his feet and went after them, moving easily, one hand thrust lazily into his trouser pocket, the other dangling a cigarette, and they were quite unaware of him as they made their way to the very rear of the room. It was darker here, for the tables were fewer, since the view of the dance floor and the band was obscured by the side of the bar, and the tables were empty, anyway, as their occupants had piled on to the packed dance floor. The girl and her red-headed escort stopped at the door at the back.

'Honestly, Ambrose, I'm not sure I think it's –' the girl said, and then the door opened and they were gone. The watcher stopped, leaned against the side of the bar and thought for a while. He had never been one to do anything in a hurry, but on the other hand he'd never been one to leave anything half completed either. This needed thinking about.

The room was dark and stuffy and at first she could hardly see a thing, for there were a lot of people there, and the small red-shaded lamps in the corners did little to illuminate the middle of the room. But then, slowly, her eyes adjusted. She looked around and lifted her brows in some amusement.

'Can't this friend of yours afford any chairs for his guests?' she said to Ambrose. He nudged at her with his shoulder and giggled in the dimness.

'Darling, don't be so boring and bourgeois,' he said, and his voice was a little shrill with excitement. 'Who needs chairs when there are so many darling cushions? Do settle yourself and I'll fetch David. He's dying to meet you but he told me nothing in this great wide world would get him out there with the hoi polloi. That's why he sent me to fetch you – now do sit, darling, I'll be back at once – ' And he disappeared into the gloom.

After a moment she sat down, curling herself as elegantly as she could into one of the big piles of cushions that were scattered about the room, and again leaned back to relax. Behind her the door through which she and Ambrose had come in opened and closed again, but she didn't turn her head.

It really was getting very late and she ought to go home now, she told herself, even though it was so bleak and alone there. It should be lovely thinking of going home to her own flat, her own beautiful modern flat full of beautiful modern furniture. Why wasn't it? Surely it was better than the old days, going traipsing home to Bessie and her clucking and the smell of Mrs Bernstein's fried fish from downstairs and hot milk and Bessie's hot water bottle. It must be – she must be very tired indeed to be thinking that hot water bottles and hot milk and Bessie were preferable to the flat in Mulberry Walk.

'Here she is!' Ambrose's voice said above her head. She peered up into the dimness and a new voice said, 'My dear, don't get up, *whatever* you do. You look too divine lying there, like Cleopatra on the most marvellous barge! *Too* delicious – let me come and join you on your floating cushions, *please* – ' Someone thumped down beside her and sat there beaming at her.

He was a solid young man, with a fat round face that was sweating richly and very curly hair that looked slightly absurd over the thin toothbrush moustache that adorned his long upper lip, but he had a charming grin and after a moment she grinned back at him.

'Hello. Who are you?'

'My dear, I'm David Damont. Your host at this madly naughty party within a party. *Isn't* it fun? Those dreary old bores out there, thinking they're having a most *glorious* whoopee of a time, when actually all the real fun is in here, with us! I heard you'd come in and when I saw Ambrose was in here with that dear man Irving and had left you outside – well, I was *livid*, positively livid with rage! That's why I made him rush and fetch you – and now here you are! *Too*, too divine – now, what will you have? A little drinky? Or some of my naughties? Did Ambrose tell you of my naughties?'

She watched as he pushed two fingers into the straining pocket of his white waistcoat, and pulled out a small flat box made of chased silver. 'He said something about – ' she began.

At once he leaned forward and pressed a finger to her lips. 'Dear one, no names, no pack drill, as those *ghastly* army types say! Not a word. Just our little naughties, and no one need know anything but that. Sugar it is, good for the soul, just a little powdered sugar. *Too* delicious and nutritious.'

He wriggled so that he was sitting closer to her and now she could smell him, a queasy mixture of Turkish cigarette smoke and sweat and expensive eau de cologne and a sick sweetish smell she didn't recognize, and she shrank back a little, frowning.

'I'm not sure – ' she began. Then suddenly there was a hand between them and she stared at it in the dimness, startled. She looked up to see to whom the arm belonged. The man who was staring down at her had a broad face with deep clefts running down the cheeks, clefts she could see clearly even in this half light, and above it his hair was thick and dust-coloured and sleeky brushed. He was stocky and not very tall and looked about thirty-five and, she thought, very boring indeed. One of those sensible types she most hated.

'What do you want?' she said rudely, pushing at the hand that was now held open, palm upwards, in front of David Damont. 'Go away and don't make a pest of yourself. David, you were saying – '

'Oh, Max, *go* away!' David said, and there was a petulant tone in his voice. 'I thought you'd gone *hours* ago – go now instead – '

'I'm going as soon as I can,' the stocky man said, and now he crouched down so that his face was on a level with theirs. 'After you've given me that box.'

'What box?' David Damont sounded more petulant than ever now, like a whining child. It was a sound that suddenly irritated Lexie enormously. She reached forwards and took the box from the place where he had hurriedly hidden it beneath his broad thigh as he sat there cross-legged beside her.

'Is this it?' she said in a loud clear voice. 'Thank you. I'd love to try some – ' She snapped open the lid and peered into the dusting of white powder that filled it.

'No, you wouldn't,' said the stocky man coolly. With a sharp movement he took the box from her, snapped it shut, got to his feet and very deliberately put it into his pocket.

'Well, of all the damned – ' she began, scrambling to her feet. 'David, who is this horrible man? Why don't you hit him or something? Why doesn't *anybody* hit him, damn it?' For no one had moved. The room, for all its crowded state, was as still as if it had been empty. No one was talking and no one was moving. They just watched silently in the dim light as Max stood with his hands in his trouser pockets and smiled at her.

'This horrible man is Max Cramer, Miss Asher. Yes, I recognized you. I saw you last year in a rather dismal little show at a hotel in Bournemouth. I remember thinking the show was dreadful but you were charming in it.'

'Thank you for nothing!' she said after a moment, then set her fists on her hips and stared at him. 'And who is Max Cramer when he's at home? I've never heard of *you*. Certainly I know no reason why you should come and spoil other people's fun. Give that back and go away. You heard what David said.'

'I say, Miss Asher – ' David was hovering uncomfortably at her shoulder. 'I say, Miss Asher, I really would rather you didn't.'

'I'm sure you would, David,' Max Cramer said. 'You obviously know that there can be considerable penalties for handling cocaine. And if you're arrested for dealing in the stuff, don't ask me to bail you out. You'll need to get yourself a new lawyer if that happens – '

Behind him the door swung and then swung again as people began to leave. It was as though by just uttering the word 'cocaine' he had filled the room with threats they couldn't bear, and they were fleeing, making small scurrying sounds as they went. Lexie looked up and saw Ambrose at the door, shaking his head at her in furious warning, before he was pulled through it by Irving. She opened her mouth to call after him to wait for her but he was gone. Furiously she turned to the man called Max Cramer, her face white with tiredness and a huge anger.

'Well, they can all behave like stupid babies if they want to! Too boring!' she said, and her voice was high and clear. 'But *I'm* not going to. Give me that box, Mr Whoever-You-Are, and go and mind your own affairs somewhere else. I'm going to have some right *now*!'

'Are you?' he said. He took the box out of his pocket and held it out towards her, balancing it on his open palm. 'Are you sure? I can't stop you, of course, since you're a grown lady with every right to go to hell any way you choose. But I rather think the papers would be greatly intrigued to hear of it. Café de Paris cabaret star is Drug Fiend! Can't you just see the headlines? And hear what the Café management would say?'

'You wouldn't,' she said, staring at him. 'You wouldn't dare!'

'Of course I would,' he said. 'Immediately. Help yourself, Miss Asher. It's all yours.'

# 18

The ringing of the phone dragged her out of a dream so confused and alarming that when she snapped her eyes open and stared at her bedside table she couldn't think where she was, what day it was, or what the noise was that had woken her. It went on and on, shrill if a little muffled by the crinoline lady doll that she kept over the instrument. She shook her head against her pillow and dragged herself upright.

'Mm?' she said into the mouthpiece, lying back so that she could rest it on her chest and jamming the earpiece between her tousled head and her pillow. 'What is it?'

'Have I woken you?' the tinny little voice clacked. 'Sorry, I tend to forget the sort of hours you theatre people keep.'

She opened her eyes wide, for they had closed as sleep threatened to overtake her again. 'Who's that?' She shook her head again to clear its muzziness. 'Ambrose?'

'Hardly,' the little voice said, and even though it was distorted she could hear the sardonic note in it. 'Max Cramer. Calling to apologize.'

She wriggled up to sit more comfortably against her pillows, staring at the opposite wall with the earpiece still pressed to her head, and tried to think. Last night she had been so overpoweringly angry that, had he telephoned then, she would have hurled the instrument through the window rather than talk to him. Now, with the thin light of the October morning creeping through her curtains and the sour taste of a disturbed night's sleep in her mouth, she wasn't sure how she felt.

'Are you still there?' the little voice said. 'I said this is –'

'I heard you. I'm thinking,' she said. 'What's the time?'

'Ten o'clock,' the voice said, and she turned and looked at her little bedside clock, squinting at it in disbelief.

'Ten – are you out of your mind? Who gets up at ten o'clock?'

'I do. That is, I get up at seven. I'm at my desk well before ten. I'm due in court in a moment so I had to call now and risk disturbing you. By the time I get out of court you could be anywhere. And my apology unoffered.'

'Court?' she said, still muzzy with sleep.

'Indeed, court. Middlesex Sessions. I'm dealing with a case of embezzlement. It's something of a speciality with me. But it'll be a long one, and I did want to reach you as soon as I could. Do you accept my apology?'

'I'm not sure. Why are you apologizing? After all, some people might think you saved me from some terrible –'

'If you thought that I'd be delighted. Do you?'

'You haven't answered my question. Why are you apologizing?'

'I was ill-mannered. I meddled. I bullied. A reasonable list of sins, I'd have thought.'

She sat and stared at the curtains moving sluggishly against her window as the chill morning air sighed through the cracks of the frame, and tried to think. Yes, he'd been officious, but all the same – even to have contemplated using that damned stuff had been lunacy. She'd seen enough of what it could do to some of the musicians she'd worked with. There was old Bixie, with his collapsed nose, his constantly wet eyes and his even more constant fights with managements when he drifted in late for rehearsals and even, sometimes, for performances. There was Sammy the drummer who had once been so amusing and lively and now wept as often as he smiled. She'd never been in the least interested in getting involved with people like that, and yet last night she'd let Ambrose and that stupid posing ass of a friend of his take her to the edge of –

'Are you still there? Or have you gone back to sleep?'

'I'm here,' she said, repositioning the earpiece against her head, for she had let it slip down as she lay there thinking.

'So, do I have an answer? Is my apology accepted?'

'Why does it matter? You've said it. Now you can go into your court and deal with your embezzler and feel pleased with yourself because you've cleared your conscience. What does it matter whether I accept or not? After all, you behaved very well, didn't you? Upright citizen concerned about the law and all that –'

'I'm a lawyer. That's what I do for a living.'

'And last night you did it for nothing. Can't you settle for that? Or do you want me to pay you a fee for it? Is that why you called? To get your reward?'

There was a little silence and then he said, 'I should have expected that, I suppose. I did interfere where it was none of my business. But all the same, I did it for the best of reasons.'

'Really? And what could they be?' She was beginning to enjoy herself now. The sleepiness had gone, though her eyes were still gritty, and her mind was working properly. Talking to this man was fun. He had none of the extravagant tricks of language used by the people with whom she worked, and yet wasn't dull as Dave and Bessie were. 'Do tell me.'

There was another little silence, then he said bluntly, 'To

protect my client was one of them. The other was to stop you making a fool of yourself.'

Her pleasure in the conversation evaporated as fast as it had come. 'Indeed?' she said icily. 'Kind of you. And who might your client be?'

'David Damont. He owns that place –'

'How nice for him.'

'And he's trying to sell it. It's no secret, so I can tell you about it. I want him to sell it because it's not good for someone like him to be involved with the sort of people who frequent that sort of nightclub –'

'People like me' she said with great sweetness.

'I don't think you're an habituée of the place. Certainly your name isn't on the list as a member. I suppose you could be a regular guest of some other member –'

'It's none of your damned business if I am!'

'Of course it isn't. But it's my business to keep David Damont out of trouble, and that means trying to get him out of the place. Last night's little episode convinces me even more that he's got to sell. I didn't know about the cocaine parties – apparently they happen often. Did you know that?'

'Oh, you're collecting evidence now, are you? This is turning out to be the oddest apology I ever –'

'Oh, for heaven's sake, Miss Asher! You're deliberately misunderstanding me! I know perfectly well you haven't used the stuff before –'

'Indeed? How do you know that?'

'Because of the way you behaved when it was offered to you. I'd been watching you, and it was obvious you weren't keen. And because you didn't look as though you're any sort of dope fiend –'

'You talk like the *Daily Mail*'.

'Ouch. You can't say worse than that, I suppose. Anyway, you don't. People who use that stuff stand out like – like –'

'Try a sore thumb. That's what the *Daily Mail* says. They like the same sort of ideas and phrases you do.'

He took a sharp breath. She heard the soft little sound across the miles of wire, knew she'd hurt him and was glad. The moment of pleasure she'd found in his conversation was quite gone now. He was as pompous and boring as a man could be, sounding just like Bessie with her worrying and nagging, and she wanted nothing to do with him. He was to

172

be put firmly in the box labelled 'Boring'.

'Look,' he said after a moment. 'Let's start again. Let's behave as though we didn't talk last night, and as though I had no reason to apologize. I just happen to have seen you at this club I was at, for reasons of my own, and remembered having seen you in a show –'

'A dreary one, you said, as I recall.'

'In a show,' he said as though she hadn't spoken, '– and now I'm calling to ask you to dine with me.'

She took the earpiece away from her head and stared at it. This was the last thing she'd expected. She was used to men asking her out, used to men leering at her, wanting to entertain her, because that was the way men were – opportunists who thought that dancers were automatically easy meat. She had learned over the years how to freeze them away, how to stop the invitations being made at all, with one sharp look of distaste. But this had never happened before, this sort of direct yet polite approach from a man like this. Max Cramer wasn't the sort who hung about theatres, wasn't the kind of man who usually came her way, and to have him behave like this – she felt a sense of dreariness settle over her and put the phone back to her ear.

'Are you there?' the little voice was clacking. 'Are you there?'

'I'm here,' she said. 'And the answer is no thank you. Goodbye.' She put the earpiece back on its hook, set the phone neatly back on the bedside table, and dropped the crinoline lady doll over it. Its little china face simpered at her and she said loudly, 'Damn!' got out of bed and went padding away to run her bath. There was no point in trying to sleep any longer. She was much too irritable now for that.


In time to come she was to remember, often, that morning in October 1926. She would only have to smell the acrid smokiness of autumn to be there again in her small flat in Mulberry Walk, feeling irritated and yet elated by that telephone conversation, had only to lie back in hot silky water to soak away fatigue to remember lying in her bathroom that morning thinking about Max Cramer and wondering why it was he had been able to make her feel so confused.

173

For that conversation was by no means the end of it. Two days later she had a letter from him, in which he repeated in spare and direct language his apology for meddling in matters that did not concern him, i.e. her actions, and asking her to dine with him. She ignored the letter. Three days after that she saw him sitting at a stageside table at the Café de Paris, his arms folded, his eyes fixed on her unwinkingly.

He almost made her lose balance, for she first caught sight of him as Ambrose lifted her into the twirls for the 'Princess in the Park' number, and she knew he knew, because he grinned at her so that the clefts in his cheeks became crevasses. She thought – he must have had dimples when he was a child, and was furious with herself for being interested enough to consider the possibility.

He came every night for a week to the Café de Paris, until everyone else in the place noticed and began gossiping about him and she had to give in. On the last Saturday night of the first run of her contract at the Café she accepted the invitation he sent as usual by the hand of Joe, the waiter who always acted as go-between for artistes and customers, and went to have a drink at his table.

After that it seemed inevitable that she would agree to dine with him, and after that first dinner, at a very small and very comfortable Italian restaurant tucked away in a side street behind St James's, refusing further invitations would have been ungracious. Anyway, she had begun to enjoy his company.

He was not boring at all, she found, but amusing in a dry sort of way, talking easily and comfortably of matters she had never thought much about before. He talked of politics, of the effect on the country of the aftermath of the General Strike that had caused so much upheaval earlier in the year; and of the new developments in Soviet Russia, where Trotsky had been expelled from the Politburo ('Who's Trotsky?' she'd asked. 'He sounds like one of the clowns in Barnum and Bailey's circus.' He'd laughed and said a little grimly, 'Something of a clown in some people's eyes, perhaps – but an interesting and important one.') He'd talked of sport, launching himself so passionately into a panegyric of praise for Jack Hobbs and his sixteenth century in first-class cricket that she'd stared at him open-mouthed, and he'd actually blushed and apologized for his interest in what had been a lifelong hobby. He talked of books, telling her why D.H. Lawrence was so important a writer and lending her his brand-new copy of his latest offering, *The Plumed Serpent* (which she didn't particularly enjoy, somewhat to Max's disappointment). They went to exhibitions and cinemas and concerts; and slowly she relaxed with him and even more slowly came to realize that he was not as other men were. He didn't produce a special sort of talk for her, designed to cajole her into bed with him, the way most men did. He had none of the silly flippant small chatter that other men seemed to think was the only kind of conversation women cared about. He spoke to her, she was certain, as he spoke to the men he worked with, and she took that as the best compliment he could have paid her.

Not that he was lacking in the graces that were obvious compliments. He sent her flowers, sometimes, so that she would come into her small dressing room at the Café de Paris, where her contract had been renewed after her short stay at the Mirabeau, to find it adrift with the scent of tuberoses or lilies, horribly expensive flowers in these dark dank winter months, or she would find a small cotton wool-filled basket in which lay one perfect hothouse peach, and that warmed the whole evening for her. He chose good restaurants to which to take her, so that gradually she learned to take an intelligent interest in wine and good cooking, and yet never once was he anything but punctiliously polite, never once did he do anything that could be construed as an unwanted advance, never once did he seem to want more from her than her company.

She was deeply suspicious at first, sure that he must have some sort of ulterior motive in behaving as he did, but as the months went by and December slid into January and brought the New Year roaring in with fog and ice that filled the streets of London with fallen horses and traffic jams, she came to the conclusion that he was just as he seemed, a pleasant friendly man who asked nothing more than her enjoyment in return for the hours they spent together, before she had to go to the Café de Paris to give her supper show.

Nor, she decided, was he like Ambrose. The fact that she was herself unconcerned with love affairs, wanted no part of the silly games that other girls of her age played, didn't mean she wasn't perfectly well aware of what such affairs were all about. She knew when a man was interested in her as a woman, and she knew that Max was. He would look at her sometimes with the pupils of his eyes so dilated that they looked twice as dark as they were, and would hold himself so rigidly apart from her when they were sitting side by side with their arms close that he trembled, yet never once would he touch her. If they were at restaurants where there was dancing, he ignored the music and made no attempt to dance. When they parted at her door in Mulberry Walk or the Café de Paris at the end of an evening he would bend his head in a sketch of a bow to say goodnight, never so much as shaking hands with her. It was all very comfortable and easy, for her if not for him.

She was also grateful to him because he made no attempt to pry into her life. He asked no questions about her history, her family or her past experiences, and she liked that. It was not, she would tell herself defensively, that she was ashamed of being what she was. To have been born in the East End was no shame, after all. But it was nothing to boast about either, and she saw no reason why she should. She also saw no reason why she should suffer again the indignity of that time at the Vaudeville in the Charlot shows when she had been taunted with the 'sheeny' label. She said as little as possible about herself nowadays, taking a leaf from Ambrose's book. He had a new voice now, with no hint of the old nasal twang of the East End streets. He spoke like any other Englishman, if in a manner a little more flowery than some, ate the same sort of food as any other Englishman, and never displayed in any way at all his Jewish origins. And Lexie, when she was at the Café, did the same. She made excuses when Bessie wanted to come to the show, telling her all the tables were booked, that anyway she'd seen the act, so why bother to see it again? Bessie, for all her quiet understated clothes and her neat appearance, was unmistakably the product of her background. She spoke in the same sort of accent that Alex Lazar did, had the same air of slightly uneasy otherness about her, and Lexie, the new Lexie, wanted no part of that. So Max Cramer's apparent lack of interest in matters to do with her origins was a comfort to her. In his company she felt properly assimilated, a true Englishwoman, and she liked that feeling.

But even there he surprised her. It was in April, when the

streets were washed clean of the winter's mud by dusty little showers of warm rain, and the windowboxes began to sprout hyacinths and daffodils along the Mayfair streets, that she discovered that he had been born not seven streets away from her.

They had been dining at one of their favourite fish restaurants, Overton's in Piccadilly, before she went early to the Café. She had changed the act again, putting in new songs, because after six months, even though it had been hugely successful, people were beginning to tire of the familiar material. As he had filled her glass with Chablis he had said easily, 'It's Passover next week. Where will you be? Is there any chance of coming to my brother's for the Seder?'

She had put down her fork with a clatter and stared at him. 'What did you say?'

'Next week, it's –'

She shook her head. 'It's all right, I did hear. It was just that – I mean, I didn't think – I didn't know –'

'That I was a Jew?' He'd smiled, and continued eating his lobster salad with equanimity. 'Why be so surprised? My name's not exactly Vere de Vere, is it? A good Jewish name, Cramer. My family lived in Myrdle Street. My brother and his wife still do.'

'I never thought about it,' she said lamely, watching him eat. Then she laughed. 'And look at you now! Lobster!'

'What's that got to do with anything? You don't have to keep every rule to be entitled to read the rulebook.'

'I suppose not,' she said, and looked down at her own plate, thinking of how bothered Bessie would be to see the lobster there. 'Except that –'

'Except what?'

'Oh, I don't know. It's just that – I do so hate it all!' And there was a spurt of anger that made him lift his eyebrows at her.

'Hate what? Seder nights and not eating lobster?'

'That makes it sound childish. No, I don't mean that. I mean – all the labels. The way people behave because – if they know that you're different.'

'Who's different?' He smiled at her, the clefts in his cheeks deepening. 'I don't feel all that different. I'm me, and you're you, and what has being Jewish got to do with it, either way?'

'You've obviously never had them jeer at you,' she said bitterly. 'No one ever called you sheeny, or you'd know what I mean. They've done it to me, and I want no part of it any more. What's being Jewish ever done for me? Why should I bother my head over it?'

'And you've never been in fights with boys from Catholic schools who shout "Christ killer" after you in the streets, and you've never lost clients because they don't want to be smeared with the label of having "one of the Chosen" as their advocates. Being Jewish hasn't actually done a lot for me, either, if I try to make out some sort of profit and loss account. But I don't. I am just what I am and there it is. I see no need to repudiate it any more than I see any need to make a great drama of commitment out of it. I'd fear I was behaving like a stereotyped Jew, one of those characters they draw in *Punch* cartoons, if I tried to work out what being Jewish had or hadn't done for me. The sort who puts a price on everything –'

Feeling the reproof in him, her face flamed. She looked at her watch, fussing a little with her cuff.

'Well, it's not something I ever thought about much,' she said as off-handedly as she could. 'Good Lord, is that the time? I really should be –'

'You've got an hour yet, my dear, and well you know it! Don't give yourself indigestion, rushing off! Have some coffee.' He beckoned to a waiter, serenely refusing to let her argue with him. 'You haven't said yet – will you come?'

'Where?'

'To my brother's. He has a house in Myrdle Street,' he said patiently. 'He has a nice wife and three dreadfully spoiled children, but I like them, and we'd all like it very much if you came to us for the Seder.'

She shook her head. 'I can't. I have a show that night –'

'Of course you have. But not till midnight. I'd see to it you were back in the West End in good time.'

'I – no thank you,' she said, knowing her voice was chilly but not caring. 'I won't be able to.'

'Well, I dare say you ought to be with your sister and the rest of your family, at that. It was just an idea,' he said amiably. As the waiter poured their coffee he began to talk about a new book he'd read which suggested that people could move about in time in their dreams, as though the

178

theories of the author were the only matters that concerned him in the world. Eventually he took her to the Café to start her evening's work, and said goodbye in his usual punctilious way without another word about the coming Passover.

She thought about what he had said a great deal, however, in the succeeding days, and actually did go to Bessie's for the Seder night service, much to Bessie's surprised delight, because Lexie had refused to do so for years, always finding some excuse not to bother. She sat there with Bessie and Dave and Fanny – Fanny looking rather haggard now and clearly far from her old self – and listened to young Monty chatter about his own doings, and to Joe, home from America for a short while and talking very importantly about his doings too, and marvelled at the effect Max Cramer had had on her. She, Alexandra Asher, to be at a family evening of her own free will? It was really ridiculous and she had Max Cramer to thank for it.

And her lips curved as she ate chopped liver and thought about him. Perhaps there was more to the business of love affairs than she'd thought, she told herself, as the noise of everyone talking at once roared around her. Maybe I should persuade him to be a little more friendly after all.

# 19

She might perhaps have pursued that thought, might have found more satisfaction in visiting Bessie and the family more often, had not it been for a combination of events that threw her life into a new set of pathways.

A couple of weeks after the Passover a particularly crowded Café audience had greeted her act with even more than its usual enthusiasm, and she and Ambrose had to perform two encores. Waiting for her in her dressing room when at last she came off, breathless and very excited, she found a big man with an exceedingly bald head who was smoking a larger cigar than even Alex Lazar usually sported. He got to his feet ponderously as she came in, and Poppy, sitting on the sofa on the other side of the small hot room, got up too, almost as heavily.

'This is Mr Welch, Lexie.' she said and set her head on one side, staring at Lexie very fixedly, as though she was trying to tell her something without using words. Then, as Lexie looked from one to the other in obvious puzzlement, she said wearily, 'He's with Mr Cochran's management, dear. C.B., you know.'

'Oh, yes?' Lexie said, and Poppy, a little surprisingly, sat down again. Usually as soon as Lexie came off she was bustling about, getting her street clothes organized ready for the change, and generally making sure all was ready and tidy for the next evening. But tonight she just sat on the sofa and stared owlishly at Lexie amid the clutter of the costumes she had worn earlier in the act. Lexie frowned sharply at the sight of them lying there, crumpled and ignored. Poppy had been getting very sloppy lately; she'd have to be told to wake herself up a little.

But now she turned her head to look at Mr Welch. 'Have we met before?' she said with an air of fine disdain. She was still feeling very elevated and excited by the tumult of approval she'd been given by her audience, and wanted better admirers than large old men with bald heads, even if they were part of the Cochran management. Then, for the first time, she fully realized what that meant, and looked at Mr Welch with rather less disdainful eyes.

'No,' he said. 'We haven't actually met, Miss Asher. Wish we had. Still, better late than never, hmm?' He beamed at her and nodded approvingly at himself.

'Yes —' she said. 'Yes, definitely—' She stood there for a moment staring at him, and there was a little silence in the hot room, underlined by the racket of voices and music coming, muffled, from the Café beyond.

'Thing is, Miss Asher,' Mr Welch said at last, 'Mr Cochran'd be glad if you could step over to his office in the morning to discuss the little matter of his new revue.'

'Oh,' Lexie said, not knowing what to say next.

'*One Dam' Thing After Another*,' Mr Welch said.

'I beg your pardon?' Lexie blinked, then looked at Poppy who was still sitting on the sofa, leaning back and staring at Mr Welch. She looks odd, Lexie thought, then dismissed the notion and looked at Mr Welch again.

'Name of the show, dear. *One Dam' Thing After Another*. Catchy, hmm? Yes. Should do very nicely, very nicely

180

indeed. We've got a great cast, great. Edyth Baker and Sonnie Hale and Mimi Crawford and a lovely score, lovely. "'I took one look at you –'" he began to sing in a surprisingly thin little voice, '– "and then my heart stood still –" Yes, a lovely score. Thing is, we need something else. Dancing, you see. Yes, dancing. And we've had excellent reports of the business you're doing here, and C.B. came and saw for himself, sent me, and here I am. So, if you could just step over to the office in the morning –'

'You want me for a revue?' she said, and took a sharp breath.

'C.B. does,' Mr Welch said reprovingly. 'He's the one who counts, you know. Me, I only count the money –' He laughed fatly at his joke and nodded at her in high good humour. 'And I can tell you this. We'll count out a lot of it for your nice little act, especially that Toytown number. It's got just what the show needs and you'll not lose by doing it. Of course, once we go into the Pavilion you can go back in your supper show. I dare say they'll hold your place here till we're ready. Business they've been doing an' all. C.B. has an understanding with them here anyway. They had money in his *Rodeo*, you know – yes. They'll oblige C.B., no question – so you see, you'll be a rich young lady, Miss Asher, a rich young lady –'

'*When* we go into the Pavilion?' She was staring at him with her eyes very bright and a little narrowed. 'How do you mean?'

He was moving majestically towards the door now, his cigar leaving a trail of smoke behind him. 'Indeed yes. The old man – ah – C.B. wants the show to be as slick as he can make it. So he's sending the acts that are new to him on the road for six weeks, in his number one tour of *The League of Nations*. Getting a bit tired that one now, to tell the truth, but the set and the costumes are still good, cost a fortune, so we're still using 'em as best we can – and then after that you come into the London Pavilion, nicely polished –'

'I don't need polishing!' she said, her face going a little pink. 'I don't have to go on number two tours to –'

He lifted one large hand in pacification. 'Now, my dear, think carefully! Don't rush into saying things you'll regret! *You* may know you don't need polishing, *I* may know you don't need polishing, but Cockie wants to do it this way, and

Cockie's Cockie, hmm? And he's offering big money, dearie, very big money.'

'How big?'

'Fifty a week,' the big man said, dropping his voice to a conspiratorial whisper, flicking his glance at Poppy, and then smiling at her with a wide avuncular grin. 'Yes, dearie,' he whispered. 'Ten big white ones every week. I dare say that'll help you feel better about six weeks on the road, hmm? You'll get it for the tour as well as for the show, and travel and digs expenses outside London, you understand. Find your own people, of course –'

'I always do.' Lexie looked swiftly at Poppy, but she was now leaning back with her eyes closed. 'It's my act and no one else's. No one else runs it or chooses the people I use, or pays 'em –'

He nodded approvingly. 'Good business head you've got, dearie. Yes.' He clapped his hat on his head, and spoke now in a normal voice. 'Excellent. Well there it is, if you're interested. Just step round to the office in the morning. About noon, you know. Not too early. Contract'll be ready as soon as you are –'

She stood and stared at the closed door after he'd gone, trying to do the arithmetic in her head. She was getting thirty pounds a week at the Café and out of that finding six for Ambrose and four for Poppy. She'd thought that was big enough money, twenty a week for herself. She'd been paying her own rent for a long time now, hadn't had a penny from Dave, was finding all her own costumes and still had a little over to tuck away. But fifty a week on the road, all expenses found – she wouldn't need to pay Ambrose and Poppy any more than she was paying now, certainly not till they got back to London and could start the supper show going again too. Fifty a week from Cochran, and thirty a week from the Café de Paris – the money danced before her mind's eye. Suddenly she threw her arms into the air and cried, 'Whoopee!' clapping her hands over her head as she performed a sharp little pirouette. Poppy opened her eyes and said drowsily, 'Hmm?'

Lexie stared at her, suddenly sobered. Had Poppy heard what Welch had said about money? It would be a damned nuisance if she had. She'd expect more for herself and probably tell Ambrose too – perhaps a small increase for them wouldn't be such a bad idea at that. Another ten bob for Poppy, maybe a quid for Ambrose.

'Did you hear what he said, Poppy?' Lexie went as casually as she could across the room to her dressing table and began to fiddle with the hooks and eyes at the back of her costume. 'Did you hear? Not bad, hmm? Come here and get me out of this, will you? What's the matter with you tonight, for heaven's sake? You look like the cat's nightmare −'

'Not feeling too good,' Poppy mumbled and made no effort to get up. 'Been feeling a bit off for days −'

Lexie turned and stared at her sharply. 'How do you mean off?'

'Sick. Keep throwing up −' Suddenly she lumbered to her feet and went across the room in a sort of half fall, half run to the basin in the corner and began to heave noisily while Lexie stood at the mirror, trying not to look at her or to hear the ghastly noises she was making. Poppy ill? It was ridiculous. Poppy was never ill − she must have been drinking or something.

Water rushed into the basin and Poppy went back to the sofa and collapsed on to it, leaning back against the wall with her eyes closed. Her face was grey and sweating, and Lexie, still standing by her mirror, bit her lip, not sure what to do. She felt suddenly very young and helpless, as though she were a small child again at dancing school and her all-powerful, all-knowing teacher had collapsed at her feet. She was frightened, and being frightened made her angry.

'For God's sake, Poppy!' she shouted. 'Have you been drinking or something? You ought to be ashamed of yourself − you're supposed to be working, not carrying on like that − for God's sake, stop being so −'

Poppy opened her eyes and stared at her, and now the fear in Lexie increased as Poppy dragged herself first into a sitting position and then to her feet. She stood swaying for a moment, her gaze fixed on Lexie's face, and then, horribly, her eyes rolled upwards and she fell with a heavy thud at Lexie's feet.

It wasn't until she and Ambrose and the stage manager had together managed to get Poppy smuggled out of the back entrance of the Café de Paris ('Can't have the customers

183

knowin' someone's got the 'eaves, for Gawd's sake,' the stage manager had said. 'Get the old cow out of 'ere fast as you can.') and into a cab so that she could be taken to the Middlesex Hospital that Lexie could think clearly again. Ambrose, already changed into street clothes, offered to go with her, his face anxious and seeming to show genuine concern.

'I'll see you there,' Lexie had said curtly, and set about getting out of her costume and changing and then tidying her dressing room as best she could. It took a long time, because the act demanded several fast changes and the frocks she wore all had cunningly hidden closures that were designed to be undone very swiftly indeed, but ensuring they were all ready to be put on and the secret fasteners prepared took time and understanding of the system involved. So it was well after three in the morning before she at last reached the big echoing casualty department of the hospital.

Ambrose was waiting for her, his coat round his shoulders in a casual sweep and sprawled on one of the long wooden benches that were arranged in rows in the great tiled hall. She stood at the door for a moment staring at him, not sure what to say or do. The smell of lysol, soap and ether was thick in the air and she felt a moment of fear as long-buried memories of childish injuries and painful remedies at the London Hospital in Whitechapel rose in her and she felt again that stab of anger that had made her shout at Poppy earlier. Bloody woman, what right had she to do this, to make such a fuss, such a nuisance of herself?

Ambrose had turned his head to watch a doctor go by, his long white coat flapping importantly, and he caught sight of Lexie. At once he jumped up and came hurrying across. His heels clacked on the tiled floor and she thought, absurdly, I could work out a super tap dance routine here. That echo makes it sound syncopated – great –

'She's dreadfully ill, Lexie,' Ambrose said, and there was a note in his voice that fed her anger even more. He sounded excited and mournful at the same time and almost triumphant. 'She won't be able to work for ages, the doctor said, if at all. She's got some liver thing –'

'Drink,' Lexie said sharply, and her voice echoed in the big room even more than Ambrose's heels had. 'She always drinks too much –'

'Oh, no, Lexie! No more than the occasional tipple! I reckon we get more from cocktails than she does from her gin and water!'

'Oh, of course she does! Anyway, what does it matter? If she can't work, she can't. It's a damned nuisance, though –'

'My God, but you're hard, Lexie!' Ambrose said, almost admiringly. 'I've always known you were tough, but blimey –'

'Oh, shut up! I've no time at all for your chatter. Where is she?'

'They've put her in a ward,' he said sulkily, and began to put on his coat. It was a long camel-hair affair, which he wore with great casualness, pulling its collar high to his ears and tying the belt tightly so that the skirts swung widely with every step to display his Oxford bags as clearly as possible. 'I've been up to see her there – they let me in because she's so ill, and there's no relatives around. I dare say they'll let you in as well, if you want to.' He tugged the belt even tighter and turned to go. 'I don't suppose you do, though, seeing you reckon it's all her own fault.'

'Oh, of course I'll go and see her. Of course I will – the thing is, I don't know what to do about tomorrow –'

'Tomorrow? The show? You'll have to borrow the girl who looks after the snake act, I suppose. Not that she's much of a dresser, I don't suppose. More of a pet-shop keeper.' He giggled, and again the echo in the great tiled space mocked her.

'That's the least of the problem,' she said savagely. 'I didn't get the chance to tell you before – we've got the offer of a six-week tour of a Cochran show, before coming to the London Pavilion with his new one. We could still do the supper show at the Café, make big money. I was going to tell you – you can have another quid a week, starting as soon as we tour, and all expenses found on the road. But without Poppy how the hell can I do it? Bad enough managing the changes when you're working from a dressing room where everything's set out in advance and you know where you are – but doing those changes when you're living out of a damned skip? Can you see it? I bloody well can't –'

'Language,' he said, but there was no real reproof in it, for he was staring at her with his face crumpled with concentration. 'Christ! A Cochran show! And here's Poppy – oh, hell, I can see why you're so mad! What do we do?'

'If I knew the answer to that I'd know everything,' she said savagely, thrusting her hands deep into the pockets of her coat and hunching her shoulders as she tried to think.

There was a brief silence between them and then he said, 'Bessie?' tentatively. She turned her head and stared at him.

'Bessie? What about her?'

'Well, I mean, she's always been interested in the act, hasn't she? Always been dead keen on you doing it, and getting on? Well, tell her what's happened, get her to come on the road with us. Bet she could do it for you. It'd be better'n trying to get someone else, wouldn't it?'

'Someone else'd be impossible. It took Poppy long enough to get the hang of those changes in the Toytown number. There's seven of 'em, for God's sake! We only managed to get so many in because we did 'em one at a time. It took two months, don't you remember? Try and do that in a couple of weeks before we go on the road and we're in real trouble!'

'I bet Bessie'd manage to learn it,' he said, turning to go. 'She's always been quick on the uptake, your sister Bessie. If anyone can do it, she can. Anyway, who else can you get? When do we have to go?'

'Week or two!' she said. 'But I'm supposed to sign a contract tomorrow. *Today*, dammit. Oh, hell, what can I do? It'll have to be Bessie – I'll get hold of her before she goes to Alex's. That'll give me time to get over to the Cochran office by noon –'

'I'll come with you –' he began, but she shook her head at once.

'No need,' she said sharply. 'No need at all. It's my act, remember. You just work for it. I'm the one who decides what happens, not you. I can go on my own.'

'And suppose I say I won't come with you?' he said, thrusting his lower lip at her, as sulky as a child. 'What'll you do then?'

'Get another man,' she said at once. 'And it won't be as difficult as getting another dresser and road manager, believe me. So make up your mind. Are you on or not?'

'Another quid a week?'

'Another quid a week.'

'Make it thirty bob.'

'Not till we come into the Pavilion. Then I'll think about

it.'

There was another silence, then he grinned and shrugged. 'What can I do, ducks? Without another shop waiting, I'd be mad to let this go. And of course if we put in a supper show as well as the revue, I get double, don't I?'

'Oh, hell, how can I say no? Depends on what we do! But we can talk about it. Right now, I've got to worry about getting us into the damned tour – go home, do me a favour. I'll go over to the East End, see Bessie first thing. I'll see you at the Café, usual time, let you know what's happening. 'Night –' She nodded sharply at him, not caring whether he stayed at the hospital or left, and went, walking away down Newman Street towards Oxford Street where she should be able to find a late cabbie plying for his last fare of the night.

It wasn't until she was almost in Chelsea that she remembered she hadn't gone up to the ward to see Poppy. And by then, she told herself, it was too late to go back.

# 20

'I told you,' Bessie said again wearily. 'I keep on telling you, it's not just that Alex is away in America and I have to stay here to keep an eye on everything. It's Fanny. She's not fit, you see. The cancer. Dave took her to Harley Street and the doctor said there was nothing he could do. Just a matter of time. How can I go?'

'But, Bessie, for God's sake!' Lexie almost shouted it and Bessie turned her head to look at the glassed doorway that led into the tea shop, her lips pursed anxiously. 'For God's sake,' Lexie said again, more quietly. 'It's just for six weeks! I wouldn't ask you if I didn't have to! I told C.B. about Poppy, told him I'd already asked you and why you said you couldn't help me, and he still said unless I put the Toytown number in there's no deal. I've got to do it, and I can't do it without you. It's not as though we'll be at the ends of the earth. No further north than Leeds, and probably no further west than Cardiff. If you had to get back in a hurry you could – and I don't suppose you'd have to, anyway. I mean, I'm sorry Fanny's ill and all that, but she's been ill for ages. It's

187

nothing new – '

Bessie stared at her, her face very still and expressionless. She's looking marvellous, she thought. The child must be exhausted, but she looks marvellous. Those new deep cloche hats suit her, make her face look even more fragile and pretty, and I like the new skirts on her. I can't think of anyone else who could wear that crooked hem and still look so elegant. Oh, if only I could just say, 'Yes,' if only I could just walk out of here with her and see her laughing and happy the way she used to look when I said she could do whatever she wanted to do, when she was little, when she was all mine. I wish she were mine again.

'But I can't,' she said, and her distress and her longing made the words come out flat and mulish, not at all as she meant them to. She felt tears lifting in her and had to school her face to control them, so that she looked mulish as well as sounding it. Lexie felt as though a great wall of rejection had reared itself between them. Fear nipped at her again and brought with it its constant companion, anger.

'You never cared about me, never!' she burst out. 'All you ever do is suck round Fanny and Dave – and much Fanny cares about you, and as for Dave – they never cared a damn about you and you know you hated her – you'd never let me go and see her, because you were so jealous – but now you carry on as though you cared about her more than anyone!'

'That's not true!' Again Bessie's self-control made her sound sulky rather than distressed. 'You always came first with me and you still do. You always will, even though you've gone to live on your own and – '

'Oh, it's that again, is it?' Lexie jumped to her feet and began to march around the office, skirts swinging as she turned on her heel at the end of each traverse of the small floor. 'Getting back at me because I wanted a place of my own, didn't want to live in that horrible flat in Hackney any more. I hated that flat! I still do. It's horrible. It stinks of food all the time and it's so dreary – so what if I wanted something better? Is that so terrible? If you really cared about me as much as you pretend you'd be glad I had my own place, you'd be thrilled that I had something better. But not you – you're so jealous and selfish you don't care – ' Now she stood still in front of Bessie glaring, her face white with anger and her eyes glittering with tears she wouldn't weep.

188

Bessie shook her head, saying nothing. She couldn't, for the flood of words had left her as gasping as though it had been a real flood of icy water. Her breath seemed to have been snatched out of her mouth and she sat there with her face as white as Lexie's own, able only to shake her head.

'All I'm asking of you is six lousy weeks, that's all! If you do it for me I can get this tour, get a really super place in a new Cochran revue, get a real foothold in the West End, and all you can do is sit there and shake your head like some stupid great cow. Oh, I hate you, you know that? I really hate you! You put on all this show of being the person who cares for me, keep on and on about how only the best is good enough, but when I set out to get it you just stand in the way. You do all you can to stop me! You'd rather suck round horrible Fanny and Alex Lazar, who isn't even a relation, than do anything for me! You're a selfish pig and I hate you.' Again all Bessie could do was shake her head, this time in a pathetic attempt at denial.

'I'll never ask you to do anything for me again,' Lexie spat it out. 'Do you hear me? Just you keep out of my way. I'll manage on my own. I don't need you, I never did!' She turned, pulled open the door and went storming out through the tea shop, scattering waitresses like startled birds as she went rushing past them, and leaving Bessie frozen in her small office.

Even before she reached the end of Tottenham Court Road regret was gnawing at her. To have said such horrible things to Bessie was dreadful. She stared at the street and its traffic, seeing it blurred through her tears, and feeling sick too as she remembered Bessie's face and that still whiteness. How could she have been so horrible to her?

And how could Bessie have been so horrible to me? she asked herself, needing to whip up her anger again, needing the fury to overwhelm the guilt that was now steadily, inexorably, rising in her. Is it so much to ask, to come away with me for six measly weeks to give me the best chance I've ever had? Is it so much?

Yes it is, when she's got to stay here, the little voice that lived deep inside her whispered. If Fanny's dying, what can she do?

But Fanny's been like that for ages. Ages and ages. She looked ill at the Seder night, and she's still not dead. Anyway, what matters most? Someone dying or someone's whole life, someone's whole career? What matters most, the person you're supposed to love best, or a sister who always treated you badly?

That's why Bessie's got to take care of her, the little voice whispered disconcertingly. Because she hated her so much at the beginning. That's why you're so angry now. Because you hate Fanny too, you always have. And now she's got Bessie dancing on her, and Dave as well, and —

Don't think about Dave. Think about how you're going to get the tour sorted out now Poppy can't go, and Bessie won't —

You didn't go to see Poppy, the little voice whispered. You went to see Cochran and you went to see Bessie, but you didn't go to see Poppy.

She had reached Oxford Circus by now, walking blindly through the jostling spring morning crowds, her small bag firmly tucked beneath her arm and her long legs striding out, totally unaware of the way passers by, men in particular, turned to stare after her. She only stopped now because a policeman on point duty held up one beefy arm to control the pedestrians so that the great drays, the swaying vans and the grumbling motor cars could get through. As she pushed against him he looked down at her and said reprovingly, 'Now then, miss, can't go breaking the law, now, can we? An' the law says you got to wait till I lets you go through.' Impatiently, she turned on her heel and went marching back the way she had come, still too distressed to do anything but keep moving. Where she went didn't matter, as long as she kept moving all the time. She had a crazy idea that if she stood still her anger, guilt and bitter disappointment about the tour would all boil up into a great conflagration that would burn her up completely.

Quite why she thought of Max then she didn't know. Had it been the policeman's invocation of the law? Or was it something as simple as the window she was passing, with its neat gold lettering reading, 'Solicitor, Commissioner for Oaths'? Whatever it was, the idea, once in her head, couldn't be dislodged, and as she reached the end of Newman Street again she stopped. After a moment's hesitation she stepped into the roadway to hail a cab. He'd advise her what to do, and maybe make her feel better about how horrible she'd been to Bessie.

His office was in Bedford Row, on the top floor of a tall red brick house that once had been very elegant but was now a little shabby. As she climbed the mahogany staircase she began to feel some of the peace she so badly needed leaking out of the quiet building and into her. She could hear the occasional muffled clatter of a typewriter, the distant sound of a telephone bell buzzing, and muttering voices, but the level of sound was low and even her own footsteps fell silently on the dull red drugget that covered the stairs. It was as though the building had something of Max about it, offering peace and strength and, oddly, time. If I talk to Max, she told herself absurdly, I'll find the time I need to sort it all out. The time to find a new dresser. The time to visit Poppy and tell her I didn't mean to be so hateful and take no notice of her illness. The time, above all, to go to Bessie and make it all right again, to make her see why I had been so angry and said such awful things.

At the top of the stairs the silence was even greater. No sound of typewriters or telephones or talking came from the other side of the glass engraved door with its quiet statement, 'Max Cramer. Solicitor'. She stood there hesitantly for a moment, almost afraid to go in. It had been a mistake to come. What could Max do to help? But then an image of his face with those narrow clefts and friendly eyes lifted in her mind's eye and, without thinking further, she tapped on the glass.

There was no answer, so after a moment she turned the knob and pushed the door open. Beyond it the office was empty, the typist's desk adrift with paper, and the chair pushed back as though its occupant had only just left it. After a moment she stepped inside and said experimentally, 'Max?'

The silence continued. She walked across to a half open inner door, pushed it open and looked in.

It was a handsome room, high of ceiling and very ornate of cornice, and as cluttered as it was handsome. Bookshelves bulged with leather-bound spines and there were piles of papers on tables and chairs everywhere. On another wall was hung a great Court Calendar, adorned with scribbles in various coloured inks. In the middle of the room a tall roll-topped desk was set, its front gaping open. Sitting in a swivel chair behind it, with his feet propped upon the desk, was Max. His head was drooping forwards and he was clearly fast asleep.

She stood and looked at him and then, in spite of her still seething anger and her misery, her lips curved. He looked absurdly young, hardly older than a child sitting there, and she let a little snort of amusement escape her. At once he moved, bringing his feet to the floor and standing up in one sleek movement.

'What is it?' he said curtly. Then, as he registered who it was, his shoulders relaxed and he looked at her in amazement. 'My dear!' he said, and brushed both his hands over his hair to restore its tidiness. 'My dear Lexie! How very strange!'

'Why strange? Have I a smudge on my nose?' She needed to seem relaxed, even flippant. She tried to laugh at him, and pulled her hat off, shaking her thick hair free of its confines to cover up her confusion.

'I was dreaming of you,' he said. His face lit into a rather sheepish grin. 'Rather a ridiculous dream, to tell the truth.'

'Really? Tell me about it.' She looked round for somewhere to sit down, and moved across the big room to a horsehair sofa set between the tall windows.

'Not interesting enough to tell *you* about, though it was interesting to me. But why are you here, my dear? It's always a joy to see you, of course, but I never expected to have you march into my office. Certainly not during a lunch hour when my clerk and typists have gone and left me in charge, and I've cheated enough to snatch forty winks. Very embarrassing.' He came across to sit beside her.

'I thought you always went and ate vast lunches with your clients,' she said, leaning her head back on the sofa's slippery headrest. She was beginning to feel weary, as at last her anger settled down from a white-hot fury to a dull aching glow and last night's lack of sleep caught up with her. She was beginning to wish she hadn't obeyed this stupid impulse. What could Max do, after all, to help her?

'Only when I can't avoid it,' he said. 'What's the matter, Lexie? Tell me about it.'

'About what?' She tried to sound light-hearted.

'Whatever it is that brought you here in this state. You

192

look devastated – tell me about it.'

She shook her head, opened her mouth to speak, shook her head again, and then to her horror the tears started and she could do nothing to control them. They ran down her cheeks, dragging her mascara with them, and clotted in her throat to huge sobs. Then she was shaking and weeping with great gulping noises and hating the way her face had crumpled and her nose and eyes were running.

Blessedly he said nothing, but just pulled a big handkerchief out of his pocket and gave it to her. Gratefully she buried her face in it and took a deep breath. The smell of him, a mixture of soap and cologne and an undefinable something that was just him, filled her nostrils and made her belly suddenly ache with a need to touch him. She wanted to feel his skin against hers, and without thinking she lifted her face and then her arms and threw herself forwards so that he had to take hold of her. She put her hands round his neck and pulled him forwards so that she could set his cheek against hers and, as its warm rather rough surface touched her own wet one, she felt a surge of need for even closer contact and she turned her head and opened her mouth to find his.

It was as though he were another person, and not his own dearly familiar self at all, for his reaction was shattering in its immediacy. He seized her as her lips touched his and pulled her so tightly against him that she couldn't breathe, but it didn't matter because she didn't want to breathe. She wanted only to have his mouth on her mouth, and his tongue hard and urgent, pushing against hers. And yet it still wasn't enough. She let go of his neck, slid her hands down to take hold of the lapels of his jacket, and pulled him against her. She let her hands do as they chose to do, and they reached inside his jacket fumbling for his shirt buttons, as he kissed her even more urgently. She pulled away from him now, not because she wanted to escape him but because she wanted to lie back and feel his weight on her.

How long that desperate hungry clawing went on she didn't know. All she was aware of was the taste of him, the smell of him and the weight of him as her hands went pushing further and further and then, suddenly, it was over as he pulled away and almost leaped off the sofa and went across the room, pulling at his shirt and jacket as he went.

'Max,' she said after a moment. She sat up and ran her

hands over her head, then touched her lips with her forefinger, for they felt bruised and swollen. 'Max? Come back – come and hold me. I want you – '

'Lexie, please go away.' He was still standing with his back to her as he straightened his clothes.

She shook her head at him, even though she knew he couldn't see her, and said, 'No.' But now he turned round, tidy at last, and stared at her. His face was blotchy and his eyes seemed to glitter a little as he looked at her. 'I don't know why you came, but I'm very sorry you did. This isn't going to get either of us anywhere. Please go away. Now.'

'But, Max,' she began. 'I didn't – I mean, I only wanted to talk to you. I didn't mean to – '

'It doesn't really matter. Just go away, please. I can't cope with this, not here. I'll meet you tonight before the show and we'll have dinner, and we can talk properly. But I can't arrange my life this way. Whatever theatre people may do, I'm still me, and I can't handle this sort of – well, I just can't.'

'Arrange your life what way? I don't understand.' She shook her head again, and after a moment reached for her bag and took out her powder puff and compact. It didn't really matter what she looked like, but she had to do something distracting, something to keep her hands and eyes busy, to stop her looking at that blotched, tense face and angry eyes.

'I'm not one of the – I'm not like the people you new women are used to. When I – when I care about a person it has to be on my terms and they're the old-fashioned kind. I have to treat people with – with respect and patience and – I can't cope with this sort of casualness. It's not my style. Making love in offices – it's sordid.'

She put away the compact and closed her bag with a little snap. 'I came to you for help, Max. I hadn't planned to make love to you. Believe it or not, I'm not made that way either. I'd have thought after knowing me for so long you'd know that I wasn't some sort of – oh, whatever it is you think I am. I was upset and lost control and kissed you. Is that so awful? If it is, I'm sorry.'

She got to her feet, picked up her hat and started to walk towards the door. 'I didn't make any dark plans, you know. I didn't set out to seduce you. Is that what you thought? That I was trying to trap you into something you don't want? Well, I wasn't. There's nothing you've got to offer me that I want.

I'm sorry I bothered you – I'll know better in future.'

'I'll come to the Café tonight, when we're both cooler,' he said, taking a step forwards. But she turned on him so sharply that he drew back.

'Don't you dare,' she said and her voice was thin and high. 'Don't you dare come anywhere near the Café. I've got better things to do than spend my time with someone who thinks I'm some sort of a – some kind of a tart. And you obviously do. So go to hell and leave me alone–' She went slamming out of the office and ran down the stairs, passing the typist, on her way up, in such a rush that she whirled to stare after Lexie with wide, startled eyes.

She ran out into Bedford Row and along towards Theobalds Road, the tears starting to sting her eyes again, and feeling sick with confusion and anger and disappointment to add to all the other hateful feelings that had come crowding in on her ever since last night's visit from Mr Welch. Twenty-four hours ago everything had been wonderful and now it was all awful. She needed someone to go to, someone to look after her. And who else was there but Bessie.

But she couldn't go to her. Not ever.

# 21

When the letter came about Fanny, she treated it in the same way as all the others that Bessie had sent – she didn't read it for several days. Why it should make any difference to put it in a drawer and then, when she happened, not really accidentally, to open that drawer again a week later to pick it up and slit the envelope, she didn't quite know. All she did know was that it made her feel more in control of the situation deliberately to delay reading Bessie's appeals and apologies. So she didn't know until well after the funeral that her older sister had died.

When she did read the letter, sitting there with a cup of watery coffee on the edge of her small desk in her practice dress and sweating a little, because she'd worked hard on the new routine that morning, she didn't feel anything at first,

195

apart from mild surprise that Fanny had after all really been as ill as that. She'd looked ill, certainly, at the Seder night service, but then Fanny had always been good at making the people around her think what she wanted them to, and she had for some time wanted to play the invalid; or so Lexie had thought until she sat there in her Mulberry Walk flat on a warm morning in June and read in Bessie's spidery writing the news of Fanny's death, at home, three weeks before. She had been just fifty years old.

She refolded the pages carefully, put it back in its envelope and dropped it back in the drawer with the rest of Bessie's letters. She had written almost every day at first after that dreadful morning behind Alex's tea shop in Tottenham Court Road, then at least twice a week after that, and the drawer was adrift with envelopes. Even though Lexie had maintained a stubborn silence, had refused to answer a single one of the appeals with which Bessie had bombarded her, she still kept the letters, and refused to ask herself why. They were just there, and that was all there was to say about it.

Now she closed the drawer and went to rewind the gramophone and start the record again. There was work to be done. Lots of work, and not a great deal of time in which to do it. Grimly she set to again. The tap routines she had devised for herself were getting easier now, and she watched herself in the big mirror she had bought in one of the back street shops in World's End, at the foot of the King's Road, appraising each twist of her head, each movement of her feet and ankles with a cool subjective approval. She was getting better, no question of it. Another couple of weeks and she'd be ready to go back to C.B., show him what she could do, force him to keep the half-hearted promise made to her all those weeks ago when everything had come crashing round her ears.

America, America, she said inside her head in rhythm with the music and the rattle of her shoes. A-me-ri-ca, A-me-ri-ca, I'm on my way, I'm on my way. She whirled and tapped and whirled again, concentrating on her work, on her sweating body and screaming muscles, on the music syncopating tinnily from the old gramophone, on everything except the news that the fortnight-old letter had dropped into her mind.

It's going to work, it's definitely going to work, she told

herself as the room dipped and leaped around her in rhythm with her flashing feet. I'll never be dependent on another person again. There'll be just me on my own, and I'll be the best they ever saw or heard. I'll show them I don't need any Ambroses or Poppies – but that thought still hurt and she didn't want to think it. She redoubled her efforts, putting in an extra step in every three, speeding up the rhythm breathlessly.

But the thought wouldn't go away and she had to let it unribbon in her mind as it wanted to, had to remember the way Mr Welch had looked at her with elephantine melancholy, and told her that C.B. was dreadfully sorry, really cut up about it, but what could he do? The thing that had attracted him to the act had been the Toytown number with its half dozen changes of costumes in as many minutes. If she couldn't deliver that, then the deal was off. No *One Dam' Thing After Another* for Alexandra Asher unless she could change costumes one after another – and he'd laughed at his joke with great delight and then looked at her lugubriously over his cigar.

'Mind you, my dear, you've got style. I'm not saying Cockie mightn't take to something else you do for some other show. He's putting together a nice little revue to take to Broadway later this year and if you can come up with a nice snappy little number for that, a classy little act like the one you had at the Café, why, I dare say he'd make a real effort to fit you in.' And he'd nodded at her, lumbered to his feet and shown her the door.

The management at the Café de Paris had shaken their heads over the act, telling her that without that Toytown number it really wouldn't pull 'em in any more and it was a breach of her original contract not to include it, so maybe she ought to give it a bit of a rest, just till she got herself together, got a replacement for her dresser – and to crown it all, Ambrose hadn't waited. He'd seen the problems piling up and gone scuttling back to André Charlot to ask for a job, and got one. He hadn't told Lexie what he'd done until he'd already been in one performance at the Vaudeville and there was no possibility he could be persuaded to back down.

Not that she would have asked him to, she told herself now, as she went into the fast end section of the new act she was devising, seeing herself as a blur in the mirror propped against her living room wall. I don't want people who don't want me, people who can't be relied on, people who scuttle and run the moment you've got problems. I don't want people at all. From now on it's just me, me, me. I'll show them, I'll show them I don't need them, rattle, tap, whirl, rattle – and the record at last ground to its hissing end. She stopped breathlessly and at once laughed herself into her scales, singing as hard and loud as she could. It was getting better, her breath control was stronger, she could sing up and down the scale now immediately after dancing without sounding like a puffing hippopotamus or looking like a fish out of water. Soon, now, very soon, A-me-ri-ca, A-me-ri-ca, I'm on my way. I'm on my way–

But all the time it stayed there in her mind. Fanny dead. Fanny no longer able to nag and needle and make Bessie look so mulish and Dave so hunted. It didn't seem possible, and for a moment she thought – it's not really true, it's just a trick Bessie's cooked up to get me to go and see them. But she knew that wasn't so, even as the idea came into her head. Bessie couldn't say a thing like that if it wasn't true; she'd think it was wicked. It had to be true. Fanny was dead.

She stopped work at last, knowing that, much as she wanted to go on, she'd reached the danger point. Push herself any harder and longer and she'd not only stop getting anything useful done; she'd actually start to harm herself. She'd had a bad fright a few days ago when she'd overdone it and her calf muscles had gone into an agonizing cramp. She'd lain there on the sheet of thin plywood she'd bought to use as a practice floor, clutching her leg, with tears running down her face, terrified at the severity of the pain and at being alone and in such agony, convinced she'd done herself some sort of permanent injury. No, overwork was a risk she couldn't take.

So she bathed and wrapped herself in her yellow satin peignoir, and went and sat in front of her open living room window, as the sounds of a July-baked London street drifted in with the fitful breeze, her bankbook and the sheaf of bills in front of her. That was something that needed thinking about, and thinking about it would keep her mind off Fanny and Bessie and everyone else too–

She ate her lunch of a thin egg sandwich, starving hungry as usual after the morning's work, trying not to worry about

198

how little she had in the meat safe in the kitchen. Half a loaf, a bottle of skimmed milk, three eggs and a couple of apples. Not much food to fuel such effortful working days, but it should see her through to the end of the week, just – and she bent her head to read her bank book, poring over the figures as though she could by a sheer effort of will make them more.

But the facts were there; the rent was paid till the next half-quarter day only, and that was just a week away; the telephone she'd already had cut off, but the electricity and gas bills were still outstanding. Another month without a job and she'd be out on the streets. She looked round at her little flat, so brave with its satin cushions, its chrome and glass tables and bent chrome chairs, and wanted to cry. She'd furnished it so expensively when she'd started out, gaily buying the best that she could find at Heal's and Maple's, choosing the jazziest of Cubist-style curtains and carpets, certain that she could afford them, and now –

But Dave was paying the rent then, she reminded herself. She'd seen no reason why he shouldn't at the time. It had seemed the most reasonable and natural thing in the world. He'd enjoyed being her supporter, she'd known that. It had made him feel he was part of the wicked raffish world of dancers and singers and performers, and he had liked coming to the Vaudeville and then to the Café as often as he could to watch her, taking a secret delight in knowing he was part of her life, albeit at arm's length. She'd known that, and hadn't minded – until the time had come when she could afford to be totally self-supporting and had dropped him completely. She'd enjoyed doing that, not least because he'd been so put out by it, and she remembered now how she had shrugged her shoulders at him when he'd tried to persuade her to go on letting him help her, and how cast down he'd been when she'd refused. Maybe now he'd like to help again and –

But she pushed that idea away. Independence, showing them she didn't need anyone else, proving that Alexandra Asher could manage her life completely on her own, that was the plan and it had to be followed. No one was going to help her, ever again. Not friends, not family and certainly not Dave Fox, with his hopeful eager eyes and his knowing stares – no, certainly not Dave Fox.

She slept for most of the afternoon. It was the best way she knew of conserving energy, and in this hot weather she needed to rest, even if her sleep was restless and dream-laden. All she had to do was put in another few days on the act; then she could go to C.B.'s office again, tell Welch she was ready for the job in America, and make them give her a sub on her first week's salary.

She woke suddenly in the late evening, as the hot air dwindled to a tar-scented dustiness in the streets outside and the traffic settled to the dull roar that ended the day's busyness. Something extraordinary had startled her. She heard it again and sat bolt upright. No one had rung her front door bell for weeks, not since those first few days when Bessie had come and waited patiently for an answer that Lexie had no intention of giving. Had she come back again? Was she trying yet again to make Lexie talk to her?

She thought for a moment of just lying down again and putting her head under the covers, but her curiosity was too strong and she slid out of bed. Pulling a peignoir over her nakedness – for she had been too hot to wear anything in bed but the thin sheet that covered her – she padded barefoot to the front door. There was a little window at the side of it, shrouded with a net curtain, through which she could see without being spotted from outside. Just to know who it was she was ignoring, that was why she was going, she told herself as she slipped silently into the tiny entrance hall of her flat.

The lights were burning in the outer hallway and she could see him clearly and she felt a lurch of shock. Keeping him out of her mind all these weeks had taken the strongest effort she had in her, and it had worked until now. She had managed not to think of him at all, but now seeing him standing there was so shocking that without thinking she actually opened the door. Not until she was standing barely a foot or two away from him did she realize what she had done, and at once she tried to close the door again. But he put out a hand and stopped her.

'Hello, Lexie. I'm sorry to have to bother you so late, but it's important I talk to you. It's a legal problem. I'd have phoned but the operator couldn't get through –'

'The phone's been cut off,' she said, and then shook her head angrily. 'I don't want to talk to you. Please go away.' Again she tried to close the door.

200

'I'm here on a *legal* matter, Lexie. I have to talk to you. For your own protection. Please—' He pushed the door open wider and stepped inside, and after a moment she shrugged and turned to go back into her living room. She was suddenly very aware of the fact that she had on only a thin satin wrapper. She pulled it round her tightly, and went and curled up in the armchair under the window as he followed her in.

'Well, you'd better sit down,' she said ungraciously. 'No, don't put on the light. I prefer the dusk.' After a moment he nodded and went and sat in the chair furthest away from her.

There was a short silence and then he said awkwardly. 'Are you well, Lexie? I was so sorry to hear about the act—'

'I'm very well.' Her voice was hard and clear. 'There's no need to worry about me. What do you want? What is this legal business?'

'I'll come to that — but I just wanted you to know how — I've been feeling dreadful about you. I hadn't realized when you came to see me that morning that you were — upset. Bessie explained it all to me — what had happened with Poppy—'

'I don't want to talk about it,' she said. 'You said there was some business to discuss. So discuss it.'

'Yes — I —' He stopped and in the dim light she saw him rub his face and realized that he was embarrassed. Just for a moment she was amused, in spite of the anger that was simmering in her. He'd hurt her a great deal that morning in his office, hurt her pride and her self-confidence. She, who had never felt the need for any sort of physical contact with any man, who had always rather despised people who did, to have been swept away by the sort of feelings she had had that morning only to have them thrown back in her face. Even thinking of it now made her throat tighten, but seeing him embarrassed in her company was pleasing and made the tightness less severe.

'Well?' she said. 'What is it? Has someone decided to adopt me and make me into an heiress?'

'I wish it were that—' He took a sharp breath. 'Your sister Bessie—'

'Has she sent you?' Lexie sat bolt upright in her armchair, pulling her wrap round her more tightly as she did so. 'Is she using you as a go-between? Or—'

201

'No,' he said. 'Please listen. After your sister Fanny died there had to be investigations into the books at your brother-in-law's office. She'd been a full partner, you see, and it was part of organizing probate for her will. Your sister had left her property to her son Monty, absolutely, and since he doesn't want to play any part in his father's business your sister's share had to be sorted out so that he could have his inheritance. And –'

'Well? What has that to do with me?'

'I'm afraid this is rather difficult.' There was real distress in his voice now. 'Scrutiny of the books has shown that your brother-in-law has been – well, shall we say he's displayed less probity over money affairs than he should have done. And when trouble started over what they were finding, Monty felt the need of legal advice and your sister Bessie sent him to me. That's why I'm involved.'

'Why should Monty want advice? He's an accountant – I thought he understood all that was necessary about money –'

'About money, yes. About embezzlement, no.'

'Embezzlement? I don't understand.'

'For some years your brother-in-law has been steadily taking money out of the business. Money that should by rights have been shared with his partner, your sister Fanny. Now Monty wants his inheritance and he wants all of it. And believing now that his father has been – well, it has to be said – robbing his mother – well, he needed legal help. He may go to court –'

'Monty's taking his father to *court*?' She shook her head in disbelief. 'Surely he can't be. Not his own father –'

'Well, embezzlement is embezzlement. Your brother-in-law has been systematically using money that by rights was your sister's. For years, I suppose. I can understand Monty's anger –'

'Maybe – but to take it to court, to make a great public thing out of it? It's not as though Monty's short of money, anyway. He's doing well enough – or so I thought.'

'He says there's a principle involved.'

'I'll bet he does. How expensive is the principle?'

'It runs to about five thousand pounds. It's a lot of money, Lexie. A lot.'

'Well, I suppose it is, but all the same – Monty taking his father to court.' She tried to imagine the scene. Dave in the dock? Monty in the witness box? How did it happen when sons sued fathers? She looked up, frowning a little. 'It's awful, all of it. But what affair is it of mine? Apart from it being my brother-in-law and nephew, I mean –'

He coughed, a dry little sound that rattled in the quiet room, and he suddenly seemed to change, to become very much a legal personage, not the man she had known for so long but a symbol of something cold and weighty that had nothing to do with individual personalities.

'It seems that some of the money embezzled he spent on you. He kept records and they've been turned over to me. It appears he paid your rent over a considerable period of time and also for some of the furnishings here.' His voice was dry and expressionless and he didn't look at her as he spoke.

She was silent for a long time and then she said uncertainly, 'Well? He was my brother-in-law, wasn't he?'

'Yes, I said that. That this could have been a family concern, a natural wish to help a young relative. But Monty says –' He hesitated.

'Well, what does he say?' She lifted her chin at him, for there was a note of distaste in his voice that was very clear.

'Monty says that if it had been simply a family concern his mother would have been involved. The fact that Dave kept it secret suggests that – suggests that there was more to it than that.'

'Oh, my God,' she said and then again more loudly. 'Oh, my God. That's horrible – that Monty –'

'I agree with you,' Max said, and she stared at him. 'I know I shouldn't feel like that about a client, and that's why I'm not taking the case any further. It's a nasty one, and I want no part of it. I've told Bessie I can't handle it, and now I'm telling you. But I wanted to warn you. The man he's gone to – he'll make the most he can out of it. He likes sordid cases like this – they make him a lot of money – and the yellow press know his cases tend to be interesting, in their terms. I'm very much afraid there's likely to be a lot of drama when it comes to court. A good deal of publicity. And I must tell you that Monty has no qualms at all about making sure that you're called as a witness. There'll be a subpoena.'

Again there was silence between them and she said in a tight little voice. 'So what can I do?'

'Be honest, I think,' he said. 'Tell them the truth. I have to

203

ask you, Lexie, because others will. Did you and Dave – were you lovers?'

'Lovers?' she said and laughed. 'Oh, my God, what a word! Lovers! It makes me sick, do you know that? Sick –' She began to laugh louder. It was a shrill giggle at first, and then as the enormity of the question swept over her it became more noisy and more uncontrolled until she wasn't laughing any more, but crying, and he was beside her, kneeling on the carpet at her feet holding her close against his shoulder.

'Hush,' he said. 'Hush, Lexie. It's all right, it's all right. It's just me, no need to distress yourself, it's all right –' He rocked her gently and crooned into her ear until the tears slowly eased and she was able to control her voice again.

'It was never like that,' she said. 'Truly it wasn't. It was just that – oh, God, however I explain it it's going to sound awful.'

'Tell me, anyway.'

'You'll hate me if I do. I hate myself,' she said and put her hands over her face. 'Because we weren't lovers, truly we weren't. But he did, just once, when I was unhappy and frightened – he did just once –'

'And you're going to tell me about it,' he said, sitting back on his heels but still holding both her hands in his. 'You'll feel better once you do. So start at the beginning and tell me all of it.'

# 22

In some ways it was worse than she had feared, but in others it was better. The bad part was waiting for the axe to fall. It took some weeks for the case to come to court, even though Monty and his eager little ferret of a new lawyer did all they could to rush it through. Not knowing what he might do when he got to court and what he might say, and above all whether she might be called as a witness, was agony for Lexie.

But the good part was the effect this new crisis in her life had had on her feelings. It was Max who had made her see that she had been unnecessarily angry with herself over her fight with Bessie, and unnecessarily cruel; that keeping herself aloof hadn't helped, indeed had made her feel worse; and it had been Max who had organized matters so that the sisters could meet again and pick up the threads of their relationship without too much embarrassment.

He had taken them both out to dinner at the Trocadero and there, in that fashionable, glittering public place, full of chatter and jazz and the clink of cocktail glasses, where recriminations and tears and hugs of remorse would have been more embarrassing than the original situation, they were able to talk of ordinary everyday things as though there had never been an argument at all, and so re-create their private links. Lexie had sat there between Max and Bessie and felt again the peace of being with people she needed and could trust, and she was grateful.

She tried to say as much as the evening wore on, but the words were halting and confused.

'I'm sorry I get so prickly, Bessie,' she began. 'I didn't mean to, but then someone says something that irritates me, and it all gets mixed up in my head, and I think they hate me so I hate them and –'

'Hush,' Bessie said, ducking her head to look into her dish of ice cream. 'It's all over. Forgotten. Let's not talk of old bad things. Just better ones. Tell me, how's the new act coming on? Did he like it, when you showed it to him, this C.B. man?'

'Yes, he liked it,' she said and bit her lip. She wanted badly to talk, wanted to say all the things that were inside her, wanted Bessie to know that she hadn't meant to be so hard and cruel, and wanted her to know, too, that it wasn't all her own badness; that there was a need in her, a feeling that was almost a pain that came when she thought about her dancing and about the act – but Bessie didn't want to talk, so that was that.

It worried her too that Max also didn't want to talk about the things she had told him. He had stayed there beside her as she'd explained, as best she could, what had happened that evening at Manor House, had tried to make him see how angry she had been, how important it had seemed to make Dave give something back for what he had taken from her. Max had crouched there, his face unreadable in the darkness, saying nothing until at last she had stopped talking and had sat curled in her armchair, exhausted but with a curious sense of relief and freedom inside her, waiting for his reaction.

All he had done was touch her hand and say, 'That's all right then. I know now. I'll know what to do if it comes up in court. I'll do my best to stop it, but at least I know the strength of it now. Thank you for trusting me with the truth, Lexie. It's always best.'

'Do you hate me for it?' she'd said then, peering up at him, for he had got to his feet and was looking over her head, out of the window into the dark street.

'Hate you? Why on earth should I hate you?' he'd said, and for a moment she'd felt his hand on her hair and put her own hand up to touch his, but he'd moved and she'd met only the empty air.

'Because I'm just a tart. That's what you thought before, and it's true.'

'No!' He'd said it so loudly that she'd jumped, and this time he did touch her, bending over to take her face in his hands and look at her closely. She could just see the gleam of his eyes in the darkness. 'No, Lexie. I never said it, nor meant it. The reason you were so angry with me that morning was that *you* felt so bad and thought it of yourself. Not because I did. I still see you as I always did.'

'And how is that?' She had said it softly, wanting him to tell her good things, needing the comfort of soothing words, wanting to feel herself made new again in good language. But he shook his head, let go of her and said lightly, 'One of these days I'll tell you. Right now, get dressed and come out to have a meal. You look famished. Are you?'

'Yes,' she'd said, and obediently had gone to dress, putting on the prettiest frock she had, a crêpe de chine with a ribbon sash around the hips in a deep blue that she knew made the most of her slanted eyes and her dark hair. He took her out to dinner at a small Italian restaurant in the King's Road, where they had talked of music and books and cricket as though there had been no break in their old friendship.

It was still the same. He wouldn't talk of the past, of his own feelings, or allow her to talk of hers, just as Bessie refused to do. She had been forced to accept that that was the way things had to be. There was nothing more she could do.

But he had talked, forcefully, of the practicalities of her situation.

206

'It's quite absurd that you should starve yourself in this fashion,' he'd said when he realized how much her resources had dwindled. 'I'll talk to your bank manager, see to it you get an overdraft. You won't be the first performer to need one, and you certainly won't be the last. You'll be back in work eventually, of course, and then you'll be able to pay it back. When it comes to money you really are very foolish, aren't you?'

She had agreed humbly that she was, even let him talk to the bank manager, and breathed again when he had cheer-fully agreed (with Max Cramer's assurance that all would be well, why shouldn't he?) to provide her with overdraft facilities for the next six months.

'If you haven't got a good new act by then, and good bookings, Lexie, you'll have to think of a new occupation,' Max told her over dinner one evening. 'But until then you're free to work at getting the act right, and then –'

'I can't see beyond this damned case,' she'd said, twisting her cocktail glass between her fingers. 'It's there every morning when I wake up and it's there when I fall asleep. I can't think of going to Cochran about his American revue, can I? If they're going to call me into court, I can't go abroad –'

'It'd be wiser not to. No one can stop you, of course, though they could call you back, I suppose. I'll see what I can do to find out how things are going. And whether they're going to call you –'

But he didn't have to do much to find out. Three days later she opened her door to a peremptory ring, to find a man in a thick serge suit and heavy black boots who pushed a piece of paper into her hand, tipped his bowler hat and went clumping noisily down the stairs, leaving her staring at the paper. A subpoena. She had to give evidence in the case of Fox *v* Fox in the High Court on 22 September 1927 – she felt sick for a moment as she read the black words, and had to lean against the doorpost to recover.

'At last,' Max said calmly when she called him. 'Better than waiting. They've put it early in the calendar, and that's good. I'll be there with you – don't panic. We'll sort it out. With a little luck there'll be a juicier case for the papers to get hold of – we'll keep our fingers crossed.'

It was a precaution that got them nowhere. Max told her, the night before the case was to be heard, that Monty's

207

solicitor had made sure that as many Fleet Street people as possible knew what was brewing. His face was pinched with anger as he explained to her what it would be like, and she listened and nodded and tried to understand, but it was exceedingly difficult to imagine something of which you have no experience, she discovered.

'Wear the simplest outfit you've got,' Max advised her as he said goodnight the evening before, leaving her as he always did at the front door of the block of flats in Mulberry Walk and not coming up. He never had, since that one and only visit he had made there, the night he had come to warn her of what lay in store. 'Make it difficult for them. They like picking on fashionable people. Dress it right and we'll be all right. Goodnight, my dear.' He'd touched her hand briefly and left her, and she had gone to bed to sleep hardly at all.

The whole episode in court was like a dream; that was the only comfort she had. It was as though it were happening to someone else, and not to her. She saw Dave and Monty sitting there as she was escorted to the witness box, saw how they were glaring at each other, and not looking at her at all, and it wasn't them, not the people she had known all her life, but stiff awkward strangers who looked like them, odd little people who meant nothing to her. She saw Bessie sitting very stiff and straight at the back with Alex Lazar beside her, and he was the only one who looked like himself, a familiar figure with a familiar grin. But she couldn't respond, for her face felt stiff and frozen as she looked at the barristers, who were the most absurd of all in their wigs and gowns. She couldn't take them seriously: they had to be play acting, it all had to be play acting.

But then they began and it wasn't play acting at all, but deadly serious. They stood her alone in the witness box and threw questions at her that seemed harmless and yet, if you stopped to think, were full of menace. Who had paid her rent at the fashionable Mulberry Walk flats? They're not fashionable, she'd tried to say, and been reprimanded for not answering the question. Had anyone else apart from Mr Fox ever paid her money, apart from payment for – ahem – normal employment? And she had tried to explain that he was her brother-in-law, that he was family, and the man who was questioning her talked smoothly of the fact that he wasn't a blood relation, of course, but her sister's husband;

208

and had he ever shown any special marks of – um – interest in her that were other than brotherly?

At this point the opposite barrister had joined in, and although the words that were used were calm and seemed ordinary enough, there was sharp malice between the two counsel as they argued – or seemed to – about whether she should be giving evidence at all. She stared at them and could feel the tension. She looked across their heads to where Max was sitting. He made the briefest of nods and she felt, momentarily, reassured. But then the questioning had started again and gone on and on and on until she hardly knew what she was saying. Not until they told her she could leave the witness box did she really feel she understood what was going on, and she wanted to tell them, wanted to explain that earlier she'd been confused, didn't really know what she was saying, please let me start again, I'll get it clearer this time –

But they were hurrying her out of court, back to the witnesses' room, and there she had to sit until Max came to fetch her. It seemed hours that she sat there, alone and frightened and very, very tired. Even a day of dancing had never left her as exhausted as that half hour standing in the witness box and being questioned. She sat with her eyes closed, her head resting against the dirty distemper of the wall, and tried to go over in her mind what had happened there in court. Would the people listening think she was a tart? That she had allowed Dave and heaven knew who else pay her money for – for what? All she had meant to do in letting Dave pay the rent was to punish him for using her as he had. That had been all it was, just getting her own back.

When at last Max had come to fetch her she had jumped to her feet hopefully, hurrying towards him with her hands outstretched.

'Is it all right, Max? Is it all over?'

'Not really,' he said, and his face was grim. 'Look, it isn't going to be easy. They've found for Monty – they're sending the papers to the DPP, I'm afraid –'

'The DPP?'

'The Public Prosecutor. That means they think there's been a criminal offence. Dave might have to go to court again. I just don't know. The thing is, the press are all over the place. They've been asking questions of everyone who comes out, and they're all waiting for you. You look all right, thank God. That suit's just right. Not too smart, not too dowdy. Put your hat on – that's it. Pull it well down. I'll get you out as fast as I can –'

'Bessie?' she said, and her tongue felt thick in her mouth. 'Where's Bessie?'

'I've sent her home. I've arranged for you to go to her place from here. No, don't look like that. They'll be hanging round your own flat, I'm afraid. I'm sorry it's worked out this way, Lexie, I truly am –' He put his hands on her shoulders, and shook her slightly, as though to force his apology into her.

'It's not your fault,' she said. 'It's mine. I should never have let him –'

'No wallowing,' he said crisply. 'It's happened, so it's happened. The thing to do now is get you out of this as fast as possible. Keep your head down and your mouth shut – come on.'

Her own footsteps rattling on the terrazzo of the long corridors as they hurried to the huge entrance doors, the smell of disinfectant and dust, the feel of Max's hand hard on her elbow – it was a dream again. None of it was really happening – and then she was out in the open air of the Strand, blinking at the hazy September sunshine as voices attacked her and lights flashed in her face and made everything she looked at seem bright green.

'This way, Miss Asher, look this way. How do you feel about the verdict, Miss Asher? Will you be going back to the Café de Paris, Miss Asher? This way, Miss Asher –' And more bright lights popping at her and Max's hand hurting her arm now as he half pushed, half dragged her across the pavement to a waiting taxi.

She sat beside him in frozen silence all the way to Hackney, staring out at the passing traffic and seeing nothing. He, to her immense gratitude, said nothing either. Even when they arrived and he told the taxi to wait, he didn't speak to her directly as he led her to the front door of the house in Victoria Park Road.

'I wouldn't get any papers tomorrow, if I were you,' he said curtly to Bessie, who had obviously been watching for the taxi and opened the door as soon as it drew up. 'It won't be very pleasant, I'm afraid. They were all there, the damned vultures. *Express, Mail*, the lot. I did my best, talking to

210

them. Gave them an angle that might help Lexie a bit – but it still won't be very pretty, even if they use it my way. I'll keep an eye on the flat, Lexie, so don't worry about that. I'll come in the morning about eight. Try and rest.' He put his hand on her shoulder and for a moment she thought he was going to bend and kiss her cheek, but he didn't. He just bobbed his head and turned and went running down the steps and back to the taxi, leaving her alone with Bessie.

She woke early, long before Bessie, and lay staring up at the ceiling trying to remember all that had happened, but it was woolly in her memory. Bessie had fussed over her, plied her with hot milk laced with brandy, and she had taken two big cupfuls. That had been all she needed to add to her fatigue, for she had fallen heavily asleep before ten and had slept deeply all night. Now she felt lumpy and slow, her eyes were sandy and she stretched and thought – I can't stay here, I've got to get out, I need some air. Quietly she dressed and, moving like a cat, slipped out of the flat and into the street below.

Even though it was only seven o'clock there were already workmen hurrying past, but none of them paid any attention to her as she hovered near the front steps. She knew she was being absurd, quite ridiculously self-centred to think anyone cared tuppence about what had happened yesterday. It had been awful at the time, but it was over now. Dead and forgotten. *Over.* She took a deep breath and began to walk, marching briskly along the road towards the Park, taking great breaths of the morning smokiness and feeling the sandiness leave her eyes and the heaviness leave her limbs. This was what she had needed: a little exercise, a chance to see things in perspective – because, after all, what was it all but a silly fuss? Just another case that would be forgotten by this time next week.

At the end of the Park she stopped to think for a moment and then walked out of the big iron gates to the road. The Park had been agreeable enough, with its dusty paths, its sooty shrubs and its emptiness, but now she wanted a little bustle, the feeling of life around her, and she swung along past the little shops, feeling better by the minute. It had all been a fuss over nothing after all.

211

She hadn't meant to go into the newsagents, but, seeing it was open, with people bustling in and out as though it were a small beehive, had reminded her how hungry she was, and its window full of models of chocolate bars beckoned her. Chocolate would be just right, something to tide her over till Bessie woke and they could have breakfast.

She couldn't have believed that seeing her own face staring up at her from a newspaper would be so shocking. She stood there by the counter with the chocolate in her hand as the carpet-slippered old woman behind the counter went shuffling away to get her change, and felt her chest lurch. Then as the woman came back she picked up the paper and said as casually as she could, 'Which paper's this?'

'Eh? Oh, that's the *Mail*. Yer want it? *Express* an' *Mirror*'s over there, *News Chronicle* and *'Erald* t'other side.'

'I'll take one of each,' she said, and feverishly scooped them up. The old woman sniffed and took her money, and with the papers under her arm Lexie ran out of the shop as though she was being chased, to run back the way she had come, to the Park. There she could sit on a bench in peace and look at them all, and find out just how bad it was.

# 23

It was dreadful. Every paper had the story, and all of them had pictures. Lexie stared at the blank-faced but surprised-looking creature who gazed muzzily out of the smudged print and thought – that isn't me. It says it's me, but it isn't. I don't look as stupid as that. Or perhaps I do? Perhaps it wasn't just the popping of the lights that made me seem so childish and silly? Maybe I do really look like that? How awful if I do.

She took a deep breath and started to read the words. 'Businessman's son cites actress aunt in cash argument,' read one headline. 'Did wife's young sister know?' ran another. The worst, in a paper liberally sprinkled with photographs not only of Dave and herself but also of the block of flats in Mulberry Walk and of Bessie and the Victoria Park Road house and even of the Café de Paris, shrieked, 'Father and

212

aunt shared love nest on mother's money alleges cheated business man.' She felt sick as she looked at the heavy black type, and crumpled the paper in her hands furiously. Then she smoothed it out and began to read the strips of type below.

She was glad she had, for it was clear that what Max had told the journalists had had an effect; the headlines were much more lurid than the story that unfolded beneath them. Monty had obviously not taken the reporters' liking; description after description presented him as hard and greedy, a mean-minded son treating his father's misdemeanours with unnecessary cruelty. Dave was depicted as a naughty but rather charming gay dog, full of waggish bonhomie; the reports made it clear that Dave had indeed been misappropriating money, but there seemed to be sympathy for him in the accounts of his doings, far more than there was for the aggrieved Monty.

When it came to their descriptions of Lexie and her part in the affair, the reporters' partiality really showed. She was described as 'charming', 'delicate'', 'sweetly pretty', 'dainty' and in spite of her distaste for it all she couldn't help but smile at that. She, the tough, hard-working Alexandra, dainty and sweetly pretty? Such nonsense. But it was agreeable all the same to know that she gave that impression.

The description of her own part in the affair was comforting. She had, they said, been an innocent recipient of her brother-in-law's generosity. One of the papers – the one with the 'love nest' headline – hinted coyly that there might have been a more-than-family affection between the two, but even then the message was that it was Dave who had been the leering naughty one (and who could blame him, when his sister-in-law was so lovely?) and she, Lexie, a helpless tool in the hands of a man of the world.

She read every word in every paper, then leaned back on the park bench, trying to get her thoughts into some sort of order. Her name was all over the cheap newspapers, and her photograph was displayed for everyone to see and smack their lips over. She'd been described as an 'actress', a 'dancer' and 'girl about town'. The fact that someone had paid her rent and bought her gifts of furniture was common knowledge. But that was all, wasn't it? No one actually knew what had happened between Dave and herself on that night all that time ago, when she had let her misery about Ambrose push her into letting Dave behave as he had. No one *knew*, so was any real harm done? Would managements stop wanting to use her because of the publicity?

She looked again at the photograph of the Café de Paris and the caption beneath it that read. 'The West End Funplace where Alexandra Asher, the girl quoted in the case, once danced', and she felt sick again. Of course they wouldn't. No one would want someone who had been dragged through the cheap papers in this sordid fashion. They'd feel she was tarnished, useless to them, and she wanted to shout her fury about it all to the dusty, tired privet hedges that lined the path in front of the bench where she sat, and at the scrawny sparrows and pigeons hunting for crumbs on the cracked tarmac.

She left the papers on the bench for the first passer by to claim and walked back to Bessie's, hands deep in the pockets of her coat, head down and cloche hat pulled well forward to shade her eyes. If she couldn't see the people she passed – and the streets were busier now as the day began to swing into top gear – she could persuade herself that they couldn't see her.

As she let herself into the house, and stood there in the squares of yellow and green and red light that the glass door insets spilled on to the lino of the narrow hallway, she could hear Bessie's voice upstairs. She was in the living room of the small flat with the door open, talking on the telephone. As Lexie pulled off her hat there was a scuttling sound along the hallway, and she peered into its recesses to see Mrs Bernstein peeping back at her.

'Such a megillah!' Mrs Bernstein, aware she'd been spotted listening to her neighbour and making a bold front of it, came shuffling along the hall, pulling her grubby apron around her and sniffing unappetizingly. Her hair was tied up in metal curlers under a tight bandeau, and her eyes glittered excitedly under its frayed edge as she stared at Lexie. 'All this in the papers an' everythin' – it's all over my *Daily Sketch*, how your brother-in-law – I mean, it's not nice, is it? Such a respectable house this is, and now your sister's phone never stops ringin' and you here. I never had a person in my house what's been in a court case like this one.' She shook her head. 'It's not nice.'

'I'm not precisely enjoying it myself, Mrs Bernstein,' Lexie said as calmly as she could. 'And you really mustn't believe all you read in the papers.'

'No? Then it ain't true? You know – that you and your brother-in-law – I mean, we all know Dave Fox. Known 'im for years round 'ere, we 'ave, but I never thought there was any – well, you know –' And she came closer and nudged Lexie with a sharp elbow. 'Is it true?'

Lexie stared at her, her mouth pulled into a grimace of distaste as she stepped back. The old woman cackled again with a lascivious leer and nudged Lexie once more. She opened her mouth to shout at her, to tell her to keep her revolting little mind out of her affairs, to go to hell and mind her own business there, but Bessie called down anxiously from the head of the stairs.

'Lexie? Is that you? I was so worried – I couldn't find you! Where've you been? There are messages for you – oh, no!'

She turned distractedly as the telephone began to shrill. 'There it goes again. It never stops –' She went hurrying back into her living room as the door bell pealed and Mrs Bernstein threw her hands up in the air and cried, 'You see? A madhouse you've made of this place, you and your carryings on! A madhouse!' She pushed past Lexie to open the door eagerly.

Max was standing there. Over his shoulder Lexie could see three men starting to walk up the path, but it was only a glimpse because Max, with rare ill manners, pushed Mrs Bernstein out of the way and hurriedly closed the door in the face of the men who had now reached the top step.

'Don't open it,' he said commandingly as the bell rang again. Mrs Bernstein gaped at him, shook her head and cried again, 'A madhouse. That there should be such goings on in my house – my poor Hymie, rest his blessed soul in everlasting peace, he must be spinning in his grave, such a megillah in a decent woman's home –'

'You're making most of the noise yourself,' Lexie snapped. 'And –'

'It's all right, Mrs Bernstein,' Max said soothingly. 'I'll deal with it all. Lexie, go upstairs. Mrs Bernstein, you go back to your own kitchen. I'll deal with everything. Off you go.' And she went, still muttering and staring back over her shoulder malevolently, but not able to withstand Max's firm hand on her back, urging her to return to her own part of the house.

'Oh, no –' said Lexie as she heard Bessie hang up the phone with a clatter upstairs and then its demanding trill as it rang again at the same time as the front door once more pealed furiously. 'What on earth are we –'

'Upstairs,' Max said firmly. 'I'll handle it.' After a second's hesitation she ran up the stairs and straight into her room, to sit on her bed and stare at the wardrobe with her heart beating like a trip hammer and her mouth feeling sour and dry. This morning on the park bench she'd thought it was all over, a fuss over nothing much – then the phone rang again in the living room.

But Max was as good as his word. After a few moments she heard the crunch of footsteps on the path and the creak of the iron gate as the men went away, and then heard Max come swiftly upstairs to her door.

'Come in,' she said drearily. 'It's open –' He stopped in the doorway, looking at her, and then came over to sit beside her on the bed.

'It's not as bad as you think,' he said gently. 'This excitement will die down. In a day or so. Certainly after the Sunday papers have picked their share of the bits off the bones. By next week it'll all be history. Except for the use people will try to make of it.'

'Use? What possible use can people make out of anything as – oh, Max.' Her eyes filled and she made no attempt to hide the fact.

He put both arms round her and held her close. She let her head droop on his shoulder gratefully and the tears ran and it didn't matter; it was all so right and natural; and when she lifted her face to his and kissed him that was right and natural too. He held her close and kissed her as tenderly as she had kissed him, and for the first time for as long as she could remember she felt good.

'Lexie, we'll get married. As soon as the fuss is over. A week or two, that's all. Then you can forget it all. Just a few weeks, no longer. Then you can push it all away. We can be comfortable and happy and I'll look after you –'

She was unsurprised, just grateful, and she held on to him and said, 'Oh, yes!' without stopping to think, for it seemed even more natural than their kissing had been. But then she *was* surprised at her acceptance of it all and she looked at him through tear-swollen lids and said, 'This is mad!'

He laughed, 'Isn't it just? But it isn't mad really. It's exactly as it should be –' Again he hugged her close and rocked her with that same rhythmic, crooning comfort that he had on that hot night at the flat when he had first come back to her after their long separation.

The telephone rang again, and he swore softly under his breath. 'I told Bessie to leave it off the hook. I'll have to go and deal with it – it won't take a moment.'

'Who is it who keeps phoning? Reporters? Like those men downstairs?'

'Some are – but most of them are managements –' He got to his feet, still holding on to her, so that she had to stand up too. She frowned and shook her head, puzzled.

'Managements?'

'They want you, of course,' he said, and there was an edge in his voice. 'Damned muckrakers.' He kissed the top of her head and turned to go, and after a moment she followed him into the sitting room.

Bessie was standing at the sideboard, the telephone earpiece pushed agitatedly against her ruffled head and the stem held so close to her mouth she could hardly move her lips to speak. Her knuckles were white with the tightness of her grip.

'No,' she was saying. 'I haven't been able to tell her yet. Yes, I will, I told you, I will. No, I can't say what other offers. No, I don't know. Yes, Mr Cochran's office has been ringing, but –'

'Bessie,' Max said gently, taking the phone from her. Bessie let it go gratefully and pulled her thick woollen dressing gown round her crooked back more tightly, grimaced at Lexie, and went off to the kitchen. Max said firmly, 'No, I am afraid not. No, I can't say. You'll have to wait until Miss Asher is available. No, I can't say when that will be.' Lexie followed Bessie into the kitchen, where she was putting on the kettle, striking the matches for the gas with shaking fingers.

Lexie took the box from her and lit the gas ring herself as Bessie leaned against the kitchen table and rubbed her face wearily with both hands.

'Tell me what they've been saying, Bessie.'

Bessie lifted her face and tried to smile at her but it was a weak and watery affair.

'They've gone mad! There've you been all this time looking for good jobs, and now because of all this, they're all – oh, it makes me sick, it really does! It's not anything to do with your dancing, you see. It's just they want you to do anything, anything at all. There was one of them wanted you to sell furniture, even – beds, as I understood it, all satin and – and another said they had this show in Soho and you – oh, it's horrible, really horrible. It's like they want to make you into a circus turn.'

'You said Mr Cochran's office had been ringing?' Lexie kept her voice as calm as she could. 'Anyone else like that? Real managements, I mean?'

'Oh, I can't remember!' Bessie sat down and rested her elbows on the table as Lexie made the tea and set the pot in front of her. 'It started so early! It wasn't eight o'clock and there's people ringing and you weren't here and – I couldn't believe it at first – there must have been a dozen of 'em. How they knew you were here I don't know.'

'There was a picture of you and this house in one of the papers,' Lexie said, and began to pour tea as Max came into the kitchen. 'Tea, Max?'

'Yes, please.' He sat down and put his hand on Bessie's shoulder. 'I told you, Bessie. Leave the phone off the hook. It's the only way to stop 'em. As soon as you're ready I'll take you to town, both of you. You can stay at an hotel till the fuss is over and then –' He looked up at Lexie, his face suddenly transformed with the widest grin she'd ever seen on it. 'Then we have plans to make and things to do. Yes, Lexie?'

'Yes,' she said, and put her hand out towards him and touched him. The peace that had filled her when they were together in the bedroom began to return. Doubts that had been jostling in her mind subsided, burying themselves deeply under her gratitude to Max, and she smiled. 'We're getting married, Bessie,' she said, and laughed a little shakily as her sister stared at her. There was a blank little silence, and then Bessie began to cry and laugh and clap her hands all at the same time.

# 24

The doubts that had come to her that morning stayed buried, or at least Lexie was able to control them. She could certainly push them away if they did come bubbling up, as the next few weeks became a hubbub of planning and excitement from Bessie who wanted to organize the biggest wedding there had ever been and had to be firmly persuaded that this was not what either of them wanted.

'Just a quiet affair, Bessie, please,' Max said. 'It's not my style to splash – all I want is the family. No one else, no one at all but ourselves.'

'After all the fuss there's been, how can we even have all the family?' Lexie said. 'We hardly want Monty and Dave, and I don't suppose Benny wants to strut around too much either. He can't be finding it easy, still living with Dave – and Joe's in America, so you can forget him.'

'Yes,' Bessie said, sobered. 'Yes, I suppose you're right,' and spoke no more about a big wedding. But there was still planning to be enjoyed, and she threw herself into it with great gusto. Alex Lazar had suggested, with an unusual diffidence for a person of his ebullient nature, that they have the reception at his tea shop, and Max had greeted that idea with real pleasure. So Bessie was in a blur of happiness as she set about drawing up the modest invitation list, devising menus and fussing over deciding which of the waitresses should have the honour of being pressed into service for the big day, which was set for the beginning of November, as soon as the formalities could be completed. It was as though none of the nastiness that had followed Fanny's death, the court case, the press hounding of Lexie, the fuss and the excitement, had actually happened. She certainly seemed not to think about it at all.

But Lexie did. She tried not to, tried very hard indeed, but it wasn't possible. As she set about packing her possessions at Mulberry Walk – for it had been decided they would live at Max's flat in Hanover Gate Mansions, near Regent's Park – and shopped with Max in Tottenham Court Road for new curtains and carpets that would make their shared new home really theirs, rather than the somewhat stern bachelor establishment it presently was, she found her mind filling with it. She kept seeing the headlines and the pictures, kept hearing the voices of the counsel who had questioned her, and, above all, kept hearing Mr Welch's plump tones, deep inside her mind.

She certainly meant no disloyalty to Max in doing what she did then. She had promised him she would turn her back on all of it; that she wouldn't go back to work ever again, would concentrate on their shared future, on being his wife and being happy, but she hadn't been able to help it. There had been the letter one morning lying on the mat at Mulberry Walk, and after she had read it she had put it in her handbag and said nothing to Max about it. She should have done, but she couldn't. It doesn't matter, she told herself defensively as the letter lay there for the next few days. It's not important. I'm not going to do anything about it, so why feel bad about it?

Then why keep the letter? asked the wicked little voice inside, although she ignored it. There were some questions that couldn't be answered.

But early in October, when the plane trees began to shed their leaves and the streets danced with them and the nip in the air bit her cheeks to a brighter red and filled her with energy, she gave up the battle, took the letter out of her bag, and went to see Mr Welch.


It was Max himself who chose the way she would tell him. He had changed a good deal during those past weeks. Although he was still blessedly himself he had become more relaxed and less puritanical about his work. Whereas when she had first known him there had been no doubt in her mind that, had his job demanded it, he would have broken any engagement he had with her, now he let his clerk deal with matters he would once have thought imperative to handle himself, and frequently took off half days in order to be with her. So when, on that particularly golden Wednesday morning, he telephoned and said, 'Let's pretend we've nothing more important to do than talk to each other. Let's drive out to the country and sit on a patch of grass and be frivolous – ' she had caught her breath and said at once, 'Oh, *yes*. Yes please.' She had been worrying dreadfully about how to tell him, and when and where, and now he had unwittingly arranged it. Her conscience bit sharply as she felt a great wave of gratitude rise in her. He was able to make her feel that so often and so easily; he seemed to have tapped a bottomless well of appreciation for him. She loved him, of course she did, but above all she was grateful to him. And now – but she'd worry about that when she had told him what she had to say.

'God bless St Luke,' he said as he manoeuvred his dark green Bentley through the clotted morning traffic of Chiswick, on their way to the Great West Road, 'letting us have the roof off.'

'St Luke?' she said, trying to pay attention. She had been gazing out at the shopfronts they were passing, not really seeing them, buried in her own thoughts. 'That's an odd prayer from a good Jew.'

He laughed. 'Dear heart, I show no nasty bigotry in these matters. If this sort of weather had been labelled by Rabbi Mendel Slotnik, then I'd cheerfully say, "God bless Rabbi Slotnik." As it is, hot weather in October is St Luke's and I appreciate it. It'll be lovely by the river. What would you rather do? Have a splendid lunch at Skindles and then walk through the fields by the water, or take the walk first and have a picnic and finish up with tea at Skindles?'

'Picnic,' she said at once, and he flicked his glance sideways at her and grinned, his eyes crinkling.

'I expected you'd say that,' he said. 'So I ordered a hamper. We can pick it up at the hotel. Lobster patties and little roast chickens and all sorts of goodies like that. We'll have a lovely day – '

'Why is it you always get everything so *right*?' she asked, turning to sit sideways in her seat so that she could look directly at him. The scarf she had tied round her head flapped in the breeze, and she pulled it off so that the wind could whip through her hair. It felt very good, and she felt again that stab of sheer joy she so often felt when she was with him. But it was immediately followed by the wave of gratitude that seemed to accompany every aspect of their relationship, and she couldn't help a frown, which she was glad he didn't see. He was concentrating on the traffic as the

221

big car edged its way through the vans and cabs and pedestrians who persisted in darting across the streets almost under his wheels.

'I don't,' he said then. 'There's a great deal I get wrong. But I do my best to make the least of those things and the best of the ones that do work. It's something I learned a long time ago. I had to – '

'Tell me about it,' she said, as the car at last moved into the first stretches of the Great West Road and the traffic speeded up. 'What were you like when you weren't the best solicitor in London, the prop and stay of Bedford Row, the scourge of all evildoers?'

He laughed and leaned back in his seat, using only one hand to steer the car and resting the other across the back of her seat. 'I was your average runny-nosed street urchin. Like all the other Jewish kids down our street. And down yours and every other East End street, come to that.'

'Never!' She laughed. 'I bet you were always tidy and had your shoes polished and never stole cherries from Mrs Berglass's stall in Jubilee Street market. That's what my friends Sammy and Barney used to do. They really were runny-nosed urchins – Awful. But you, you stayed at home and read good books. Tell the truth.'

He made a face. 'I suppose I might have been a bit of a swot at times. But not all the time. Not to start with. But after my father died – well, there wasn't any other way out.'

'Out?'

'Out of the street,' he said. 'I go back there now, and I'm happy to do it. It's good to see my brother Phil and his wife and the children – but when I lived there, it was different. I had to get out, any way I could. It was the most important thing in my life.' He stared at the road ahead, his face quite expressionless, and Lexie looked at his profile and tried to imagine the solemn child he had once been.

'Why?' The wind snatched the word from her mouth and he didn't hear her, so she repeated it loudly. It sounded more demanding and peremptory than she had meant it to and he glanced at her, his brows a little raised.

'Need some history, do you, so that you know what it is you've committed yourself to marrying?' he said lightly. 'Well, I dare say you're entitled to know. So, where do I begin? When my father died, I suppose – '

The road unwound beneath the big wheels, and the sun glinted off the chrome of the bonnet as they sped westwards. He talked and she listened and didn't see the glossy new factories they were passing or the tidy little suburban villas with their privet-hedged gardens full of dahlias and scrubby chrysanthemums. She saw only the small boy in the poky little flat in Myrdle Street, so like the place in Sidney Street where she had grown up, but much less comfortably furnished, for there was no rich Aunt Fanny to supply the hand-me-down furniture. She saw him with his head bent over his schoolbooks, night after night, while his brother ran and played in the streets below and his mother spent all her time wearily washing and ironing, for, now she was a widow, that was how she kept her sons alive. Lexie could almost smell the reek of heavy yellow soap and bleach, and heard the hiss and thump of the heavy flat irons his mother lifted from the constantly burning kitchen range, felt the sweat that trickled down the small boy's back as he worked in the overheated room on hot days, and knew too the hunger that filled him. Not all of it was a hunger for food (though that was not unheard of in the small flat, for his mother, despite the long hours with her laundry tub, earned precious little with which to feed her family, often needing to collect baskets of charity food from the Board of Guardians or the 'Schnorrer's shop' as the better-off neighbours scornfully labelled it, the rich women's settlement in Spitalfields) but a different kind of hunger, for a better life he could not have described but which he dimly perceived must be possible.

She saw him as he grew bigger and tougher, finding a series of evening jobs in the markets of the East End, humping bags of potatoes, onions and carrots for hours on end for a couple of coppers and a bag of half-rotten food, saw him getting up in the mornings long before his brother and mother to study hard so that he could get first a scholarship to the Raine's Foundation School in Arbour Square and then, eventually, to University, to read law. She watched him as he made his steady way onwards, through articles to an old-established City firm and then a junior partnership in an East End office, until now at last he had his own place in the splendours of Bedford Row. There was much he didn't tell her, being spare both of self-pity and self-aggrandizement, but she could see it clearly for all that, the long lonely years that gave time only for work, with none for fun or friendship, and she thought suddenly – it's all right. I'm worrying for nothing. We're the same. I'm worrying for nothing, he'll understand, he *will* – and her spirits lifted. She leaned forwards and kissed his cheek and he protested, laughing, warning her she'd make him swerve and kill them both. But she didn't care and kissed him again and he hugged her briefly with his free arm, as he steered the sleek car expertly to the side road that was the last stage of the run down to Maidenhead and the river.

They sat in a patch of long grass high above the river bank, with a clear view of the slow-moving water and the tired sunburnt reeds drooping their heads into it, steeped in the dusty gold of the afternoon sunshine. They had eaten the lobster patties and the little roast chickens greedily; the air, for all its lazy autumnal warmth, had enough crispness in it to hone their appetites. They had also drunk a whole bottle of hock and now were feeling replete and at peace.

She moved after a while, pulling the rug he had spread for her back from the check cloth the hotel had so thoughtfully packed in the hamper, and stretched herself out on it. He watched her, smiling, sitting there with his arms around his knees, a stem of long grass held between his teeth. He had taken off his jacket and tie and opened the neck of his shirt. Lexie could see the dark hair growing at the top of his chest and was amused by that, for the hair on his arms, clearly to be seen now for he had rolled up his shirt sleeves, glinted gold in the sunshine.

'Your arms look like hot buttered toast,' she said lazily. 'How did you get such a tan?'

'I spoiled myself back in April.' He got to his feet and came over to sit beside her, looking down at where she lay with her arms behind her head as a pillow. 'I went to the South of France and sunbathed and swam – it was glorious. We'll go there together soon. Will you like that?'

'It sounds dreadfully expensive.'

'It is. But I only have you to spend money on, and I want to.'

'But your family? Don't you – ' She stopped, embarrassed

for a moment, feeling she was prying, but he laughed comfortably and lay down beside her, stretching out and staring up at the sky like her, squinting a little against its soft brightness.

'My love, I can assure you you are not marrying into a family of indigents. My brother makes his own living – he'd be mortally offended at the idea that I pay him. He still lives in the East End because he likes it. He feels right there. He's not as ambitious as I am – never was. He's a trouser presser and he's happy that way, and so is his wife – and he makes a good living for them all. He costs me nothing. And my mother died two years ago.'

'I'm sorry,' she said automatically, and turned her head to look at him. His profile was sharply etched against the blue-gold sky. 'Is it good to be ambitious, Max?'

'Good? I don't know,' he said and rolled on his side, propping his head up on one hand so that he could look down at her. 'I just am. I always have been. I knew there had to be something better for me than Myrdle Street and there was. Just as I knew one day I'd meet you. I was always ambitious for you.'

'But how could you be? You can't be ambitious for someone you don't know.' She caught her breath, wanting to talk about what it was that was pushing more and more urgently against the barrier of her tongue, knowing she would soon have to say it, but wanting to hear what he had to say, too.

'I knew.' His voice was a little husky. 'I just had to wait until you arrived. But I knew you would – '

He bent and kissed her, gently at first and then more urgently. Lexie let her arms go round his neck, enjoying the contact but wanting to talk to him, needing to tell him. She opened her mouth to speak and that made his kiss more urgent, and then they were clinging together, their mouths hot and desperate, and she stopped caring about talking. She wanted only to touch him, to feel his skin under her fingers, and suddenly she was stroking that dark-haired chest and this time he didn't pull away, as he had that dreadful day at Bedford Row. Instead he rolled back a little, so that she could reach him more easily, and his own hands were caressing her body as hungrily as she was caressing his. It was as though they were one mind inhabiting both bodies, as though each

225

knew what the other wanted without having to explain or show.

The sun was cooling now as the afternoon drifted away, and Lexie shivered a little as the chill wind touched the bare skin of her thighs, for her dress was now crumpled under her as she twined her legs about his and that little movement seemed to make him even more urgent in his caressing. Almost before she knew it was happening they were locked together in the closest of embraces and her body was moving in rhythm with his. It was not at all as it had been that first time, when it had hurt so much and she had hated it all so dreadfully, when her body had screamed its loathing of what was happening and she had felt as though she were not there at all — just her body was. Now it hurt but in a totally different way, a marvellous way, a way she enjoyed and wanted, and she pushed herself against him, feeling the pain and glorying in it, trying to increase it, to make it climb a hill of sensation that would, she knew, explode into a shower of splinters of excitement. She threw back her head and felt her mouth widen into a rictus of a grin that showed her clenched teeth, felt her face and then the rest of her body get hot and hotter and hotter still, and then at last she was there, riding out the waves of sensation and hearing high thin cries that were good in her ears, marvelling at them and yet knowing that they were coming from her own throat. Then, and only then, did she become more aware of Max, of his face hot and wet against hers, of his breath thick in her ears as he too lifted his head and showed his face, a sweating face with eyes shut and a look as ecstatic and intense as it was possible for a man's face to be. And then he collapsed, panting, against her. She could feel his heart pounding against her ribs, matching the speed of her own.

They lay together under the slowly darkening sky, aware only of their own bodies, feeling the world drifting beneath them and time passing them by, not caring about anything. It was enough just to be there, as they were, together.

# 25

Max's solicitousness for her comfort, his concern that she had been as satisfied by him as he had been by her, was so touching that she felt tears sharp against her eyelids, and she said gently, 'My dear, I'm not made of sugar! I won't break up and disappear. You didn't hurt me – or not in a way I didn't want, at any rate. Please – don't worry – ' She touched his cheek as he knelt beside her, looking down at her in the soft light of the early evening, and she smiled up at him. 'Only now I'd like to tidy myself.' He nodded and scrambled to his feet, turning his back on her, and with almost ostentatious politeness began to pack the hamper.

When he'd finished and she was as neat as she could make herself, considering the grass stains on her silk frock, he held out his hand to help her to her feet, but she shook her head, staying where she was, sitting back on her heels on the rug, hands folded on her lap.

'Not yet,' she said a little huskily. 'There's something I've been wanting to say to you all day. I must say it, now. Before we go back to the hotel.'

He grinned, and at once set the hamper down on its end and sat on it, folding his arms. His happiness hung round him, an almost palpable thing. His eyes were bright, his cheeks were still flushed and he looked more like a boy than a man of thirty-five.

'Yes'm,' he said, his eyes crinkling with the laughter in him. 'Immediately, ma'am. Tell me you love me. Tell me we're going to be the happiest married people who ever – '

'No,' she said urgently. Although she hadn't meant it that way, it came out as a sharp little bark and slowly he unfolded his arms and set his hands on his lap.

'What is it?' he said after a moment, and she bent her head to look down at her own hands on her knees. Away across the river the sun was setting in a pool of crimson. Streaks of eggshell blue and the most tender of pale greens were streaked across the sky making it more like the lid of a chocolate box than a real sky, and she turned her head to stare at that; anything rather than look at his face.

'I – what you were saying before, Max. About ambition. How important it always was to you – do you still feel like that?'

The puzzlement was clear in his voice. 'I – darling, what is this all about? Yes, I suppose it is. I mean, I care like the devil about working hard and doing my best, and I promise you I'll always look after you, that I'll give you the best home I can, and all your needs and more besides and – '

'No!' She knew she sounded almost angry now and didn't care. 'Damn it, I'm not asking you to – to give me a statement of your possessions or your earning capacity! I'm not talking about money – that's not important. I mean, it *is* in that it shows you've achieved your ambition, but it's not the most important part of it.'

'No, I know it isn't.' He sounded guarded now. 'I know that.'

'It's the doing – it's being *you* and making people know it's you, and getting it right and making them listen.'

'Yes,' he said gently, and then came across and crouched in front of her and set one finger beneath her chin, trying to make her look at him. But she pulled her head away irritably and after a moment he got to his feet again.

'This is bad, whatever it is, isn't it, Lexie?' His voice was clipped with anxiety. 'I'm sorry – I should have known better – but it just seemed so right. We were here and the sun and grass and the smell of the air and the water singing down there, and we're to be married so soon. I didn't feel it was wrong, and I didn't realize it would upset you so much – '

'Oh, of course it hasn't! It's not about making love that I'm worried!' she said, and now she did look at him. 'My darling, that was wonderful! It just had to happen. It was wonderful and I'm glad I did – but it's about getting married – it's about that, you see, that I have to talk to you.'

He was so still and so silent that she said sharply, 'Max?' and he stood there with his back to the paint-splashed western sky, silhouetted against the exhausted orange disc of the sun that was slowly disappearing behind a stand of distant elms.

'What about getting married?'

She scrambled to her feet and stood there with her hands clenched behind her back, looking at him and squinting a

228

little against the light.

'I want to, I truly do. You must know that. But – '

'How can there be any buts? We're getting married in two weeks' time, Lexie! If we weren't do you think I'd have – that I could have – what do you think I am, Lexie? I love you – I never thought I could love anyone as much as I love you. I didn't think it was possible. Don't tell me now you don't believe that? How can you doubt me now?'

'I'm not doubting you. It's me.' She shook her head, took a deep breath and tried again. 'Max, I saw Mr Welch a few days ago. I've been trying to think of a way of telling you ever since, and then when you phoned this morning I thought – today – today – I'll tell him today – '

'Welch?' He sounded amazed, as though she had suddenly spoken in a new language that he didn't comprehend. 'What on earth are you – '

'Cochran wants me for his New York show,' she said baldly. 'I thought at first he was like all the others, only wanting me because of all that horrible publicity, but of course it isn't like that, not for New York. They won't have seen any of the fuss – so they really do want me as a performer. It's a marvellous chance, Max. Six months in New York and then he said – he *promised*, I can have it in the contract, he didn't just say it – then I can have a lead part in the next London Pavilion show. It's what I've been wanting all my life, Max. It's the chance I've always prayed for. I know I promised you I'd forget all about the business, that I'd give it all up and just be married to you, but then it was easy to promise. I'd lost my act at the Café. The only offers I was getting were for the wrong reasons. It was easy to promise. Now it's different. He wants me – *me* – and what he's offering is – well, you can see, Max! Featured billing on Broadway, and then a West End lead. It's too wonderful to be true – I can't say no.'

'Six months?' he said after a stunned little silence. 'Six months? You're saying that – '

'I'm just asking you to postpone the wedding till I come back. Or, if you like, we can be married before I go and then – but I didn't think you'd want to do that. I thought you'd rather wait and then when I'm back and in the new show at the Pavilion, it'll all be so easy.'

'You knew this when you – when we – ' He gestured at the

grass with an oddly shy little movement. She set her head on one side, puzzled, and he said, 'You were going to say this to me and yet you didn't stop me from – '

'But my darling, why not? How could it make any difference? We're us, we're still ourselves. I still love you – why not?'

'How much can you love me to talk of going away for six months? Never seeing each other for half a year – only letters – '

'It'll hurt like the devil. I shall miss you dreadfully,' she said at once. 'Don't think I don't know it. But you have to pay for what you want. Don't you? You did. You spent all those years working and studying and never went anywhere and never had any fun and you thought it was worth it.'

'I didn't know *you* then,' he said, and his voice sounded heavy in the dim light. The colour had disappeared from the sky now, leaving it a rich cobalt. The trees and the grass and the river were rapidly draining their colour away too, becoming a soft monochrome, and she could feel the dampness of the dew all around her. 'If I had, I – I don't know what I'd have done. I would have dropped everything for you.'

'Then you'd have been wrong!' she said vigorously. 'You must know that! Work and plans to do what you want to do – you can't just drop them because of – I mean, it's marvellous that you love me and I love you. I want us to be happy, but it's not enough – '

'Not enough?' he said, and even though his voice was its usual quiet self there was a sort of wail in it and she put one hand out towards him.

'Oh, darling, I didn't mean it to sound like that, truly I didn't. I just want – '

'Being married to me won't be enough to fill your life. That's what you want to say.'

'Would it be enough for you to be married to me? *Only* married to me? If I said to you, drop your work, close the office, give up all you've struggled for, leave it all behind and come with me? Suppose I said that, said I could earn enough for both of us – and he's offering marvellous money, I have to tell you – if I said that, would you regard that as reasonable?'

'Don't be absurd, Lexie!' For the first time he sounded

irritable. 'You can't ask a man to – '

'But you can expect it of me? Is that what you're saying?'

'You promised. You told me, when we first talked of marriage, you promised me to give up the theatre, to be my wife. I want us to have children, Lexie, to be as other families are – '

'I want children too! One day, I suppose. Not yet, but one day – but even then, I can still go on working. If I take care of my figure and work hard I can go on dancing. There were girls in the Charlot revue who'd had babies – I could as well. Why not? I wouldn't want children yet anyway – so I could go to New York, get this marvellous start and then when I get back and do another show or two – '

'And then another and another,' he said. 'And then, one day, we'd both be too old. And perhaps too strange to each other to care any more. You'd be so busy about your dancing – '

'And what about your work?' she said. 'Your work's important to you. You've spent years getting to where you are – don't you think it'll come between us sometimes?'

'No,' he said. 'I wouldn't let it.'

'You couldn't stop it.'

There was a silence between them and then he said, 'You're saying that you need your work more than you need me?'

'Not more, Max.' She said it as gently as she could. 'Not more. But I need it perhaps as much. I don't know. All I do know is that if I have to miss this chance – '

'What? That you won't be happy?'

'I don't know. I truly don't know. But I think that I'd be angry and hurt and maybe bitter, and one day I might even resent you for taking away something I wanted. And I don't ever want that to happen to us. I want us to be right and – and natural together. As we were when we made love here.'

'And if we hadn't been getting married in two weeks' time, it would never have happened,' he cried. 'Can't you see that? I am what I am, Lexie! I believe in the – the right way of doing things, the real values, the real standards. To be married, that's the right way – '

'*Real* values? What's so valuable about what you're trying to do to me? What's so real about telling someone you love them in one sentence and then in the next that because you love them you won't let them do the one thing they most

231

want to do? What's real or valuable about that? It's like you're trying to own me, not love me! I want to dance, Max. I have to! I want to marry you, too, but I have to dance! And if I can't, then – '

The words hovered unspoken in the air between them and she contemplated them, aghast. She loved him. She loved him more than she would have thought it possible to love anyone, and here she was throwing him away, telling him she didn't want him, trying to tell him – what? That the long hours of stretching her muscles way beyond the limits of their trained endurance, that the interminable days of aching legs and screaming calves, smelly dusty backstages, exhaustion and terror as the curtain rose and the great mindless leviathan of an audience was revealed, waiting to eat her up and spit her out, was better than what he had to offer? Was that what she was trying to say? She stood there in the twilight with her head up and looked at him and shook her head, wanting to call the words back, and yet relieved and glad that she had spoken them, for it was out now, and he had to decide.

'If you can't?' he said it quietly. 'If you can't you'll do what?'

'I don't know,' she said miserably. 'I really don't know. That's the problem we've got, Max. What are we going to do about it?'

'I don't know either.' He stood very still, his face too shadowed to see clearly, so that it was some time before she realized that he was crying.


Long after she had gone to bed in her half packed-up flat at Mulberry Walk she lay and stared at the ceiling, unable to think clearly. The journey back to town had been misery. She had sat curled up, as far away from him in the passenger seat as she could get, while he drove in grim silence, both hands set tightly on the steering wheel and his face fixed in a hard mask. She had wanted to talk, wanted to tell him it was all right, she'd changed her mind, she didn't want to dance any more after all, it had all been a ridiculous fuss over nothing, she hadn't meant a bit of it – but the words had dried in her mouth and refused to be spoken. Because she *did* want to.

232

In spite of his misery, in spite of the pain of seeing tears running down his cheeks and having to pretend she hadn't noticed – for she knew how bitterly ashamed he would be if he had thought she had been aware – it was what she wanted and there was no point in saying otherwise. The thought of New York hovered over her mind like a mist; no other concern was so near to her, not even the wedding that had been planned. All she felt now about Bessie and her excitement was irritable boredom; she loved Max, of course she did, but she didn't want a wedding, certainly not now. In a few months' time it would all be different. After New York, after the chance of a lifetime –

He had left her at the flat and spoke then for the first time since leaving Maidenhead.

'Tomorrow, Lexie. It's all more than I can cope with at present, I have to admit. This afternoon – and then – I can't cope. Tomorrow I'll call you and we'll sort this out – one way or another, I know we can. Just remember I love you and want what's best for you. Promise me you'll remember that, and that this afternoon was – that making love with you was all I knew it would be. I love you so much, Lexie.' He'd kissed the top of her head, no more, but with such rough passion that it left her shaking as he turned and ran back to the car and took it screeching away down the quiet street towards the King's Road.

And now here she lay in bed in her flat, with all her possessions in packing cases around her, even her clothes mostly packed ready to be taken over to Max's flat. It had been agreed that she would leave Mulberry Walk on Friday, the day after tomorrow, that she would move into an hotel and live there for the last week of her single life. Her furniture and bric-à-brac was to be put into store until they should decide which to keep and which to get rid of. It was all planned down to the last detail, and now she lay and tried to see herself following that plan. She tried to see herself walking out of a hotel in the quiet Mayfair street, and into the car that would carry her to the synagogue in St Petersburg Place in Bayswater where they were to be married. Then she tried to see herself at Alex Lazar's tea shop, dancing with Max, her own husband, at her own wedding.

But she couldn't. All she could see was herself with her luggage on a porter's truck being carried before her up the gangplank of a liner, and herself in a stateroom as the ship pulled away from the shore, and then herself in New York, walking along the Broadway that she knew so well from the Hollywood films she had seen, flickering over the dim screens of the cinema in the King's Road. She lay in bed and saw her feet dancing on a Broadway stage, her name in flashing light bulbs above a Broadway theatre front, her face in American magazines and newspapers, being hailed this time not as an unwitting participant in a sleazy court case, but as a star, a real star, a dancer everyone knew and loved.

By five in the morning she knew what she had to do, and how she was to do it. There was an inevitability about it that couldn't be avoided. Then at last she slept, safe in the knowledge that her alarm clock would wake her at seven. There was a great deal to do, and not much time in which to do it.

# 26

The rain had been coming down relentlessly for over an hour, making gutters run like rivers and the sidewalks an obstacle course of pools where potholes had formed between the broken stones. Lexie stood under the awning of the coffee shop, trying to hold her umbrella so that it protected her legs as well as her body, and wondered bleakly whether they had special clouds of their own in New York. She would never have believed it possible that such sheets of water could be hurled down so violently for so long.

At last amid the squealing traffic she saw a squat chequered cab without a passenger. She ran forward, waving furiously, but again she was too late. This time it was a man who pushed her roughly aside, not caring that he drenched her as he rushed past to grab the door and get in. Lexie stood there wanting to cry with frustration and loneliness and – although she wouldn't have admitted the possibility a month or so ago – sheer homesickness. No one in London, she told herself with furious misery, would treat a woman so; in London it rained, but never as cruelly as this. Horrible city, horrible – and then, as she went splashing back to the sidewalk, had to grimace at herself. Because it wasn't a horrible city. It was the most dramatic and electric place she had ever been in, and ever since she had arrived six weeks ago she had been in a fever of excitement.

She had needed New York's drama, needed it badly after the five days at sea, because it had distracted her. The journey had given her too much time to think, too much time to be frightened about what she was doing, above all too much time to think about Max and to a lesser extent about Bessie. She had sat on the glassed-in deck aft of the great saloon, her legs wrapped in a thick tartan rug and a cup of beef tea beside her, struggling with the letters to them.

Bessie's, first, because that had been the easier, but still hellishly difficult. To explain to her why she had gone without even telephoning, let alone going to see her to explain properly – it just wasn't possible to get all she needed to say into the words that came into her mind. All she could manage was a bleak little statement of fact. That she loved Max dearly. That she didn't want to hurt him, but that she knew she had to take this opportunity Cochran had given her. That if she had stayed and talked to either of them, she knew she'd be dissuaded, and that in the long run that would just lead to more problems. She had to do what she was doing and that was that. And please, would Bessie cancel her appointment with Alex Lazar's niece Hannah, who had been making her wedding dress, and tell her she was sorry and some time she'd come back to Mary Bee Couturière and she would try again. That it wasn't a for-always thing, not a cancellation, but a postponement. That was all. Just a postponement. And she sent her love to Bessie and would write again as soon as she could.

Then the letter to Max. She had tried over and over again to say it all, to explain it to him so that he wouldn't merely understand but would applaud, would send her a cable to say, 'ALL FORGIVEN STOP AM FOLLOWING TO NEW YORK AT ONCE STOP WILL MARRY THERE STOP NO MORE PROBLEMS STOP YOU WILL DANCE WE WILL MARRY.' But of course that had been impossible. However hard she tried in her mind to force him to see it her way, however hard she worked at creating long imaginary conversations with him, it never came out right. She would explain in the most impassioned of words, deep in her mind, as she stared out at the heaving grey water beyond the glass that enclosed the deck, how desperately important it was to her to have this special chance to prove that Alexandra Asher was the real performer she knew herself to be, and then try to make the shadow of him say the words she wanted, but it never worked. She could see only his face with those deep clefts staring blankly back at her, and sometimes the tears that had streaked it that evening by the river at Maidenhead – and then again she would bend her head to the writing pad and try to get the letter right.

In the end it was even more bald than the letter to Bessie had been. 'I do love you,' she had written, 'but I've got to do this. If I don't, I'll never feel right again. I will come back, truly I will. I hope you can wait for me. It won't be long.'

After that, arriving in New York had been what she needed. No more sleepless nights in the narrow bunk of the SS *Ascania*, rocking queasily across the November-angry Atlantic, but sleep born of the exhaustion of bewilderingly busy days and the newness of it all.

The people at the Cochran office, a small and crowded pair of rooms over a delicatessen on Forty-third Street, had been almost overwhelmingly friendly. At first she had thought that was because they had been told such good things about her, from the London office. It was a week or more before she realized that this was the local style; that everyone was extremely everything – either very friendly and very helpful or very laconic and very rude, but always very immediate. There was none of the restrained, cool politeness that she had always taken for granted at home, but a noisy, sometimes almost overwhelming, openness that she found sometimes very beguiling, occasionally very irritating, and always very fatiguing. But never mind, she told herself, it filled her mind to the exclusion of all else, and that was a good thing.

They set to work immediately. In vain did she protest that she needed some time to find somewhere to live rather than stay at a costly hotel, that she wanted a day or two at least to find her feet. Pete Capitelli, the dance director of the show she was to join, pooh-poohed that.

'Listen, lady, a place to live in you can find in a coupla hours. We got try-outs in Boston and Philly in less'n a month – you want we should all sit around waiting while you go househuntin'? Cochran says you got to be second lead in this show, and that means we got to get you workin' right away. I'll call my cousin, Frankie. He's got connections down the Lower West Side, he'll find you an apartment quick –'

'But I thought I'd try to find my own family here,' Lexie said, still struggling to do things her own way. 'It's not that I want to live with them, you understand, it's just that I thought they'd be the best people to make sure I chose the right sort of place –' and don't find myself being cheated, she thought privately, though was too polite to say so. But at once Pete nodded vigorously.

'Listen, you got family, o' course you go to them! They make sure no one tries to do you down! Family you can trust. Even my cousin Frankie, he'd try it on a bit, business being business. This way you got to be better off. Okay, so who are they, where do they live? We'll call 'em, tell 'em they should start lookin' for a place for you, and we can start work this morning. I gotta raw line-up of girls there I got to whip into some sort o' shape fast – I can't be doin' with hangin' around no more. We got to –'

She gave up trying to keep control of her own actions, then. She told him about her half-sister Busha and her brother-in-law Nathan Marks and the three children and how they had come to New York when she had been a baby; that she had never met them herself but that they had written letters occasionally to her other sister in London, and that they lived just off Intervale Avenue in the South Bronx. He had nodded and grunted, 'A nice neighbourhood, got a good few Italians there –' clearly feeling this to be an index of its niceness, and reached for the telephone.

So it was that she met her niece. She had spent the morning in a dusty rehearsal room behind the Alvin Theatre where they were ultimately to open after their out-of-town try-outs, working harder than she could ever remember doing. Pete Capitelli was a friendly man, and a helpful one, eager to get the best out of *Cochran's New Revue* that could be got, and particularly eager that she should be as perfect as she could be in her dances and two singing numbers; but he was the hardest taskmaster she had ever had. Not since her first lessons with Poppy Ganz all those years ago had she been so aware of shrieking, aching muscles and pulled tendons, and as she went over the complex routines that had been devised for her, doggedly repeating them over and over again, she remembered Poppy Ganz with real affection and a great wash of guilt. After she had become ill and been sent off to convalesce in a small nursing home at Broadstairs, Lexie had never thought of her again. She had visited her a couple of times while she had been in the Middlesex Hospital in London, had sent her fruit and flowers, but then, once she was out of sight and wasn't at any risk any more, had dismissed her from her mind. Now, pushing herself through Pete Capitelli's agonizingly athletic routines, she promised herself, breathlessly, between high kicks, that she would write to Poppy at once, today, to tell her what she was doing and ask her how she was.

When at last Pete called a break and she went off, almost hobbling, in the wake of the chattering girls who were the chorus backing up her solo numbers, rubbing the sweat from her face with a towel, she hardly noticed the anxious little woman hovering in the corner by the door that led to the small room where coffee was waiting for them all, until she coughed awkwardly and stepped forward.

'Er – would you be Lexie, maybe?' she said with a little gasp, and then bobbed her head and her nose – a rather long thin one, and went a sudden pink. Lexie stopped and stared at her.

'I thought maybe – you have kinda the look of my brother Sidney. I mean, you're real pretty and Sidney ain't pretty, but you got a kinda look of him. I'm Barbara Marks. I guess you're my aunt. It's really crazy having an aunt younger than you are, but I guess I'll get used to it.'

She was small and painfully thin, with hair that was dust-coloured and meagre, crimped into tight waves as part of an attempt to look fashionable. Her clothes, too, tried very hard to be smart, but somehow missed. Her frock of green tartan was just a little too heavily trimmed with braid. Her coat, in another shade of green that managed to clash disagreeably with the frock, had just a little too much fur on it, and both were a good deal too young in style for a woman who was obviously well into the second half of her thirties. She stood there looking at Lexie with an expression of nervous hope on her face and blinked at her as Lexie rubbed her face once more with the towel, staring at her.

'Hello,' she said uncertainly. 'Yes, I'm Lexie. It's awfully nice of you to come and see me here. I mean I didn't expect it. Pete – Mr Capitelli – told me he'd left a message at your phone number but–'

Barbara's face split into a great smile that transformed her, and made her look, for a moment, quite young.

'I just love the way you talk! It's great – I could listen to you all day! Just imagine! You're my very own aunt and you talk like that. It's real nice. Sure, I got the message and I asked for time off from work, and they said sure I could come. I said to them I got this new relation arriving and she's a famous dancer and all, and Mr Guz, he said sure, as long as I make the time up, and I said sure I will, no problem, don't I always do like you want? So here I am. It's real good to see you, Lexie. I never thought I'd get to meet any of my folks from London. Momma used to tell me a lot about you all, when we was kids, you know, on account I'd forgotten all about it – I was nine years old yet when we came here – but now she lives in Seattle with Sidney so I don't get to talk to her so much no more. I told her in a letter already that you was here, and she'll be that excited, I just know it. And Melvin – he lives in Duluth, of all the crazy places. He'd be real pleased too if he knew, only I don't get to hear from him so often, you know how it is with brothers, they don't care the way women do, do they? Oh, gee, there I go again, just jabberin' on and on – Momma always said I could talk the birds off the trees and tails off donkeys and all, but living on my own the way I do and not getting the chance to talk that much to people, and being so excited about you coming, well you can understand it, can't you? I sure hope you can. I'd not want you to feel bad about me or anything–'

Lexie laughed. She couldn't help it, for this odd chattering little creature was very disarming in her delighted excitement and there was something very likeable about her, and again Barbara produced that great transforming beam and said, 'So, listen, maybe we can go eat a little lunch? I got all day off, you know, and it'd be great – we could go to the deli, just, and have a sandwich or maybe – I mean the deli don't cost too much and–' And her nose went suddenly redder as she fell over her embarrassed tongue.

Lexie shook her head, even more amused. 'It's all right,' she said. 'I'm not short of money, if that's what you mean. Cochran paid my fares and expenses to get here, and I'm getting a rehearsal salary, and even though I'm living in an hotel I'm not doing too badly. But I can't eat now. Never do eat much midday while I'm rehearsing. Maybe we could meet this evening? When we've finished? Would that suit you?'

'It'd suit me fine!' Barbara said, her face blazing with pleasure, and she bobbed her head and gasped and laughed and smiled all at the same time until Lexie feared for a moment she'd choke with it all before she went bustling away down the stairs, promising to come back on the dot of six to meet her.

It had seemed the most natural thing in the world after that first evening that Lexie should move in with Barbara. She assured Lexie earnestly that it would be no trouble to have her there, none at all, that the apartment was too big for her since her folks went away, that she could afford it easily – but then when Lexie had insisted on paying her share of the costs she had tried to protest that she shouldn't, that relations were relations. 'If we don't take care of each other, who will?' she had finished shyly, and Lexie had leaned forward and patted her hand and said firmly, 'I insist. Half of everything. Or else I don't come.'

They'd agreed it all very easily, because Barbara was so desperately anxious to please her. It was almost pathetic, Lexie thought, to see the excitement in her as she took her uptown on a bus and showed her the neighbourhood, pointing out the local sights, like the synagogue and the best grocery store and the library, and to see how proudly she walked along the narrow streets nodding and greeting her neighbours – half the district seemed to know the other half by sight if not by name – with her interesting new relation in tow. Twice she stopped to introduce her to passers by, begging her to talk, to 'say something in that great accent', and Lexie to her own surprise had been much amused and willing to oblige. Anyone of her family in London who had made such a fuss over her would have got short shrift, yet now she took no offence at all at Barbara's excitement. She couldn't; no one could.

The apartment was really rather small and poky. At first Lexie's heart sank as she looked round the tiny living room. It was very reminiscent of the first home she could remember, in Sidney Street. But after Mulberry Walk with its glass, its chrome, its elegant furniture, which she had enjoyed all to herself, how, she asked herself, could she live here in this boxy place, with its noisy neighbours and the sound of the elevated railway thumping through the thin walls? She looked at Barbara and was about to say something to that effect but closed her mouth, for she was gazing at her with such proud pleasure it would have been impossible to say anything that might hurt her. So she said nothing, just promising herself privately that as soon as possible, once the show was established on Broadway after its out-of-town try-outs, she'd be able to find somewhere better, somewhere she'd be more stylish and comfortable.

But in fact she forgot that plan quickly. Barbara absorbed her into her life so thoroughly and made such efforts for her that she knew she could never be as comfortable anywhere else. She cleaned and cooked, much as Bessie always had, but without ever making Lexie feel, as Bessie somehow always had, that she wanted anything back for herself. If Lexie was too tired after rehearsals to talk, that was fine with Barbara, who would sit and listen to her radio contentedly, leaving Lexie to be alone in her room as much as she chose to.

The room itself Barbara worked on with great diligence, while Lexie was in Philadelphia and Boston for the first weeks of try-outs, so that she came back to New York to find it freshly papered and furnished. It was rather like Barbara herself; furniture just that little bit too fussy in style to be elegant, curtains and carpets that little bit too frilly, but the overall effect was also like Barbara: warm, affectionate and unquestioning of Lexie. She could be herself there in a way she would not have thought possible so far away from all that was familiar and homelike.

So they had settled together well enough; if there was any problem at all it was that Barbara, like Bessie, was a shade too solicitous for her health. The least hint of pallor on Lexie's face would make her bustle about anxiously with aspirin and cups of hot broth and the offer of hot water bottles to supplement the apartment's steam heat, and that was tiresome for Lexie because she was often pale, and often looked out of sorts these days.

There were many reasons why she should be so. The amount of work that Pete Capitelli was demanding of her increased rather than eased as rehearsals and then perform-ances went on; she was enjoying the work, was certain that the routines she had been given were ideal for her style of dancing, and knew that once the show opened on Broadway she'd get the sort of attention she'd always wanted, for the try-out audiences were loving her. But for all that it was a gruelling pace that he set, and its effect showed on her face.

The newness of the food she ate upset her too; she wasn't used to the vast quantities of corned beef sandwiches and Danish pastry and coffee they all seemed to eat with such relish, nor to the amount of sugar everyone seemed to regard as normal; the doughnuts were too sweet for her and the cheesecake too rich. She found herself eating erratically and then, when she did succumb to hunger, eating food that disagreed with her. It made her feel queasy sometimes and occasionally she actually threw up. She would emerge from the washroom behind the rehearsal rooms or in the dressing rooms pale and shaken and with her head spinning, to pull herself together as best she might to get back on stage and start working again.

Add all that to this dreadful climate, she thought now, back under the coffee shop canopy and peering out in search of a cab that she could get to before other determined New Yorkers could beat her to it, and no wonder she'd been feeling so bad lately and looking so peaky. It would have been nice to tell Barbara, to ask her to come with her to see a doctor to get herself sorted out, be given a tonic perhaps to bring her up to strength, but that would have been such a drama – it would have made her feel worse. It was bad enough that Barbara already worked so much overtime at the millinery factory where she was chief trimmer, to make up for the hours she lost running around doing things for Lexie; to ask her to take off even more time would be impossible.

She had to find a doctor for herself, and now, waiting for a cab, she told herself sourly that by the time one did come she'd probably have pneumonia and really something to tell him. She sniffed a little dolorously and pushed away a wave of homesickness as at last a cab did come and she could scramble in and tell the driver breathlessly to take her to 177 East Eighteenth Street, an address given her by one of the girls in the chorus line when she'd asked casually for the name of someone who could give her a check-up. She had just an hour before she was due at the theatre for the last rehearsal before tomorrow's opening; she had to get her tonic now and start taking it and be really ready for what was to come. The first night of her first Broadway show, and she hugged herself trying to raise a wave of excitement and pleasure to wash away the misery she had been feeling.

But it didn't work. She only felt queasy and she sank back in the corner of the dusty cab and stared out of the streaming windows and tried not to think of Max at home in London, three thousand miles away, concentrating instead on controlling her rebellious stomach.

# 27

'Jesus!' Lily said and stared at her. 'I thought you English girls was too ladylike to get yourselves knocked up.'

'Knocked up?' Lexie said, trying not to sound as angry as she was getting. She'd had to ask someone to help and this girl, of all the girls in the line, had seemed the most sensible, but already she was regretting speaking to her.

'Sure knocked up! Ain't that what you call it? What do you say in London, then?'

'Pregnant,' Lexie said, and then had to shut her eyes and lean back. Lily tutted softly and reached over and pulled on her shoulders, making her bend forwards with her head down.

'Listen, sweetie, you feel faint, lean over, not back. You ought to know that. So, listen, what you want to do?'

'That's why I asked you,' Lexie said wearily and sat up. The feeling of nausea had gone again. 'I can't think straight – I don't know what to do – I keep going round in circles.'

Lily pulled her chair round and sat on it back to front so that she could rest her arms across the top. Her exceedingly long legs looked even longer in that posture, and in her skimpy costume she looked frivolous and glittery, but her eyes behind the heavy mascara were friendly and cheerful and Lexie thought – I was right, she will help – and looked at her with a travesty of a grin on her face, trying to be as relaxed and sensible as she could, even though inside she was screaming with panic.

'So listen,' Lily said. 'Who's the guy? Is he in the company? That Pete's been eyeing you a little more than somewhat –'

Lexie shook her head. 'No,' she said shortly. 'It's – he's in London.'

'Hmm. So tell me, you cable him, say, "I'm knocked up, come at once", does he come, or does he go running like a scalded cat in the opposite direction?'

Lexie shook her head. 'I'm not telling him. No, don't argue with me. That's one thing I'm sure about. I don't tell him –'

She got to her feet and started to prowl around the dressing room, holding her wrapper firmly round her, not caring about crushing her sequin-dripping costume. 'It's not fair, it's just not fair!' she burst out. 'I've always been so – I'm not one of those girls who does this sort of thing! Just once, once it was and now – it's not *fair* –' And she felt tears prick her eyes again.

'Anyone told you life was fair was a lousy liar,' Lily said dispassionately. 'Don't go crying your eyes out over somethin' you can't do nothin' about. Men gets away with it, and girls don't. That's a fact. Bad girls don't get knocked up, only good girls do. That's another fact. Bad girls is too clever to let the bastards lay one on 'em that way. It's good girls like you, real shlemiels, get themselves in this sorta jam. Okay, you don't want to tell this guy, you don't want to tell him! What can I say except I think you're crazy? It's his kid an' all, you know. But okay, okay!' And she held up both hands to stave off Lexie's protests. 'So you got to think it through. Got any money?'

'Only what I make.'

'That'll be better after tonight,' Lily said and grinned at her, amiably. 'If I had your sort of personality, baby, and a big part like this, there's no way I'd let 'em get away without paying me big, big bucks. Really big bucks on account you're goin' to bring 'em in like they was flies. You're all right, believe me.'

'Am I?' Lexie said, looking at her uncertainly and then made a face. 'Damn it, I know, I've always known I could do it, given the right chances. And now I've got one, and – oh, Lily, what do I do?'

'You go down to Hermann's,' Lily said promptly. 'He'll take a hundred and fifty off you and there it is. No more problem.'

Lexie stood very still looking at her. She'd heard about what could be done, of course she had. No one could spend so many long nights backstage in a theatre full of young performers and not know. She'd heard the same story she was telling now so often before, heard other girls crying over this dilemma, heard the names of 'helpful' doctors swopped, and she had been scornful of their stupidity. She had looked at them sideways and told herself what fools they were – and now here she was, far from home, alone, frightened and as stupid as any of them. Again the tears threatened.

'No, sweetie, no bawlin'. You'll ruin your face and screw up your performance. You want Hermann's address?'

'Yes,' Lexie said. 'What else can I do?'

Lily was right, as right as her own instinct had been. She was an undoubted hit. She knew it before the end of the first act. Even at the height of her Café de Paris success in London she'd never had a welcome like it from an audience. They shouted and whistled and stamped their feet. As she stood there listening to it she caught Pete Capitelli's approving eyes from the wings and felt the mixture of reactions from the chorus line behind her – jealousy of her success together with gratitude that she was giving the sort of performance that would mean a long run, and therefore regular work for all of them – and all she could feel was anger. All these years she had known she could do this, had been certain that one day she'd be a real star – not just a cabaret performer, but a real star – and it was ruined for her. Ruined by a man she thought she loved and who had sworn he loved her. As she stood there hearing the applause for her first act finale she hated Max, hated him with all the energy she had. He had loved her and thereby ruined everything.

That thought stayed with her all through the rest of the show, which went even better than the first half if that were possible, all through the excited hubbub which erupted in her dressing room afterwards as the producer and the staff from the office and Pete Capitelli and a whole horde of evening-dressed people she'd never met came rushing to congratulate her and tell her how marvellous, plain incredibly marvellous she was, a real honey of a dancer, the greatest hoofer they'd seen come out of England – and all through the party after the show. She hated Max for what he had done to her. She closed her mind tightly to her own behaviour, not admitting that she had been as eager, if not more eager, for him as he had been for her, and certainly did not admit the fact that, had Max had his way, she would have been safely married to him now, glad and happy to be bearing his child, not hating it, feeling as though her body had been invaded by a parasite that had to be torn out to make her whole and happy again.

When she burst into sudden noisy tears halfway through the party and had to rush off to the bathroom of the big plush hotel suite that the management had hired for the evening, to throw up noisily and then lean, grey-faced and sweating, against the bathroom wall, the people who saw put it down to exhaustion, to natural excitement, to the rigours of being Broadway's newest star, and she was grateful to Lily who said as much in a loud voice and offered to take her home. For the first time she wished that she'd asked Barbara to the party. She could have taken her home and they could have kept it in the family.

The family, she thought, sitting huddled in the corner of the cab into which Lily had put her, after being told firmly by Lexie that she could manage fine on her own now. The family. At least there was Barbara; she had felt so alone when that doctor had told her as though it was the most ordinary thing in the world that she was pregnant. The baby was due in early August by his reckoning, but there was Barbara after all. She was family, wasn't she? And she climbed slowly up to the apartment to find Barbara still sitting up although it was well after midnight, waiting eagerly for news of how the show had gone, and was glad that she was there.

'I'll get tickets for you tomorrow night,' she said abruptly as Barbara, her nose pink with excitement again, leaped to her feet. 'I suppose I should have got them for you tonight but I –'

'That doesn't matter!' Barbara said at once, and hurried to take her coat and fuss around her as she settled her in a chair. 'I know I'll get to see it when you're ready – how did it go, Lexie? Was it great? Did they shout and stand up to clap an' all that? I bet they did. I bet you're a real star now, hey? I told Mrs Beekman down at the grocery tonight. I told her my aunt Lexie, who is so much younger'n me, it's crazy, she's gonna be a real star, you'll see, and Mrs Beekman she said she didn't doubt it, on account you look so cute and talk so nice – I got some broth all ready and –'

'No broth,' Lexie said, leaning her head back on her chair and closing her eyes. 'Barbara, I'm pregnant.'

'Oh,' Barbara said after a moment, and sat down abruptly. 'Oh,' and Lexie opened her eyes and looked at her. She hadn't been sure what sort of reaction she expected. She hadn't even realized she was going to tell Barbara until the words came out of her mouth, and now she sat looking dumbly, waiting.

After a moment Barbara said, 'Oh,' again and tried a little smile. 'Usually people say mazeltov, don't they? Do you want I should say mazeltov?'

Lexie looked at her and then suddenly laughed. 'Oh, Barbara, I do like you! You're like Bessie, only I think a bit better – no, that's unkind of me. Bessie's – well, she's Bessie. She worries a lot. But you're –'

'I worry too!' Barbara said, and now all her face was pink and not just her thin nose. 'I mean, I want you should be happy. I like you too. You're a real great aunt to have –' And she giggled. 'That sounds stupid but you know what I mean. It's more like you're my sister. I always wanted a sister, what with Melvin and Sidney being so – well, anyway, I want to help you any way I can. Are you –' She chewed her upper lip for a moment. 'I mean – the guy – is he –'

'No one you know,' Lexie said crisply. 'I don't want to talk about him. Not now nor ever. It's no one here, anyway.'

'So you won't be getting married or anythin' like that?'

'Nothing like that.'

'Oh,' Barbara said again and sat quietly waiting. It's odd, Lexie thought. She can be so noisy and chattery but so still as well. Lexie began to relax, to feel calmer, and the panic that had been hovering inside her all day and been so close to the surface these past few hours subsided and lay lower in her belly, like a slumbering animal.

'So, what are you goin' to do?' Barbara said carefully. 'I mean, the show an' all –'

'Of course, the show and all,' Lexie said and again leaned back and closed her eyes. 'I've got the name of someone who'll help – I'm going tomorrow morning to see him. I –' She opened her eyes then. 'Will you come with me?'

247

'Yes,' said Barbara and nodded. But her eyes looked bleak and a little shadowed, and when she smiled reassuringly at Lexie it wasn't with quite the comfort that had been there before.

The notices in the papers were lyrical, and she sat up in bed to read them after Barbara had brought them to her with a tray of coffee and a bagel, which she couldn't eat, much to Barbara's distress. They should have made her feel marvellous, but all she could think of was the slip of paper in her bag bearing the address of Dr Hermann, way down on the Lower East Side. He was waiting for her like some sort of spider in a web, she felt, and she was being drawn towards him against her will, helplessly. Then she shook herself and got out of bed and went padding off to take her bath. This was ridiculous; no one was forcing her to do anything. She was pregnant, but it was vital that she should stop being so, and Dr Hermann was to help her. He wasn't bad, but good. If anyone was bad it was Max, who had made this happen to her.

But that thought wouldn't work, wouldn't shape itself fully in her mind. It went skittering away as she soaped herself and tried to think only of what she was doing, of each separate movement of her hands. And she managed to do just that, until she soaped her belly and sat there in the water staring down at it, trying to see what lay there behind the smooth flesh, tried to visualize its present concavity as a curve, a bulge, a person – and again she shook her head and tried to fix her thinking on the here and now. She had to see Dr Hermann. That was all there was to it – Dr Hermann.

Dr Hermann's office was in an ordinary tenement house, one of a long sweeping row in a street filled with market stalls and shouting women and men lounging against walls. She and Barbara stood outside gazing up the broken front steps at the open door and the clutter of children who were playing there, blue-kneed and runny-nosed in the biting December air, and peered again at the piece of paper in her hand. But it was the right address, and after a moment she went up the steps. Barbara followed her, wordlessly, and they made their way past the staring children and up the stairs.

248

The building was old and neglected and smelled of years of greasy cooking and cats and incontinent drunks in corners. The staircase was rickety and the balustrade greasy, and Lexie drew back fastidiously from the walls with their streaks of ordure and marks where bugs had been swatted and left to rot. This building couldn't contain a doctor's office, surely? There had to be some mistake – or perhaps once inside his set of rooms it would all be different? Despite her doubts she went on, right up to the fourth floor. And there the door was, with a small, dog-eared card pinned to it. 'Dr D.W. Hermann,' it read. 'Knock twice.'

'Let's go away,' Barbara said suddenly. 'I don't like this place, Lexie. It don't look the way a doctor's office should look. Even Dr Levy up on Hundred and Twentieth, he's only a half-dollar doctor, he's got a better place than this. It don't feel right, Lexie –'

But Lexie shook her head at her and knocked twice on the door. After a long pause there was a shuffling sound and the door opened a crack.

''Oo's dat?' The voice was gruff and thin at the same time and Lexie said loudly, more loudly than she meant, 'Is this Dr Hermann's office? I was given his name –'

'So don't shout, already –' the voice said, and the door was pulled open a little wider so that she could see the speaker, a tall man but rather bent, with a straggling beard that covered a scrawny throat revealed by an open-necked and far from clean shirt. He was wearing sagging trousers and carpet slippers and he looked at her over the top of smeared spectacles, one side of which had been mended with sticking plaster. After a second he said, 'So wait a moment already,' and shut the door again.

They stood there uncertainly, and again Barbara said urgently, 'Please let's go, Lexie. It just ain't right the way this place feels –' but then the door opened again and he stood there nodding at them and beckoning them in. He now had his shirt buttoned up and a bow tie clipped into it, though it had been set in place so hurriedly that it lurched sideways, giving him an absurdly rakish look. He had put on an ancient jacket, too, and had combed his beard. He looked a little less unkempt now and certainly seemed more alert, and after a moment Lexie took a deep breath and walked in. There was nothing else she could do, she told herself, trying to force

249

down her fears and her deep doubts about the place she was in. Who else would help in this awful mess? She could hardly go marching into a Fifth Avenue clinic, impeccable with chrome and antiseptic perfection, and demand a doctor who would get rid of her burden, who would break the law for her and –

'I'm pregnant,' she said baldly. 'And I was told –'

'Tush!' the man said. 'Such stupid ways to talk you girls got! You got a few period problems, is all. This we can talk about. You got a bit irregularity, you don't feel good, you need a little something'll bring on your naturals and shoin fertig – it's all done. I got the right medicines to make a lady feel good, to make her regular. This is all I got. No talk of nothing else here, you understand? I don't want no crazy talk.' And muttering beneath his breath he went across the room towards a high-backed sofa covered with cracking leatherette. Beside the sofa was a table covered, rather ominously, with a dingy piece of unhemmed sheeting which was lumpy with the objects hidden underneath it.

She looked round the room as Barbara stood hovering at the door, at the sink in the corner with a few dirty dishes stacked untidily on the drainer beside it, and at the curtained off alcove behind which she could see a grimy stove with more dishes piled on it. There was a divan bed in the corner, with a frayed patchwork counterpane pulled roughly over it. Everywhere there were piles of books and papers, and over it all hung a heavy smell of elderly coffee and thick pine disinfectant and cheap alcohol. Brandy, Lexie found herself thinking, he drinks brandy –

'Lexie!' Barbara hissed at her at the same moment that Hermann turned round to peer at her over his glasses.

'All right, then, miss, you should come over here, get on the couch and bend your knees up and out. You have to take off your panties first, naturally, and then we sort out these little periods of yours. Slippery elm, that's the medicine you need, just a little slippery elm, put in the right place, an' by tomorrow, maybe the next day, you got your periods natural –'

She stared at him, her face feeling so tight she could hardly say the words. 'Tomorrow? I thought – now. I mean, Lily said – the girl who told me about you – she said you'd do it right away –'

'Tssk,' he said. 'Such stuff these wimmin say. You think I

250

let it happen here? You think I'm crazy? I tell you what I do is to get the periods behaving natural. It's all I do. I make periods behave natural. I got this, you see?' And he fumbled beneath the cover on the table and pulled out a chipped enamel dish and held it out to her. There was a piece of what looked like a rough twig lying there.

'Piece of slippery elm, that's what it is. It's a natural thing what grows – natural, not one of your nasty metal instruments. Natural. It likes liquid, you understand? It's what they call hygroscopic.'

He grinned suddenly and his teeth were surprising large and yellow. She looked at them, fascinated.

'Yes. Hygroscopic. That's doctor's talk. I learned it when I was a medical student. Long time ago. Yes. So, okay, this piece o' slippery elm gets put in the opening to the womb, sucks up all the liquid it can get so it swells bigger and bigger, makes the womb open – pfft! A period. You understand? A period happens. It makes you regular. But it don't happen right away, no sir, not right away. At home, tomorrow, your friend should be there to help you, on account it might give you the cramps a bit, and you bleed a bit more than normal with periods – tomorrow, the next day when the elm is all swollen, it happens. But not here. It ain't right, here.' And he looked around at his room and then at her and somewhere behind his wet eyes she could see a glimmer of shame.

'You got the money?' he said then, and the glimmer had gone. 'That you got to have first. No money, no slippery elm. It comes expensive, this stuff. Normal periods, they come expensive. Your friend, she told you how much? Hundred an' fifty, that's what it costs, this bit of elm. You got it?'

He put down the dish on the table, tucking it under the cloth again, and grinned at her, displaying the big yellow teeth once more. He came towards her and now Barbara moved, almost jumping forwards to seize Lexie's elbow and pull on it.

'No!' she said shrilly. 'No! No money. We ain't got no money. Lexie, this man's a bad man – come on outa here – please come out. You can't stay here, it ain't right. He'll kill you, you hear me? I had a neighbour once, she had this slippery elm stuff put in her and she was so sick she near died.

251

She had to go to the hospital, have transfusions – Lexie! No! If I have to call the cops you don't have this man do nothing to you! I won't let you. I'll take you away –'

But she didn't have to. As soon as she had said the word 'cops' the old man moved so fast they were hardly aware of what was happening. He pushed them both towards the door and then shoved past them to open it and bundled them out into the dark stairwell and slammed the door on them. They heard the bolts pushed home and the key turn and then his thin gruff voice shouted, 'Go away! I don't want to have nothin' to do with you! Go away, or I call the cops, you hear me? I'll tell 'em you're hookers makin' trouble – go away – you hear me? Go away –'

They stood there in a stunned silence and then, suddenly, Lexie started to retch. But oddly, even though she felt so physically sick, she didn't feel as bad inside as she had. The panic had gone.

# 28

The snow started late in March and, because it was so bad, the theatre had to close for three nights till the streets were cleared and the out-of-towners could get in to fill the audiences again. That helped because it gave them the extra time they needed. Lily came over to stay, helping them carry the suitcases filled with Lexie's costumes, and the three of them sat with their heads down over their needles, working as carefully as they could, and with all the skill that Barbara had – which was considerable – to guide them.

It was a curiously happy time for Lexie, and she would sit there at the table in Barbara's poky little apartment with the radio on, its jigging music punctuated by the hissing and knocking in the steam radiators, and feel glad to be one of this small enclave of women. From time to time Barbara would bustle away to make coffee and Lily would stop and light a cigarette and tell them outrageous tales of her life in the old vaudeville days when she had been on the road, sometimes reduced to dancing in burlesque shows, making them both laugh till they wept. Then they would settle again to their sewing, making Lexie's costumes cunning facsimiles of what they had been to start with, but now with all sorts of secret fastenings and tapes and flaps that made them able to expand as much as Lexie might need them to, while still not displaying her state at all obviously.

For the decision had been made and plans been laid. Lexie was going to have her baby. That morning in Hermann's dingy little room had done more than frighten her off an abortion. It had filled her with a deep well of gratitude to Barbara, for she knew she had had a very fine escape. She no longer felt the child within her as a parasite; she felt no affection for it, no sense of pleasure in its existence, no joy in the knowledge that she and Max had made it, but there was now a strange sense of wonder. She would look at passers by in the street, and then down at her still flat belly and think – there's a person in there. A person. And the feeling that went through her at that thought was extraordinary. Not pleasure, not satisfaction, not excitement, but a sort of vast surprise. It was a feeling she quite liked. She learned how to summon it up deliberately, and often did as the show took off and lines formed day after day at the box office, and the weeks sped on towards spring.

But all the time she had refused steadfastly either to tell Barbara and Lily who the father of the baby was, or to let him know of her situation. Although both of them had at first tried to persuade her otherwise, they had soon given up; she was adamant on that score and they knew it.

But she was willing – indeed eager – to talk about all her other plans, and they would discuss for hours, long into the night, how it would be. Barbara would stop working at the millinery factory in the summer, when the baby was born. 'They're already paying me more than enough to keep us all,' Lexie said, when Barbara had looked alarmed. 'And I'll be getting more after three months. Someone's got to look after the baby, and if it isn't you it'll have to be someone else. And that'll cost money and – '

'No,' Barbara had said at once, with great indignation. 'No, Lexie! You don't go getting strangers to look after your own! If you're gonna pay people, so okay, I'll do it!' And she smiled then, a tremulous little grin as her nose went a particularly bright pink. 'I'll like that. I guess I'm not gonna get married ever, like Melvin and Sidney always said, but to

253

have a baby to look after – I'll be – ' She had shrugged her thin shoulders and made a face and laughed and sniffed all at once, and her eyes had been very bright. Lexie, embarrassed suddenly, had looked away.

'And I can always get a box of outwork from Mr Guz, if we get a bit short,' Barbara said then, her voice bubbling with optimism, 'when he gets busy, it's real murder there. He'll be glad to have me, and I can do a dozen hats while a baby's sleepin'. Oh, Lexie, I *am* so happy!' Lexie had lifted her brows at her and said sardonically, 'Well, I'm glad someone is!' and then laughed and hugged her briefly as her face fell. 'No, don't fret. I'm happy enough.'

And she was. Once the panic had gone, she knew she could cope. The show was an undoubted hit, and when she had asked for a bigger salary there had been no demur. She had a contract not only for this show but for the one to follow, for she had told them firmly that she loved New York so much she didn't want to go back to London as Mr Welch had planned, and Pete Capitelli had been immediate with his promise to manipulate Mr Welch and Mr Cochran the way he wanted them to go.

'We've got a first-class hit,' he said jubilantly. 'And after this one we're gonna have a grade A tip-top *double* first-class hit, as long as we got you. Never you mind about London, Lexie. You stay here with us and we'll sort it all out. With the money you'll be makin' you can get yourself a first-class apartment too. Riverside Drive maybe and – '

'No,' Lexie had said at once. 'I think I'll stay in the Bronx for a while.' He'd shrugged and said, 'Suit yourself,' and she had gone back to work happily. That she could hide her pregnancy for several months she was confident. With her costumes modified and Lily to help her, there was no end to what ingenuity could do, she told herself optimistically, and there was the summer break to come, time to have the baby quietly and get back to work. She wouldn't be the first performer to hide a pregnancy almost till the last minute. Many had done it before her, with judicious use of corsets and careful trimming of costumes, and she could do it too, she was certain. Her own costumes for this show were, fortunately, designed to shimmer and float; they could have been dreamed up to help her hide her changing shape, and now it was all settled she felt much better. The nausea had stopped and she had regained her appetite; now she had to stop herself from eating too much rather than try to force herself to take in some nourishment, and she bloomed. The audiences loved her and sighed over her. Office girls began to imitate her thick bobbed haircut with its heavy fringe and make up their eyes to look as slanting as hers were, and hardly a day went by but a magazine or a newspaper wanted an interview. And the way she lived had a great effect on the journalists who came twittering into her dressing room to gush and chatter and write their fulsome praise of her.

She had decided to stay with Barbara rather than to seek a bigger, better apartment, partly in order to save money (after all, she would tell herself, I can't be certain the show will go on, or that the next one will do well, even though deep in her heart of hearts she was so certain) but also because of the anonymity of the Bronx. She could lose herself in that populous neighbourhood as she could never have done in a fashionable apartment building. Once she left downtown with its staring tourists and knowing Broadway journalists and gossips she felt safe from prying eyes, for now that the local people were used to her they paid no more attention to her. She was Barbara Mark's relation from London, just another of the neighbours, and they got on with their busy lives and left her to get on with hers. It seemed to balance the evenings spent in the glare of the footlights and the great spotlights, dancing her heart out on the stage, wrapped in those glittering floating costumes while everyone stared at her.

It was this decision that endeared her so greatly to the journalists. They found her modest style of living democratic, they told her, not at all stuck up as they would have expected a snooty English performer to be. She behaved like a real down-home-style American, and they loved her for it. The articles about her in the magazines and the paragraphs in the gossip columns were always good, and the show's management basked in the satisfaction of having a hit as spring turned the streets of New York from cold greyness to a more hopeful warmth, and the trees in Central Park lifted their heads and began to breathe again. There were window-boxes filled with daffodils in the Bronx and barrows of them at street corners in midtown Manhattan, and slowly Lexie began to feel as much a New Yorker as she had once been a

Londoner.

It was a metamorphosis that was helped by her determination to shut Max out of her mind. She knew perfectly well that if he knew of her situation he would come at once, that none of her anxiety for her future was justified. He loved her, he wanted her, and would be overjoyed about the child she carried. But deep inside she was ashamed. It was this as much as everything else that sealed her mouth, and made her refuse to let anyone in London know what was happening to her. She knew the shame was irrational; she knew she had done nothing she need feel guilty about. But it was there, and she had to work hard at forgetting London and the people who had once been such important parts of her life.

So she wrote only the most scrappy of letters to Bessie, telling her that the show was a success, that she had met Barbara, the only one of the Marks family still to live in New York, and adding no more than inconsequential chat about the weather. Bessie would write back long rambling letters full of gossip about Alex Lazar and his niece, about Benny, who seemed to be coping well enough on his own without Fanny to take care of him, and about everything and anything except Max and Dave, and her own feelings about Lexie's absence. It was clear she had decided that she would play the game according to Lexie's rules, and Lexie would read the close-written pages and remember the letters that Bessie used to write, long ago, during the war, and she would fold them back in their envelopes and wait a couple of weeks before answering. That way she stopped Bessie from intruding on her awareness too often, and kept that ever-threatening guilt at bay.

She treated Max in the same way, too. He had answered her first letter, the one she had written on the ship, addressing it to the Cochran office, and it had been linked with a desperate appeal to come back, to allow him to come and get her, assuring her that somehow, *somehow* they would make an arrangement that would make it possible for them both to be happy. That she could work, of course she could, that he hadn't realized how much it meant to her, but please, they must be together, must talk –

But it had been too late by the time that letter had reached her. The time it took for mail to cross the Atlantic meant that when she read those eager pages she already knew she was pregnant. And that meant she had to say no. How could she go back to him now, in this state? So she told herself, and knew she was being absurd. Who better to tell than the child's own father? But whether it was her own stubbornness, or a new bubbling up of ambition which distrusted Max's assurance that he would let her work, or whether it was due to an alteration in her thinking caused by her pregnancy, she didn't know. She only knew that she had to keep quiet and do things her way.

By May she was having to wear a much firmer corset to contain the bulge in her belly and a tighter breast binder, too, to give her the fashionable skinny look that hitherto she had had naturally. Now, for the first time in her life, she had breasts that needed controlling. She would ease herself out of the tight garments, gently massage the taut, swollen skin and rub away the itching of her darkened nipples, and stare at herself in the long mirror in the bathroom and again feel that vast surprise. Her belly was round but not excessively so, considering she was now around seven months pregnant. There was a fine dark line that ran from her navel down to the smudge of dark hair in her groin, and she ran her finger down it and saw suddenly a vision of herself at five years old sitting on a wall in Jubilee Street with stolen cherries in her pinafore lap, listening to Barney and Sammy talking about where babies came from. She could almost hear the piping childish voice come down the years, lapping against her ears. 'They come outa their bellies,' Mossy had said, small Mossy with the adenoids and the big round eyes. 'They come outa their bellies. They splits open and they comes outa their pippicks − ' She laughed and then, ridiculously, felt her eyes fill with tears. Bessie, she thought. Bessie and Jubilee Street and Madame Gansella and the years before the war when it was all so easy and I was looked after all the time.

And I'm looked after now, she told herself sturdily. Putting on her wrapper, she went to sit in the little living room so that Barbara could fuss around her with little dishes specially made to tempt her now capricious appetite, and then dozed and relaxed until it was time to dress again and go to the theatre.

In June the heatwave started: the streets sizzled as water was poured on from the passing carts and the children whooped and shrieked around the hydrants. The theatre was impossible as temperatures climbed steadily into the nineties. Audiences thinned out and at last reached the stage where they fell below the essential level for profitability. Much to Lexie's relief, the notices went up. The show would close on 11 June and come September, the management promised, they would be casting for the follow-up to this great success: all members of the company invited to keep their names on the lists.

Now at last she could stop wearing the corset and the bust binders, and she sat about for most of the day as June became July and July limped into August, and found that the surprise and wonderment had all gone now. She was tired all the time, irritable and very, very bad-tempered.

Barbara did her best to keep her happy, scurrying home from the millinery factory to clean the apartment and prepare their meals, but it was a losing battle, and she became quiet. Her nose seemed to be a permanent pink now as she drooped silently around the apartment doing all she could to keep out of Lexie's way, while at the same time still looking after her. The fact that Lexie knew how hard Barbara was trying, and how unjust she was being herself, didn't help matters. It just made her more bad-tempered than ever.

Then, at last, on a night so hot and stifling that Lexie could only sit out on the fire escape gazing into the thick darkness, listening to the people shouting on the streets below and the crying children in the neighbouring apartments, it started.

All day she had been feeling restless. Her usual lassitude had been replaced by a spurt of nervous energy, and she had actually prepared a meal for Barbara and herself, which had cheered Barbara enormously. Her face had lit up when she had come in and seen the bowl of salad and the sliced cold corned beef ready on the table. Maybe Lexie had only bought at the deli, but she had done it, that was the point. Barbara had beamed at Lexie and been her old chattering self for the evening, which had made Lexie feel even more restless and irritable.

When it actually started Lexie felt like an excited child at a fairground standing under a roller coaster which she both feared and wanted to ride. The fatigue, the restlessness and the irritability left her and surprise and wonderment came back in a great wave. She sat bolt upright on her rocking chair so that it swung wildly, with her hand on her belly, feeling the contraction ride across it. She had been having contractions for weeks, of course, the painless kind that did no more than make her breathe a little more deeply, but these were different. These were the real thing, demanding peaks and troughs of tightness that made her feel as though her body were an unoiled machine that was creaking with each long, slow turn of its cogs.

She let it go on for several hours, sitting there on the fire escape, long after Barbara had gone to bed, counting the creakings and timing them, as the city slept fitfully in the exhausted heat, listening to the occasional wails of the police sirens. Then, as the sky thinned and lost its murky blackness, and the first daylight came creeping through and the colour slowly slid back into the buildings and the children in the surrounding apartments woke and began to cry again, she went heavily indoors to wake Barbara.


The baby was born at two a.m. the following day, after twenty-four hours of those creaking pains, then two hours of sweating, heaving and desperate pushing as Lexie struggled to free it from her body. She felt sometimes that she was turning inside out, that it wasn't a baby she was trying to expel but her own heart as the sweat ran down her face and stung her eyes, and she grunted and gasped and grunted again. But it was a baby and not her whole inside, and she lay and stared at it, her face creased with puzzlement, when they showed it to her and told her she had a daughter.

She looked round the labour room, squinting at its gleaming white tiles and the nurses and the doctor standing there, and said weakly, 'What?' The doctor laughed indulgently and said, 'You have a fine daughter, Mrs Asher. Your husband will be a real proud man.'

'No husband,' Lexie said. She closed her eyes and then opened them again to stare at the baby. It had a face so crumpled and red it looked furious, and it was streaked with some sort of yellow waxiness that made her grimace with distaste. She said, 'A girl?' and the nurse leaned over and gave it to her to hold. Lexie looked down at the crumpled face just as the eyes opened and stared at her.

Big eyes, they seemed, big dark eyes, full of knowledge and wisdom and a sort of scorn. Almost without thinking she put out her hand and touched the cheek beneath one of those eyes, and at once the small mouth moved and turned sideways. The little head followed the movement too and the yellow-streaked lips reached Lexie's fingertip, took it in and began to suck furiously. She laughed, a little breathy sound, as the nurse laughed too. 'Guess she missed her supper, hey? You'll be able to feed her later.' At once Lexie pulled her finger away.

'No,' she said, turning her head away from the bundled infant in the crook of her arm. 'No – Barbara. Give it to Barbara. She'll feed it. She bought bottles. She'll feed it. Give it to Barbara.'

# 29

'I don't know why, Barbie. I just feel I've got to,' Lexie said. 'It's the best offer they've ever made, and anyway –'

'And anyway, you want to go there.' Barbara leaned back in her chair and tried not to show how agitated she was. If she'd learned one thing in all these years with Lexie, it was the importance of not displaying naked emotion. If there was anything almost certain to send Lexie off on her own stubborn path it was any hint of pressure from someone else, and today, clearly, it was necessary to be particularly careful. It was rare indeed for Lexie to use Molly's cosy name for her. She must be very strung up.

'I suppose I do.' Lexie got to her feet and went over to the big window to stare down at West Fifty-seventh Street nine floors below. There was the usual elegant bustle down there, cabs drawing up at the entrance to the Henry Hudson Hotel, dog walkers from the Parc Vendome apartment block on the corner of Ninth Avenue, flower shops and candy stores with their indolent, expensive customers. For a moment she felt a surge of certainty that she did not, after all, want to leave it all behind. It had taken her long enough and money enough to get here, heaven knew. She thought of the cramped little rooms they had shared in the old apartment near Intervale Avenue, of the hot nights sitting out in the breathless humidity of the fire escape, and told herself she was mad, quite, quite mad even to think of behaving so stupidly. Here she was in one of the nicest parts of Manhattan, living in real comfort and security and not a little style. She'd left the fire-escaped buildings and the rattle of the steam in the old pipes and the smells of the delis and street stalls far behind long ago. Why let go of it all now?

'I don't have to leave it all for good, of course,' she said then, still staring down at the street. 'After all, it mightn't work out there, and then—'

'Sure it'll work out,' Barbara said at once, almost automatically. 'When did any show you were in not work out? But — I'm not sure what you mean?' And she looked at Lexie's back, keeping her own very straight and trying to keep her voice relaxed and unanxious, though she knew she wasn't really succeeding. But Lexie seemed not to be aware of that; she still stood at the window with her hands clasped in front of her, and her head bent.

'I mean, why do I have to upset you and Molly, just because I have to go? It could be a short run, after all. The way things are there, who can say? And anyway, I could have it in the contract. Got to come back soon — say six months — how would that be?' Lexie whirled round and looked at Barbara with her chin set at a sharp angle and her eyes very bright.

'I don't reckon I quite see what you mean,' Barbara said carefully. 'Are you saying that—'

'I'll go on my own.' Lexie sounded impatient. 'I know I said I'd take you both, that we'd just start again there, but for God's sake, why do I have to upset you two? Molly's happy in school, isn't she?'

'Very happy.' Do I sound relaxed? Barbara thought. Do I sound as though I don't really care either way? Please let me sound relaxed. 'She's real good at arithmetic, Mrs Seligson said, and her writing's getting better all the time.'

'So why take her away? She's doing well — going to a new school, and in England yet — it'd be sure to upset her, wouldn't it?'

'Well, I guess it would,' Barbara said. 'I mean, any child changing schools gets kinda upset. She fussed a bit when she started, didn't she? And when she had to leave Mrs Ross's grade. But now she just adores that Mrs Seligson, never stops talking about her.'

'Yes,' Lexie said. 'Yes, of course that's the way to do it – if you can manage, that is –'

'Oh, sure I can manage.' Barbara went over to her armchair to get her knitting. She didn't want to knit, but it would give her something to do with her hands. 'But what about you, Lexie? Won't you sort of miss her?'

'Of course I will,' Lexie said. 'Of course I will. Like the very devil. But she won't miss me, will she? She won't be upset, and –'

'She *will* miss you, Lexie. Truly she will – she loves you so much that –'

'Yes,' Lexie said. 'Yes, I know. We've been through all that before. But she won't miss me the way she'd miss you –'

There was nothing Barbara could say, and a silence grew between them, thickening until it was almost palpable. Barbara could only sit and gaze miserably at Lexie's back, for she had turned to stare out of the window again. She looked as good as she ever had, even in a plain crêpe de chine frock, with hips as slender and legs as fine as they had been when she was a girl, for all her thirty-seven years, and her thick dark hair was still cut in its elegant bob. Other women wore their hair fashionably marcelled with crisp waves marching over their heads in regimented lines, but Lexie maintained her own style and managed to look as modern as tomorrow. Other women fretted and fussed at beauty parlours and at Lexie's age had skins that were already showing signs of sagging, but Lexie still had her English complexion. Barbara lifted her hand and touched her own lined face and then, embarrassed at her own foolishness, concentrated on her knitting again.

'Well, I guess I'll have to think about it a bit more,' Lexie said abruptly. 'It's a marvellous offer, but all the same –'

'It's the way things are there that worries me.' Barbara couldn't help it. She'd meant to say nothing, had tried so hard to say nothing, but the words pushed themselves out past her teeth. 'Joe downstairs was saying he reckons there'll be a war in Europe before Christmas. He's got all day to read the papers and he listens to all the news bulletins on the radio all the time and –'

'Oh, for God's sake, Barbara, the *janitor*? A lot he knows! Do you suppose they'd be rehearsing new shows if there was going to be a war? It's the new game everyone's playing, that's all. Every party you go to, everyone you hear, all they can talk about is war, war, war. You'd think they want it to happen, the way they go on! I don't believe it! I saw enough last time not to believe it. Those soldiers we used to do the show for, the way they were – no one wants that again, no one wants another war.'

But she didn't believe what she was saying, and she knew Barbara didn't either. For weeks she'd been reading the papers herself without letting Barbara know how worried she was, sitting in her dressing room at the theatre eagerly scanning the pages for any scrap of news out of London. She knew it was true. War wasn't an impossibility any more. The question was not will it happen, but when will it start?

And how much is my wanting to take this offer to do with all this war fuss? she asked herself drearily, still looking down at the sunlit Manhattan street below, but trying to visualize grey London streets and London buildings and London people. Ten years it's been, more than ten years, and I've refused every offer they've made. God knows there've been enough of them – Cochran never stopped asking me. The better I did here, the more he wanted me home, and I wouldn't go – but now that it looks like trouble's in the wind, I can't make up my mind to say no. I must be stark, staring mad.

Bessie, she thought then, with a sudden spurt of anger, Bessie, why doesn't she *write*? All those years of letter after letter, full of gossip and questions and chatter, and now, when I need to hear from her, when I'm aching for that damned chatter, silence. Why doesn't she *write*? Anxiety tightened in her again and she moved sharply away from the window.

'What time is she due out of school?' she said, not looking at Barbara.

'Half after three.' Barbara had her head bent over her knitting now. 'I usually leave around fifteen after. Unless you want to fetch her today?'

'Do you mind if I do?'

'Lexie, for heaven's sake, don't be that way!' Barbara burst out. 'You make me feel like I'm trying to–'

'Oh hell, I'm sorry. I didn't mean to upset you.' Lexie tried to smile. 'I mean to keep my promise, but every so often it just creeps up on me. I'm sorry–'

263

'Me too. Sorry I bawled,' Barbara mumbled. 'Listen, we need some ice cream – I didn't make any dessert for tonight yet. Would you get some on the way back? The drugstore on the corner of Fifty-eighth and Eighth has that bilberry one she likes best. If you get a quart I can keep some for tomorrow and then–'

Lexie laughed. 'You're a set of French windows, you know that? You know perfectly well if I stop at the drugstore she'll want a soda–'

'Well, it won't do her no harm. Once in a while it's not so bad–' Barbara said, still mumbling. 'And anyway–'

And anyway it'll give you two time to be together, and you aren't together that much. The words hung unspoken in the air between them and after a moment Lexie nodded and went to the door. 'I'll go now,' she said. 'I'll walk round the block the long way. I need the exercise.' And time to think. 'Don't worry if we're a bit late, then. I guess she'll take her time over the soda. At least ten minutes deciding which flavour.'

Barbara gave a stilted little laugh and bobbed her head, and as she heard the front door of the apartment close behind Lexie and then the distant whine and clang of the elevator she went to the window to watch her go down the street. She won't be around a lot longer for me to watch, she told herself bleakly, because she'll go. She'll take that offer, I know she will. And she couldn't decide what made her feel so bad about it: the thought of Lexie far away in an England threatened by war (she had a hazy image of a tiny island being shot out of the sea by huge German gunners in aeroplanes) or the deep-down knowledge that she wanted Lexie to go and leave her alone with Molly.

Molly, she thought, and felt the spring of delight that even thinking about the child could lift in her. Molly with her slanting dark eyes and her thick dark hair and pointed little face; Molly with her chatter and her giggles and her ready hugs, her tears, her tempers, her cooing; her Molly.

But she isn't mine, she told herself, and went out to the kitchen to start getting supper ready. She isn't mine. She's Lexie's. I'm just her aunt, and Lexie's her mother.

But she doesn't know that. She thinks I'm her mother, and we've let her think it. It had seemed so natural and easy, because the baby had called Barbara by her first name right from the beginning. She'd not been like other babies with strings of mamamamas and dadadadas; she'd said bababababa – and then learned to make them into Barbie. It had been simpler for her infant tongue to handle, that was the point. That was why she had called for Barbie when she'd been fretful or feverish, or had a pain or a bad dream or just wanted company. It wasn't that I wanted to take her away from Lexie. It just happened that way.

And after all, it was you she knew best, wasn't it? It was you who looked after her and fed her and changed her diapers and burped her. It was your face she saw first thing in the morning and last thing at night. How could it be otherwise when Lexie had to go to the theatre every night and was gone when it came to bedtime, and was still sleeping in the morning when the child awoke? How could it be otherwise when it was you who took her to play in the park, to walk along the paths beside the playground and feed the birds with breadcrumbs? How could she not feel best with you who took her shopping for clothes when she needed them, took her to the dentist and the doctor and all the rest of the ordinary everyday things that Lexie couldn't do? It wasn't Lexie's fault that she couldn't do such motherly things. She had to go out each day to work, to dance and sing and make the money that kept them all so comfortably and indeed elegantly in the smart section of the West Side that had been their home for most of Molly's life.

And where, Barbara remembered now, slicing carrots into a saucepan, where she had become Molly. Lexie had chosen to name her baby Milly after the mother she had never known, who had died giving birth to her. Barbara had liked that, for she could just remember her grandmother, and had loved her, so Milly the baby had been. Until they had moved to 333 West Fifty-seventh Street and the fancy neighbours had misheard when they'd been told the pretty baby's name, and had assumed it was Molly; and Molly had somehow suited the elfin infant in her handsome beribboned bassinet, so Molly she had become – Molly Rowan because we were as foolish about her surname, as we were foolish about so many things, but at the time it had seemed best. Lexie had put her own name of Asher on the birth certificate, of course, but had added another one: Rowan, the name of the character she had played in one of the sketches in the show she had been in at the time of her pregnancy, and somehow they had both drifted into the habit of using that additional forename as a surname. It was easier and less embarrassing for the unmarried Lexie, and for Barbara too. So the child had just stopped being Molly Asher and had become Molly Rowan.

Just as I had become her mother in everyone's eyes, and Lexie her aunt. It had seemed too complicated to explain when people made the assumption. Easier to let them think she was a widow, a sad widow with a baby to rear, and wasn't it lucky she had her dear young aunt to live with her and provide for her? After all, she told herself, as she set the carrots on to cook, after all, it had suited Lexie too, hadn't it? Broadway stars don't look good as illegitimate mothers. It was important that she gave the gossip columnists nothing they could hold against her. Their living had depended on it, all of their livings, but specially Molly's. So without discussing it, without planning in any way it had happened. Molly thought Barbie was her mother – when people spoke to her of her Mommy it was always Barbara she looked at, not Lexie, just as it was always Barbara she ran to when she was in need of comfort – and it would be dreadfully complicated now to explain the reality of the situation. Bad enough the way it had been when she had asked why she didn't have a father like the other children at school. Barbara remembered that day with painful clarity – how she had felt her chest lurch at the question as they walked home from school during Molly's first week there, and how she had opened her mouth to say something, anything, to say he was a traveller, he was Mr Rowan who had had to go away, and Molly herself had created the answer before she could say a word.

'Jenny says her daddy died of the flu and she said it happened to a lot of people, dying of the flu, and she guessed it happened to my daddy too, and if it had we could be best friends because then we'd both be the same and I want to be Jenny's best friend, so is that what happened to my daddy? Did he die of the flu like Jenny's did? Say he did, Barbie, say he did. Jenny's got a kitten at her house and a garden with a sandpit, and I want to be Jenny's best friend for ever and ever –'

So Molly was given a daddy who died of the flu, and she and Jenny had been friends for almost the whole of the semester. By the time they stopped being best friends it was there, part of their lives; a dead daddy and Molly as happy and cheerful as anyone could want.

And now, Barbara thought as she scrubbed potatoes to bake in their jackets the way Molly liked best, now what? Lexie in England and us here – is that how it will be? And what about money? She hadn't said anything to Lexie about that, though from the moment she'd heard about Cochran's new offer and how Lexie was actually considering taking it, it had been nagging at her. Will she take me with her? Or will I have to go back to the factory? How would I pay the rent here if I didn't? Will Lexie still pay for everything even though she's away? Will she be able to earn enough in England to pay for us all, for two homes? It was a lot to worry about, a lot to fret over, but underneath was the gaping, stretching, wicked, selfish hope that Lexie would go, even though it was so risky, and leave Molly for Barbara. All to herself.

Lexie, walking with her swinging stride along Eighth Avenue, knew exactly what Barbara was thinking. How could she not know every aspect of her thinking, every shade of her feeling? It was ten years they'd been together now, closer than any marriage could ever be, two women sharing the burden of caring for each other and for a child. Oh, Molly, Molly, Lexie thought as she moved swiftly through the strolling passers by. If only I didn't care about you so much, how easy it would all be! I could see you run to Barbara and not care. I could hear you calling her in the night and not be hurt. I could sit back when you won't come to me because you're tired and miserable and it's only Barbara you want, and not mind. But I do care and it does hurt and I do mind and now I'm thinking of leaving you and letting Barbara love you even more and invade you even more and take you over altogether. How crazy can a person be? What is there in England that makes me want even to think of going back?

Work, her little secret voice whispered, it's work, isn't it? Some of it's worry about Bessie, some of it's worry about a war and wanting to be at home if it happens, suddenly being English again after ten years as an American, but mostly it's work. Because what else is there now? You've done it here; you've taken Broadway. It's yours any time you want it. There isn't a producer anywhere in town who wouldn't whoop and grab if he knew you were available for a show; there isn't a producer in Hollywood either who wouldn't be cock-a-hoop to get you for one of his films. They've asked you often enough, haven't they?

So why not go west? she asked herself as she reached the school, seeing the mothers waiting for the bell to go and the children to emerge and slackening her steps so that she could loiter well away from them. Why not go to California, make *that* the new mountain to climb and slice into little molehills? If you're bored here because you've made it, need a new excitement, a new set of problems to solve, a new ambition, go to Hollywood. Everyone else does.

Because I want to show them at home, she found herself whispering. I want to show them there that I'm the best performer they ever had. Me, Alexandra Asher, top of the heap. That's what I want them to know. Who knows in London what I'm doing here? The managements do, I dare say, a few flitting travellers, the Noël Coward crowd, but I want more than that. I want everyone to know I'm the best. I want all of them to see me and marvel and know what they let go.

And Max? whispered the little voice again. At once she stopped loitering and marched to the school doors to join the waiting women, smiling vaguely at them as at last the bell rang, the doors clashed open and children began to rush out. I don't give a damn about Max, she told herself firmly, standing on tiptoe to scan the cluster of tumbling shrieking bouncing children who were pouring down the steps. I never think about him, so why think about him now?

Because you think about him all the time, the little voice jeered at her. All the time. Every day he slides into your head, every damned day that ever comes. You want to go home to show him, that's what it is. You need to find him again. All these years, having all the fun the gossip writers say you do, all those friends and still the untouched, the unsullied. You're famous for it, there isn't a performer within ten miles of Times Square who has your reputation for virtue. And all because every day you think of Max, one way or another, you think of Max. You idiot.

And then at last she was there, her slender body standing out among her sturdier classmates the way a dove's stands out among pigeons, her small head poised on her delicate neck the way a sweetpea flower is poised on its tough pale stalk. Lexie smiled widely and waved as Molly looked around, then saw her and stopped very still for a moment before running towards her.

'Hi, Lexie.' she said and tucked her inky hand, warm and sticky with the day's busyness, into hers. 'Is Barbie okay? She's not sick?'

'Of course not, darling,' Lexie said, and made herself sound as she always did with Molly, cool and sensible and unfussed. 'She's making supper and she said she needed ice cream for dessert. So I thought we'd go together and get it, hmm?'

At last Molly seemed pleased to see her and held on to her hand tightly as she began to jump up and down. 'The drugstore, the drugstore,' she carolled. 'Can I have a soda, Lexie, please can I have a soda, huh, can I? A mint, or maybe a chocolate – or maybe strawberry? Or shall I have a pineapple and will they have fudge malted maybe or–'

Lexie laughed, and together they turned and went back towards the drugstore and home. Whatever I decide, whatever happens, she told herself as the child chattered and jumped along beside her, I have her now, just for this little while. Just for a soda's time. After that I'll decide what to do. After that.

# 30

The ship slid into Southampton on a day so misty that the air felt wet to the touch and the sirens cried mournfully to each other across the heaving greasy water, but she was glad of the grey dampness because it matched her mood. All the way across she had worked hard at being glittering and gay, the sophisticated star returning to take the lead in a glossy new show. It was what the other passengers expected, and she had delivered a performance as good as any she had ever given on stage. But all the same, she was miserable. Even before the ship had left she had known she was wrong to leave them. She had stood there at the rail, staring down at the pier below at Molly, in her blue tweed coat and hat and leather gaiters, clutching a streamer in one hand and Barbara in the other, and had wanted to push her way through the crowds back to the gangplank and run down to pick her up and hug her.

But of course she hadn't. She had just held on to the other end of Molly's streamer and gone on holding it long after the ship had made its stately departure from the pier and the streamer had torn, and lay tangled with the myriad other streamers that hung down the ship's great flanks. She was leaving the person she loved most in the world with someone else, leaving security and comfort and success, and for what? Uncertainty, loneliness and probable war, and all because of this crazy hunger to jump on a stage and scream at them all, 'Look at me! Pay attention to me! I'm Alexandra Asher and you've got to love me!'

She had not told the Cochran management when she was arriving. She wanted no flurry of reporters to greet her at Southampton, no publicity at all until she was ready for it. There was Bessie to be seen and – there was Bessie to be seen first, she told herself firmly. And I have to get myself settled and organized before I get involved with the show; that's why I don't want any fuss at Southampton. But she knew she lied to herself. She needed to know where Max was and what he was doing, to be ready to cope if he chose to make contact with her again – or allowed her to do so. But she wouldn't think about that. She dared not.

London felt odd; standing in the echoing expanse of Victoria Station as the crowds eddied and scurried past her, her chin up as she let the sounds and smells and sights of the place come back to her, she thought – it's changed. It still smells of soot and horses and bus exhausts and apples from the fruit stalls and damp newspaper and sweating people, yet it's changed. It's edgier and noisier and there's fear in the air. Suddenly tears pricked her eyelids and filled her nose. She was amazed at herself as a wave of homesickness far greater than any she had ever known while she was in New York rose in her belly and threatened to engulf her entirely. She was actually trembling with it as she followed the porter with her luggage to the taxi rank and told the driver to take her to the Savoy. She wouldn't stay there for long – much too

270

costly, even at her level of income (Cochran had agreed to pay her handsomely for rehearsal time as well as for the run of the show), but it was a good starting point.

The sense of nostalgia lingered all day; she seemed to be walking in a sort of a dream as she booked into the hotel, and then afterwards as she walked along the Strand to look at the Adelphi Theatre where the show was to run. Everything seemed particularly poignant in its familiarity, yet frightening in its strangeness. She almost panicked for a moment, fearing she was ill, that she was losing control of herself, for she felt like another person, as though she weren't inside her own skin at all, but was a separate ethereal entity that hovered over the slim woman in the suede coat with the fur collar pulled up to her ears, watching her with a beady critical eye. But then she reached the theatre and it was as though everything clicked into place, as though that ethereal otherness slipped back inside her skin where it belonged, for the posters outside were huge and garish and shouted at her: 'The New Cochran Revue, Opening Here Shortly! *Happy Returns*, starring that dancing sensation of Broadway, Alexandra Asher with Flanagan and Allen, Beatrice Lillie and –'

She stood with her hands thrust deep into her pockets and laughed aloud. *Happy Returns*. What a perfect title. She was home now, well and truly home and she felt the familiar excitement and that hot, hungry feeling rise in her, the feeling that meant she was ready to work, to create new routines, to learn new songs, to rehearse till every muscle shrieked and every joint complained. A lovely feeling, a joyous feeling, and slowly the memory of Molly on the pier at New York staring up at her from under the brim of her blue tweed hat receded at last.

Once she had been to the Cochran office and the formalities were settled, contracts signed and rehearsal schedules arranged, she was free to deal with more personal affairs: finding somewhere to live and – she had to deal with it now – contacting Bessie. All the time she had been telling herself how much she wanted to see Bessie, but now she was free to do so she was curiously reluctant, and had to make herself pick up the telephone immediately after breakfast next morning to call her number. But she did it and then sat on the edge of her bed listening to the distant tinny double ring, feeling faintly sick with apprehension, not knowing why.

271

After all, there was no need to fear Bessie, not good old Bessie – was there?

There was no answer and she put down the telephone, her brows slightly creased. She had called early to make sure she caught her before she left for work, and she looked at her bedside clock and frowned even more. Surely Bessie hadn't gone already, at just after eight? But then, remembering how punctilious she had always been in matters to do with her job, Lexie knew she could have done, and called the number of Alex Lazar's office behind the tea shop in Tottenham Court Road.

The voice that answered wasn't Bessie's but a harassed waitress's which said firmly that no, there was no Miss Ascher there, and no, there never had been in all the time she worked there and that was nigh on six months, and why don't she call 'ead office down in the City? Lexie raised her brows – a City office! Lazar had come on in the world, clearly. She called the number she was given and at last reached Alex Lazar himself.

'Who?' the voice clacked in her ear. She could hear the muffled note as he spoke round his cigar, and grinned suddenly at the image of him that rose in her mind.

'Lexie, Alex. It's Lexie. I'm trying to get in touch with Bessie.'

'Well, I'll go to – you're in London?'

'The Savoy. Got here yesterday. I'm opening in Cochran's new revue at the Adelphi – the posters are all over the place.'

'So I don't go reading posters! Is it my fault I don't know you're here? You should have written, sent a cable or somethin' – why didn't you?'

'I like to surprise people,' she said. 'But I'm the one who's surprised. I didn't know you had a City office, and I didn't know Bessie didn't work at Tottenham Court Road any more. Where is she? I can't get an answer from the flat.'

There was a short silence at the other end of the phone and she said sharply, 'Alex? What is it? Where is she?'

'In hospital, dolly. No, don't go gettin' yourself in a state! It's all right, now –'

'How do you mean, all right now? What happened?'

'It wasn't all right – she had somethin' a bit nasty there – women's things, you know how it is –'

'Not unless I'm told,' she snapped. 'For heaven's sake,

Alex, you don't have to be coy with me. What happened to her? Where is she? How is she now? And –'

'So let me get a word in sideways already! Okay, I won't be coy, though she'll kill me for talkin', I dare say. She got cancer of the womb, all right? She was lucky, she got very anaemic, passed out here at the office one day, so I took her to a doctor. If I hadn't, God knows how long she'd have gone on as she was. The doctor said another few months he wouldn't ha' been able to do nothin' for her. It was lucky she bled a lot, got so weak, or I'd have never known. As it is, she's had a big operation – a *big* operation, you shouldn't know of such things, they took half her insides out, poor girl – and radium and now she's on the mend. Been ill for months –'

'Oh, God.' Lexie said it in a whisper. 'And I was angry with her for not writing –'

'Ah, you know Bessie. She can't say somethin' good, she won't say nothin'. Probably didn't want to worry you –'

'Yes. I suppose – listen, where is she? I want to see her.'

'Of course you do,' he said heartily. 'I got her in a nice little convalescent hospital down at Bournemouth. She's got another three weeks there, then she's back in London at home and soon back at work –'

'Oh, yes, of course,' Lexie said, and couldn't keep the sardonic note out of her voice. 'She must get back to work, mustn't she? It would never do to upset the office, would it?'

'Lexie, you're a fool.' He said it easily, with no hint of anger in his voice. 'You don't know from nothing, you know that? If you want to kill your sister for good and all, you take her job away. She's good for my business, sure she is. I been missing her something chronic. But I'm good for her and my business is good for her. Without us she ain't got much, has she? You in America these ten years and all –'

Lexie was silent for a moment. Then she said abruptly, 'Yes, I'm sorry –'

'No harm done,' he said equably. 'So tell me, already, how are you? Doing well over there, hey? I come over a few times, always your name everywhere, wanted to get to see one of your shows, but you know how it is, when you're travelling on business – you can't do all you'd like to –'

'I know how it is,' she said. 'Yes, I'm doing very well. And you?'

'Me? I'm thriving, dolly, thriving. Got more tea shops now than you can count if you take your shoes off as well as your gloves! And three theatres – and shows on the road. Thriving, that's me. And my niece, you remember my niece Hannah? She's a lady now. What do you think of that, hey? Lady Lammeck, that's who she is! Her husband, lovely fella, lovely, he's Sir Marcus and –'

'Yes,' she said abstractedly, not listening any more as he launched into one of his usual panegyrics about his beloved niece. Bessie, ill – it was hard to imagine. She had never been ill; always frail, of course, with that twisted back of hers and her fragile bones and her pale face. But ill enough to be unable to work – Lexie couldn't imagine it. She managed to stop Alex's chatter about Hannah long enough to get the address of the Bournemouth nursing home from him, then hung up the phone and sat staring blankly at the wall. She had always seen Bessie as someone to lean on, someone who was always there in the background to be used and relied on, but now *she* was someone who needed care. It was an odd idea.

Lexie decided not to let the nursing home know she was coming. It would be easier to face Bessie and assess her situation if she didn't expect her. Bessie had always put on a show for her, she knew that, and she wanted no show. Just the reality.

They told her Miss Asher was outside, and she walked through the hallway, her heels clacking on the polished parquet, past the low tables with their bowls of crimson dahlias and chrysanthemums and out to a stone terrace that overlooked a garden running down to the edge of the pine-filled chine. She stood uncertainly, staring down the lawn at the basket chair and its blanketed occupant, then took a deep breath before walking across the grass towards her. The turf sprang under her heels, making her unsteady, and when Bessie turned her head to look at her Lexie swayed for a moment, almost losing her balance. Bessie tried to stand, to reach towards her, and Lexie, hurrying forwards to stop her, finally did lose her balance and landed at her feet. Staring up at Bessie's astonished face, she laughed shakily.

'Well!' she said breathlessly. 'How's that for an entrance! Throwing myself at your feet, no less. How are you, Bessie? Why didn't you write me you were sick?'

'You're home.' Bessie's voice was thin and yet husky. 'You're *home*. Are you? Really?'

'Really,' she said. 'Really home. A new Cochran revue –'

'Someone told me they'd seen a poster with your name on, in London, but I didn't believe it. I didn't dare. I said it was a mistake –'

'No mistake.' Lexie laid her hand on Bessie's and felt a jolt of shock at how thin it was. Her face had always been thin and looked much the same now as Lexie remembered it, and her body was hidden in blankets, but that hand told all the story for it was shell-like in its delicacy. For a moment Lexie's grip tightened and she leaned forwards and hugged Bessie to her. Under the blanket she seemed to be as a fallen leaf at the end of the autumn, a tracery of its former self, a translucent shadow of the robustness that had once been there, a fragment that could blow away to dust unless it were watched over and protected.

'It's all right, Bessie,' she said, her voice slightly muffled by the blankets. 'It's all right. I'm home. I'll look after you and you'll be well again –'

'Yes.' Suddenly Bessie's voice sounded like its old familiar self. 'Now I'll be really well. Oh, Lexie, I've missed you so! It's been the same every day since you went, it never got no easier. Tell me everything – I want to know what you've been doing, what the shows have been like and – oh, everything –'

Lexie sat back on her heels and smiled at her. 'There's time, plenty of time. I'll get round to it. When you're well and we're settled in a nice flat somewhere.'

'A flat? But –'

'You'll live with me, won't you, Bessie? With me and Barbara and –' She stopped suddenly and the smile disappeared. She took a breath and said awkwardly, 'You know I lived with Barbara in New York –'

'She's coming here? To live?'

'Yes. I haven't arranged it all yet, but I'm going to. I – Molly, too.'

Bessie looked blank. 'Molly?'

'I never told you –' Lexie wanted to tell her the truth, needed to. She opened her mouth to say it and was amazed at the words that came out.

'Barbara has a child. Her name's Molly. She was named

275

after Momma, but it sort of got changed. She's Molly. You'll love her, Bessie. She's – she's a beautiful child and you'll love her.'

Bessie shook her head, opened her mouth to speak and couldn't, then shook her head again and was suddenly crying, the tears rolling down her cheeks. But she gasped and wiped her eyes with the backs of both hands and said, 'I'm sorry. This happens sometimes. I'm still a bit on the wobbly side, you see. But it's getting better all the time. I'm fine, really – Molly! Barbara with a child! What happened? I mean, she's a widow, or what?'

'A widow,' Lexie said after a moment, then bent her head as she searched in her bag for a handkerchief for Bessie. 'A widow. She doesn't like to talk about it. The past or anything. When she comes, don't ask her. It – it upsets her. And Molly too. Better not to ask –'

'No – I – Barbara, a child! I can't imagine. She was just a baby herself last time I saw her – when are they coming? Where will you live? Will you come to Hackney, to me? Mrs Bernstein, rest her soul, died last year, so I got the downstairs as well now. Not that I use it, you understand, but it's so nice to have the place to myself. Neighbours can be good, but no neighbours can be better.'

Lexie laughed a little shakily. 'I know, I know just what you mean. No, I don't think – not Hackney. I'll get a house somewhere, for all of us. We can all live together and –'

Bessie shook her head. 'It's kind of you, but no, Lexie. Victoria Park Road – that's home for me. I don't fancy living anywhere else. I'll be fine there. You get your house and come and see me often, hmm? More often than the old days, maybe?'

'We'll talk about it.' Lexie smiled at her again, putting all the anxiety and affection she felt for the fragile little bundle in the chair into it. 'Maybe we'll find a way we can all live together and all be happy – we'll talk about it. It'll be better than the old days.'

Bessie looked down at her fingers laced on her lap, almost transparent in their whiteness against the rough redness of the blanket.

'Have you seen – talked to anyone else since you got back, Lexie?' she asked softly. But Lexie heard the question as clearly as though Bessie had shouted it.

'No,' she said. 'No, I haven't. I've talked to Alex, of course, but that's all. Only Alex. What news of – of everyone? Dave and Monty and –'

'Dave went away,' Bessie said, still not looking at her. 'Went to live in Palestine. Said he'd always wanted to be a real Zionist, so now he lives in Haifa. He writes sometimes – Monty I never see. I – it was never the same after the – you know. And Joe and Benny, well, they moved away too. You know how close Benny always was to Dave, so he went after him and he lives in Haifa now. And as for Joe – he never writes no more. Haven't heard from him in years. Last I heard he was in California. Of all places, California.'

'He was always like that,' Lexie said. 'Always doing something different.'

The question hung unanswered between them. There was a long pause and then at last Bessie looked Lexie straight in the eyes. Lexie was very aware of her pallor, of the violet smudges in the temples and beneath the eyes that gave her a bruised look.

'Max got married,' she said after a moment. 'Six years ago it was. He married one of the Damont family. They're relations of Alex Lazar's niece, you know. Nice people. He married one of them.'

# 31

They called it the phoney war, and sometimes Lexie would wonder how she could have been so frightened of what war would mean to England, when she had come rushing back to London at the end of 1938. Now, with Munich a forgotten promise, Chamberlain a ridiculous joke and the actual declaration of war oddly like an anticlimax, they had come to terms with the idea. They worked and ate and slept and worked again, and paid no attention to the piles of sandbags in the parks and the 'Shelter' signs at street corners. It was all nonsense, really, a shadowy absurdity happening over the Channel and nothing to do with real life at all.

At first they had talked of evacuation, she and Bessie and Barbara, seriously considering sending Molly back to New

York and safety, but Molly had wept so bitterly at the suggestion and had thrown such tantrums at the mere mention of the possibility of being parted from Barbara (they had been told that the chances of getting a passage on an evacuee ship for her were slender, American citizen though she was) that they had abandoned the idea.

It had never been a realistic suggestion as far as Lexie was concerned. The thought of letting Molly go away from her again was much too painful; the six months it had taken to sell the apartment on West Fifty-seventh Street and get them over from New York had been misery for her. She had busied herself well enough of course, not only with the show, which did marvellously well, but also with renovating the Victoria Park Road house (for she had agreed in the end that they should all live there, faced with Bessie's total refusal to consider moving away). For all that, however, the separation had seemed interminable. To let Molly go again, even to protect her from the risk of air raids, was more than she could cope with. And anyway, as no air raids happened and the strange state of limbo persisted, the anxiety faded. If it ever got really bad, they would go and live in the country, Bessie would tell Lexie cheerfully. And Lexie would agree, if still uneasily.

But as more and more of the mothers and children who had been evacuated out of London to the fields and woods of Suffolk and Norfolk and Devon came drifting back to their familiar old Smoke, as people began to tell themselves that there was no real risk, that it was all a lot of rubbish, that they'd finish Hitler and his stupid Huns before Christmas, she became more and more uneasy. The news from over the Channel was ominous, as Hitler marched into Denmark and Norway, and the British Expeditionary Force dispatched to Norway to deal with the matter failed signally to deal with anything at all, and she began to remember, hazily, the things that had happened in the last war. The Zeppelin raids that had so frightened everyone, those big silver cigars that had come floating in so silently to do so much damage, came back into her mind, and she told herself fearfully that it was obvious it would happen again. The first air raid warning over London, the one that had come on the very first night of the war, may have been a false alarm, sending everyone scuttling unnecessarily for bolt holes in cellars and under stairs, but it wouldn't always be like that. Sooner or later, and she feared rather sooner than anyone thought, there would be bombs again and fires and terror and the thought would send her hurrying back to Hackney after the show to try once again to persuade Barbara and Molly to leave London.

But they wouldn't. They would sit there beside Bessie's cosy fire, preferring her half of the house to their own, with Bessie on the other side of the grate, and look at her and smile and shake their heads when she talked of finding a place for them in the country. They were happy, happier than she could imagine. They weren't frightened. They wanted to stay where they were.

And Lexie had to admit that Molly *was* happy. She had arrived in England a sulky leggy creature who had changed surprisingly in just six months. Lexie had met the ship at Southampton and was taken aback at how much she'd grown in just half a year. She had walked soberly down the gangplank rather than skipping as she had been used to do, looking very calm and adult. The difference between ten and almost eleven was clearly a significant one, for she looked quite altered. Lexie had been puzzled at first, and then a little saddened, for Barbara whispered to her that Molly had 'grown up,' and 'become a young lady,' and then had blinked and nodded and grinned and made a mysterious face all at once. It had taken a moment or two for Lexie to comprehend her, but then she had, and had looked at Molly and felt a pang of regret. To reach adolescence so young – it seemed too soon, much too soon.

Her first weeks in London had been stormy, for apparently she liked nothing she saw. Lexie took her and Barbara from place to place, showing her the sights of London as Europe crept closer and closer to war during those summer months of 1939. But then the war had really started, and that seemed to change Molly most.

She had watched the children of Hackney being evacuated, seen the floods of belabelled, gasmask-carrying young ones going past in bus after bus on their way to the railway stations, and had clung closer to Barbara and to Bessie, to whom she had clearly taken a great liking, and said urgently, 'Don't make me go, will you? I want to stay here in London, in Hackney. I like Hackney.' Lexie had relaxed at last, grateful to see the child content. She liked her school, one of the few that remained to offer any classes to the child-depleted neighbourhood, and she had found enough other stay-in-London children among whom to make friends (certainly she was often out in the evenings on the occasions when Lexie was able to come to Hackney before going to the theatre), so Lexie stopped worrying, as best she could, and settled for a day-to-day existence. That was all any of them could do.

*Happy Returns* closed after a reasonable run, and at once she was put into another show, this time at the Palladium Theatre, and that meant a great deal of extra work, for the show there played twice nightly. It was a gruelling schedule and she was forced to take a one-room flat in the middle of town, since travelling between Hackney and the West End every night became too much of a chore. She needed to be within walking distance of the theatre, and the flat she found, in a tiny block just behind Marble Arch, was ideal.

Ideal for work, that was, but not so ideal when it came to seeing Molly, for somehow whenever she did manage to get over to Hackney she wasn't there. Barbara would smile and shrug her shoulders when Lexie asked sharply why she was always out, and murmur about her friends and how much the child enjoyed being with them and how important it was for her to see them, for after all, there were so many children out of London, and Lexie would have to accept it and go back to the West End in time for the early show, swallowing her disappointment as best she could.

She had become very good at swallowing things that were unpalatable, she discovered. The news of Max's marriage had shaken her a great deal more than she would have thought possible. She should have realized he wouldn't sit alone and bear the willow for her for ever, she told herself over and over again during those first weeks in London while *Happy Returns* grew in rehearsals, and then opened to packed houses and cheerful reviews. Why shouldn't he marry? I walked away from him all those years ago, kept aloof, what did I expect? That he'd sit and weep and wait till I chose to return?

That's exactly what you did think, said her interior voice, sneering again. Arrogant creature that you are, that's exactly what you did think! Well, he didn't. Swallow *that* as best you can, madam. He *didn't*.

I'm glad he didn't, she would argue back at that other part of herself. I'm glad, because now I don't have to tell him anything, do I? If he'd waited for me, if he'd still been around ready to try again, then I'd have had to tell him. He'd have had to know Molly, share her – and I share her enough. Bad enough with Barbara. If Molly had Max as well, and loved him too, I couldn't bear it.

And so the weeks plaited themselves into months and the first winter of the war slid away in waves of irritation at the blackout and mutterings about the way rationing was biting: first there had been the tea ration, and then butter and other fats, and then they'd announced that there was a shortage of eggs which was something to make everyone moan for a week on end. But for the household in Victoria Park Road, life was very tranquil, in spite of the dark nights and shortages. Bessie had recovered quite well from her long illness, though she needed to go to bed rather earlier than she had once done, and tended to go rather white about the mouth if she didn't get there early enough. But having Barbara and Molly with her seemed to have lifted her spirits amazingly. Alex Lazar, on one of his flying visits (and he was up to his ears in war work, busy as he was with ENSA, the entertainments service that had been set up by the government to provide shows for service men and women and people on war work, running shows all over the country for army camps and hospitals) commented on that approvingly and told Lexie that she'd 'saved Bessie's life and that's a fact'.

'You brought that child here, and it's made a new woman of her. Don't let 'em evacuate her, Lexie, not unless they take Bessie too. And she can't go because she has to run my shops. So there you are.' He'd laughed and grinned at Molly and dug into his pocket to find her some chocolate (a rare treat these days with long queues at every sweet shop), then departed to plunge himself back into his war work, whistling as he went. For Alex Lazar war work was the greatest pleasure there was, and he blossomed under his burdens.

And so did Lexie, curiously, for although she too was doing extra work for ENSA, spending almost as many hours at the Drury Lane Theatre, the headquarters of the division, as she did at the Palladium, she didn't get as tired as she would have expected. The people who came there, the soldiers on leave, the nurses snatching a night out from their long hours in the wards, the airmen exhausted by the boredom of waiting for something to do in this phoney war, showed their appreciation of all that was done for them so vociferously that they made her feel needed in a way that not even the most enthusiastic Broadway audience had been able to do.

The only drawback to her life now was the infrequency with which she saw Molly. Sunday was now the only day she could get over to Hackney, although on most evenings she did manage to telephone the child. But that was not really satisfying, for Molly was no longer the chatterbox she'd been when she was small: there was an aloofness about her, an unwillingness to talk, that Lexie found baffling.

'What are you doing this evening?' she would ask, and Molly's voice would reply thin and cool down the line. 'Oh, nothing much. Seeing my friends.'

'Oh. Who?'

'Well, Susan and Lilian – no one you know. I've got to go now, Auntie Lexie. I'll be late.'

That had made Lexie first angry, then hurt, that 'Auntie' label. Up to now Molly had always used just her first name, as she did with Barbie, which had helped blur the confusion of the situation not only for outsiders but for Lexie herself. To be cast now so firmly in this peripheral role – it was not something she was happy about, and as soon as she could she tackled Barbara about it.

'Honestly, Lexie, I don't know why she calls you that,' Barbara said wretchedly. 'It's her idea, not mine. Bessie told her to call *her* "Auntie", so I suppose she just thought – I didn't make no fuss about it. I mean, it'd only confuse her if I did, wouldn't it? Unless you want to tell her – I mean, I suppose she ought to know sooner or later.'

She had looked bleakly at Lexie over the knitting that occupied her so interminably, and made a small shrugging movement. Lexie had stared back at her, knowing there was nothing she could do. Molly was happy, settled. To start trying to change her view of her world now would be cruel – Lexie couldn't do it. She'd have to know the truth some day, but not now.

The summer of 1940 limped on its way, June rolling into sluggish July and then, in August, the phoney war abruptly lost its phoniness. Air raids that were aimed at the RAF started in the second week of August. For ten days people went around London as strung up as violins, certain that at any moment the raids would spread from the south coast airfields and installations to the City, but it seemed the Luftwaffe had instructions to keep away, and some Londoners began to think they never would come.

Until late one Saturday evening, after the show had finished and the pubs were turning out. Lexie had hurried out of her costume as fast as she could, eager to get over to Hackney. This week, she had promised herself, as she wiped make-up from her face, this week I'll really try to talk more to Molly, try to get her to relax, talk more to me. Maybe even tell her the truth – though if I do I'll have to tell Bessie as well, of course. Oh, hell, if only we hadn't let the stupid thing start in the first place – she's mine, mine, not Barbara's.

Outside the Palladium on the dark pavement there was the usual crush looking for the few available taxis, exacerbated tonight because it was Saturday. Even those who felt safer staying at home all week ventured out on this traditional night. She stood there for a moment peering around in the dimness and then decided it would have to be a bus. They weren't as quick or as comfortable but at least they ran, and they got there, so she swung out into Oxford Street, pushing her way surefootedly though the crowds. The long months of the blackout had trained her to see in the dark and had given her confidence, but when she got to the bus stop that confidence crumbled, for there was a hubbub there that took her unaware. There were policemen about, all of them besieged by shouting, questioning people. After one startled look round Lexie made a beeline for one of them and pushed her way to the front.

'I don't know no more'n what I told you,' he was shouting, lifting his hands in the air to hold off his importunate questioners. 'I told yer – no buses running east at present on account of enemy action over at Stepney and Bethnal Green. Soon's we know more, we'll tell you. Bus inspector's on the blower now.'

She felt sick as she stood in the middle of the eddying crowd and stared up at the policeman's pale face in the darkness. Enemy action at Stepney and Bethnal Green? Victoria Park Road lay neatly tucked behind the two areas: a

283

ten-minute walk down Mare Street to Cambridge Heath Road and that was Bethnal Green, and Stepney wasn't much further. Lexie caught her breath sharply and pushed her way back to the kerbside. If she had to walk all the way she'd get there; find Molly, get her out, make her leave London for the country. It was too risky to keep her here, she'd have to go.

There was a nightmare she often had: she would be struggling to get somewhere, desperately needing to catch a train or a bus, to find a taxi or someone to give her a lift, and in her dream she would run and shout and wave her hands frantically as the vehicles she needed passed her heedlessly. Her steps would be sluggish and heavy, as though she was trying to drag her feet out of the clay; and now the nightmare came alive. She ran along Oxford Street towards Tottenham Court Road, swearing aloud at the people who stumbled in her way, knowing only that she had to get to Molly, and as people swore back at her and shouted after her in the darkness the tears started. She who hardly ever cried found tears blurring her eyes, and suddenly she remembered herself crying once before; saw a picture of herself sitting on the side of her bed in the flat towards which she was now running so frantically, with Max holding her and kissing her and saying, 'Lexie, we'll get married as soon as all the fuss is over.' That was the last time she could remember really crying, and that had been the start of Molly. That had been the moment when Molly first became a possibility, and now here she was crying again, this time not for Max but for his child. The thoughts and tears jumbled together in her head and mixed themselves up with her gasping breath until she didn't know where she was or what she was doing, only that she had to run, to get to Molly, to scoop her up and get her out of London.

# 32

She managed to get a lift from a passing lorry at the top of Holborn. The driver good-naturedly went out of his way to take her to Hackney when he saw how distressed she was. It gave her time to recover her control as she sat there in the swaying rattling cab as he pushed his way through the City, going east. He shouted encouragement all the way, assuring her that those bleedin' 'Uns'd never do no real 'arm, not to London, they wouldn't bleedin' dare, she'd see, it'd all be as right as ninepence, no need to get 'erself into such a two'n'eight, she'd see.

And he was right. The street was quiet in the warm darkness, untouched by any bombs, though there was a faint scent of burning wood in the wind that blew up from the south. As the driver drew up at the end of Victoria Park Road, so that she could jump down, he grinned and cried, 'See? Told yer it'd be all right, ducks! Keep yer pecker up – don't let the buggers get yer dahn.' Then he went rattling away into the night, leaving her to run up the road, let herself into the quiet house and lean against the front door with her eyes shut and her mind blanked as she tried to relax.

'Who is it?' Bessie's voice came anxiously from the top of the stairs.

Lexie called softly, 'It's only me, Bessie – not to worry.' She walked slowly up the stairs, exhausted now by the agitation of the past hour. 'Did you hear anything? They bombed Bethnal Green tonight, I heard –'

'Bombed?' Bessie drew her dressing gown closer around her. 'I heard a bit of noise, but I thought it was thunder – it's been quite hot today. But bombs – oh, Lexie, is it going to begin, the way they all said it would?'

'I think it must be,' Lexie said heavily. She went into the living room and threw herself into the armchair by the dead fireplace. The room looked as it always had. Downstairs in Barbara and Molly's share of the house there was the most modern of comfortable, chintz-covered furniture and Heal's chairs and tables, set against the most elegant of new wallpapers, for Lexie had spared no expense in the redecoration, but here it was all as it had been when she'd been a child. Bessie liked the familiar and the beloved, however shabby, and refused any changes to her home.

'Molly's going to have to go, you know, Bessie. She can't stay here – it's more than I can stand. I don't think I've ever been as terrified as I was tonight when I heard – the journey back here was –' She shivered. 'Did Barbara and Molly hear the noise? Did they think it was thunder? Or do you think they realized? I'll have to ask – what time did Barbara go to bed?'

Bessie looked uncomfortable. 'She hasn't yet. I was just waiting for them to come in.'

Lexie sat bolt upright and stared at her. 'Waiting for them? What do you mean? They're out? Both of them?' Her voice rose shrilly. 'Bessie, are you mad? They can't be out at this time of night – Molly – it's almost midnight, for God's sake! Where are they? What are they doing?'

Bessie looked wretched and her face crumpled like a worried child's. 'I said the same. I told them they shouldn't, but Barbara said – and Molly got all upset so I – I mean, I don't see why you can't be told, but Barbara said you'd get angry – oh, dear!' And suddenly tears were welling out of her eyes and streaking her cheeks. She rubbed the back of one hand against them and sat down abruptly. She was pale and looked as ill, suddenly, as she had that day when Lexie had first seen her again, at the Bournemouth nursing home, and with a little rush of compunction Lexie ran over to her chair and crouched in front of her.

'Bessie, love, don't upset yourself, please. Just tell me, quietly, what it's all about. No, don't look like that, I won't be angry – I just want to know – come on now. You'll feel better if you tell me.' And it took every bit of acting ability she had to keep the fear out of her voice. Box clever, she thought. Box clever to get what you want. I must know – Molly and Barbara out of the house at this time, while there were enemy aircraft in the sky which could come back at any moment to blast them all into infinity – I can't think about it. I can't. 'Tell me, Bessie. You'll feel better if you do.'

'I *can't*. I promised them – but you make them tell you. It's so silly, all this secretiveness. As if it wasn't the same for you – you did it, why shouldn't Molly? I can't understand why it is –'

There a distant thump as the front door below opened and then closed. Lexie was on her feet at once, running for the sitting room door.

'Molly?' she called as she reached the top of the stairs. 'Molly? Barbara? Where the hell have you been? What's going on, for God's sake? It's midnight – where the hell have you *been*?'

They came upstairs quietly, Molly first, and her chin went up as she stared at Lexie with her brows raised, looking

286

extraordinarily old suddenly. It was like looking at a stranger, Lexie thought as she stared back, not my Molly. She could have been any age – twenty, even more, not the twelve-year-old I know her to be. It's less than a month since her birthday, yet she looks now as though she's lived in the world for so many weary years that she's sickened of it.

Lexie hurried after her as Barbara brought up the rear. Reaching forward she grabbed Molly's arm, tugging on her. 'Where have you been?' she said again, and knew her voice was shrill with worry. 'Where the blazes have you been at this time of night?'

Molly looked down at the hand on her arm and then, very coolly, at Lexie. 'I don't see what you're fussing about,' she said loudly. 'I've been out with Barbie. Can't a person go out with her mother without all this fuss?'

Lexie stared at her and then whirled to look at Barbara. 'What is all this? I came rushing back here because of the bombing and –'

'We heard about it,' Barbara said, pulling off her hat and then her coat, fussing as she folded the sleeves and set it neatly on the back of a chair, anything not to look at Lexie. 'There weren't any buses because of it – that's why we're a bit late. We had to walk back – but it wasn't so bad, it seems. There were some people hurt over at Stepney, someone said, and –'

'Barbara, where were you?' Lexie's voice was as sharp as a new knife and Barbara almost winced as she looked up at her.

'It's nothing so terrible, for heaven's sake,' she said, her voice thin and almost petulant. 'But you know how you are – when I said in New York that it'd be kind of nice if Molly went to ballet classes you nearly went crazy, and said she shouldn't, not ever, it was bad for kids to go to dancing class. I thought then you were making too much of it, but you got so upset that I – anyway, when Molly wanted to, I told her not to tell you. It'd just have started a fuss and I knew I could pay for it out of the housekeeping. Oh, Lexie, don't look at me that way! She wanted to, and I didn't want a fuss and –'

'*I* said not to tell you.' Molly's voice came in cool and light and as relaxed as though they were talking about the weather. 'It was a secret between Barbie and me. Nothing to do with anyone but us. And Bessie.' She turned and smiled at Bessie, sitting curled miserably in her armchair. 'I told

Bessie, only it was a secret, wasn't it?'

'I told you I hate secrets,' Bessie said, not taking her eyes from Lexie's face.

Molly turned away from her and shrugged. 'Well, anyway, it was a secret, because Barbie said you'd fuss—'

'What secret, for Christ's sake?' Lexie shouted it now, no longer caring what she sounded like. 'You're all talking nonsense.'

But they weren't and she knew it, remembering only too well the way she had lost her temper when Molly was four and Barbie had in all innocence tried to enrol her for ballet classes at the local school. She could remember still how white-faced Barbara had been as she had stood there, letting Lexie's tongue lash at her.

'I go to dancing classes,' Molly said loudly. 'So there! Barbie pays for it, so why shouldn't I go? You don't want me to have any fun, not ever, but Barbie does, and if she says I can dance, I can! It's up to her, not you—' She stared at Lexie challengingly, her arms folded over her narrow chest and her jaw thrust forwards. 'I said not to tell you, to keep it a secret 'cos I don't like rows, and I knew you'd make one. You are now – look at you! Barbie, tell her it's all right. You said I could, didn't you?'

At last she was sounding like a child again, not a remote adult, and that made it possible for Lexie to take a deep breath, to relax and simulate calmness. She sat down at the table, resting her elbows on it, and stared over her clasped hands at Molly.

'My love, I hate rows too! I'm not making one now – I only shouted because I was worried. I'm sorry – I won't shout again. But there were bombs and I thought – I was afraid they'd fallen here. I'm still afraid they will and I think it's time, whether you like it or not, to think about leaving London, to go on somewhere safe where the Germans won't come. But I didn't mean to make a row, as you put it. Not that I'm not sorry about the dancing lessons – ' She swallowed and managed to smile a bright tight little grin. 'It's something I know about, dancing. It's the toughest, most miserable business – '

'You're a dancer. It's not hurting you! You're a star in all these shows, you dance and sing – why not me? Don't you think I'm good enough?' Molly was still standing in that

288

challenging position. 'Why did you tell Barbie I mustn't ever do it? Does it make you jealous or something?'

'Molly!' Barbara gasped, but Lexie shook her head at her.

'No, Molly, I'm not jealous. Just – ' She looked down at her hands for a moment and then back at the stubborn little face that was scowling at her. 'I love you, that's all. And I didn't want you to go through the hell I did. I worked all the hours God sent, and I don't think I ever stopped hurting, and the people were – it's a rotten life, Molly. I want better for you. Good schooling and maybe university and to be happy and comfortable and – '

'I want to be a dancer,' Molly said mulishly. 'I told Barbie. I told her I want to be an actress too, and I shall be, you'll see. You can't stop me, not if Barbie says I can. Can you?'

There was an icy silence, broken only be a sharp intake of breath from Barbara. Then Lexie got heavily to her feet. 'No dear, of course I can't,' she said, keeping her voice as expressionless as she could. 'Of course not. Not if Barbara says it's all right. Is that where you were tonight? At a class? It was very late – '

Molly flushed and her eyes suddenly lit up as she unfolded her arms at last and came skipping over to the table to stare eagerly into Lexie's face. 'No!' she carolled. 'No, it was something much better! We did a show! It's the first one ever, and it was marvellous, because there's only six of us, what with all the kids being evacuated and all, so I was in every number, every single one, and they all applauded so much it was wonderful! Lilian, she fell over in her solo and Susan made ever so many mistakes, but I was great, wasn't I, Barbie?' She lifted her chin exultantly and laughed aloud. 'I was great! And Miss Alicia says now I'm twelve I can start work properly and – '

'What did you say?' Lexie said loudly, looking at Barbara. 'What did she say, Barbara? Classes is one thing but – '

Barbara bit her lip and gazed at Lexie with eyes that were both triumphant and alarmed. 'I didn't think it'd go that far, Lexie, honestly. It was just something she wanted to do, and I couldn't see no harm in it, though I knew you wouldn't like it. That's why I didn't – anyway, there was this Miss Alicia's Academy we went past one day and Molly said let's ask, and we did, and she got Molly to try a few steps, and she said she was a natural, a real natural.' She reddened even more then.

'And why shouldn't she be? It's in the family, after all! Isn't it? And she learned real fast. Miss Alicia said she could do solo numbers – and then she said about this show they've got. It's going to tour all the places where the children are evacuated, Miss Alicia says. It's got those ENSA people organizing it – we heard about them from Bessie because of Mr Lazar, and he fixed it for Miss Alicia, and well – now Molly's twelve, she – Miss Alicia – says it's all legal for her to be in a show. She'll have proper lessons, of course, because the law says she has to, and there'll be this teacher who'll travel with them, and the show'll only do one performance a day, mostly matinées at schools –'

'It's going to be called *Here's London!*' Molly said, almost bouncing with excitement. 'It's to help the children stay where they're evacuated, instead of them getting all miserable and coming back to London and getting bombed, and I'm going to sing that song "A Nightingale Sang in Berkeley Square" and "Goodnight, children everywhere" and –'

'They want me to go with,' Barbara said huskily and she moved forwards and put her hand on Lexie's arm. 'I knew I'd have to tell you now, because Molly's dead set on doing it, so I'm real glad you're here, though I wish you hadn't found out this way – well, anyway, I was surely going to tell you. It's a way of going out of London, you see, isn't it? We can be together, Molly and me, and she can do what she likes doing and we'll be safe, won't we?'

Lexie was trying to get her head into some sort of order. She wanted Molly out of harm's way, wanted her out of London as much as she had wanted her here a few months ago. The hour she had spent getting to Hackney from Oxford Street had convinced her, as nothing else could, that evacuation was a must. Even if the bombing didn't get any worse than tonight, even if there were no more raids, the fear of them was enough. And here she was being shown the one way to get Molly to go happily, because it was the one way to ensure she would have her beloved Barbara with her. The rules about evacuees were clear; mothers of under-fives could be sent away with their children. Mothers of twelve-year-olds – no, there was little hope of finding a billet for both of them together, except this way.

But what a way. She thought of the long miserable years of the last war when she too had been a child dancer on the road, of the cold digs and the colder trains and charabancs, of the dreadful food and the long hours of practice in cold icy drill halls and dusty scout huts, of the leering men, not only backstage but in the audiences, and the way they had grabbed for her as she'd gone dancing among them with her collection box, and she closed her eyes to blot it out. Was this going to happen to Molly, too? Hadn't she promised herself a better life for Molly, better than her own mother's had been?

She opened her eyes then and looked bleakly at Barbie. Own *aunt*, she thought, and wanted to laugh. I worked and planned for Molly, and what did it get me? Cast as the aunt, lost the lead role, cast as the aunt, not the mother, and she actually began to laugh, weakly at first and then more loudly until she could hardly catch her breath.

Molly stared at her and then at Barbara. 'Is it all right, Barbie?' she asked, moving to stand closer beside her. Through her laughter-slitted eyes Lexie saw how tall she was now, the same height as Barbara, but so much more beautiful, so much more hopeful and alive and eager, and the tears of laughter thickened and threatened to become tears of misery. She took a deep breath, found a handkerchief and blew her nose.

'What can I do?' she said. 'You've got to get out of London, that's for sure, and if there's no other way you'll go –'

'Of course there isn't!' Molly said and laughed, a clear bell-like sound that was full of the most natural childish merriment. 'I'd run away if you tried to make me go anywhere I didn't want to go – I'd keep on running away until you let me stay in London. But if I'm in a show, that'll be different. Then I'll go, because we'll be in different places all the time, and it'll be marvellous, really marvellous–' She laughed again and hugged Barbara and kissed her cheek, but made no attempt to come and hug and kiss Lexie.

Later, when at last Molly had been calmed down from her towering excitement with a cup of hot milk and sent off to bed, and when Lexie had brushed away Barbara's confused attempts to explain, to expiate her sin of secrecy, and then had also gone to bed, Bessie wearily got to her feet.

'I need bed too. Thank God it's Sunday tomorrow – this morning. I'll be able to lie in. Not that Molly's likely to let any of us sleep all that long. I never saw the child so excited–'

She moved heavily to the door, pulling her dressing gown around her. Looking at her, Lexie thought with a pang, she's getting old – yet she isn't really. Only sixty – not all that old, is it? But she looks more.

'No,' she said. 'I don't suppose she will. Go to bed, Bessie, I'll sit here awhile, have another cup of tea, then I'll go too. Goodnight, and sleep well.'

'Goodnight,' Bessie said, but she lingered at the door, still looking at Lexie. Then she sighed softly. 'Why didn't you tell me, Lexie? You could have told me, you know.'

'Told you what?' Lexie looked up. 'Told you what?'

'That Molly's yours. You could have told me. I'm Bessie, remember me? You can tell me anything.'

Lexie stared at her, face blank and mouth drying with surprise. Bessie, who had always been so quiet, so easy to manipulate, so biddable, to talk so? It was as though a passing cat had opened its mouth to bark like a dog.

'I suppose she's Max's, too.' Bessie turned again to the door. 'You'll have to think a lot about that, you know, Lexie. He has a right to know if she is. And so has she, of course. Goodnight, my dear. Don't sit up too late.'

# 33

At first, when she got to the island, she was scared to sleep. After the long weeks of nightly bombardments and daily bone-shaking journeys in ill-sprung lorries, lurching over hot sand and rough shale, she had got into the habit of grim endurance. To be able to lie in a real bed, rather than a makeshift canvas and lathe construction in a tent, to be able to black out the night with closed lids and slide into oblivion with the comfortable certainty that the morning would come and she would still be alive – it was difficult for her to get used to that. That there was a real future available, a tomorrow that was certain to come – that was an idea she had come to do without.

She had learned to cope with each moment as it was, not thinking about the minutes just gone or those about to come, just the immediate now. It was the only way she had managed to survive those interminable months in North Africa with a show every night, and sometimes in an afternoon as well. Seven days a week, month after month after month.

When she had joined her first travelling ENSA group, just after Molly and Barbara had left London for Winchester and the start of their *Here's London!* tour, all she had wanted was that sort of unremitting grind. If I'm working all the time I can't be worrying, she'd told herself, and recklessly had accepted everything they threw at her; tours of north-east England factories where they did four shows a day, for each of the shifts of whey-faced munitions workers, then of the Welsh coalfields where boys who looked barely old enough to be out of school came climbing black-faced and weary out of the pits to sit sleepily in their canteens watching Lexie dancing and singing, and Dave Calleff, the comic, cavorting and miming at them. But she had discovered very early on that it was possible to work herself to a state of numb exhaustion and yet still worry.

The image of Molly never left her: when she was herself struggling into her costumes in icy cold odorous lavatories, for want of any other dressing room, and trying to paint her face to some semblance of glamour in speckled broken mirrors, she could see Molly doing the same; when she sat slumped in corners of cold trains as they waited forlornly in sidings for the chance to get out on to the main line amid all the troop trains, she felt the misery that Molly must be feeling in the same situation, and the hopelessness of it all built up in her until she was almost at breaking point.

She hadn't broken, of course, but when her Welsh tour was over and the few letters from Molly and Barbara made it clear that they had no intention of giving up their mad progress – for that was how Lexie now saw it – she had almost in despair agreed to take the North African job. It would be a small company, they had told her: the accompanist and the comic, if they could persuade them to go, but mostly herself. No, she couldn't have a dance partner; she'd have to devise a show that the boys would enjoy, that would bring some agreeable excitement and the memory of home, but all on her own. With the minimum of costumes and props. There was no way they could travel great skips for her. She had to be able to carry her kit herself wherever she went. Furthermore, they said, it would have to be an open-ended contract; they couldn't spare transport space to bring them home to England on leave. Whatever time there was for leave would have to be spent in Africa, so it could mean being away for a long time.

She had nodded dumbly and signed the contract, flying out of Brize Norton aerodrome one bitter December night in 1941, hunched in the back of a cold Dakota with Dave Calleff grumbling in a constant monotone on one side of her and Larry Peters, their lugubrious accompanist, slumped silently on the other. There seemed no reason to stay in England any more; there were managements who were casting shows again for the West End, in spite of the ever-increasing raids that were pummelling London so mercilessly, optimistic that the Luftwaffe would give up eventually, that life would get back to normal, but she hadn't wanted to stay for that. To be in England, to know that Molly was somewhere within reach and yet not able to see her – that would be hell, and the thought of going out to work with the soldiers in what she thought of as the front line – even though she knew this war wasn't in any way like the last one, with its trenches and lines and fall-back areas – was less painful than staying at home.

Lying now on her back on the springy turf with the scent of rosemary and basil hot in her nostrils, she tried to remember how she had been that night she had left England, more than two years ago – it didn't seem possible in some ways that she had been away so long, and yet in others it seemed like a century.

She had not received a letter from Molly for two weeks, and on the last night she had begged permission from the station commander at Brize Norton to use the telephone. Grudgingly he had agreed, and she had sat there in his cramped, stuffy little office struggling to persuade the operator to find a route that would connect her with Molly. She had known she was somewhere in Gloucestershire, because the last letters she had received had said they were covering that county for three weeks, and when she'd gone to ask him Alex Lazar had emerged from the maelstrom of activity that was his home at Drury Lane Theatre to tell her that according to his schedules – and the English school tours were in his bailiwick – that was where they'd be.

'But there's no need to worry over them,' he'd said,

patting her on the back in his avuncular fashion. 'If my Hannah had been there I'd have had more peace of mind, I tell you. As it is – ' And he had grimaced and shaken his head and she had said nothing, knowing how hard the war had hit his precious niece, and had taken gratefully the list of addresses he had given her for the *Here's London!* company.

'No promises, mind!' he had warned her. 'These bloody schedules change like they're made of candle grease, but as far as I know that's where they're supposed to be the next couple of months. Don't worry, doll. I'll keep an eye on 'em while you're gone, just like I will on Bessie. Though, thank God, *she's* keepin' an eye on my affairs. Without her the whole lot of the tea shops'd be down the drain. She's a marvel, bless her – ' She had nodded and folded away the list, and then, later, at Brize Norton, had used it to try to reach Molly.

At first she had intended just to go quietly to North Africa, to make no attempt to say goodbye, to be as unfussing and unfussed as it was possible to be, but she had found that beyond her. She had to say goodbye properly, had to hear Molly's voice say it too. It became the most important thing in the world – more important than the long hazardous flight to North Africa that lay ahead of her, more important than the risks she was taking going to work in a battle area, certainly more important than her immediate physical discomfort.

At last she had managed it. As Dave Calleff had hovered outside the office door and hissed urgently at her that they were loading the plane, that they were calling for her, she had got through and had sat there with the phone pushed so hard against her ear that it hurt and shouted in her anxiety, 'Barbara? Oh. Thank God, I've found you – Barbara, is she all right? Where is she? Can I talk to her?'

'She's fine, Lexie, believe me, she's great. She's so good in the show, they all love her, the other dancers and all. Everyone likes her, and in her solo, the one about Christmas trees, you know, she's really – '

'Where *is* she, Barbara? Let me speak to her – put her on the phone, Barbara, please – quickly – I've got to go and I must talk to her – '

'Oh, Lexie, I can't – she's not here right now – she's gone out – the show finished early tonight and – it was lucky I was

295

still here when the phone rang. I was just going back to the billet and – she's out, Lexie – '

'Out? Where out? Where can a kid go in a dead and alive hole like that this time of night?'

'Local fish and chip shop! They've got one here that still gets some stuff in – it's not so dead and alive, really. It's a nice town, Cirencester, you'd like it – the stage director took her there – one or two of the other kids, too – he's giving them a special supper. Oh, Lexie, are you all right? Where are you? Where are you going?'

'Africa,' Lexie had said and shook her head savagely at Dave who had now pushed the door open and was gesticulating furiously at her through the crack. 'I'm going to Africa. Tell Molly – make her write to me, Barbara. I miss her so, make her write – ' The line had crackled and gone dead, and she had had to follow Dave out across the frosted tarmac to the looming hulk of the plane, wanting to cry but not able to. She had never felt so desolate and miserable as she had that night.

Even remembering it now, lying under a hot Mediterranean sun over two years later, she felt the dull ache of misery in her, and she opened her eyes again to squint up at the sky. I'll be able to sleep here, be able to rest. It's not like work at all, here. It's all right. And Molly's fine, and soon, surely there'll be letters, and a long one from her? There must be. It's been almost six weeks and I haven't heard a word and until I do I won't sleep, even here where there are no guns and no low-flying planes and no urgent shouts in the night, night after dreary night.

Behind her there was a faint tinkle of a bell and she turned her head and there, its jaws grinding superciliously, was a goat. It stared at her with haughty eyes, then walked away with mincing little steps that set its bell tinkling gently. Lexie laughed suddenly and rolled on to her belly to lie on the turf with her chin propped on her fists, staring down at the sweep of the hill below her and the sea beyond, letting her senses wallow in it all. The scent of the herbs, even with a faint, musky overlay of goat, was delicious, and the heat on her back through her thin army-issue shirt was like a blessing. All she could hear was the roar of silence, that ringing in her own ears that she had not heard for so long a time, interrupted only occasionally by the buzz of an insect or an

296

even more distant goat bell, and again she laughed.

The world had gone mad. She had seen bombs that gouged great holes out of the desert to send a shower of shattered cars and men and tents over vast areas. She had seen men lying in hospital beds, so drugged to relieve the pain of their injuries that they seemed unaware of the fact that a real person was standing in the middle of their ward singing to them. She had seen planes fall out of the sky in great waves of smoke and flame – but all the time there had been this place, this patch of green and broken stones and butterflies and goats, high above the sea on Cyprus. Apollo's Temple is here and always has been, yet we shoot each other and fight and scream, and my child is so far away from me I can't really believe she exists any more.

She got to her feet then, brushing down her khaki slacks to get rid of the shreds of grass before setting off at a swinging march down the hill, back towards the base. It was getting hotter now, and anyway there was a show this afternoon. This place might feel like a rest cure after the hell of Tobruk, but it was still a naval base, and there was work for her to do. A show this afternoon for the ratings, then one tonight for the officers, and another tomorrow for the townspeople who would come pouring out of Limassol and the villages into the base to sit and chatter and breathe garlic at each other and watch her dance. She laughed at the thought. What did they care for the tango and the tap–dancing routines and the romantic dreamy numbers that made up the act now? They had been devised to please men far from home lost in a nostalgic yearning for suburban streets and cinemas and Ginger Rogers. Could they offer anything to people who had Apollo's Temple on their doorsteps and who lived under this burning blue sky? Again she laughed, a little grimly this time, and told herself not to be so stupid. She had work to do, and to hell with the audiences for which she did it.

Dave Calleff was sitting on a wooden chair against a whitewashed wall, his head thrown back and his face wreathed in a beatific grin as he lifted it to the sun. He opened his eyes into a squint as she came up to the door of the billet and grinned.

'Nice turn up for the book this one, eh, ducks? Beats bleedin' Sidi Barrani, and no error. Not a bloody gun for miles, as far as I can tell. A right cushy number, and I'm told they've got a bleedin' banquet for us tonight after the show. The officers here don't do bad, I'll tell you. Roast lamb they're givin' us, a whole bleedin' roast lamb, done over a bonfire. Bos'n of the *Predator* told me, and reckons we're in for a great night. Officers here really are officers – none of your palsy-walsy stuff like the Eighth Army – '

'Lovely,' she said. 'I'll look forward to it. Have you been to see if there's any post?'

'Tonight, lovey.' Dave closed his eyes again. 'Went down this morning, I did. There's a supplies plane due in while we're working. They'll bring anything coming to us down to the nosh up.' He grinned, still keeping his eyes closed. 'Got a birthday, lovey? That's what it is, is it? Waiting for your pretty cards?'

Dave never had any real mail: he had a wife long since abandoned somewhere on the road during one of his pre-war tours, and grown-up children who had hardly known him and now cared too little for him to write letters. The most he ever got was a scribbled postcard from an old pro, and when he did he would sit and natter for as long as anyone would listen to him of the old days at the Leeds Empire and the Met down Edgware Road when old Stubby and Joe the seal trainer had tied on a big one. Lexie, recognizing the desperation of loneliness when she met it, would listen and say nothing when he jeered at her for her anxiety over her own mail. When you have no one to worry about, she told herself, people who do become enviable.

Yet hers wasn't an enviable position to be in. She ached for Molly, yearned for her in a way that she found startling. The scrappiest of letters from her would be enough to illuminate a week or more. She would carry the letters in her shirt pocket or tucked down her brassière under her spangled costumes and they warmed her as though they had been actual burning coals, even the most meagre of them. She often thought of Bessie when she read the letters, remembering the sort she used to write to Bessie during the first war, and how long and chatty Bessie's had been in reply. Like mine are now, she told herself, and felt the stab of her own young cruelty as keenly as if she had been Bessie herself.

She did all she could to make up to Bessie now, writing her letters as long and as amusing as she could make them, and greatly valuing the long screeds Bessie sent back – when they arrived, that was – but still, it didn't make up for the pain she now felt as Molly's thin missives came fluttering out of Barbara's envelopes. Thank God for Barbara, at least, who told her in faithful detail of all Molly's doings. Lexie was grateful to her, even when the news she gave, written so artlessly and honestly that it was clear Barbara had no idea what she was telling Lexie about her daughter, was so alarming.

And it often was. Molly, moving through her teens, now almost sixteen, spending so much time with the stage director, a man of thirty with a taste for Gin and It in any quantity he could get. Molly being sent flowers and even, amazingly, in these days of desperate shortages, chocolates by men in the audience who followed her about from performance to performance. Molly going to parties at local army camps and aerodromes and being escorted back to her billet by good-looking young men. Barbara's letters prattled on about it all, and Lexie felt her chest constrict as she read it. Please, she thought now, as she made her way to the tarpaulin-covered space which was their makeshift stage, please, when the post comes tonight, let there be a letter, and let it tell me that Molly's all right. That she's still a child and not – that she's a child, my Molly, still a child.

The afternoon performance was fun and she enjoyed it, to her own amazement. For a long time now dancing had been a chore, singing an effort. The old days when work had been all that mattered, when giving a better show, getting on, being a star, had been so essential, seemed an eternity away. She had forgotten the marvellous excitement of having a happy audience that concentrated entirely on her instead of listening with one ear cocked for enemy planes or guns. She had forgotten it was possible for an audience to be relaxed and happy, to applaud wholeheartedly, to enjoy a performance for its own sake rather than for what it reminded them about. The sailors stationed here in this quiet backwater of the war were a cheerful lot, well aware of their good fortune in being here, and dancing for them was actually a delight.

It was a delight that lasted, too. After the show she went back to her billet, slept dreamlessly for three hours and woke refreshed and actually eager for the performance that was to come. She hadn't felt like that for ages – she couldn't remember how long it had been – and some of her old ambitions lifted in her unexpectedly. I'm going home. It's time I went home. I won't sign on for another overseas stint. I'll go into a West End show. I've earned it. The raids have eased up, they say. London's all right again, or nearly all right. Certainly it's not as bad as North Africa has been. I'll go home again, see Cocky.

She found time to press her costumes, which had become rather more than a little bedraggled, put on her make-up with real care rather than the usual slapdash haste, and knowing she looked good made her give a better performance than she had for many months. She knew just how good she was as she drifted across the expanse of the makeshift stage with Larry's thumping piano accompaniment doing its best for her, knew the effect she was having on the rows of attentive officers sitting there in the glimmering darkness under a sky so heavily dusted with stars that it looked as though it had been frosted, for the waves of approval, even love, that came to her from them washed over her and made her lighter than ever. She danced and sang and then danced again, and when at the end the men got to their feet to shout and whoop and stamp for her she knew she had given a performance that deserved their ovation. She stood very still in her pool of light, thrown by a lorry parked alongside the stage, with her head up, as Larry thumped away cheerfully at the piano and the men in the darkness there before her poured their adoration at her feet, and she knew her ambition had not completely died. This was what she had always wanted. This was what living was for.

Somewhere behind her she could hear a muffled conversation, even though the noise from out front was so tremendous, and she turned her head to look, peering into the wings made by the folds of tarpaulin. There was a young officer standing there, his head bent over some notes. Then, as he caught her eye, he came out on to the stage a little awkwardly and held up his hands to the audience.

'Gentlemen, gentlemen, please! A moment, please!' Slowly the applause slackened and the noise level dropped. The young lieutenant grinned at her, his face sweating under the lights, and then lifted his chin and spoke again to the audience.

'Listen, you chaps, give a man a chance! I've got to introduce the skipper, so that he can do the honourable! Do shut up!'

Lexie laughed as there were a few more whoops and shouts, then at last the audience was captured and the sweating young man began to read from his prepared notes. He talked of how delighted he and the lower-deck chaps had been to be given such a wizard show by such a lovely star as Miss Asher, of how lucky they'd all been to have a special performance, and how much the senior officers wanted to thank her too – and went on to introduce the representative of the 'chaps with all the scrambled egg on their sleeves' to offer his thanks too.

'Gentlemen, be silent, if you please, for our skipper, who has a few things of his own to say. Miss Asher, gentlemen – Commander Cramer!'

# 34

'Dolmades,' Max said. 'Vine leaves stuffed with meat and rice. Will you have some more?'

'No,' she said. 'Thanks. I just wondered what they were called.' She pushed at the food on her plate with her fork, trying to behave as though she were hungry, as though everything was normal and that she could eat just like everyone else.

'You'll have to try the lamb when they bring it,' he said. 'Greeks get very upset if you refuse their food. And it really is delicious.' He leaned across to pour some more wine into her glass and she felt his sleeve brush her bare shoulder, and it was as though she had been stung.

The table stretched away on each side of her, lined with young men chattering and shouting and laughing and eating and drinking as fast as they could, and she felt a stab of anger. She could have enjoyed this, could have been sitting here at the centre of their attention, flirting a little, laughing and eating as cheerfully as they were, but all she could do was feel the tightness in her throat that made her want to get up and run away into the darkness, down towards the sea that lay on the other side of the stretch of beach where their celebration was being held. But she couldn't get up and run because if

301

she did she knew her knees would give beneath her.

'Did you know I was coming here?' she said abruptly, not looking at him.

'Yes.'

'When did you know?'

'The signal came ten days ago. They said you'd had a rough time in North Africa, been with the Eighth Army through all the worst of it, and that you'd had a bad ride. Needed a rest, and we were to look after you. Are you all right, Lexie? You look wonderful.'

She ignored his concern completely, fanning the small flame of anger that was lurking deep inside her.

'Then you could have found me and talked to me any time this last three days. Why wait till tonight? Why be so dramatic about it?'

His laughter bubbled clearly under the hubbub that surrounded them. 'Actresses aren't the only people with a taste for the dramatic. I'm a lawyer, remember? All that courtroom stuff – we're quite good at it.'

'So you were just amusing yourself?'

'No,' he said after a moment. 'No. I thought it would be safer.'

This time she did look at him, briefly. 'Safer?'

'You'd have to stand there with me, there on the stage. Couldn't run away. Not in front of several hundred men –'

'Why should I run away?'

'Why did you last time?'

She caught her breath sharply and he put out one hand and set it on her arm. 'You did run away, Lexie. You didn't give me a chance to sort it all out, to talk to you, find out what you wanted, to – to explain –'

She jerked her arm away. 'Tell me about your wife.'

It was as though she had slapped him, even though he didn't move, still sitting there with his hand on her arm, his fingers warm against her bare skin, for he seemed to recoil from her. There was a silence and then he picked up his fork and began quietly and methodically to eat.

'A calm person. Very quiet, but fun. A sense of humour that could surprise people. It often surprised me. Hard-working. Kind. What more can I say about her? You'd have liked her. She was a likeable person.'

She frowned then. 'Was?' she said uncertainly.

302

'Yes,' he said equably, and ate another dolmades. 'She was killed in a raid in '41. She'd been ambulance-driving in the East End and went right into the middle of an incident. They told me it was almost certainly a direct hit. I hope so.'

'I'm sorry,' she said, and closed her eyes for a moment. 'I'm so sorry. That must have been dreadful for you.'

'Yes,' he said and put down his fork. 'Yes. It was a tragedy. She was forty, just. The same age as you. Almost exactly. Her birthday was in February – just a couple of weeks after yours.' She caught the glimmer of his eyes in the light of the charcoal fire over which the lambs were roasting in front of the long table, and felt her own eyes get hot and sandy with unshed tears for a woman she'd never known, who had taken her place with this man.

'It's all right, you know,' he said gently. 'I can talk about it now. It's been three years, you see. You can learn to live with anything. I learned to live without you. I've learned to live without Laura.'

'Did you have children?' She had meant the question to be a kind one, an interested query, no more, but it came out harshly and she bit her lip, but he wasn't looking at her now. His head was bent as he stared at his plate.

'No,' he said after a long moment. 'No. That was the real tragedy for Laura. She wanted children very much, but there it was – sometimes I think it was better for her that she died when she did. To have gone on, into her older years, without children – she'd have been very unhappy about that.'

'And you?' She shouldn't have asked, she didn't want to ask, but the question couldn't be held back. 'Does it make you unhappy?'

'Yes,' he said, making no attempt to disguise the depth of feeling there was in him. 'Yes, dreadfully unhappy. I always wanted children.' He looked at her then. 'You knew that, didn't you? How much I wanted children?'

She shook her head.

'You must have done.' He said it almost angrily, startling her a little. 'You must have known it was part of how – oh, well, it doesn't matter now, I suppose. But it was part of –' He grinned suddenly. 'I used to see her, you know. Our daughter. It was always a daughter I imagined, somehow, to start with. Then there'd be boys, I thought – ridiculous, isn't it? I sound like *Home Chat* magazine. Tell me about you,

303

Lexie. More than I know already, I mean. I've watched your career, of course – read about you in the American magazines. You were hugely successful, weren't you? You deserved to be. I thought I knew how good you were, but tonight – I really saw tonight what it was you had. Still have. You danced like an angel tonight, Lexie.'

She was staring at him, not hearing his words, just watching his face moving in the glow of the charcoal fires, and trying to see Molly in it. He had wanted a daughter, she thought. He wanted a daughter and there's Molly, and she's part of him just as she is of me, and she should be there in his face, and for a moment she thought she saw her there, almost saw that eager expression that had been so much a part of small Molly, growing up on the West Side of Manhattan. But then the image faded and she could only remember the closed little face that had stared at her over folded arms in Bessie's living room at Victoria Park Road the last time she had seen her. There was none of that watchful stubbornness she remembered in Molly in Max's face now, none of her self-absorption. He was interested in her, Lexie, not in himself as he talked on about articles he'd read about her, showing how eagerly he had collected news of her during the long years while she had lived and worked in New York. Suddenly she wanted to put out her hands, to touch him as he had touched her, to tell him everything that was in her, of the loneliness of those long years, of Molly and Barbara and –

It took a physical effort not to do it, and she sat with her hands tightly clasped in her lap as he talked. She was grateful when the waiters who were serving their meal came bouncing round the table, following one of their number who was bearing a great platter of steaming, fragrant roast lamb while they played bazouki music and sang at the tops of their voices. The men sitting round the long table began to applaud, banging their knives on their glasses and Max made a face and gave up trying to talk. He couldn't compete with the din and she was grateful for that, for she could turn away and concentrate on separating herself from him.

It was all still there, that was the trouble. The old comfort she had found with him, the old certainty that he was interested in her, really interested in her for herself, and not for what he might get out of her.

He was exciting in a way she had forgotten he could be. In

the years that had elapsed between that October afternoon beside the Thames at Maidenhead and this dark May night on a beach in Cyprus there had been many men who had wanted her, who had looked at her with that dark gleam in their eyes that showed how much she stirred them. There had been men she had danced with and dined with, men she had laughed with and men she had enjoyed talking with, but there had never been one who had made her flesh move on her bones the way this man could. Her reputation on Broadway as untouched and untouchable had been rooted in reality, unlike many Broadway labels. She had really not been interested in sex, and for a while had even thought that she was completely unlike other women in that she didn't need passion. But then she had wondered, when she thought of the matter at all, whether she had in some way transformed her feelings from one kind of wanting to another. She had wanted success as eagerly as some women wanted to be kissed and caressed. For her the excitement of being greeted with a huge roar of approval from an audience was a greater exhilaration than being greeted with a surge of need in just one man's loins. Why waste energy on one man, she had asked herself sometimes, when I can control a theatre full of them, when I can meld several hundred separate individuals into one great yearning creature with one great yearning desire – to love me? Who needs lovers when they have what I have?

So she had thought till tonight, sitting at a trestle table covered with bed sheets and decorated with rough pottery plates and thick glass tumblers, eating peasant food served in peasant style under a Mediterranean sky, surrounded by a horde of half-drunk naval officers. So she had thought until she had seen Max Cramer's face again with the deep clefts that split his cheeks into familiar planes and the thick dust-coloured hair that shaped itself to his head so neatly. He looked older yet unchanged, the same yet totally different, and she ached for him and trembled for him and was amazed at the strength of her own feelings.

The noise eased a little as the lamb was served and the young men began to eat. She tried to eat too as the man on her other side, a Surgeon Commander, began to talk to her, and slowly she regained control of herself. It had been a bad moment that, she told herself, a bad moment. I almost told him about Molly. I almost told him.

Later, waking yet again from her fitful sleep to lie staring up at the low ceiling of the small whitewashed room she had been given at the taverna, listening to Dave Calleff's snores coming from the adjoining room, she thought suddenly – why? Why am I so worried about telling him? Would it be so terrible to tell the truth now, after so long? He wants a daughter, and God knows Molly needs a father. Perhaps it would be the best thing for everyone if I did tell him, let him know what he had always wanted was available?

She drifted into a half waking, half sleeping fantasy in which she told Max about his daughter and Molly about her father, and they both came hurrying back from their wartime wanderings so that they could throw their arms around each other's necks and come to live with Lexie in a small house somewhere near the Park. Hyde Park, not Victoria Park, she told herself, watching the scene she was creating grow behind her closed lids. Hyde Park, in a perfect little white house, and Bessie and Barbara will live with us and we'll all be happy together, Max and Molly and me – and the scene behind her lids changed, became a stage, and she was dancing in the middle of it, in a skirt made of myriad layers of the most delicate tulle, floating in a dance that was all grace and spun sugar delicacy as she sang – Max and Molly and Me – just Max and Molly and Me –

The next time she woke it was daylight, the sun already slanting across the mass of blue-green sea grass that fringed the beach across the road from the taverna, and she sat on the windowsill staring out at the gently heaving sea licking the sandy shingle and knew herself for a fool. As if she could tell Molly she had a father when she didn't even know who her mother was! That's the real problem I've got to deal with when I get home. I've got to tell her. She's old enough now, she won't be as hurt as she would have been if I'd told her when she was six or ten or twelve. Sixteen – she's almost grown-up.

I've got to go home and tell her. After that, I can think about Max and what I tell him. And she wanted to laugh, suddenly, sitting there curled up on a windowsill in her shabby silk pyjamas which showed in every seam the rigours of the past two years of travel, and plotting how to rebuild relationships she had once deliberately destroyed. Why do I always get it wrong? I got it wrong with Max, timed it all wrong. I got it all wrong with Molly, too. I had him and I lost him and now I want him. I had her and I gave her away and now I want her. I can time a dance, why can't I time my own life?

She hadn't remembered how much it hurt to cry – it had been so long since she had done it. It hurt dreadfully, making her eyes burn and her chest feel tight and her belly like cold lead. But though it hurt, it helped. For a little while.

# 35

They had told her that she and Dave and Larry Peters, the accompanist, would probably be on their way home from Cyprus within a week of getting there, arriving in London some time at the end of the first week in June, but then suddenly all that changed.

She was doing a show for the whole base, both ratings and officers, including some different numbers but mostly the stuff they'd already seen and were delighted to see again, when she became aware that there was some activity in the audience. Even while she danced one of her most vigorous numbers, a jazz affair that made her head snap round so that the whole stage and auditorium swirled in her eyes, she could see what was happening: messengers coming to whisper in the ears of the senior officers sitting in the front rows, and then people getting up and leaving. At first she was irritated, and then alarmed. In North Africa that sort of behaviour had always meant trouble on the way – a German attack, perhaps.

But it wasn't a German attack, she discovered. Indeed it was quite the reverse. As soon as she was off-stage and had changed and cleaned off her make-up there was a messenger waiting to take her to Max Cramer.

'Developments, miss,' the seaman said in response to her demand for news of what was going on. 'Don't know no more'n that, I'm afraid. Developments. But I dare say

Commander Cramer'll know. 'E said to bring you as fast as I could.'

The big room he took her to was alive with people and sparking with excitement. It was a little while before Max could detach himself from the group of officers with whom he was talking, heads down over a big map, but he caught her eye and grinned at her, a huge excited grin, and for a moment she felt a lift of delight in his pleasure and grinned back as widely. And then she thought – is it over? Is this why they're all in such a state of barely controlled excitement? Is the war over?

'Invasion,' Max said when at last he came over to where she stood just inside the door of the big operations room. 'At last, the second front. Not a word to anyone, for God's sake, but it's scheduled for the next few days. France. We've got to send support vessels, and – well, anyway, it's going to be as hectic here as it's never been. We've had it too cushy for far too long and now it won't be cushy any more, thank God. But it means you're stuck here for a while. We can't send any ship out of here except to the invasion area – at least not for a week or two. There's no hope of air transport, the way things are. Can you just settle for a rest? I doubt there'll be much chance for shows – once we really get going every man's going to be hard pressed to find time to eat and sleep, let alone get any recreation. It'll be a bit dull for you.'

'Dull?' she cried, jubilantly. 'Dull? It's the most exciting thing – oh, thank God! This bloody war really could be over by Christmas – they've said that so often, and now it could be true.'

He nodded. 'It's going well in Italy, too. Your Eighth Army is well on the way.'

'My Eighth Army!' She laughed then, feeling the absurdity of it. 'They're not mine, bless 'em – though I spent enough time with them to feel I was theirs – oh, Max, will it be all right? No more bombs at home, no more need to worry about Bessie and Barbara and –'

She stopped, just in time. She'd nearly said Molly's name.

'No more bombs,' he'd said, grinning at her again so that his face slipped into the familiar clefts, and she wanted to reach up and touch his cheek and had to clench her fists in her pockets. 'You can sleep well at night and stop fretting. Bessie'll be fine –' He frowned then and said interrogatively,

'Barbara?' but she ignored that, and began to ask eager questions about the likely progress of the invasion. France? Where in France? Would it work at once, did he think? Would they get a foothold fast enough to send the Germans running back to Berlin? Was it just a British operation or would the Americans be in on it? Where exactly were they going to land? And –

He laughed and told her she'd have to contain her curiosity as best she might. As soon as news was available she'd get it – and now go to bed. Everyone had work to do and she was in the way, and that was the last thing they needed.

She obeyed at once. Her long trailing round North Africa with the army had filled her with as much discipline as any of the soldiers she'd entertained. She left the big map room buzzing with its barely contained exuberance and drama to go back to the taverna and an attempt to sleep.

But she slept poorly that night, and indeed for several nights after, as the base slid into full gear. Ships moved in and out of the harbour so fast that she couldn't keep up with what was going on, and the men stopped being the friendly chattering companions she'd become used to and became abstracted and too busy for conversation. She would spend long hours sitting up in the middle of the ruins of Apollo's Temple with her arms clasped round her knees, staring at the sea below and all the activity, trying to imagine what was happening at home in London.

News came at the end of the week that the local weather in France had held the invasion over from its originally planned date of 31 May, and the next week was agony for all of them. The shipping movement had eased now, with most of the base's complement already away, ready to provide whatever back-up they were scheduled to offer in the cold waters of the English Channel. Lexie stared at the horizon as the days limped away in a vain attempt to imagine what was going on there, aching for news, sometimes almost crying with the anxiety and the sickening tension of hope deferred.

And then, late in the afternoon of 6 June the news came and spread round the base with the speed and crackle of a newly lit fire. It had been Normandy, no it hadn't, yes, it was, they were in, it was all on its way, a beachhead had been established, it hadn't been established, the British were alone, no they weren't, there were Canadians and Americans too, they were six miles from the coast, they were still on the beaches – and then at last as real news began to filter through and the reality hit them the camp settled to a strange stillness.

She sat in the NAAFI canteen, clutching a cup of thick black Bovril in both hands, and watched the few men who were free to come there sitting in silent groups, worrying and hoping for the news to keep on coming, to be good, to be a real promise of the end of the war. The five years they'd already been through seemed to hang over them all as it never had before; they were tired, everyone was tired and emotional and yet controlled. She gazed into the inky depths of her Bovril and wanted, again, to cry. It had to work, this invasion, this second front. It had to.

She saw nothing of Max as the days crept by, and she was both aggrieved and grateful for that. One part of her wanted to be with him very much indeed, She had to work hard at preventing herself from going over to the big operations room where he spent all his time now. I've done without him all these years, she would tell herself furiously as she went striding about the base, in aimless search of exercise. I've never needed him or any other man all this time. I'm free, I'm independent – I don't want him.

But the ever-present little voice would laugh at her, would jeer and sneer. Oh, don't you? Then why are you getting yourself into such a state? If you don't need him, why do you see his face all the time, why can't you get him out of your mind? You're no better than any one of those stupid girls you used to sneer at, no better. You've got the same itch in you they had. You're just another candidate for the farmyard, just another stupid female – just a besotted –

I'm not, she would protest passionately, staring at the road beneath her feet as she walked. I'm not. I'm a dancer, I have a career. I'm not interested in just being domestic – and the little voice would jeer back, liar. You're a liar, and not a very good one at that. Liar.

So she was grateful that she could not see him. If she had been with him, she told herself as the days tightened into a fortnight, hobbled on to become a month, if I had, God knows what would happen. I'd stop thinking for me, I'd start thinking for him as well and that would be dreadful.

Dreadful? whispered the little voice. Why dreadful? Would it be dreadful for Molly? What about her? Isn't it time she

310

knew she had two parents? Two real parents? When are you going to face it, Lexie? You've been a fool. You should never have let it happen and now you've got to do something about it.

For the first time she had good cause to be glad that she had so long to think. As the long hours dragged past she found it all shaping in her mind. She would find Molly as soon as she got home to England and be candid with her. It would be painful and difficult, but she would tell her and beg her forgiveness. Then she would tell her of her father. That was what she would do, she promised herself as the days got hotter and the scent of flowers and herbs thickened until it filled every corner of the base. That will make her forgive me. Won't it?

The one person she tried not to think about was Barbara. How she would feel about Molly being told that the person she had always regarded as her mother was no more than a cousin didn't bear thinking about.


When the news came that there was a berth on a ship, that she would be on her way home to England within twenty-four hours, her first thought was to find Max, bid him goodbye, make a plan to see him again as soon as he too returned to London – which surely couldn't be long now? The success of the invasion had filled them all with the certainty that the war was at last counting out its last days. Soon all of them would be going home, starting real life again. But he was off the base, and no one could – or would – tell her where he was. 'Official business' was the most the senior officer in command would say, and she had to accept that. She wrote a short note to tell him she was on her way home and that she'd be living at the old address with Bessie. 'Perhaps,' she wrote rather stiffly, 'you'll call on us when you get home leave. Yours sincerely –'

The journey home seemed infinitely longer than the weeks she had spent in Cyprus, for now she was going back her impatience grew and spread through her till it was like a physical thing, an itch she couldn't scratch. As the elderly frigate went lurching and rolling through the Med and then bucketed across the Bay of Biscay she fretted and fumed and became so bad-tempered that even good-natured Dave avoided her.

Then at last the morning came when she left her berth in the cramped quarters deep in the ship and came up on to the wet deck to see land on each side as they slid slowly up the Bristol Channel. It was a cold blustery morning. She pulled her coat up to her ears against the rain and leaned on the dripping rail, staring out at the dull greyness passing her in the faint mist, and for the first time realized how lucky she had been. All that time in North Africa, working in gunfire and bombs, culminating in the long journey just behind her through a Mediterranean infested with German shipping during which they had seen and heard nothing remotely dangerous, and here she was, whole and unhurt. Suddenly she was deeply and passionately grateful.

I'm here, she thought jubilantly. I'm home, and it's all right – it's nearly over and I'm all right. She wanted to thank someone and didn't know who. Religion had never played any real part in her life, but standing on the deck of a shabby frigate as it made its slow way up the Bristol Channel on that wet June morning in her forty-third year she felt a need to be grateful, and in a muddled way put some sort of prayer together, aiming it she didn't know where, feeling it necessary to do so none the less. Then, sharply and unexpectedly, she felt a stab of acute guilt. All those years when I thought only of me, she told the passing green smudge of the bank. All those years when I just danced and pushed and wanted and danced some more, and now I'm safe. And Molly and Barbara and the way I've treated them – I've no right to be so lucky.

Her self-critical mood lasted well into the day, saw her all through the noise and confusion of their landing at Bristol, through the tedium of the port authorities' red tape, right on to the train to London. The parting with Dave Calleff had been surprisingly emotional. He was on his way north to Leeds, where he had friends, he said vaguely, who'd help him get a nice little place in a nice little show somewhere, sure to want an old trouper like him. She had hugged him and seen him on his way, her eyes hot with regret for the parting, and then had made her way to her own train to sit for the long hours it took to amble through the drenched fields and dripping trees to London.

Larry left her, too, choosing to stay in Bristol for a while.

'I've had enough travel to last me a bloody month of Sundays,' he told her before disappearing into the crowds at the station. 'I'm off to find a pub somewhere and I'll not come out till Christmas. 'Bye ducks. Keep your powder dry.' And now she sat in a corner seat staring out of the grimy windows at the rain, past the strips of peeling anti-splinter paper that were criss-crossed over them, and tried to see how it would be when she got there. Bessie – where would Bessie be? At home? At Alex Lazar's office? I'll phone as soon as we get to Paddington. She laughed aloud because the word sounded so commonplace, so blessedly ordinary after the place names that had been so much a part of her life for so long. Tobruk and Cairo, Tripoli and Sidi Barrani and Limassol and Apollo's Temple.

London felt odd, decidedly odd. She stood in the middle of the eddying crowds on the concourse of Paddington Station, smelling the reek of oil and soot, listening to the steam hissing and grumbling behind her and stared round, bemused and lost. I'm home, she thought, I'm home. But no one seems to care, no one seems to have noticed.

And why should they? she asked herself as sturdily as she could, humping her kitbag on to her shoulder as she looked round for a vacant telephone booth. Why should they? It's only me – I may have been away on a battlefield for all this time, but they've not had a marvellous time either, looking at them. For the people who moved past her were tired people; faces looked grey and pinched and tight with irritation, and the voices she heard weren't the familiar old jovial ones that had been so much a part of her London before she left. People were bad-tempered, snapping at each other, pushing past rudely when once they'd have lifted their hats and stood aside, and she frowned sharply as someone shoved past her and sent her rocking on her heels without a word of apology.

There was no answer from the telephone in Alex Lazar's office, and as she stood in the stuffy little telephone box listening to the burr of the ringing she felt suddenly old and tired and very, very lonely, and tears stung her eyelids. I'm home and no one knows and no one cares, she thought, as she recradled the phone and pressed button B to get her money back. I'm home and who gives a damn? With a savage little gesture she scooped the two pennies out of the machine and went to spend them on a cup of tea at the buffet while she

313

waited until Bessie was likely to have reached Hackney.

She bought a paper, too, and that was when she discovered why everyone looked so strained and grey, why London, far from being full of relief and excitement because the invasion was going so well, was more tense than it had been even at the height of the blitz.

Doodlebugs they were calling them, though their real label was V1 rockets. With a gradually deepening sense of dismay, Lexie read of the effects of Hitler's last despairing attempt to win this war, of the way the things came overhead roaring ominously and then, even more ominously, fell suddenly silent, making people stare fearfully upwards as they prayed that this time the thing would fall on someone else, not on them.

That was the worst part of it all, said the article she was reading. In the first blitz we all worried about each other as well as ourselves, the reporter wrote. This time we put our own skins in front of someone else's. Not British at all, he scolded. Not British at all. We must be as brave and caring as we were in 1941, he went on. Soon Monty and his chaps will break through to the Pas de Calais and get rid of the wretched things' launching pads. Soon he'll be as pushy as he ever was in the Desert Rats campaign – just hold on, London – the journalist became rhetorical and bombastic – hold on and be your old courageous self! We'll get through this last convulsion. Relief will come soon.

She dropped the paper in the salvage bin and went to try the phone again. Home, she told herself as she joined the queue that was waiting for the kiosk. I'm home and I'm not sure why I was so eager to get here. She grimaced at herself and shifted her heavy kitbag from one shoulder to the other. There you go again, being ungrateful. This morning you were praying to say thank you, and now you're moaning. Will you ever know what you want, Alexandra Asher? Will you ever get yourself sorted out?

# 36

'I can't believe it,' Bessie said again. 'I just can't believe it! I kept thinking, hoping, I'll get a telegram, a message maybe, but I never thought you'd just arrive this way. It's marvellous. Oh, Lexie, it is marvellous, isn't it?' She stood there on the doorstep staring at her, and Lexie laughed and gently pushed her backwards.

'It'd be even more marvellous if you let me come in,' she said. 'It's cold here on the doorstep. I don't think it's ever going to stop raining.'

Bessie was at once thrown into a fever of apologies and fuss as she ushered Lexie into the house and hurried her up the stairs, chattering breathlessly all the time of how amazed she was to see Lexie and that was why she'd kept her standing there on the step, until Lexie was at last detached from her coat and kitbag and settled into the biggest armchair and Bessie was bustling about in her kitchen making tea and shouting through the open door.

'I tried and tried to get news of you, but even Mr Lazar couldn't tell me any more than you were on Cyprus and all right, and no one knew when you'd get away, what with the invasion and all.'

She appeared in the doorway and waved the teapot at Lexie, her face red with excitement. 'And what do you think about that, then? It's nearly all over, now, should be over by Christmas, that's what they're all saying. Mr Lazar reckons it'll be a bit longer than that, but he says it's all over bar the shouting.' She disappeared again as the sound of the kettle's whistle began and the smell of toasting bread came creeping out of the kitchen. Lexie leaned back in the chair and took a deep sigh of relief.

Last night had been dismal. She'd gone to one of the small hotels that clung dispiritedly to the skirts of Paddington Station to spend the night in a dingy room which smelled of damp and which offered lumpy cold beds, and had slept little. Call after call to Bessie's flat all through the evening had failed to raise her and Lexie had been frightened for a

315

while, wondering where she could be; hurt in one of these new doodlebug explosions perhaps? That didn't bear thinking about. She must just be out for the evening, she told herself at eleven o'clock. I'll call her in the morning. She had slept fitfully and uneasily until six-thirty and had then had had to get up. She couldn't bear the grimy, miserable hotel another moment and had decided on impulse to take an early bus and go straight to Hackney instead of waiting to telephone.

The sight of Bessie on the doorstep in her dressing gown, staring at her incredulously, had more than made up for the misery of her first night back in London after so long. Now she sat with her head back against the familiar old armchair, dreamily staring up at the even more familiar pattern of cracks on the ceiling, and let herself really relax.

Bessie came hurrying in with the tea and toast and, she proudly pointed out to Lexie, a pot of real marmalade, for which she'd had to save ration points for weeks.

'It'll hide the taste of the margarine,' she said cheerfully as she poured the tea. 'It gets more like axle grease every day. People think I can get black market and all that, just because of the tea shops, but you know Alex Lazar – no hanky panky for him, specially now he's working for the government. He's marvellous, he really is, the way he keeps going. Seventy-six he was, the other day! You'd never think it to see him. He's all over the place – now, tell me about you. Where've you been and what have you done, and what did the–'

'Lots of time for that,' Lexie said. 'Bessie, how are they? Molly and Barbara? Are they well? Where are they?'

Bessie sipped her tea, throwing an anxious glance at Lexie over the rim of her cup. She seemed to be pondering a decision, and then to reach it, for she put her cup down and said firmly, 'In Scotland. That's where they are. They're fine – but they're in Scotland.'

Lexie felt her belly plunge sharply with disappointment. 'Scotland? Ye Gods, what are they doing there? It's the back of beyond–'

'And the rest,' Bessie said, and pushed the toast towards Lexie. 'Eat, Lexie, already. You look as thin as a rail. You need your food – it's good marmalade.'

'What are they *doing* there?'

316

'It's a show. Not an ENSA one – they stopped doing that a while ago, once the managements got into action again. She's doing ever so well, Lexie. Barbara says it's amazing to see how they eat her up. Even the difficult audiences go mad for her. She's really very good, Barbara says. I wish I could see her –' And she looked wistful for a moment. 'It's funny, isn't it? I could never see you in your shows in the first war, and now in this one –' Her voice dwindled away and there was a little silence between them.

'Yes,' Lexie said after a moment. 'Yes, it – Bessie, I know now. And I'm sorry.'

Bessie's forehead creased and she looked anxiously at Lexie. 'Know? Know what?'

'I treated you badly. I know now just how awful I was in those years when I just didn't – well, I dare say I could have got to London sometimes, while we were doing *Babies on Parade*, but somehow – I just –'

Bessie had gone very red and Lexie stared at her and suddenly saw beyond the thin lined face and the wispy grey hair tied into curling papers to the Bessie of her childhood. She'd always thought of her as a plain dull little thing. Just Bessie, dear old familiar Bessie, but not handsome as Fanny had been or richly ripe like Poppy Ganz. She'd just been old Bessie, but now Lexie saw the shape of the bones beneath the skin. She had lovely eyes, grey-flecked and wide, and the shape of her forehead was broad and pleasing above them. Impulsively Lexie leaned forward and kissed the papery cheek and hugged the narrow bones of Bessie's twisted shoulders.

'It's so good to be back with you, Bessie. I really have missed you and I do love you a lot, you know. I haven't shown it much, and I've treated you awfully badly, but I do love you –'

For a moment Bessie sat rigid, then her shoulders relaxed and she clung to Lexie with an urgency that left them both breathless and then as suddenly as it had come the surge of emotion passed. Lexie was leaning back in her chair again and sipping tea as Bessie, head down, fiddled with her spoon.

'The thing is, they should be back in London very soon,' Bessie said abruptly, covering her embarrassment as best she could. 'I got a letter from Barbara the other day. She says she's coming down this week – there's business things she's got to settle and–'

Lexie sat bolt upright. 'They're coming to London? When? That's wonderful!'

Bessie shook her head. 'I said Barbara's coming to London. Molly can't leave the show. She's the star, you know. Not seventeen yet and she's the star! So when it's business Barbara has to come on her own.'

'What sort of business?' Lexie demanded, and again with increasing uneasiness Bessie shook her head.

'I can't say, really,' she said. 'I mean, Barbara didn't say much–'

'Where's her letter?'

'It's around somewhere,' Bessie said vaguely, but she made no effort to go and look for it and after a moment Lexie nodded. 'I see. It's like last time, isn't it? Secrets. Things I mustn't know.'

'It's not for me to say, Lexie,' Bessie said wretchedly. 'It's awful, it really is, the way I keep getting in between. I never mean to, but it just sort of happens to me. I feel like a walnut sometimes between the crackers. All I want to do is love you all and keep you happy, and all that happens is I get in the way.' She peered agitatedly at Lexie. 'When you went away it was like that, and now here you are, only one day back and here we go, starting it all over again.'

'I'm sorry,' Lexie said after a moment, and again leaned forward and hugged Bessie. 'I suppose you're right. I'm sorry, lovey, I didn't mean to upset you. Just tell me, when will Barbara be here?'

'She wasn't sure – next few days was all she said. She'll phone me as soon as she gets to London. It's so hard these days to plan anything properly – the trains are so bad and–'

'I know,' Lexie said. 'I know. I suppose I'll just have to wait. Maybe, once she gets here, I can arrange to go back to Scotland with her. See Molly there–' And Bessie, relieved, smiled radiantly at her and began to fuss again over her lack of appetite for breakfast.

The waiting days were dreadfully difficult. It wasn't that she had nothing to do; she had a great deal to do, for the flat downstairs needed opening up, needed to be filled with fresh air, to have its windows cleaned and its floors swept and curtains shaken out, and she enjoyed the domesticity. It made her physically tired, which helped her to sleep and pleased Bessie, who nodded happily at the way the lines of fatigue slowly dissolved from her face and her thin frame filled out a little as the meals Bessie insisted on providing each evening had the desired effect.

There were other things she could do, too, like getting back in touch with her own career. She'd been oddly nervous about calling the Cochran office at first, and then had chided herself. She, who had been working so hard and so continuously for so long to be afraid that she wouldn't be wanted any more? Ridiculous! She had sorted out the clothes she had left behind in her wardrobes and chosen the most becoming of her pre-war suits, a smart tailored affair, and perched the most outrageously cheeky of her hats on her head and gone up to the West End to see what was news in the world of entertainment.

It was dispiriting. The theatres were all open again, and had been ever since the first blitz had spluttered to its end. In the last few months the lightening of the blackout to a dimout had given many of them a new lease of life, as audiences came back to the West End aching for a little entertainment to relieve the eternal grinding effort of making war. But in the last few weeks fear had returned again, and though performances went on − with a sign on-stage throughout each show warning audiences there was an 'Alert' (it was rare that anyone had time to post a warning once a doodlebug came) − the audiences were scanty and abstracted, always keeping one ear cocked for the ominous silence that meant a rocket had chosen them for a target.

So, although she was welcomed with open arms wherever she went, and Cockie's office talked optimistically of how they hoped to do all sorts of things once the war actually was over, and though other managements she visited made it very clear that they'd take her like a shot if they put on another show worthy of her talents, the hard fact was that there was no real offer of immediate work. Lexie felt a sudden twinge of fear as she sat in the Savoy having a meagre afternoon tea late one afternoon when she'd been home just over a week. Was this the moment that every performer feared, the moment when the pedestal on which they'd stood and lived and pirouetted for so long began to crumble, when other pedestals threatened to be raised by other stars? Was she to find herself on her way out so soon after working so hard for the war?

She tried to push the idea away, but it clung stubbornly to the edge of her consciousness. She had seen it happen to other dancers, seen the years catch up with them. Couldn't it happen to her? She was, after all, well past forty. Had her time come so soon? For a moment she thought of Max and ached for him, thought of the small house of her Cypriot fantasy, the small white house near Hyde Park, and shivered apprehensively.

But she pulled the shreds of her courage and her dignity about her and went home to Bessie, telling herself not to be such a fool. Once she saw Barbara, really sorted out what was to happen about Molly, she'd get her confidence back. That was all it was, she told herself as her bus went swaying eastwards towards the familiar security of Victoria Park Road. I'm unsettled, can't put my mind to things till I've told Barbara what's to happen. Once I have I'll be fine again.

Because she had made her plan. Barbara was to be told first – that was the only fair way to do it. She owed Barbara a great deal, she knew that, and she was determined Barbara should know how grateful she was. But she was equally determined that the time had come for her to reclaim the daughter she hadn't meant to lose, and even if that hurt Barbara badly, it had to be done.

She had planned the conversation in her head over and over again; how she'd sit down with Barbara and explain to her that she had never meant to use her as she had, that it had just seemed right at the time, but the time has changed.

'I'm blessed in my family,' she would tell Barbara. 'Bessie has been more than a mother to me, and you have been more than a mother to my child. But now it's different, and we have to put it right. Because Molly needs a father, and until she has her mother, that can't be given to her. You do understand, Barbara, don't you?' In her imagination Barbara would smile and nod and say with sweet reasonableness, 'Of course I understand, Lexie, dear, of course I do. I'll stand back and forget all the years when I looked after Molly for you – I'll just be her cousin now, and you can be her mother and –'

But then her imagination would let her down badly, for

the image would shiver and disintegrate and she would hear only Barbara's impassioned voice shrieking at her, 'No! No – you mustn't – you can't – she's mine –'

The uncertainty came to an end at last. One evening, just as they were separating to go to bed, Bessie's phone rang. It was Barbara, and Bessie stood there with her eyes bright as she held the phone pressed to her ear so ferociously that her fingers went white, nodding and crying loudly, 'Yes – yes,' as Lexie stood in a fever of impatience to take the phone from her. But as she seized it from Bessie's hand the line went dead and she literally stamped her foot in her frustration.

'It's all right, Lexie,' Bessie said eagerly. 'Really it is. I got it all from her – I never talk much when she rings because it always happens like that, the line getting cut. It's awful – but she's getting the overnight train from Inverness tomorrow. She should be in London by ten in the morning if they're lucky, and she's going to the Regent Palace Hotel. But she's going first to some business meeting – there's a contract to be signed, she said – and then she'll be at the Regent Palace at about half past twelve. She has to go back to Scotland the same night, so she said I was to meet her there. Only we'll both go, Lexie, shall we? It'll be a great surprise for her, just as it was for me. We'll see her at the hotel the day after tomorrow and then you'll hear about everything. Only another day, Lexie. That's all.'

# 37

A grey day, threatening rain but thick and hot, dewing the hands and face with sweat, so that the air was heavy and oppressive and that matched her mood. As she sat beside Bessie on the bus coming into the West End from Hackney, staring out at the passing streets, she had a sudden memory of herself sitting on another bus and looking out at rain and feeling dreadfully, agonizingly unhappy. Puzzled, she teased at the shred of the image, trying to remember when it had been and why she'd felt so bad; and suddenly it all came back to her. Alf. No, Ambrose. She'd loved him so much, she remembered, gazing out through her own reflection at the crowded pavements of Holborn as the bus trundled on its way. *I loved him so much and I haven't thought of him for years.* She marvelled at how desperately important he had been to her, and how easily she had forgotten him, and felt a sharp stab of sadness at the passage of time.

She'd never worried much about time before, had always been rather scornful of those who frantically denied their real age, and hid from themselves the fact that time was passing with silly stratagems like make-up and clothes. She had always dressed in the way she felt best, not in the way that made her look youngest, and yet here she was now, thinking sadly of her lost youth, grieving over the child who had once sat in a bus in tattered finery and broken her heart over a boy who cared nothing for her.

Remembering Ambrose and the years when they had danced together triggered other memories and she said abruptly, not looking at Bessie but still staring out of the window, 'I wonder what happened to Poppy Ganz? I should have seen her before I went to America, but somehow –'

'Oh, she's doing well enough,' Bessie said. Lexie jerked her head round to stare at her, dumbfounded.

'You know?'

Bessie looked at her in surprise. 'Well, of course I do. I mean, you don't just lose people, do you? Not people you know as well as I know Poppy. I mean, it's been over thirty years, hasn't it? We go back a long way together –'

Lexie shook her head and managed a tight little grin. 'You make me feel really bad sometimes, Bessie, you really do. I lose people all the time, don't I – I sort of lost Poppy –'

'Oh, well, it's different for you,' Bessie said. 'You had your career to think of and all –'

'You had yours too,' Lexie said. 'With Alex.' And suddenly Bessie went rosy pink.

'I never thought of that as a career,' she said, dismissing it, but she sounded pleased all the same. 'It was just a job, to make sure we – just a job.'

'It was a career,' Lexie said. 'Still is. And you kept up with – where is she, then? Poppy? How is she? Well?'

Bessie grinned suddenly. 'I think she's well enough. Tough Poppy Ganz is, always was, but since she had that illness she carries on like she's a real nebbish. Always watching her liver, you know? Clever, I grant you. Meant

322

she got special rations – she's been at Hemel Hempstead, little place out the other side of Watford – for years. Went in 1938, before Munich – said there was goin' to be a war and she wasn't hanging around London to get bombed. There were people who laughed at her, but she wasn't all that wrong, was she? Runs a dancing school there. Does all right, I think. I saw her a year or so ago when she came up to see her sister-in-law, after Lenny died –'

'Lenny Ganz died?' Lexie tried to see back through the years to the sharp-faced little man who had sat there beside her on a rug in Cephas Street, and she frowned. People shouldn't die that easily, she thought with a sudden surge of fear. They shouldn't –

'He left London soon's he could when the war started, went to live in Coventry to be safe, and poor chap got caught in the raids there. Terrible they were. He was injured – broke his back – and he never got over it. Lingered a long time after, but –' Bessie shrugged. 'It was a blessed release when it came.'

Lexie turned her head to look out of the window again. Not far now; another three or four stops and they'd be at Piccadilly Circus and then they'd walk into the Regent Palace Hotel and there would be Barbara and they'd sit down and –

Once more her mind sailed into one of her imagined conversations, and she shook her head at her own reflection and frowned again. There's no sense in this, she told herself. No sense at all. Think of other things. People – all the people who were so important to me, and now where are they? What happened to them all? Are they dead too, like Lenny Ganz?

'Have you heard from anyone else lately?' she asked Bessie abruptly. 'Joe or –'

Bessie made a little face. 'It's all right, Lexie,' she said. 'I mean, you don't have to feel bad because you aren't like me. Not everyone has to be the same – I got the time to write letters and keep up with news. You haven't. It's no sin –'

'It's bloody selfish,' Lexie said with a sort of violence and then managed to smile. 'I am selfish, aren't I, Bessie?'

The bus was at Oxford Circus, now, turning left into Regent Street, and Bessie began to pull on her gloves. Whatever the weather, Bessie always wore gloves in the street. 'Selfish?' she said, and there was a considering note in her voice, as detached as though she were discussing the price of a yard of blackout cloth. 'I wouldn't say that. It's more that you're sort of single-minded, you know? You can't think of too many things at the same time, because when you think about things you think about them very deeply. You were always like that when you were small. If you wanted something there was nothing else in the world. Just what you wanted, and you had to have it. You used to – oh, it's hard to explain.' She looked at Lexie almost shyly. 'You used to make things happen the way you wanted them to happen. Just by being the way you were. It was like – oh, like you had a searchlight in you. It used to pick out what you wanted the way searchlights pick out planes in the sky, and when the light's on the plane you can't see nothing else. Everything else just disappears. You were always like that. Me, I sort of have an ordinary light on all the time so I can see everything, and remember everything. But it don't mean you're bad and I'm good. It just means that you're you and I'm me. That's all –'

The bus stopped at the corner of Glasshouse Street and the conductor called loudly, 'Piccadilly Circus, *Picc*adilly Circus. Alight 'ere for Rainbow Corner and America – you'll find plenty of 'em if you want 'em, the 'ole lot, overpaid, oversexed and over 'ere, that's all that's the matter with 'em – *Picc*adilly Circus and Rainbow Corner –' Two American servicemen sitting behind Bessie and Lexie laughed and bantered with the conductor as slowly the bus emptied and Lexie and Bessie found themselves out on the pavement. Lexie wanted to say more to Bessie, wanted to tell her she was sorry for being the way she was, wanted to explain to her that she didn't mean to be so selfish, would prefer to be like Bessie, remembering people, keeping in touch with them, but the moment had passed and all she could do was tuck one hand into Bessie's elbow and guide her along Glasshouse Street towards the hotel.

I'll tell her tonight, she promised herself as they walked, her hand firm against Bessie's thin arm. After I've talked to Barbara and sorted it all out. And I'll try to say it to Barbara too, help her to see I didn't mean to be so selfish with her, didn't mean to use her so. Because I did use her, I know that now. She was always there, always so willing, and I used her and I've never told her how grateful I am, and how much I

324

care for her. Suddenly she felt a little wash of emotion for Barbara and knew it was love, a real undemanding love, and it made her feel good. We'll be all right, she told herself with a lift of certainty. We'll be all right, and so will Molly and so will Max. All all right, every one of us –

The street was clotted with people, the American servicemen who used the social club called Rainbow Corner, round in Shaftsbury Avenue, and the girls who hung around to snare them. Even at this time of the day, just before one o'clock and lunchtime, they were there in strength, their faces garish with rouge and their lashes beaded with heavy mascara. Bessie stared straight ahead as they made their way between the groups, clearly embarrassed by them, and equally clearly quite terrified that one of the lounging soldiers would misconstrue her presence among them and speak to her. It was one of the best-known pieces of mythology that no respectable woman could walk anywhere near Piccadilly Circus, and Lexie smiled involuntarily. To think of her dear straitlaced Bessie with her grey hair in its wispy bun and her crooked shoulder being molested by a lascivious soldier – it was a ludicrous image and she enjoyed it so much that when one of the big sergeants leaning against the window of a tobacconist's winked at her and called, 'Hi, sweetie, fancy a li'l gum?' she hardly noticed him.

They reached the corner of Glasshouse Street and were about to cross the road towards Denman Street and the hotel when it started. The sound had been there in the background for a few seconds, Lexie realized suddenly as people stopped all round them and looked upwards. A heavy thrumming was filling the air, making itself heard even over the rumbles of vans and buses and the clatter of wheels from the cabs that were arriving at the hotel. Then it seemed even louder as people stopped talking. Heads craned and eyes stared upwards, and then Bessie cried shrilly, 'I can see it – look, I can see it –'

At that moment others saw it too. Voices were raised and hands pointed and some people began to push urgently towards the end of Glasshouse Street where the steps led down to Piccadilly tube station. Someone began to shout – 'Take cover, take cover! The bleedin' thing's goin' to cut out – take cover, take cover –'

It was an extraordinary moment. The sound stopped with

a sharp little cough and then there was silence. People seemed frozen where they stood. Even the buses in Piccadilly Circus behind them seemed to be aware of the need for quietness. There was a breathlessness in the very air that made Lexie's chest feel tight. Even in North Africa, when gunfire had spluttered all round her, there hadn't been fear like this. There she had always felt she could dodge, that she'd be all right because the guns were fired by men, and they weren't aiming for her. It had been an irrational feeling, but it had protected her from terror none the less. Now she was filled with it, for the thing overhead, silent and gliding downwards, was not under the control of any man: it had no real target. She tried to take a deep breath, tried to reach out to pull Bessie away, back towards the tube station and safety, but she couldn't move.

Above her head the whistling sound started, grew louder, more peevish, more shrill, and then almost casually hit the corner of the hotel with a roar. She felt the shock wave rock her on her heels and she fell awkwardly on to her back, but she was lucky, for there was someone behind her to break her fall and it didn't jar as much as it might have done. After only a moment she was up again, trying to pull Bessie to her feet, for she too was lying on the pavement.

All round them the shouting started. People were calling to each other, telling each other to phone the ambulances, call the fire brigade, get the wardens out, and somewhere someone was swearing comprehensively in a loud Brooklyn voice and she wanted to giggle, for it sounded so incongruous. Then there was a warning shout from ahead and as she turned her head to look she saw that a whole corner of the huge building had been shattered, and pieces of masonry were still falling, making slow, ominous shapes in the air as they tumbled.

There was a smell now, a mixture of explosives and dust and burning and a whiff of coal gas. Then at last bells were ringing and fire engines were thrusting their scarlet way through the cluttered street. Wardens appeared from nowhere, pushing people along, urging them away from the corner where the masonry was still tumbling.

'Oh, God, Barbara!' Bessie said, urgently. 'Barbara's in there.' Moving with a speed that didn't seem possible from so small and frail a body she darted across the street, almost under the wheels of a fire engine, and into the building. After one startled moment Lexie followed her, almost wrestling with a warden who tried to hold her back and shouting at him, 'I've got to go in there – I've got to get my sister –' She ducked under his arm and plunged across Sherwood Street and through the big revolving doors into the building.

It was bedlam inside. She stood blinking in the dust and smoke, trying to spot Bessie, but there was no sign of her. She pushed through the crowds towards the desk which was besieged with people, all trying to reach the telephones, while one desperate clerk was trying to hold them back as outside the noise reached a crescendo of shouting, fire brigade bells and wardens' whistles.

There was still no sign of Bessie in the hubbub, but it would be unlikely she could be seen among so many people, small as she was. Lexie stood uncertainly for a moment, then as the clerk turned his head towards her she called desperately to him, 'Hey – my sister – we came to find my cousin. She just arrived at the hotel, I think – Miss Marks –'

The clerk stared at her, then shook his head, wide-eyed with bewilderment and terror. She saw he was just a youngster, probably barely sixteen, not old enough to be in the services and therefore able to do this job. She wanted to reassure him, but all she could do was shout. 'New arrivals – have you had new arrivals this morning?' After a moment he nodded dumbly and said, 'Winter Garden – someone went to the Winter Garden – said to tell anyone looking for her Winter Garden – I just told someone – the Winter Garden –' Someone else suddenly leaned over the desk and seized him by the lapels of his jacket and he threw one despairing look at Lexie and tried to understand what the excited Frenchman wanted who was holding him so tightly.

The crowds in the lobby were thinning now as people were cleared away by the wardens and the initial shock of fear receded as those who weren't hurt tried to get out to the street and see what was going on.

At last Lexie saw the sign to the Winter Garden, pointing off towards the right, and she pushed her way into the corridor as fast as she could, but stopped short. Over the heads of the milling people she could see a wide conservatory, glass-lined, where windows hung shattered in their webbing of crisscrossed strips of gummed paper, and the

327

floor was piled with rubble. She felt sick as a new wave of fear rose in her. It made her rougher than she meant to be as she shoved through the knot of men and women standing staring and craning and someone said indignantly, 'Hey, no need to push people around, for God's sake – '

But Lexie didn't care and pushed on till she was in the front of the crowd. There were ambulance men there, busy with stretchers. She saw them carrying a laden one out on to the street through the door on the far side, and looked round frantically for someone to ask, someone who would know, who had been here in the Winter Garden when the blast hit it and then seized on a man in the hotel's uniform.

'Where are they taking them?' she said urgently. 'I was meeting my cousin here. I think she may be – where are they taking the injured?'

The man peered at her and then lifted his head and called. 'Hey, lady – this the lady you're looking for?' Lexie whirled in a great upsurge of hope, but as she saw Bessie pushing her way towards her her face fell.

'No,' Bessie said. Her face was crumpled as well, for she too had looked incandescent with hope until she saw Lexie. 'No – we were both meeting her – can't you find out if she was here? Can't you, please – find out if – '

He shook his head at them, clearly sympathetic, but helpless. 'Sorry, lady, really I am, but we won't be able to know where we are for a bit yet – I mean, we'll have to check the hotel register against the people here. I'd go up the hospital if I was you, lady. They'll be going to the Middlesex, I reckon. It's the nearest. I'd go there. They'll be able to tell you who they've got in there – just cut through Berwick Street and then up to Oxford Street and cross over. They'll tell you who they got there from here – '

As they turned to go he said awkwardly, 'I wish you luck, lady, I really do. They're buggers, these doodlebugs. I do wish you luck – ' But he looked bleak as he said it.

# 38

They had been sitting in the echoing waiting hall of the casualty department all afternoon and into the early evening before they had been given the bag, and now they sat with it on the bench between them, staring ahead at the tiled walls, silent and alone in their loss.

They were free to go but didn't want to. It was as though they'd reached a tacit agreement that leaving the hospital meant leaving Barbara for ever. And they didn't want to do that yet.

Daylight was only just beginning to fail, and a hospital porter began to put up the old blackout shutters ready to switch on the lights. Some of the waiting people, the alert and cheerful ones, called encouragement to him, warning him with heavy jocularity that the doodlebugs hadn't got eyes to see where they were going, but could smell out lead swingers at forty paces. It was as though nothing special had happened, as though it were just another ordinary day, as though Barbara was still alive.

'Should we phone her?' Bessie whispered. Lexie turned and looked at her uncomprehendingly.

'What?'

'Molly. Shall we phone her? Or – ' The question dangled, unaskable, between them.

'She's got to be told,' Lexie said. 'You can't keep it from her. She's got to be told – but not on the phone.' She moved stiffly, tensing her aching buttocks against the hardness of the bench. 'I'll go and see her. Oh, God damn it all to hell!' She stamped her foot on the terrazzo floor so sharply that the slap echoed, and people turned their heads and stared at her curiously.

'I know.' Bessie's voice was thin and very tired. 'I know. It seems so – all these years outside London to keep them safe and now when it's all supposed to be nearly over, the second front happening and all, now – it's so stupid. Stupid – ' She began to weep helplessly, letting the tears slide down her face unchecked, just sitting with her hands resting on her lap.

After a while Lexie looked at the handbag on the bench between them. 'Is this all there is?' she asked, and Bessie nodded, reaching in her pocket to find a handkerchief and scrub at her reddened nose.

'The nurse said her clothes were too ripped to be – I said we didn't want them. I suppose she used it as an overnight bag. It's a big one, isn't it?' She too turned her head to look at the bag and they sat in silence a little longer. And then, moving sharply, Lexie picked it up.

'I'll have a look,' she said, twisting the clasp that kept its plump sides closed against the bulk of its contents.

But once it was open she couldn't put her hand inside. She looked at the change purse and folded envelope that lay on top of a neatly folded cotton nightdress, and remembered something she'd read somewhere, and found herself saying it aloud.

'And they saw those things 'a didn't want seen, and they touched those things 'a didn't want touched – ' Bessie caught her breath and turned her head away.

'I've got to,' Lexie said. 'Haven't I? Help me, Bessie – I've got to!' Bessie laid a hand on hers and then reached into the bag for the change purse.

'She never liked carrying a lot of cash,' she said. "You never know who's going to hold you up or anything," she used to say. I told her, this is London, not Chicago like on the pictures. People don't have guns and do hold-ups here, I said. But she used to say, "You never know", and she used to work out just how much she needed and that was all she carried with her – ' Again the tears began to trickle down her thin cheeks.

'The envelope – it's got nothing written on it and it's sealed,' Lexie said, turning it over in her hand. 'Shall I open it?'

Bessie almost snatched it from her. Her cheeks had developed uneven patches of red and her eyes looked very bright. 'In a minute,' she said, and folded the envelope and set her hands over it on her lap. 'Do the rest first.'

There wasn't much to do. The nightdress was the bulkiest item. They found a toothbrush, a tin of pink tooth powder and a sliver of soap wrapped in a dry flannel inside its neat folds. There was a small comb and a mirror and a clearly much prized powder compact, a stub of lipstick in a matching tube, and, staring at them, Lexie could remember seeing them on Barbara's dressing table at home in Manhattan. She said, 'It's my fault. All of it. If I hadn't come back she'd still be safe in New York. So would Molly – it's all my fault – '

'Don't be so silly,' Bessie said sharply. 'Don't be so *silly*. You start talking like that, you start blaming yourself for the whole damned war. It's just the way it is. That doodlebug could have hit any one of us. Only it didn't. It was meant for Barbara. Nothing you did or said would have made any difference.' Lexie looked at her, at the sudden ferocity in her face and the glitter of anger in her eyes, and reached forward and took her face in both hands. 'Thank you,' she said. 'Thanks. I know I'm stupid but – thanks.'

'We'd better go, Lexie,' Bessie said after a while, when they'd repacked the bag with its pitiful contents, apart from the envelope which she still held in her hand. 'There's nothing else we can do. I've told them what they have to do about the funeral and all – ' Lexie whitened, and she said gently, 'It's something you have to think about, isn't it? I've phoned the synagogue and explained. They said she can go near Momma and – she's family, so she should be near the family. She'll like that.'

'She'll – she's dead, Bessie! How the hell can a dead person like where she's buried? Don't talk that way – I can't stand it – '

But Bessie shook her head, unusually stubborn. 'People know,' she said. 'They do. When they buried Momma and I saw it was right in the middle of a row and there were people she'd known near her, I thought then, Momma knows. She'll be happier here. People don't just disappear. Even when they're dead you have to look after them – ' Lexie opened her mouth to argue and then wearily closed it again. There seemed no point in puncturing Bessie's fantasy of happy dead people. If it helped her, who was Lexie to take away the comfort? If I could believe something like that myself, I'd feel better, she thought, as slowly they made their way out of the hospital, Bessie leaning rather heavily on her arm now. But I can't. Barbara's dead. I never told her I was sorry, and there's not a damned thing I can do about it. I timed it wrong again.

She found a taxi to take them home, ignoring Bessie's

protests at the expense, and as they sat side by side in its dustiness, watching London unravel alongside them, she tried to remember how she had felt that morning, sitting in the bus on the way to meet Barbara, and she couldn't. It was as though she were a different person in a different world. Whoever that Lexie had been this morning she was gone now, as dead as Barbara was. I'm just a lot of dead people, she told herself as the taxi at last reached the flat. I perch on top of a great pile of dead Lexies, the small Lexie who was a searchlight and this morning's Lexie who was so remorseful, and all the others in between. She began to laugh at the thought, and then, as Bessie looked anxiously at her, took a deep breath and managed to control the incipient hysteria.

'I think we'd better take sleeping pills tonight, Bessie. Both of us. I think we need them. 'I've still got some I brought from New York. I'll make you some soup and then you go to bed. We need to, both of us – '

'If you wait for the funeral Molly'll get agitated,' Bessie said. 'One day later coming back than Barbara said won't worry her – she knows the trains play up. But three days – she'd be frantic and it would be awful to tell her on the phone. Though I'll have to tell her brothers in a letter, won't I? Thank God Busha didn't live to see this day, her only daughter dead – it would have killed her – ' She shook her head at her own foolishness and managed a small smile. 'You'll have to go now, Lexie. It's all right. I can cope with the funeral. Alex – Mr Lazar'll come, he'll help me.' She went pink. 'He always does when I need him.'

She insisted on coming to Euston to see her off, despite Lexie's protests that she could cope perfectly well, but when it came to it Lexie was glad of her company. The train was an hour and a half late leaving. The station was packed with irritable people waiting to get on the few trains that were running, and having Bessie to keep her company as the long minutes crept away helped a lot. They talked little, exchanging only desultory comments about the other people sharing the vigil with them, listening to the conversations of others nearby, exchanging smiles with other passengers, but it helped for all that.

When at last the train arrived and they were allowed to board, Bessie came with her to the barrier, pushing her way busily forward to make sure Lexie was at the front of the queue so that she'd have a better chance of getting a seat. The long haul to Scotland sitting on a suitcase, or worse still standing against the windows, would be hell on earth, she told Lexie. It was important to push ahead and get herself settled.

'And take this with you,' Bessie said as they reached the barrier and she pushed her through. 'Molly'll explain it. Don't get angry, Lexie. And phone me when you get there –' and then the crowd surged forward and Lexie found herself hurrying along the platform to the train, staring down at the envelope that Bessie had thrust into her hand.

Once she was on the train and had managed not only to get a seat, but that great prize, a corner seat which would give her a firm window surface against which to lean when she fell asleep, she turned the envelope over and over in her hands, not wanting to open it. The envelope that had been in Barbara's handbag; was it something she ought to open? Even Barbara must have secrets of her own; maybe this was a private letter, nothing to do with anyone else? Maybe it would be better to throw it away unopened. She frowned. What was it Bessie had said? 'Molly will explain it – don't get angry – '

Bessie knows what all this is about, she thought, and remembered the uneasiness there had been when she had asked what Molly was doing in Scotland, the way Bessie had behaved. Secrets again, secrets –

The train lurched forward, throwing the passengers in the now heavily crowded carriage against each other. The man standing in front of her lost his balance and trod painfully on her feet and she tucked them under the seat as neatly as she could as she slipped her thumb under the flap of the envelope and slit it open.

At first she was bemused. It was the flimsy copy of a contract. She'd seen plenty of them in her time: just a standard contract for a performer's services, with a few typewritten additions in the margins, and she'd turned it over in her fingers, puzzled, and then started to read it.

It was as though she were sitting with her feet encased in ice, and the chill was rising in her. The words trembled under her eyes as the train rattled over the points, through Hampstead and Hendon, going north with shrieks from its

333

whistle and great gouts of soot-stained steam painting the night sky, and Lexie had to read the words over and over again to get the sense of them.

The contract was for the services of Miss Molly Rowan for the next five years. She was to give her services solely and wholly to the company herein described, Carter Enterprises Ltd, for a salary that would be negotiated upwards at six-monthly intervals, commencing at the date of signing at fifteen pounds a week. She was to make herself available for all forms of work on stage and screen, and would consult with the company, said Carter Enterprises, on all matters pertaining to publicity, exploitation of moving picture rights, still photography rights, endorsement rights, etcetera, etcetera – the company offered certain guarantees in exchange to protect the interests of said Miss Molly Rowan in every way necessary, to promote her career to the best of its ability, and would take her to Hollywood for the purposes of film making as soon as hostilities ceased, or shipping lanes were open to passenger traffic, whichever was the sooner.

The clauses ran on and on, each more unctuous than the last and then at the end there were the spaces for the signatories. Two signatories for Carter Enterprises. One for Miss Rowan. And there was Barbara's signature, neat and upright, showing how heavily she had pressed with her pen through the carbon paper, for the image was much clearer than that of the others. In brackets, after her name, she had written 'parent and guardian'.

Lexie folded the flimsy paper very carefully, slid it back into its envelope and stowed it deep inside her bag. Outside it was completely dark, and she sat with her forehead resting against the dirty window and watched the reflection of the carriage fleeing over the shadowed landscape. Above her head the blue lamp burned dimly, for, relaxed blackout regulations or not, the LMS Railway had no intention of fitting their trains with better lighting until they were certain there was no further risk of air raids. It wasn't possible to distract herself with reading; deciphering the contract had been difficult enough. All she could do was stare out at the patterned darkness and the occasional glimpse of a car's dimmed headlights on the road and think.

All through the long hours of the night as she slept fitfully, wriggling from time to time to ease her cramped limbs without encroaching too much on the space of her snoring neighbour, she tried not to think of what that contract meant, but by the time the daylight came edging slowly up the sky and revealed the carriage in all its bleary unsavouriness she gave up the battle. She had to think about it and she did, over and over again.

Molly in Hollywood? Molly in films? She felt a sharp edge of anger rise in her and tried to persuade herself it wasn't what it felt like. It wasn't the anger she used to feel when other people in shows in which she had been cast seemed to have better numbers to sing, better choreography. It wasn't like that; how could it be? She couldn't be jealous of her own daughter, a child of only sixteen who'd done no more than dance in a few provincial shows over the past couple of years or so. It was ridiculous. It was because she was so exhausted that such hateful ideas came into her head. It was because she was so hurt by Barbara's death. It was because of anything but the truth. She *wasn't* jealous. Hollywood was hers as well, for the asking. It had been any time during the ten years she had spent in America. Why feel that edge of anger now, because it was offered to Molly?

Because she's too young. Because it's a cruel place, a madhouse. They'll spoil her, take her childhood away from her, turn her into some sort of simpering creature that men will leer at and want to handle and . . . She shook her head at the fields and patches of rough moor now speeding past the train windows in the thin light of dawn, and told herself to stop being so wicked, *stop* being so wicked, in time with the rattle of the train wheels. *Stop* being so wicked, *stop* being so wicked, *stop* being so –

For the last hour of the journey she did manage to sleep, exhausted as she was, and when at last, late in the morning, the train slid wearily into Inverness Station she was able to leave her narrow seat feeling less poised on the edge of collapse. Her eyes were gritty and her face felt tense and swollen, but she was awake. She could face Molly and tell her the sad news and help her cope with her grief and be a mother to her.

She managed to find a taxi to take her to the address that Bessie had given her, and had time to comb her hair and make herself look at least presentable. She had to look her best to meet her daughter.

# 39

'Och, no – it canna' be true!' said the little fat woman in the dirty overall. 'Not yon Miss Barbara! A bonny wumman, a fair bonny wumman! Och, 'tis a wicked world, at that. An' that puir bairn away up the stair mitherless! Och, 'tis a wicked world–' She shook her cloth-capped head lugubriously and went waddling up the stairs to show Lexie the way to Molly's room. She sounded so absurdly Scots that Lexie immediately thought of those caricature performances the comics used to put in the shows in New York; any moment now she'll cry, 'Hoots awa'' and start a sword dance, she thought, and a laugh rose in her throat and threatened to escape her tightly closed lips. The hysteria was still in her, she realized. She'd have to work hard at being controlled and sensible when she started to talk to Molly.

It was a small solid house, built of stone and good oak, with doors that were heavy and swung quietly on their hinges. She was able to go into the room without waking Molly and close the door behind her, much to the disappointment of the avid landlady.

Molly was a hump in the middle of the tousled bed, a few wisps of curly hair emerging from the sheets, her breathing steady and peaceful in the quietness. Shall I wait till she wakes and just sees me? Lexie asked herself, and bit her lip with uncertainty. Won't that alarm her more than being roused? And she stood there in the middle of the floor with the drift of Molly's clothes around her feet, for the room was in a considerable state of dishevelment, and tried to decide what to do.

But Molly seemed to sense in her sleep that she was no longer alone, for the hump in the bed heaved, more rumpled hair appeared and she said sleepily, 'Wha's 'a' matter? 'S'at you, Barbie?'

'No,' Lexie said as gently as she could. 'It's me, Molly. It's Lexie.'

The hump remained very still for a couple of seconds and

then slowly Molly rolled over and sat up, peering out from beneath her tangled hair and rubbing her nose with the back of her hand.

'I'll open the curtains, shall I?' Lexie needed something to do, and she went across the room to fumble with the drawropes of the heavy curtains as Molly stared at her, her mouth a little open.

I can't look at her, Lexie was thinking frantically. I can't. I haven't seen her for so long and now I can't look at her—

But she turned and forced a smile, and as she saw Molly's small pointed face she thought – oh, my God, but she's grown up! She's a person. She isn't a child any more – she's grown up – and without thinking she said, 'Oh, Molly darling, you look so different! You've grown so much!'

'Where's Barbie?' Her voice had a deeper ring to it now, a richness that was disconcerting in its maturity. Lexie gazed at her and tried to see the child she had left behind in London four years ago and couldn't find any trace of her. There was just a young woman in a white cotton nightdress that stretched across full young breasts and showed a slender neck and arms, a woman who seemed poised and confident, in spite of the fact that she was rumpled and still half asleep.

'Where's Barbie?' she said again. There was a trace of shrillness in her voice that made Lexie feel less shy of her.

She came and sat at the foot of the bed and said as steadily as she could, 'I've got bad news, Molly,' and then stopped. In all the thinking she'd done since Barbara's death the one thing she hadn't let herself consider was how she was going to tell Molly. She had shied away from it like a terrified child and now she had to face it; and with no resources to help her, no plans behind her to concentrate her mind, it came out as roughly as a blow, and she saw Molly actually flinch as the words hit her.

'She's dead. She was caught in a doodlebug raid at the Regent Palace Hotel, and died in hospital later. I came up because I didn't want to tell you on the phone—'

It was dreadful. Because she hadn't thought about what she would say to Molly, Lexie hadn't really considered how Molly would react, but even if she had, she could hardly have expected what happened, for Molly shrieked, a great cascade of sound, an eldritch wail that filled the room and struck Lexie's ears with a shock that was like a physical blow. She sat bolt upright in the crumpled bed with her fists clenched on each side of her head and screamed steadily, hardly stopping to draw breath, over and over again.

Behind the aghast Lexie the door flew open and the landlady came bustling over to plump herself down beside the shrieking girl and wrap her in her fat stubby arms.

The noise went on and on, though muffled against the landlady's billowing front and after a moment Lexie reached forward, tentatively, not knowing what to do, too shocked by the din to be able to think. But Molly was totally unaware of her and went on shrieking monotonously as the landlady rocked her and crooned at her until it seemed to Lexie that she would rock her right out of bed and on to the floor.

At last the screaming lessened as exhaustion took over, and then Molly began to cry, great tearing sobs that were piteous to hear. Lexie came to her other side, to try to get her away from the landlady, but the other woman made no effort to relinquish her grip and just stared at her with a malevolent gleam in her little eyes. Lexie was nonplussed: to fight over Molly would be stupid and undignified, but she couldn't let this horrible interloper sit there and keep her from her child when she was so distressed, and she said sharply, more sharply than she meant, 'Go and get some coffee. At once. I'll look after her. Go on now –'

The landlady glared defiantly at her as Molly went on and on with her great racking sobs, and Lexie was afraid she was going to refuse. But she stared her down, and at last the woman let go of Molly and went slowly to the door, her old slippers slap-slapping insolently against the floor in a way that made Lexie's anger rise even more.

But it wasn't really anger, she knew, as at last the woman went and she could wrap her own arms round Molly and hold her tight. It was her own grief that was threatening to overwhelm its boundaries, and as Molly rocked herself back and forth, fists still held to her head and elbows tightly against her sides, so that although Lexie had her arms round her she couldn't really feel any response in her, she felt her own tears begin to fall. Barbara was dead, dear comfortable eager Barbara who had loved them both and looked after them so well for so long. Barbara was gone and the world was a grey and bad place to be in in consequence.

But after a while she took a long breath and swallowed her

tears, using every scrap of self-control she had to calm herself. Across the room there was a washstand with a blue china jug and bowl on it. She let go of Molly, who still showed no awareness of her presence at all, and went across to find a towel and dipped a corner of it in the stale water in the jug. She wanted to use it to cool Molly's hot face, to soothe away the scalding tears that streaked her cheeks, but before she could turn back from the washstand the door flew open again and the landlady returned with a cup and saucer in one pudgy hand. She made unerringly for the bed and thumped herself down beside Molly with one triumphant glance at Lexie, and began to coax her to drink.

The tears eased at last as Molly obediently sipped the muddy brew and Lexie, glad to see it, controlled the flash of fury she had felt at the woman's encroachment. She sat down on the other side of the bed and watched her.

'I'm sorry, darling,' she said gently. 'I truly am. But you had to be told, and Bessie and I decided I should come and –'

''Oo are you, anyway?' the landlady said pugnaciously. 'To come here upsetting this puir wee bairn so – why did they no' send her family, then? 'Tisn't fittin' that strangers should –'

'I am – Barbara was my cousin,' she said icily. 'Now, thank you for your interest, but we can manage perfectly well, thank you –'

But the landlady ignored that, looking at her with her head on one side. 'The cousin, are you? An' never been near them all the three months they've been in this show and in this house? Not till now – tush, there's a –'

'She's not my cousin,' Molly said suddenly very loudly. 'She's not –' And she began to weep again, noisily, clutching the landlady and turning her head to bury her face in her apron.

Lexie stared at her, her eyes dilated with amazement. 'Molly!' she said in a breath and then, more loudly, 'Molly! What do you – I don't understand – what did you say?'

Hope was lifting in her, a mad hope that after all Barbara had understood, had realized the time had come and told Molly herself, but then Molly pulled herself away from the landlady's grip and stared at her, eyes wide and glittering in her white face.

'Coming here and telling me Barbie's dead – and all you

339

can say is, "Molly, darling, you look so different, you've changed so much!"' Her imitation of Lexie's voice and speech rhythms was uncannily accurate, her own voice with its lingering trace of an American accent completely disappearing, and Lexie blinked at her, startled, and tried to speak, to explain, but Molly just rode over her.

'With Barbie dead that's the first thing you can say – that I've grown! It's so *stupid*. I hate you, you hear me? I hate you – to tell me Barbie's dead–' The tears began again and she pulled her knees up and wrapped her arms round them and buried her head in the curve of her own body till she was a bundle as small as it was possible for her to be.

Never taking her eyes from her, Lexie spoke in a voice as low and controlled as she could keep it to the old woman who was sitting staring avidly at Molly. 'Get out. Do you hear me? Get out. At once.'

The woman opened her mouth to speak but Lexie went on more loudly, 'If you don't go, I'll put you out–' and the old woman went scuttling to the door.

'As soon as ma man gets in, I'll be havin' you outa here, do you hear me? I'll not be spoken to so in ma own hoose–' she cried shrilly and then went slapping down the stairs muttering all the way. Lexie took a deep breath of relief.

'Molly,' she said quietly, and then, as there was no response, said it again, more loudly. 'Molly. I'm sorry, truly I am, that I had to bring you such dreadful news. But don't be angry with me, darling. I'm as bereft as you are. Bessie too. It's a dreadful thing to have happened–'

'I want Barbie,' Molly said in a muffled voice. 'I want my Barbie.'

'I do too. I'm going to miss her dreadfully.' Lexie put out her hand to touch Molly, but she pulled away, huddling back against the head of the bed and staring at Lexie with eyes as glittering as they had been before, but her face now flushed and damp.

'No, you're not.' She almost spat the words. 'You didn't love her. You didn't love me. You just went off and left us.'

'Molly!' Lexie looked at her aghast. 'But it wasn't like that! You wanted to go on the road with that children's show and–'

'You could have come with,' Molly said. 'You could have if you'd wanted to. But you didn't. You stayed in London

340

and –'

'I had my job to do!' Lexie couldn't believe what she was hearing. 'My darling, you know that! And then I had to go abroad with ENSA. You knew that too. I wrote so many letters – I kept on writing – you hardly ever wrote to me, but I kept on sending you –'

'Letters!' Molly almost spat it at her. 'What good are letters? People who love people don't just send letters – you didn't have to go abroad. You could have done what Barbie did. You could have come with. That's what other mothers did –'

There was a long blank silence, then Lexie said carefully, 'Other mothers?'

'Do you think I didn't know? Do you think I didn't know you didn't want me? You gave me away, that's what you did. You gave me to Barbie and now she's dead and I haven't got anyone –' And the tears began yet again but this time they were piteous, the tears of a terrified child feeling herself completely alone. Lexie leaned forward and, despite Molly's resistance, put her arms round her and held on to her. For a brief moment, as fragile as a bubble's life, they clung to each other. But then, moving awkwardly, Molly pulled away and scrambled out of bed to the washstand, poured water out of the jug into the basin and began noisily to splash her face.

Lexie watched her for a while and then opened her mouth to speak as Molly scrubbed her face dry, but Molly seemed to know what she was going to say and interrupted her.

'Don't you go thinking just because Barbie's dead you can get mixed up in what I do. I won't have it. I'm a grown-up now – no one'll tell me what to do.'

She lifted her face from the towel. 'Did Barbie sign that contract?' she said sharply. 'Did she? It's why she went to London.'

Lexie bit her lip, thinking for one wild moment that she could deny it, but she knew she couldn't. Quite apart from the rights and wrongs of lying to Molly, there were the practicalities of it. Barbie had signed a contract with the Carter people and they'd want to enforce it. They'd tell Molly if she didn't.

'Yes,' she said gently. 'But –'

'There's no but about it.' Molly turned her back on Lexie and reached for clothes that were lying scattered about the

341

floor. She began to dress, making no effort to hide her nakedness, and Lexie saw the curve of her hips, the rich roundness of her belly, her long slender legs and knew what she said was true – she was grown up.

'Barbie signed and that makes it legal. As soon as they can they're taking me to Hollywood. I'll be a star and you can't stop me–'

'It's not a legal contract, Molly,' Lexie tried to sound reasonable. 'How can it be? You seem to know the truth – and it wasn't a truth I ever meant to hide from you–'

Molly whirled round, her face twisted into a sharp little sneer. 'Not legal? When did you ever bother with *legal*? I saw it, you know, that birth certificate. When we were packing up the apartment to come to London. I saw it. You put a different name on it and everything – you never cared then whether it was legal to give me to Barbie and give me a different name. Well, you did, and everyone knew Barbie was my mother, and so she is, even now she's dead. She signed that contract and if you try to – if you say anything to anyone and try to spoil things for me, I'll tell everyone what you did. I will, I will, you see if I don't–'

'I don't want to spoil anything for you, Molly.' Lexie felt that she wasn't really there; that she was sitting watching the whole scene played out on a screen. For a wild moment she thought that it had already happened: Molly had gone to Hollywood, and this was a film in which she was the star and in which she, Lexie, had a bit part, and there was a sick heaviness inside her that wouldn't budge, that pinned her to her seat and made her very voice sound flat and dull.

'I want you to be happy. It's true I did behave stupidly when you were born but it wasn't meant the way you think it was. I loved you so much – I still do. If I tried to explain now you wouldn't understand how it was then. One day you might, when you get your own career going. You'll know what it means to be where I was when you were born, when I saw my big chance. But – I'm not making excuses, Molly. For a long time now, for years, I've been feeling more and more dreadful about you, but there was nothing I could do. There was Barbie, loving you and wanting you and not wanting you ever to know–' She shrugged. 'It happened. Leave it at that for now. There's no sense in going over it again, not when we're both feeling so – when Barbie's only

342

just died.'

'When I get my own career going?' It was as though Molly had heard nothing else that Lexie had said. 'You mean you're going to let me – that you aren't going to spoil the contract?'

'Not if it means that much to you.' To her own amazement Lexie felt a yawn threatening her. Exhaustion point was very close suddenly. 'I think you're very young for the sort of people you'll have to deal with. I've met some of them and they're –' She shook her head. 'But I'm not stupid. I can't see that you're going to pay any attention to what I say –'

'Of course I'm not,' Molly said. 'Why should I?'

'Indeed, why should you?' Lexie's head drooped and she looked down at her hands on her lap. 'I've been a lousy mother, haven't I? But I meant well. Oh, I meant well. It was just –' She found she had a little spurt of energy after all, and lifted her head to look at Molly. 'I had to earn a living for us all. I had to take care of you the only way I could. Earning money. There was Barbie who could give you the same things I could – loving and looking after and someone to be with – except for one thing. The only way she could have made a living for us was working in a millinery factory, and she didn't want to do that any more than I wanted her to. I had the stage – and –' She was struggling now. 'And I wanted the stage. The way you do. Can't you understand that? The way you do –'

There was a brief silence, then Molly turned away and went to the dressing table to pick up a comb and start pulling it through her rumpled hair.

'Well, if you know I want the stage,' she said at last, 'you won't stop me from going to Hollywood.' It was as much a statement as a question.

'I've already told you I won't spoil anything for you,' Lexie said. 'That I only want you to be happy.'

'The only way I'll be happy is going to Hollywood,' Molly said. 'Barbie wanted me to go –' Her voice trembled and she took a breath, then went on more steadily. 'It's right for me. We talked about it a lot. I'll stay in this show, touring Scotland until the war's over, and that won't be long now, everyone says so. Then as soon as there's a ship, I'm going to America.' She stared at Lexie's image in the mirror. 'Is that settled then?'

'It's settled.' Lexie stood up. 'Will you come out with me

now? Show me the theatre? Show me the sort of work you're doing? I'd love to meet some of the people in the show – the director and –'

'I'd rather you went back to London,' Molly said, and now she looked only at her own reflection in the mirror, pulling the comb through her hair over and over again till it shone like a piece of coal, for it was darker even than Lexie's hair, thicker and richer. 'I'm all right here. Everyone looks after me. Like Mrs Sturt downstairs. She's a bit of an old nuisance, but she thinks I'm lovely, so –' She shrugged, and now she did shoot a swift glance at Lexie. 'I can look after myself. I've been looking after Barbie for years, really. Keeping her happy while I did what I wanted, my way –' And again her voice wobbled and she speeded up her combing, dragging it ferociously across her scalp.

'But money and –'

'I've plenty of money. I've looked after it for both of us for ages. Barbie only took what she needed when she went to London. I've got plenty, and I get good money in this show and I'll be getting some from Carters. I told you, I'm grown up now. I don't just look it. I *am*.'

She turned back once more to Lexie. 'I want you to go back to London. Give my love to Auntie Bessie. I'll write when I can. Goodbye, Lexie. Just leave me alone and I'll be all right.'

It wasn't until the train had left Scotland behind and was well into the north of England that Lexie realized that Molly hadn't asked her who her father was.

# 40

As the war dragged out its last weary days, Lexie set about trying to reshape her life. Peace was coming; even though the terrifying autumn days when the second wave of rockets, the silent V2s, arrived and left London shattered and even more shaken than after the blitz and the threat of the first doodlebugs, everyone knew that. People started to talk about 'after the war' as a real time that would happen rather than as a fantasy, and beneath the exhaustion and the irritation that made people snap and snarl at each other there was a flicker of real hope. There *would* come a time when the streets would be bright at nights with lamps and unshuttered shop windows; a time when those shop windows would be piled high with goods as they had been long ago; a time when no one would ever again have to queue for hours for a box of matches, a packet of cigarettes or the rare treat of fresh food. There would be cosy nights beside the fire with no fear of death falling out of the sky, and holidays by the sea where now barbed wire befouled the beaches. There would be a time when you could live your own life and follow your own interest instead of the national one.

Lexie tried very hard to feel part of this new hopefulness, and to cut out of her conscious mind the memory of Barbara's death and the loss of Molly, but it was exceedingly difficult. For all her efforts to be rational, all her attempts to tell herself she was being ridiculous, even hysterical, she could not stop herself from feeling that Molly was dead too, that her child had been lost as irrevocably as Barbara.

Her only remedy was work, she told herself, as she sat one afternoon late in February on the windowsill of Bessie's living room, staring out across the road at the dripping trees in Victoria Park. Work had been Bessie's salvation; after Barbara's death and the news that Molly had refused to return to London she had seemed to shrink a little, to become greyer and wispier and even more tired. For a while Lexie had been sharp with anxiety as she watched her struggle through each day; was she going to lose Bessie too? Hadn't she been punished enough already? But Bessie had gone on in her stubborn way, insisting on going to work at Alex Lazar's City office all through the V2 rocket days, in spite of the risks, and she had been right to do so. Now she was still frail, still clearly tired, but there was a strength in her that sustained Lexie and reassured her, and helped her live through the passing days.

It was now more than half a year since she had last seen Molly and been so firmly excluded from her life. But the loss still bit keenly, though with Bessie there to lean on she could cope with the pain. Now it was just a steady ache, and only hurt enough to bring a little rush of tears to her eyes when she deliberately reminded herself of what had happened, much as a person with a sore tooth deliberately bites on it to feel the thrill of sensation it causes.

But I can't go on like this, she thought as she watched the mist rising dankly beneath the trees in the park. There was a thick acrid smell in the winter air that was squeezing its way in through the cracks of the window frames and she coughed a little, feeling the rawness of the cold and hugging herself against it. There was no coal to be bought anywhere and they'd used most of their meagre ration before January was out. To light a fire before Bessie came home in the evening would be gross self-indulgence, she told herself mournfully, and again pulled her heavy cardigan more tightly round her body.

Work, she thought again, I must get back to work. If I'm fit to work, that is. Six months and she hadn't danced a step, hadn't practised a moment, six months of just pottering around the flat, cooking for Bessie when she came in, and sitting for long hours staring out at the park. It was a dangerous way to be, she realized suddenly, because she didn't mind it. To have buried herself in domesticity would have once seemed to her as bad as literally burying herself alive, yet now she had done it and hadn't noticed how stultifying it was. I must get back to myself, she thought with sudden panic, and the thought brought her to her feet and she began to prowl around the living room, walking round and round the table with her head bent as she lectured herself silently. I must have been mad to let this happen; to rot like this, just because of − at once she pushed away the memories that had begun to rise in her, preventing herself from wallowing in them, determined to think forwards; I must have been mad and it's got to stop.

She looked at her watch. Two o'clock. Two o'clock on a Wednesday afternoon: still time to do something with the day. She ran downstairs to her own flat and her icy bedroom, switched on the light and sat at her dressing table. I must fix myself up, go up to town, see what I can sort out −

The face that stared back at her from the mirror was like a stranger's, pinched and pallid, the hair lifeless. Panic rose in her sharply. Had she changed so much so quickly? There were lines there she hadn't seen before, surely, a softness about the jawline, a dullness in the skin that was so unfamiliar as to be chilling. She said aloud. 'I'm forty-four,' then bit her lip and went on gazing at her image. 'I'm not supposed to be so old, am I? When was I thirty? What happened to twenty? I'm forty-four, forty-four –' She caught her breath in a sharp little hiss and began to scrabble in the drawer where she kept her precious supply of make-up, a dwindling resource in these days of shortages of everything, and began to put it on.

Her old skill was still there; under her quick fingers the pallor eased and became just an interesting background for the soft flush of rouge, the shadows under her eyes were lost as she applied darker, richer ones to the lids, her lips lost their harshness as she curved them with colour and when at last, with a flick of mascara, she completed her canvas and could lean forward and stare in the mirror again and feel the panic begin to subside. She didn't look all that bad now, surely? Forty-four, perhaps, but not a decrepit forty-four.

'I can,' she whispered to her reflection. 'I can,' and didn't know quite what she meant by it. But she did know that she'd reached a corner of her road and was taking the right turning. It would have been so easy to say, 'I can't,' and sink back into the morass of depression and domesticity of the past six months, so easy to flee from her reflection when it had stared back at her so dully, but she hadn't. She'd changed that alarming image, restored it to some of its former excitement, and with that change of appearance she had changed herself. 'I can,' she said again, but this time loudly, pushing back her dressing table stool and going across to her wardrobe. There were clothes there she hadn't worn for months; she could look good again and she would –

When she reached the front door, looking elegant and assured in a chalk-stripe suit and a small hat that was a nonsense of feathers and veiling perched over one eye, there was a letter on the mat. It was one of the familiar blue airmail letters that he'd been sending with almost religious regularity ever since she'd come back to England. She bent and picked it up, turning it over and over in her gloved fingers.

Would she open this one, or would it be one she put away in a drawer and left, waiting till she could cope with it?

She wouldn't answer it, that was for certain. She'd decided that when the first of them had been waiting for her when she'd come back from that dreadful journey to Scotland.

347

How could she speak to him again when he couldn't be told of his daughter? How could she tell him of his daughter when the child – no, the young woman – had so determinedly and so firmly rejected her mother? Bad enough she was suffering the hurt of that rejection; no need to hurt him, too, giving him a child and snatching it away in the same moment, for surely Molly would be as uncaring of him as she was of Lexie? Why should she care, after all? She didn't know him. Better he shouldn't know of her. So Lexie had argued when that first letter came, and she had reminded herself of that argument with each subsequent letter. Now she dropped this one back on the doormat and walked over it. Let it lie, she thought as she pulled the door closed behind her and went clattering down the steps into the street. Let it lie. I'm going back to work. I can't confuse myself with him. Not now.

It was dark when Bessie got home. She stood in the hallway putting her keys back into her bag and listened for Lexie, but knew even as she strained her ears that she wasn't there. She had always been like that with Lexie. From the time she had been a toddler, Bessie had known instinctively where she was in the house and how she was feeling. It was a closeness that had been born long ago in Sidney Street when Shmuel had been alive, and which had been reforged in these past six months. Bessie had found her child again and had been happier than she would have thought possible, even though she'd known that Lexie was grieving, that she had been blanketed in a deep depression that had slowed her steps and dulled her eyes and made her lethargic and silent. So now she knew that Lexie wasn't here, as the hint of her old favourite perfume in the air made her spirits plunge, even as she felt glad that Lexie was so much better.

She'd known this was coming; she'd seen it develop over the past few weeks, seen the depression lighten, just as the mist in the park across the street did on winter mornings, first heavy and wet, completely shrouding the trees and the park benches and the truncated walls where once the railings had stood proudly – the railings that had long since vanished to be made into bullets and tank housings – and then swirling a little, becoming thinner in places so that just the ghosts of the tree trunks showed through and then the outlines of the

348

benches and finally the grey grass itself. So it had been with Lexie and now, Bessie told herself as she reached for the light switch to illuminate her way up the stairs, now the mist has gone altogether. It's still grey days with her, but she's out of the fog. She's on her way, and she'll leave me behind again.

The light sprang on and the letter on the mat seemed to shout at her and she bent and picked it up, staring at the crisp writing on the back. Commander Cramer, it said, and then the string of numbers that was the coded address of his ship. She turned it over. Alexandra Asher, he'd written; no attempt to use the polite address; no 'Miss'. Just her name, uncompromising as a headline on a theatre poster. Bessie put the letter down on the hall table and went upstairs. She was bone-tired and there was the fire to be lit and supper to be made and her lips curled a little wryly. How like the old Lexie to have gone out so impulsively, without stopping to think of Bessie coming home to a cold, empty and foodless flat; she's getting better. She's her old self again, almost, thinking first of Lexie and then of Lexie and again of Lexie, then feeling bad because she remembers other people afterwards. Darling Lexie, Bessie thought, I'm glad you're better and I wish you weren't — but I'm really glad —

She dropped her coat on her bed, then went into the living room to take their precious box of matches from behind the clock and use only one to light the fire. As the paper caught and then the handful of sticks, she crouched for a while holding out her hands to the sudden blaze, grateful for its thin heat but mostly for its bright light. Soon the sticks would disintegrate into dull ash, once they'd done their job of igniting the briquettes made of wood shavings and coal dust that were all the fuel they had left this winter. There would then only be, if she was lucky, a dull glow as the briquettes gave up their heat with great reluctance, so this moment of brilliance was to be relished, and she breathed in the smell of cheerfully burning wood, absorbing the scent of it and glorying in the moment while it lasted.

When the phone rang she felt almost irritable. It was probably Alex, she told herself. He'd not had time to come to the office for weeks, so busy was he with his ENSA work at Drury Lane and with his niece Hannah's affairs — for as she slowly came to terms with the loss of her husband in the blitz and restructured her life, her demands on her uncle became heavier than she perhaps realized – and there were matters of business they had to discuss.

But it was Lexie and her spirits lifted absurdly, took a little somersault and made her voice sound glad and eager. She hadn't just gone out impulsively concerned only with her own doings. She had been concerned for her, Bessie, coming home to the empty flat, and she cried joyously, 'Lexie! Where are you? I just got in and –'

'I know.' Lexie's voice came thin and distorted through the phone, but there was a crispness in her tone, a purposefulness that had been missing for a long time. 'I've been calling every ten minutes since half past six. I should have left a note, but I was an idiot and forgot. I didn't want you to worry –'

Bessie felt the tears fill her nose and, childlike, rubbed it with the sleeve of her coat. 'I wasn't worried,' she lied, grinning at the phone as though Lexie could see her, could recognize the pleasure in her. 'I wasn't worried –'

'Good,' Lexie's voice clacked. 'I was, leaving like that. Listen, Bessie, I'm going back to work. I suddenly decided this afternoon that I can't – well, anyway, I'm in Cockie's office and there's a tour they're putting together for the suburban houses. Wimbledon and Streatham and Golders Green – it's a revue of bits from several of the old shows, just to tide them over, they say, till they can get a really good one together for the West End. They've made a place for me – we've got to sort it out and I won't be able to get home for a while yet. So don't worry, will you? It might be quite late. I'll try to get home in time to tell you what's happening but – anyway, don't *worry*. Have you lit the fire?'

Bessie grinned in the flickering light. 'I've lit it,' she said. 'I'm all right, Lexie. It was nice of you to worry – thanks.'

'I should have left a note,' Lexie said. 'Bye.' The line clicked and went dead and slowly Bessie recradled the phone. Lexie, to worry like that about her? To take time out from a business meeting to call me? Again her nose filled with tears. She sniffed noisily and went back to the fire, to coax the smouldering briquettes to burn more cheerfully.

A suburban tour, she thought, and now the tears couldn't be held back. Her Lexie in a second-rate suburban tour? Once she'd have laughed at the mere suggestion, and indeed no one would have made it. Alexandra Asher was a West End star,

350

not a stopgap for a tired tour round the edges of London. It must have hurt her dreadfully to be offered that. Dreadfully. Bessie got to her feet and went to the larder to see what sort of meal she could scrabble together, trying all the time not to let the tears overwhelm her.

It wasn't till she was eating her meagre supper of toast spread with margarine and enlivened with the dried-out end of the week's cheese ration that she found comfort in the thought that, though Lexie must have been hurt by the poverty of the offer she'd been given, she'd still accepted it. She hadn't flown into a rage, or made a fuss; she'd accepted the unpalatable fact that after the years she'd spent out of the public eye, touring the army and naval bases, she was no longer the star she'd been. She was ready to climb back the hard way from the bottom.

If only, she thought, as she washed up her dishes, if only it had all been different, and she slipped into her favourite daydream, the one in which Lexie hadn't run away to America, but had married Max and settled down in England and had Molly and been secure and safe and properly looked after and –

She stopped rubbing at the plate she was holding and stared down at her hands in the washing-up bowl. They looked gnarled and twisted under the distortion of the water and she thought suddenly, 'I'm getting old – sixty-five – ridiculous,' and then bit her lip, trying to decide whether the idea that had slipped into her mind had any right to be there. It was so unlike any idea she'd ever had before, that was the trouble. I never was the sort to push at things, to make them happen the way I wanted. I'm not like Lexie. I'm me. I just let things happen, don't I?

But after a while she took her hands out of the water and dried them meticulously and then went downstairs to fetch the letter that lay on the hall table.

# 41

'I've heard of black Mondays,' the stage doorkeeper said, and spat into the dust outside the stage door. 'But this is bleedin' ridic'lous. Blackest Tuesday I ever saw in all my natural.' He went back into his cubbyhole, slamming the glass door behind him as on the stairs beyond the black corridor there was a rush of feet and the shouting of jubilant voices. Lexie made a face at the man beside her and turned to go to her dressing room.

'You'd think he'd manage to cheer up today, at least,' she said. The man laughed as he followed her towards the stairs and his own dressing room. 'I only asked him if there were any letters for me, and I get a lecture about how miserable he is.'

'That's Arthur, love. Never been known to crack a smile, that one. Everyone hoped the doodlebugs'd get him, but there it is – still grousing and still in amongst us. Doesn't deserve it! Black Tuesday? He ought to be strung up.' He nodded cheerfully at her and went hurrying away to his own dressing room to change out of his costume and go to join the hubbub outside.

She could hear it even from here: the shouting of voices, the raucous noise of hooting buses and vans and people singing and, from somewhere fairly near, the wail of an ill-played saxophone. London was shrieking its corporate head off in relief and didn't care who knew it. It may have been bad for business – and Arthur had been right about that: she couldn't remember ever playing to a smaller house, all through the run – but it was an incredible night for all that, and she sat in her chair and stretched and yawned before beginning to wipe off her make-up.

The end of the war: it didn't seem possible and after a moment she got to her feet, went to the window and pulled at the dusty black fabric that had been nailed over it in 1939 as a permanent blackout. It resisted her for a moment and then gave way in a shower of dust that left her coughing but it opened at last on to the warm May evening and she could smell the excitement coming in from the streets beyond. Victory night. It was over, all over. No more bombs, no more sirens, no more deaths on remote battlefields. It was over, in Europe at any rate, and she rubbed her face and tried to let the excitement fill her too.

She went back to her dressing table and set to work again on her face, trying to concentrate on what she was doing, but it wasn't easy. There beside her on the table, her sticks of make-up on top of it, lay yesterday's paper. Just a bit of rubbish, fit to wrap up fish and chips, she told herself savagely, or for lighting a fire. It's rubbish, yesterday's dead news. Not important. Why let it fret you so? Not important.

But of course it was, and once her face was clean, and she'd reapplied street make-up and dressed, she picked it up again. To deny it was there wouldn't help. She had to accept it, had to come to terms with it, and she unfolded the pages carefully so that the photograph was on top.

It was a boring pose they'd put her in. Just the same as those they'd all used in the old days, before the war, perched on a rail with a grinning sailor alongside her. She sat with her legs crossed to show her pretty knees and the long expanse of shin, her head up, smiling directly into the camera. Is it just to me that she looks so alive, so ardent, so marvellous? Lexie thought. Is it because I've got this special feeling for her? Or does she really look like that? She had to admit it was because Molly truly did have that vitality and eagerness that could make people breathless, because the photograph was absurdly large on the page. It dwarfed all the other items there, even the jolly little stories of children reunited with parents in London, as reverse evacuation brought the hordes pouring back home again, and the snippets of news about gloomy prisoners of war going on hunger strikes in distant camps, and who–cared–anyway–about–prisoners? jokes. Clearly the editor had been as enchanted with Molly as was the journalist who'd written the glowing, gushing words that captioned the picture:

Delectable seventeen-year-old Molly Rowan. Delightful, Delicious, altogether the most Disarming young lovely of the Peace poses for our lucky photographer at Southampton as she prepares for her adventures in the New World. Off to Hollywood to leave us weeping at our loss, saucy Molly promises she'll be back one day soon to see us all.
'You mustn't forget I'm American by birth,' she carolled to me when I told her how sad we were to see her go. 'I came to do my bit for good old

353

England, and now we've beaten the Hun, I'm off to Hollywood to make my first picture. But I'll be back, if you'll have me–'

If we'll have you, Miss Rowan? I don't know how we could bear to let you go – but go with our love and gratitude. You have indeed done your bit for old Blighty, and we're grateful. Come back soon!

Lexie had known it was going to happen. She'd seen the contract with her own eyes, so it had only been a matter of time. Yet it had hurt dreadfully; she had opened her newspaper so casually, had leafed through it the way people always did in these new peaceful days. The time when you seized on every edition with as great a hunger as if the words were printed on cake had gone; now people weren't concerned any more. It was over. The war was over and no newspaper now could shock and distress as they had all through the bad years. But there it had been, and she had felt it as sharply as though she'd been kicked in the belly, had actually caught her breath with surprise so that Joe Damian, the acrobat, who was sitting beside her in the canteen noisily drinking tea and arguing with the dance director over horses as they always did during the show breaks, had swivelled his eyes at her anxiously and asked her if she was well.

'I'm fine,' she'd said as calmly as she could, and had folded the paper away in her bag, but ever since then it had hung over her head like a cloud. Molly's picture filled her mind's eye, Molly's wide challenging smile haunted her, Molly's hair blown in the wind over Southampton Water mocked her, Molly going to Hollywood.

Now, moving swiftly, Lexie packed her handbag, took one last look round the dressing room, closed the door and made her way through the corridors to the stage door. Home, through the shrieking crowd celebrating the arrival of peace, home to Bessie and a different kind of peace. Tomorrow I'll try to sort it out in my head. Tomorrow I'll decide. Somewhere deep inside her Lexie knew she'd already made up her mind, but she didn't want to face up to the implications of her decision. Not yet.

She could hear Arthur's grumbling voice long before she turned the corner that led to the last corridor and the street. He was haranguing someone who spoke only occasionally in a softer voice, and there was something about the sound of it that made her set her head on one side and slow her steps.

'Much as me bleedin' job's worth,' Arthur was complaining. 'I can't go lettin' every Tom, Dick an' 'Arry as asks go wanderin' around 'ere just like that. Could be bleedin' Fifth Column for all I knows, couldn't yer? Yers, I know the wars over – to listen to the way everyone's goin' on you'd think it was going to make a lot o' difference, but it ain't. All it's going to mean is blokes out'a work like I was for three years after the last bleedin' lot –'

She had to turn the corner then, for she had heard the soft voice speak once more and now she knew, and there was no point in hiding. There had been a clink of coins too, and that meant that Arthur was going to decide miraculously to be obliging after all, so any moment now he'd come and find her skulking there. She took a deep breath, and walked out to meet him.

'Hello, Max,' she said. He twisted his head sharply, looked at her, and then, very slowly, grinned.

'To think I could have saved myself ten bob,' he said and grinned even more widely as Arthur snorted and slammed himself into his cubbyhole. 'You look marvellous, Lexie. Really marvellous. Are you well?'

'Fine,' she said. 'And you?'

'Never better. Home again, you see. They promised they'd get us back before the last day, and God bless their Lordships of the Admiralty, they did. Docked at Pompey last week, managed to get shore leave this morning. Came straight here.'

She looked at him in the dim light of the single dirty bulb that swung above their heads in the draught created by the bustle as some of the cast came pushing past with mutters of 'G'night', dropping their keys on the sulking Arthur's shelfed door. Max was in uniform, looking remarkably handsome for a rather plain man, and somehow exactly right in his well-tailored and gold-emblazoned jacket and peaked cap, and Lexie was very aware of the interested stares the chorus girls gave him as they went past.

'You look well,' was all she said, and then with a sudden sharp little frown, 'How did you know where I was?'

'*The Stage*,' he said. 'They're still publishing it, you know! I got a copy in Portsmouth and saw the notice of the tour. I'd have called you at home, if I'd managed to get to London in time, but the train was late, of course, so it was easier to come straight here.'

'Yes,' she said, feeling as shy as a child suddenly. He

seemed to understand, for he said, 'Let's go and see the fun, shall we? It was hell getting out here from Waterloo. The underground was going mad – people dancing in the aisles! Come on –' He tucked a hand into the crook of her elbow and led her out into the street. She followed, very conscious of the warmth of him through the fabric of her sleeve.

Outside the street was a heaving, roaring mass of bodies. The noise hit her ears and made her pull back a little and he laughed and shouted above the hubbub, 'I reckon they're happy,' and she nodded, unable to shout back. He grinned reassuringly, and then, leading the way, began to push through the crowds that milled round the theatre.

She realized he was making in the general direction of the tube station and followed with her head down, grateful for his guiding hand firmly holding hers.

They were baulked after a while by a particularly noisy knot of people who were dancing a conga in a closed circle, and he pulled her closer to him and put an arm about her shoulder. She shivered even in the warmth of her coat on this May evening; he held her close and said in her ear, 'Won't take long now. Let 'em work it off and then we'll go –'

It doesn't matter that he's back, she told herself fiercely, staring at the glazed eyes of the dancers as they went weaving and ducking in front of her. It makes no difference, I've decided –

'I wish we could go up to the Heath,' he shouted in her ear. 'It must look wonderful up there, looking down on London with the lights on again.'

'We'd never get home,' she roared back. He made a face and nodded.

'I suppose not – pity, though –' Then the crowd in front of them broke and the dancers went shrieking and reeling away, leaving a clear pathway. At once he used the advantage he'd been offered and went plunging forward, pulling her with him.

They were breathless when they reached the comparative calm of the station, and as he bought tickets for them she ran her hands over her rumpled hair and took a deep breath. The panic and excitement of the interlude in the crowd was over, she told herself firmly. Keep your head, Lexie. For God's sake keep your head. Whatever he says now he's here, you've decided.

They sat on a bench at the end of the platform for a long time, waiting for the train. They were still running, the woman guard told them very definitely. Probably held up by the passengers acting daft, but still running. There'd be one in soon, ready to turn round and do the run back to town. Just wait, she said, just wait.

So they waited, sitting side by side, and Lexie stared over the lines to the platform on the opposite side, at the shaded blue lights, the empty chocolate machines, and the torn posters warning that Careless Talk Costs Lives and demanding whether their Journey was Really Necessary, and tried to behave as though this was any other night; that she was just going home after a show to a bad house, and tomorrow there'd be another performance and then another till the end of the week, and then back on the road again. Till the tour was over and she—

'Are you as well as you look, Lexie?' he said abruptly. She turned to look at him, surprised.

'I didn't know I looked that well,' she said. 'I'm fit enough.'

'I wasn't thinking of health so much as – oh, it's more than that. You look – eager, I suppose is the word I'm looking for.'

She laughed then. 'Eager? What for? A tatty show that can't even pull in the crowds on a Victory night?'

He shook his head. 'No show could pull 'em in tonight. There's more fun to be had on the streets for nothing than you'll ever get in a theatre. It isn't every night we win a war, after all. Not that it'll do us much good. There are times coming that'll be so grim they'll wonder they celebrated.'

She frowned at that. 'What do you mean?'

'Wars have to be paid for,' he said shortly. 'We've been living and fighting on credit. Now we've got to pay the debts and that's going to be hell. But–' He shook his head. 'No need to talk of that now. Not tonight.'

'You sounded like your old self then,' she said. 'Not a bit like a sailor.'

He laughed. 'A sailor! A hell of a sailor I was! Running a ship's like handling a complex law case. You have to think of half a hundred things at the same time. I may be in uniform, but I'm still a lawyer. Don't be beguiled by all the scrambled egg.' He touched the gold braid on his sleeve briefly and looked at her comically, and she smiled. It was fun to be with him again, after all.

Somewhere down the track they heard a rattle of wheels and they both peered to see if the train was coming, but it was a false alarm. They leaned back on the seat again and relaxed, staring ahead of them at the faintly gleaming lines snaking away in the darkness. After a moment he stirred and turned to speak to her, just as she in turn opened her mouth to speak to him.

'Lexie,' he said, just as she said his name. He stopped and shook his head, but she refused to go on and he started again, and it was clear now that he was strained and uncomfortable. She had felt the tension in herself, and knew it had to be in him too, but now for the first time since she had seen him standing talking to Arthur at the stage door she could feel it.

'All right,' he said after a moment. 'All right. Me first. I don't know what you were going to say, but I hope – I'd like to think it's as important as the words I've been practising ever since I left Pompey.' He threw a small glance sideways at her, then looked back at his cap, which he was turning rhythmically between his hands, snapping the brim with his thumbnail. 'I've practised them for years, I think. Lexie, will you marry me?'

She sat for a long time watching him play with his cap, and tried to think. It would be so easy to stop trying. To say – I'm tired. I've done what I wanted to do, I showed them, didn't I, that I was a star? I was the biggest and best Broadway had. I showed them. So can't I be quiet and easy now, and say, 'Yes, of course I'll marry you and be comfortable and–'

'No.' She was almost surprised to hear the words come out of her mouth. It was as though it were someone else who had spoken. 'No, I can't.'

He was very quiet and then he said, almost conversationally, 'Oh. Can't or won't?'

'There's a difference?'

'Decidedly. *Can't* implies some sort of impediment. *Won't* displays lack of will. Can't isn't as cruel to me as won't. So, which is it?'

She was silent for a long time. Down the line the signal flapped and a gust of wind brought a sudden burst of singing from the streets outside the station.

'Can't,' she said at length. 'Can't.'

He took a deep breath. 'Thank God for that. All right. What's the impediment? Have you married someone else?'

'No.'

'Have you stopped loving me?'

Another short silence, then she said carefully, 'I feel about you as I did when we – when I didn't marry you last time.'

He laughed, a sound full of real amusement. 'That'll do. That'll do fine. Can you tell me the impediment?'

'I'm not sure I understand it myself,' she said, suddenly irritable with herself, with him, and with the delay of the train. She got up and went marching to the edge of the platform to look down the line, and after a moment he followed her.

'Try,' he said invitingly. 'Have a go. You'll be surprised how easy it is once you start.'

'Stop being so bloody professional with me,' she flared. 'I'm not one of your blasted clients –'

'*Touché*,' he said and grinned. 'It's a bad habit lawyers get into. All the same, it's good advice. Try it.'

Again the little silence, then she turned and stared straight into his face, sick of the evasion, tired all the way through of the whole confused state she was in. She let the words rip out of her, making no effort to control or modify them in any way, not trying to make herself seem any better, just throwing out raw honest facts, and he stood and listened as she talked, never taking his eyes from her face.

'I'll tell you why,' she said. 'I'll tell you why. Because I'm a failure at the moment. Because I'm forty-four. I'm getting old and I'm on the bottom. If I get married it has to be when I'm on top, when I'm winning. No one, no one at all, is going to save me from failure but *me*, do you understand? I want no help from anyone. I'll give myself as a great prize when I'm ready and the person I marry will know not that he's saved me, not that he's being good to me, but that I'm being good to *him*. I'm going to America, back to Broadway. I was a star there and I can be again. I'm going to be again. Then, when I've shown you and I've shown Molly and I've shown all of them what I am and what I can be you can ask me again – if, that is, you want to be given a gift, rather than to be the one who does all the giving. All right? Do you understand? No one helps me but me – so I can't marry you.'

359

She stopped as suddenly as she'd begun. He stood looking at her, his hair blowing a little in the light breeze that had struck up, and she saw the hurt in his face and hated herself for it. But she felt better, hugely better, certain now that she'd made the right decision. Broadway. That was where she was going, as soon as she could get there. No more lousy suburban tours, no more aching at the sight of photographs of Molly in the paper. Her own life again, her own career.

But again her own words let her down. 'I'm sorry, Max. You deserve better,' she heard herself say. 'I'm a lousy bitch, you know that? A lousy, greedy bitch. You deserve better. Go and find another Laura, Max. You don't want to waste time on me.'

At last the train came, rattling into the station in a glitter of light, and she said desperately, 'I'll get into the last carriage – for Christ's sake don't come with me. It's a big train – go sit somewhere else. Pretend you never saw me tonight. It's really the easiest way. Forget you ever saw me.'

# 42

'It was wonderful, really wonderful,' Bessie said, and tried to get to her feet. 'Now I'll leave you to get yourself ready and go to your party and –'

'No!' Lexie said, pushing her back gently into her chair. 'You sit there and Tina'll give you some coffee or whatever. Then we'll go together. And it isn't a party, exactly, to start with. It's supper. At Sardi's.' She looked sideways at Bessie to see if she understood the significance of that, then shook her head. Clearly she didn't.

'People always go to Sardi's after a Broadway opening,' she said as Tina helped her out of her costume and gave her her wrapper. 'It's a sort of tradition. If you've got a hit, they applaud you – all the people there. It's quite a moment. Of course, if they don't applaud you, you want to die.'

'They'll applaud you,' Bessie said confidently. 'They'll applaud you all the way. You were marvellous. So's the show. Sometimes a performer's good and a show's bad, and sometimes it's the other way round, but this one's got everything. Good music, good show, and you.' She nodded wisely and Lexie leaned over and hugged her.

'Oh, it's so good to have you here, Bessie,' she said. 'I can't tell you how much. I never thought you'd do it. God knows I've tried hard enough to persuade you –'

'Couldn't spare the time,' Bessie said, a little pink about the ears but clearly pleased. 'Alex – Mr Lazar needs me, you know how it is. He's not so young any more and now with all this work he does for Israel and all –' She shook her head. 'Couldn't get away before.'

'Listen to her, Tina!' Lexie said to her dresser. 'Do you hear her? This Mr Lazar she's talking about – her boss – he's eighty-two, eighty-three or so, I grant you, but she's not exactly a spring chicken any more herself! Flew here, would you believe! There are men half her age terrified of crossing the Atlantic by air, but this one won't come any other way, because she couldn't spare the time by sea –' Tina grinned and began to brush Lexie's silk grosgrain suit, ready to help her into it.

'I thought there'd be a lot more people in here,' Bessie said hastily, wanting to change the subject. 'Don't they all come round after a first night the way they do in London?'

'They do if you let 'em.' Lexie was leaning close to the mirror, applying her street make-up in long careful strokes, covering the fine lines that traced their patterns round her mouth and under her eyes. She frowned a little as she looked at herself – fifty? Damn it all, *fifty!* – and she added a little white highlight beneath her eyes to soften the smudges there. 'But I don't let 'em. They just get in the way while I change and jabber, and anyway I like to get myself looking right before I go on show again.' She leaned back in her chair and looked at herself appraisingly. 'Will I do?'

'You look lovely,' Bessie said. Lexie flashed a grin at her and began to climb into her suit. She wasn't just being polite when she said she was pleased to have Bessie with her – she really had been warmed and excited when she'd arrived. In the six years since she'd come to New York and begun the painful climb back to her old pinnacle, she'd asked Bessie many times to come and see her, but she'd always been evasive. There was Alex, she'd say, and she saw a good deal of his niece Hannah these days too, which was nice, and the business had grown, and – excuse had followed excuse, and

361

Lexie had fretted over that. Always at the back of her mind had been the fear of losing Bessie, the conviction that one day illness would eventually overcome that crooked frail little body, but somehow Bessie just went on and on.

She'd had a severe attack of flu that had turned to pneumonia in 1948, and Lexie had been frantic when Alex had cabled to beg her management to let her go home to see her. And she had flown back, braving the terrors and discomfort as well as the huge expense of the flight over the Atlantic, only to find Bessie at home from hospital and getting ready, as usual, to go to the office. Lexie had sailed back to New York feeling more lonely than she would have thought possible. She wanted Bessie's company as she never had before; needed her reassuring commonsense, her unquestioning support, the essence of her, almost physically. She would lie awake and think of her and worry over her and then be angry with herself for being so stupid. Wasn't life going well for her now, better than she could have hoped? It hadn't been the easiest thing in the world to get back on the Manhattan theatre circuit, but she'd done it.

Now, getting ready to go to Sardi's after the opening of her biggest and most ambitious show yet, one in which she had actually had a share of the production responsibility, she felt happier than she had for a very long time indeed. The early years in New York had been marred, often, by news of Molly. The combination of feeling that could be aroused in her by a newspaper photograph, a magazine interview, a radio show, was as queasy as it had ever been; the bitter sense of loss combined with the sharp bite of resentment that her daughter clearly had Hollywood by the tail, the sick sense of failure as a mother mixed with her pride in Molly's success as a performer – it had all dogged her, but for the past year or so it had been easier. There had been less about Molly in the popular journals, and more about Lexie. The balance had been restored – and now here was Bessie, right here in Manhattan, and again she looked across at the small figure perched on the edge of her chair and grinned at her.

'This Sardi's place we're going to,' Bessie said casually. 'It's where everyone goes, you say, after a first night?'

'Absolutely everyone! Lexie picked up her bag and looked for the last time in the mirror. 'Even if there's a party. You can go on to the party afterwards, but going to Sardi's first is a must. So, come on, Bessie! Hold my hand. Your baby needs you!' Bessie laughed, reddened and got to her feet, tucking her claw of a hand into Lexie's elbow.

'Do you have a table booked? A special one, I mean? Or do you just get put where they've got space?' Bessie asked as they came out of the theatre into Shubert Alley. She shivered and moved closer to Lexie as the bitter cold of the February night air bit into her. 'And can everyone in the restaurant see everyone? I mean, will they all see you?'

'They'll see me,' Lexie said a little grimly. 'Have no fear about that. They'll see me. Hold on to me, now, I tell you. This makes my knees shake – Peter wanted to come with me – you remember? I introduced you, he's the director – but I told him I had you and we'd be fine on our own. So, here we go –'

The noise inside the restaurant was discreet, a pleasant hum of voices and clatter of glass and silver, and Lexie stood there for a moment in the doorway taking in the rich flavour-filled scent of gin, flambéd food, expensive cigars and brandy and then she tilted her chin, pulled Bessie a little closer to her, and walked forwards.

For a dreadful moment she was afraid it wasn't going to happen, feared they'd all sit at their tables with their heads together studiously staring at the pictures of famous performers on the walls, at their menus, at their waiters, at anyone but her. Then at last it started: a small spatter of applause from a table to the left of her, and then another as people saw she had arrived and then, finally, it went all round the big elegant space, like long grass bending before an affectionate breeze, and she felt the smile start to grow on her face all by itself, completely out of her control, widening until she knew she was grinning like a Cheshire cat.

Memory sparked in her, and she saw herself as though she were a long way away down a vast corridor, a small remote figure on a brightly lit stage. She was walking into a big restaurant, where people glittered and chattered and paid her no attention at all, and she was wearing ordinary street clothes, a beret, a simple dress, and was embarrassed because of that, but Bessie, who was with her at the end of that long vista, she wasn't embarrassed at all. She walked jauntily into the great threatening room, towards Alex at a table, and suddenly Lexie laughed to be standing here in Sardi's in 1951,

363

and thinking of London in 1918 – it was absurd.

'Bessie,' she said joyously, turning to look down at her. 'Bessie, do you remember that time we went to the Trocadero, after going to a show one night? To see Alex? And he introduced me to André Charlot's chap and –'

But Bessie wasn't looking at her. She was walking beside her with her head in the air, clearly searching for someone.

'What is it, Bessie?' Lexie said as the applause went on and on around her. 'Who are you looking for?'

At once Bessie went crimson and ducked her head. 'No one,' she muttered. 'No one – this is lovely. Lexie, I told you they'd all applaud, didn't I? I told you –'

'You told me!' Lexie said and laughed, letting Bessie's odd behaviour go, putting it down to the excitement of the moment. 'You're never wrong, Bessie, my love, you're never wrong –' And then they were there in the centre of the restaurant where Peter and Danny the choreographer and Bruce the costume designer and Frankie who'd done the music and all the rest of them were at a big round table all applauding as hard as they could, and she and Bessie sat down in a great flurry of excitement.

It was, Lexie told herself deep inside her mind, the best moment she'd ever experienced, but as the thought came into her head it was followed by a sharp pang of anxiety, as though in just thinking it she was disposing of it, as though in labelling the moment as a peak she had doomed herself to a headlong fall into a trough out of which perhaps she would never be able to climb.

She almost shook herself at the absurdity of the notion, but the chill remained with her and made her more vivacious, more glittering and more sparkling, as the praise for the star that was an essential part of the proceedings was heaped on her. The director, the designer, the musicians, all deserved as much credit as she did; she was well aware of that, and knew how big a debt of gratitude she owed them, but it was traditional to lay the credit for all the success at the star's feet, and she'd earned it. She smiled and smiled and gloried in the moment and wondered, somewhere so deep inside herself it was almost inaccessible, why she felt such a sense of emptiness.

They had reached the coffee stage when at last Bessie beside her seemed to wake up. She had been sitting quietly, eating little, only smiling and nodding when people spoke to her, seeming content to sit in Lexie's shadow, silent and unobserved. But now, suddenly, she sat up very straight and began to chatter very rapidly and totally inconsequentially to Danny, who was sitting on her far side. Lexie, who had been talking to Danny across her, was a little startled for a moment, but, then remembering that Bessie rarely drank and now had a glass of wine in front of her, turned to speak to her other partner. But he was occupied with the girl on his other side, and for a moment she was alone in the middle of the big party and could catch her breath.

Ahead of her she could see a mirror on the far wall and she moved her head slightly, to catch her own reflection. And saw instead two people sitting at a table against the wall. She sat very still for a long moment and then whirled in her chair to look back over her shoulder.

'Oh dear,' Bessie muttered. Lexie flicked a glance at her and said incredulously, 'Bessie? You knew they were here? *Together*? You knew?'

'Once you said everyone came here, I knew they'd come. I thought there was a party after the show, like they have in London, and I thought they'd go there, and it'd all be a lot – well, I didn't know about here, how it would be. But I thought, well, he's a sensible man, he'll know what happens, he'll know what to do – where you'll be –'

She was gabbling now, totally unlike herself, and her face was as bright a red as Lexie had ever seen it.

'I saw them come in just now,' Bessie was murmuring. 'I got worried at first when they weren't here, but then I saw them and I got even more worried – Lexie, don't be angry with me.'

'Angry?' Lexie said and she knew her voice sounded flat and dull. 'Angry? Should I be?'

'Well, I don't know. Maybe. But it seemed to me to be so silly and he told me what you said about if you were a success again you'd – anyway, I told him about this show and all you'd said about it. It sounded like it could be the hit you've been wanting – and –' She shrugged. 'So I told him he ought to come –'

'More wine, Lexie?' Danny leaned over and filled her glass. 'And you, Bessie? You're some lady, you know that, Bessie? We'll have to find a show that's right for you, and make you a star like your baby sister here – come on, have some more wine – it's the best. French. None of your domestic stuff –'

It was a few minutes before Lexie could escape from the general conversation, could turn back to Bessie and demand more, and all the time she answered mechanically to what people said her thoughts were whirling. It was crazy, it was impossible, it was ridiculous and what had Bessie done, for God's sake? How could they be –

At last the talk shifted, became less general and she was free to talk to Bessie again. She turned her head and said stiffly, 'Why together, Bessie?'

Bessie reddened even more and ducked her chin. 'Because it was so wrong,' she mumbled. 'All wrong. I couldn't bear it. You were so miserable and – it wasn't right, so young as she was and so far away, so I told him –'

'When?'

'When? Oh, a long time ago. After Barbie died and you were so miserable and –' She shrugged. 'A long time ago –'

'Did he know when –' Lexie swallowed. 'Did he know before he came back to England after the war?'

'Yes, he did.' Bessie looked at her defiantly. 'It wasn't right, that child going so far away and not knowing who her father was and no one to look after her properly. So I told him – and I told her, too. I wrote her a long letter all about it and explained how it all was, to the best of my knowledge. Barbie had said to me how it was. We were together a lot, Barbie and I, when you were in ENSA during the war. You must have known she'd talk to me about the old days when you two were here in America. You must have known she would. So, I understood how it had been with you, and I told Molly. And then, after you went to America, Max went to see her –'

She peered up at Lexie anxiously. 'You're not too angry, Lexie? It just wasn't right, you see. Someone had to tell them both. They're entitled, aren't they? A man's entitled to his child – and she's entitled to her dad.'

But Lexie sat in silence. Around her the party was breaking up as people made complicated plans about cars and taxis to take them on to the party that Peter had organized for the cast over at his hotel. Lexie sat in the middle of the flurry letting them go, assuring them that yes she'd follow on, she'd get

366

there, no problem, but she just had some people to see first; and then she saw in the mirror that behind her he had got to his feet and was watching the table where she sat. His image disappeared and reappeared as people passed in front of him and then, at last, there were just herself and Bessie left as he came purposefully towards them.

# 43

Bessie had gone, gathering up her bag and gloves and scuttling away like a small frightened animal to sit with Molly. As she had gone hurrying past Max he had put out a hand to delay her and murmured something that made her look hastily over her shoulder at Lexie and then smile, an anxious little smile; and then he had looked at her too and she had closed her eyes.

Now he was sitting beside her. She'd felt the table rock slightly as he'd pulled his chair closer to it, had felt the warmth of him near her and she could keep her eyes closed no longer. He looked tired, very tired; there was a heaviness under his eyes and his face looked thinner. But then he smiled, and at once he was the old Max and she smiled too; she couldn't help it. Seeing him had made the whole excitement of the evening complete; it was as though his appearance at Sardi's had been the climax of the show; the emptiness she had felt inside her had been filled, and she put out her hand and set it on his.

'You'll have to tell Bessie it's all right, you know.' He spoke as though he was continuing a conversation they had started ten minutes ago but which had been interrupted just for a second or two, rather than as a man who had not seen her for almost six years. 'Bless her, she's terrified. Convinced you'll scalp her for her meddling. I told her you wouldn't, that you'd be as glad as I am, but she needs to hear it from you. You are glad, aren't you?'

'Yes,' she said after a moment. 'Yes, I think I am. I – I feel a bit odd. I mean, to see you, with her, after all this time – it's very odd. It'll take some getting used to – '

'It took me no time at all. Once I knew.' He turned his

367

hand over so that her own fell into his palm and he could hold it, closing his fingers over hers. 'It was almost as though I'd always known, really, but hadn't got round to thinking about it. She's lovely.'

'Oh, yes, Molly's lovely,' Lexie said and felt the little chill come back. 'She's got a marvellous face – '

'I meant as a person,' he said, almost reprovingly, and she blushed a little.

'I can't say what sort of person she is,' she said. 'I tried very hard to know her after the – when Barbie died. But she was very angry then, and she wouldn't – well!' She shrugged. 'I dare say she's told you all about that.'

He shook his head. 'No, Lexie. She doesn't talk about you much at all. She won't. There's some mixed-up feeling there, I know that. She won't talk about it to me. But – ' He tightened his grip on her hand. 'But she agreed to come here with me today. I told her what I was planning to do, to come here to see you after the opening of the show, and she said she'd come. I met her in Chicago, after she'd come up specially from the coast last week, and we came in on the *Twentieth Century* yesterday. So you see, she loves you.'

Lexie lifted her brows at him. 'Does she? Because she won't talk about what happened between us? Because she took a train ride? Is that evidence of love, Max? Lawyer's evidence?'

She hadn't meant it to show, the bitterness and hurt; the last thing she had ever wanted anyone to know was how the anger had built up in her over the past six years. When Barbie had died and Molly had reacted as she had, she had understood, or tried to, but as the years had passed and the letters she had sent to Molly had gone unanswered, as her attempts to reach her by phone when she knew where she was filming had ended in total failure, the bitterness had curdled and now lay heavily in her. She had a daughter who wanted no part of her – was it any wonder she was filled with resentment?

But Max was shaking his head. 'Not because of the fact she came, Lexie. Because of the person she is. I've spent a lot of time with her these past years. We've made up for a lot of what we never shared. It's been good, and I know her now. We have a lot of fun together, Molly and I. Whenever I come to Los Angeles – and that's been a couple of times a year, ever since the end of the war, because I took on a couple of directorships of American corporations – whenever I come, we're together. And she's marvellous, Lexie, truly she is. She's so straight – says what she has to say without any messing about and – '

Lexie lifted her brows. 'Is that a virtue? To blurt out everything without stopping to think what it might mean to other people? You admire that?'

He laughed softly. 'You are funny, Lexie. There's a lot of that in you, for heaven's sake! Directness, I mean. When you want something you want it, and nothing deflects you. When Molly wants to say something she says it and no one deflects her. What's the difference?'

'All the difference in the world,' Lexie retorted. 'I never set out to hurt people, or – '

'But you did it all the same,' he said quietly. 'You never meant to, I'm sure, but you did. You had to do what you did, and Molly has to say what she says. And remember, Lexie – she says nothing about you. Even though there's clearly something that – well, that isn't quite comfortable between you. She's straight, but she can bite her tongue when she has to. But look, let's not just talk *about* her. Let's talk *to* her. She's here because she wants to talk to you, but – '

'But what?' She knew she sounded harsh, and couldn't help it. It had been so good to see him, so comforting, but now all that was gone, all the pleasure and all the relief. The emptiness inside had come back. 'She could have talked to me any time this past six years. We've been in the same country, for God's sake, and if she was able to take the train from Los Angeles when you asked her, she could have taken it to find me. I wrote to her. I called her. All I ever got was a stonewall silence – and now you're telling me that I've got to smile sweetly and talk to her, because she wants to? So that she can tell me these straight things you so admire, is that it? Do you want to sit and watch me suffer just because – just because – ' She had to stop, because her voice was rising and beginning to shake and the people at the next table were looking curiously at her.

He was still holding her hand and again his grip tightened. 'Want to see you suffer? Oh, Lexie, if you only knew! I'm here because I want you. You told me that you couldn't marry me when I asked you, last time, not that you

369

wouldn't. Well, now you can, can't you? You're a success again. I saw the show – it's going to be an enormous hit, you know that. So now you can marry me, and now you're going to. We've wasted far too much time already. But Molly – she's part of it too, isn't she? Part of us. I'd have said as much that night at Golders Green Station if you hadn't been so adamant that you couldn't marry me. But you were, so there was no sense in telling you I knew about her. Even though you made a slip of the tongue and spoke her name to me.' He grinned a little crookedly. 'Anyway, I had to go and see her for myself. Suppose we hadn't got on? Suppose she'd given me my marching orders? Why start a drama unnecessarily? But now it's different. We're going to be married, and our daughter surely is included in that – '

She held on to his hand tightly, trying to stop herself from shaking. 'But suppose she gives *me* my marching orders?' she said. 'She did once. She could again. Maybe this time, now you know her and – she's so important to you, maybe this time it'll be you who can't marry me.' Her eyes slid away from his. 'Won't marry me.'

'You do want us to be together, then?'

'Oh, yes.' She said it impatiently, as though it were the most obvious thing in the world. 'I wanted that even the last time when I told you I couldn't. But I wanted the – I wanted what I've got now as well. I had to have it. Well, I've got it, that success. I've shown them I can do it. Twice. I'm fifty, and I'm a star again, and no one can change that. But now I'm tired and I can't go on being the way I was. I want to stop wasting time – yours and mine – but now there's Molly.' She lifted her eyes to look in the mirror and saw that she was sitting there staring across the restaurant at her, as beside her Bessie chattered and laughed. Their gaze locked for a moment and then Lexie looked away, back to Max.

'So there it is,' she said wearily. 'I do want to marry you. I'm sorry I took so long about it, and I hope I'm not too late. But if you prefer to have Molly, I'll live with it. Somehow.'

'There's no choice to be made!' he said. 'I didn't have to make a choice, for heaven's sake! She'll be as happy as I am – '

'You haven't told her yet?'

His face looked suddenly red, almost angry. 'Told her? D'you think I'd tell anyone we were to be married until you knew? That'd be crazy.' And then she laughed. His anger

370

was so ridiculous that there was nothing else she could do. She was still laughing as Molly crossed the restaurant in response to Max's signal and came to stand there beside him. Lexie looked beyond her to Bessie but she, in her usual self-effacing way, was hurrying across the restaurant towards the ladies' room and Lexie looked at Molly and managed a smile.

'Hello, Molly,' she said and thought – God, she's beautiful. Was I as beautiful when I was twenty-two? Was my skin as translucent as that, were my eyes so vibrant, did I have hair that gleamed like that?

'Hello, Lexie,' Molly said. Her voice was even richer, now, a deep huskiness that carried a trace of an American accent, just enough to make her sound intriguing to both English and American ears. 'Congratulations!'

Lexie went as pink as Max had and looked sideways at him, but he was looking at Molly. 'I didn't know you – '

'It's a great show.' Molly was pulling out a chair, and Max hurried to help her. She settled herself at the table as coolly as any other table hopper in the place, as though she were just an old acquaintance saying hello after a few weeks' break in a friendship. 'The music is the best I've heard on a stage for ever. He's good – has he done any films? If he hasn't he should – '

'Oh, yes, the show,' Lexie said. She giggled suddenly and looked at Max, who grinned broadly back at her. 'I'm glad you liked it. One way and another, I'd almost forgotten we opened tonight. It's been an – well, it's not been an ordinary opening night, has it?'

'Hasn't it?' Molly said and looked up at Max. 'Seeing us, is it that that's made it different? Well, I can understand that.'

'You never answered my letters,' Lexie said after a moment. 'Or came to the phone when I called. You must have got some of those messages. Didn't you?'

'I got them,' Molly said. 'But it was best not to answer.'

'*Best?* How could that be best? I just wanted to – '

'Because of Max,' Molly said, as though that were the most obvious thing in the world. 'If you'd talked to me, you'd know we'd met. And he said you weren't ready yet to see him again. He didn't say why – ' And she shot him a swift glance. 'Just that it wasn't time – so – ' She shrugged her shoulders. 'So it was easier not to answer when you called or wrote. I'm sorry.'

'Are you? Really?' Lexie meant it to sound like a plea, wanting Molly to know the depth of her hurt, wanting her to love her, Lexie, as much as Lexie had loved Molly, but it came out as a sharp little bite of a phrase. Molly looked at her, her brilliant eyes showing no expression, and said, only, 'Yes, of course.' She turned to Max and grinned at him. 'Hi, Max. Happy?'

'Very,' he said gravely. Lexie looked at them, saw the bond that lay there between them, and felt the sharpest bite of anger she had never known. They were there because of her, because of *her*, Lexie, yet they shared a closeness that excluded her, and she got to her feet so quickly that she almost stumbled. But Max was too swift for her. He was on his feet before she was, holding her elbow and keeping her close beside him. Looking down at Molly he said, 'I'm happy because we're tidying things up, Molly. Getting married. It was always supposed to happen, you know. We just got a bit out of synchronization, one way and another. What with wars and things like that – '

Molly sat for another long moment and then she too got to her feet.

'Well, well!' she said to Max. 'Out of synchronization – that's a cute way to put it. When are you getting married?'

'We haven't got round to that yet,' he said, and his hand was warm on Lexie's arm. 'There are things to sort out. This show'll run for a while yet, obviously, and Lexie'll be held here in New York, but there are plans we can make. I have to come to the States a good deal, and I dare say I can find other companies who need me here, and come to and fro more often – '

'You'll wear yourself out, doing that,' Molly said sharply. 'Toby does that flight sometimes. He says it's a killer.'

'Toby?'

'A friend.' She brushed that aside. 'Eighteen hours – it's exhausting.'

'Better than five days at sea,' Max said. 'Aren't you going to wish us happy, Molly?'

There was a tiny pause and then she said, 'Of course. Very happy.' She leaned forward and kissed Max's cheek and then after a tiny pause kissed Lexie's. Her lips felt cool and dry on her skin and she was gone almost immediately, but Lexie touched her cheek and was startled to find it wet. She hadn't

372

realized till then that she was crying.

'Molly,' she said then, almost desperately, and not caring whether it showed or not. 'Do you mean that? That you really want us to be happy?'

'Of course.' Molly smiled and her face took on a new set of planes and patterns and her eyes seemed brighter still, and a separate, dispassionate Lexie observing the scene from a distant corner thought, Oh God, but she's beautiful. 'Of course I do.'

'Then you'll have to stop being that way with me.'

'What way?' Molly lifted her brows slightly and looked at Max, amused, almost as though she were saying, what *is* she on about?

'I don't know what it is – but you're cool – you don't seem to be – ' She shook her head. 'I can't say, exactly. It's just that I feel you aren't happy about this. That you're angry – '

They were still standing beside the table as waiters and other diners eddied round them and Molly bent her head slightly and looked up at Lexie from beneath her lashes, a sharp considering look.

'I wish you happy,' she said levelly after a moment. 'Make no mistake about that. I want you to be happy because I want Max to be happy. He's – Max is a very special person in my life now. So, of course I wish you happy. But it's no good thinking you can suddenly turn into a loving Mom, just like that, after all these years. We're strangers, aren't we? Barbie was my mother. Sure, I know you had me, I know that. But it's Barbie I think of when I hear the word "mother". I can't change that in five minutes, can I? I'll do my best to be what you want, but there's no guarantee I'll succeed. Personally, I think it'll be difficult. But I'll try.' She lifted her chin then. 'So there it is. I wish you very happy indeed, and if Max isn't happy I'll be very – well, disappointed, I guess. Yes, that'll do. Disappointed.'

She kissed Max again. 'Settle for that, okay? It's all I've got. Listen – ' She looked over Lexie's shoulder to the table where she had been sitting. 'There's no sign of Bessie. I'd better go rescue her. You two love birds go. I'll get Bessie back to her hotel. Where's she staying?'

'The Algonquin,' Lexie said. 'But, Molly – '

'Great. I'll take her there. So long, Lexie. Goodnight, Max. Take care of yourself – ' She walked swiftly away, her

373

long legs moving under the satin of her dress in a way that made the men still lingering at the tables and the yawning waiters stare after her with a new alertness as her parents stood and watched her go.

# 44

In the event, they weren't able to marry until the summer. The complexity of organizing a marriage in New York between a pair of British citizens was too tedious, Lexie said, to waste energy on. 'As soon as the show closes,' she promised, 'I'll come back to London. I'd sooner be married in London, anyway. Bessie won't have to come back here then, and I can't be married without Bessie to see, can I?'

And it will be harder for Molly to be in London, her secret voice murmured in her ear. Be honest; that's why you don't want a New York wedding. You'd be embarrassed to have your daughter there – but she stifled the idea, not wanting to admit the truth, and worked her way through the run of the show as patiently as she could. Now it was all agreed, she wanted to be married very much indeed, so much so that even her huge success in the show gave her small pleasure. She'd achieved what she'd set out to do, and now her patience was running out.

She was frightened too, frightened of her own reactions. She would lie in bed at night, remembering the long years of loneliness without him, marvelling at her own stupidity. What imp of cruelty had made her turn her back on him so often? That she loved him had never been in doubt, yet how often she'd turned him away. Why had she been so captious?

Because I'm greedy, she would tell the darkness above her head. Because I'm greedy and want the mindless attention of an audience more than I want the constant care and attention of one man; greedy and stupid. And then she'd argue back, passionately, that it hadn't been like that; that her hunger for success hadn't been just a vulgar longing for applause, but a need to prove to herself that she was a gifted person, that she could be what she wanted to be. That was all it was, she would cry wordlessly into the night, that was all it was – and

374

I can't trust that need not to come calling me again, making me turn away from him, making me miserable again – I must marry him soon. Please, let the show end soon, let me go home.

He came to see her almost twice a month while the show ran, going straight from the airport to work at his New York office all day before coming to her at the theatre, looking almost grey with the fatigue of the eighteen hours spent on the BOAC Stratocruiser, as well as the strain of the day's dealings. She would hold him close and feel the taut muscles relax under her fingers and watch him sit half slumped in her dressing room as the exhaustion eased and his colour and energy came back. But she was worried all the same; he looked his age now, and he had never done that. She worked it out and it was a cold little shock to realize it. He's almost sixty, she thought. Oh, God, how could I have been so stupid, how could I let myself waste both our lives like this? She would send Tina to fetch hot coffee for him before she went on stage for her next number and try to convince herself that she did have to finish the run, that it wouldn't be right to break her contract and go home now – but she wanted to, very much indeed.

Molly had gone back to the West Coast and wrote occasional cool notes in response to Lexie's letters, but she showed no sign of demolishing the barrier that stood between them, in spite of Lexie's efforts to make her letters cordial. One evening, when she and Max were dining at their favourite corner table in the Algonquin's Oak Room, she let him see how much that hurt.

'Will it be better once we're married, Max? Will she start to show me any affection then? The sort she shows you? And why does she manage to love you so well when she didn't know you when she was a child? I was always there, always cared – yet now you'd think that – oh, I don't know –' She stared down into her wineglass and shook her head.

'For an intelligent woman you can be very obtuse, my darling,' he said. 'It's because she *does* love you, because she *did* grow up with you, that she's so difficult now. It's easy to care about me, I arrived out of the blue when she'd grown up, a ready-made father, and maybe even a rather glamorous one, what with being a naval officer at the time; so falling in love with me was the easiest thing in the world. I've got no

375

blemishes, you see – I never stopped her from doing what she wanted when she was small, or disciplined her, or gave her any memories of being a hard-done-by child. She could take me on as an equal and be as loving as she liked. There aren't any risks in loving me, are there? But you – you're deeply embedded in her. If you like, you were a sort of father to her – but only the heavy sort – earning the money, making the painful decisions about moving her home from New York to London, all those things. And to add to that there's her feeling of loss over Barbara and over you – she lost you too, you see, when she discovered what she did about you and Barbara at the age she was – she must have felt bereft, out on her own. Can't you see that? Can't you see she behaves to you as she does because she loves and needs you, and she's furious about that? That until she stops feeling the need, she won't be able to allow herself to show the love?'

She had been staring at him all the time he talked, turning her glass between her fingers, and now she laughed a little shakily. 'My darling,' she said as lightly as she could. 'You sound like Peter from the show, after he's been to see his shrink. It's the fashionable thing to do these days in New York, to go to a psychiatrist, and he's nothing if not fashionable. He talks like that after one of his sessions –'

'If his psychiatrist talks as clearly as I did, then he's an unusual psychiatrist,' Max said a little tartly. 'It's not that I mean that I'm such a miracle of clarity – it's just that all those I've ever met spout the most frightful jargon. No, Lexie, don't try to dodge it that way. You know what I mean. You're not stupid.'

'No,' she said and ducked her head, not wanting to look at him. 'No, I suppose not. But I'm hurt and –'

He took her hand, making her relinquish the wineglass. 'Of course you are. But it'll get easier. Just give her time. Once we're married, it'll be easier. When she's learned to live with her jealousy –'

'Jealousy?' Her head snapped up at that. 'Molly, jealous of me? When she's so young and so beautiful and –'

'Well, of course she is! You're a top liner, and she's still trying to make it – she gets only small parts. You know, that was a lousy contract poor Barbara signed for her, a dreadful contract. She's been cheated all down the line – she gets very little money, and when any decent part comes up Carter's refuse to release her. She's been a difficult character at the studios and they're punishing her for it. It's not unusual in Hollywood, you know! I've done my best to sort things out for her, legally, but it'll be a couple of years yet before she finally gets rid of Carter's, and in the meantime she barely scratches a living. You get all the attention and the money and –' He hesitated. 'And me, I suppose.'

She felt a sudden stab of shock. 'And you?' she said, hating herself for the idea that came into her head. 'She's jealous because you're marrying me?'

'I think so. She thought I was hers, when you didn't know we'd found each other. And now you've come between us. From her point of view, of course. Not from mine.' And his hand tightened on hers. 'Never from mine.'

She made a grimace of distaste. 'You can't mean that –' She shook her head. 'It's a revolting idea.'

'What is?'

'That she'd be jealous of me because of you – you make it sound –' She tried to laugh lightly, and it came out as a sort of giggle. 'You make it sound like something out of a bad French novel. All that steamy illicit sex.'

He stared at her for a moment and then nodded, understanding. 'Well, I hadn't thought of that, but I see what you mean. No, she doesn't have any sexual feelings for me, Lexie. You needn't worry about that. But she does need a man she can feel safe with.' He hesitated. 'She's very bad at men. She's had some unhappy affairs these past few years. Ever since she got to Hollywood. It wasn't easy to be a seventeen-year-old there in the last year of the war. The place was packed full of uniforms and doom, and she wasn't very clever at dealing with all that –'

'My God, but you know a lot about her!' she burst out. 'Does she tell you everything about herself? Even about her love life?'

'Yes,' he said simply. 'Who else has she got that she can trust?'

'There's me, for God's sake. There's me! I'd have listened, I'd have helped. I wasn't that far away.'

'She felt you were. Please, Lexie, don't punish yourself this way. You can't change the way things are with you two overnight. You've got to take each day as it comes, between you and Molly. But not between us. We're all right. Isn't that

377

what matters most?' He looked at her with his face suddenly full of naked fear, and she leaned forward and touched his cheek with one finger.

'Yes,' she said. 'Yes, of course it is. I'm being greedy again. I want everything and I want it at once. You and Molly too. And I can't have that, can I? But I've got the most important part, and I wish I hadn't been a fool and waited so long.'

They made love that night, back at her apartment, a tiny box of a place on Central Park West that she had moved into as a stopgap when she had come back to New York six years earlier, and had never got round to leaving. For the first time she was glad it was so small and so very intimate, for it made it all so easy and natural. He had taken her back there after dinner and she had put her key into his hand when they had come to her door on the eleventh floor, and he had looked at it and then at her and then opened the door. There had been no talk, no drama about it; they had just quietly gone to her small bedroom and undressed and slipped into each other's arms as though it was something they had done every night of their lives for twenty years, and as Max said, later, when they lay drowsily curled up together listening to the distant wail of police cars and the hum of the traffic far below them. 'Time doesn't matter any more. Does it? It's always been like this.'

'Yes,' she said and yawned and fell asleep as suddenly as a baby. She slept dreamlessly all night, to wake refreshed and comfortable to make love again, but this time it was more passionate, more hungry, and much more urgent, and it left her shaken and breathless, for he showed in every possible way that his need for her was as intense as it had been twenty-four years earlier. And, what was even more surprising, his touch woke in her an intensity of desire that amazed her. All through the long years of working and struggling and assiduously courting her voracious god of success she had ignored sex; she hadn't believed it mattered to her, had returned in her mind to the long-ago days when as an almost-adult, just emerging from the chrysalis of childhood, the sweating leering appetites of men had seemed to her to be boring and stupid. It had been then, as it had for the past long years, something irrelevant in her life; her body had belonged to her and only her, and no one, she had been

378

certain, would ever invade it. Even that first time they had made love, she and Max, on the river bank at Maidenhead on that glowing October afternoon, it had not been like this, and she was almost afraid of what happened to her that morning.

But he touched her cheek and kissed her and went padding away to the little bathroom to whistle his way through a shower and struggle with her delicate little razor to deal with his stubble, leaving her to stare at the sunlit window at the foot of the bed, her mind in a turmoil. How had she been able to live without this sort of satisfaction for so long? How could she have been so blind about herself, so totally unknowing of her own needs, to have let time eat up so much of her life in such a sterile way?

And that thought had frightened her, made her tumble out of bed herself to shower (a crowded giggling operation in the available space) and then make breakfast for him, anything to stop herself thinking of that. She had success, enormous success; to consider even for a moment the possibility that it had all been hollow, a spurious and useless substitute for the real life that had been waiting in the wings all this time – it was out of the question.

The show closed in June, in spite of the fact that she had been awarded one of the much coveted Tony awards for her part in it, and the management gave a vast farewell party for her. She was glad Max couldn't be there, because one of his most important clients was fighting a big fraud case in London. That meant she could really put a full stop to this side of her life. She had made up her mind that she would never return to the Broadway stage; that she would leave it at the full flood of her achievement, and if Max had been there, much as she loved him, that would have blurred the edges of the old and the new. He was tomorrow and Broadway was – had to be – yesterday. If there was a tinge of regret in her determination to cut clean she would not recognize it. She spent the evening at the party at her glittering best, chattering and laughing and teasing the people who actually wept because she was leaving, and refused to be distressed.

'I'm changing everything!' she told them joyously, one after another, as people told her she was mad to go when she could earn a fortune, write her own contracts for any future shows, could enjoy New York as her private empire. 'I'm going to the new world, my new world – I've finished with this one – quite, quite, finished.'

And so she had. She went back to England by sea, wanting to use the five days of the journey to sever completely the links with her American life and they were married in London seven weeks after she got back. They had talked about having a 'proper' wedding, a religious ceremony in a synagogue followed by a reception, but Max, a little surprisingly, refused.

'I don't need a canopy in shul,' he said. 'Not unless you do. And I know you don't. I don't want you going through something you don't care about just to please me. I can be a Jew without keeping all the rules. I told you that years ago, do you remember? Well, it's the same now. So no shul. And no reception either – just the people we care about, that's all. Quite apart from anything else, to be getting married at our age is really a little comical, isn't it? Can't you imagine the sort of publicity there would be if we tried to make any sort of fuss over our wedding?'

So it was a quiet affair at Caxton Hall, with just Bessie and a now clearly elderly but very dapper and vigorous Alex Lazar and Max's brother and his family as guests, then a quiet dinner at the Savoy for them all, and home together to Max's flat at Hanover Gate, just outside Regent's Park. And that was that.

And yet, of course, it wasn't. The meagre nature of their wedding celebration opened the door to a richness of marriage that Lexie would never have believed possible. Each succeeding day brought them closer together, brought new satisfactions and delights in each other's company. They retraced some of their old steps, going to the same sort of places they had gone to all those years ago when she had been in cabaret at the Café de Paris, but interspersing these outings with long peaceful evenings at home, sitting either side of the fireplace, 'for all the world like Darby and Joan', as Max said ruefully, reading or listening to the radio or, sometimes, watching television.

It was that which brought her back to work. She had had no intention of ever working again; had made up her mind to it that now she was to be Mrs Max Cramer and that was all, but he had laughed at that.

'Darling, do be reasonable!' he'd said when she'd torn up

yet another letter from New York offering her yet another part in a new show. 'Of course I don't want you to go back on the stage – unless you want to. I know better than to say you shouldn't do what you feel is right for you – but if you do nothing at all you're going to die of inanition. You need something more than pottering around the flat and cooking dinner occasionally. Anyway, you know perfectly well that I'm happy to eat out as often as you like. I've no special affection for home cooking. In my experience a chef who's paid to feed me does it rather better than even the most loving of enthusiastic amateurs.'

He'd kissed the top of her head as he made for the front door and the day's work at his office in Bedford Row and the Law Courts. 'Think about it, darling. Television, perhaps? They seem to need some real talent, going by the thing we saw last night.'

So she did think about it, and after a few weeks of vacillation went to see one of the agents she remembered as being good, and almost shyly offered herself for what might be available.

'Just for fun,' she'd assured the man who sat and stared at her thoughtfully from behind the sort of heavy glasses that accountants wore. He was as unlike the agents she had worked with in New York as it was possible for a man to be; none of the old flamboyance and glamour about entertainment these days, she told herself, looking round his neat office with its shelves of ledgers and box files. This is high finance, not fun. For a moment she wondered if she was right even to consider working in this new medium; perhaps she was too old now to change to new ways and new ideas.

But she wasn't. She was offered an involvement in a short run of a sort of panel game, in which members of the public pitted their memories of past entertainers against those of the entertainers themselves, and she succeeded so well that the show was given an extension, and she was elevated to a major part in it. She enjoyed it, since it involved just one day's work a week, and came to find a little gratification in the status it gave her as a celebrity again. She was recognized when she went shopping in Harrods or Harvey Nichols, asked for her autograph when she went to the theatre or dined out. It was amusing, and Max seemed to enjoy it too, basking in her reflected glory. So she accepted one or two more such television engagements, and spent the rest of her time being Mrs Cramer.

That kept her agreeably busy. Max often needed to entertain clients or their contacts, and he now found it was much more agreeable to do that in his own home than in a restaurant. Lexie, with the aid of a local woman who came to clean and help with their dinner parties, became an adept if not too adventurous cook and was certainly an elegant hostess. She enjoyed the evenings spent charming dusty lawyers and abstracted businessmen, and took real delight in winning them over, as she would discover she had when Max came home jubilant with success after his cases. So with such small matters, and her regular visits to Bessie – who was still working contentedly, if for rather shorter hours, in Alex Lazar's City office – time passed extremely agreeably.

The years slid together with alarming ease. Their first wedding anniversary seemed to arrive quickly enough – their fifth even more suddenly. They were busy and happy and could have gone on being as they were; there was their work, and their many acquaintances – though they had few close friends, needing them so little, content as they were with each other – their regular letters from Molly (but no visits, although Max saw her occasionally on his many business visits to the States) and the rich fullness of the minutiae of daily life. Lexie would not have believed it possible she could be so happy while not pushing desperately to be successful at work, would not have thought there could be so much contentment in small things. She felt she had at last found the river that had led to her safe harbour, that the years of fighting her way to survival on the high ocean of her ambition were safely behind her. She was content at last; she wanted no more, could not imagine ever needing more, and could have gone on as she was for always.

And perhaps she would have done if Molly hadn't at last decided to come to England to see them.

# 45

It has been a hot and heavy day, with people lying listlessly around on the yellowing grass in Regent's Park and the air smelling faintly of melting tar as the traffic chewed up the roads and drivers swore irritably at each other. She had walked in the park for a while that morning, but had escaped home again gratefully, feeling the tension in the very air, as full of unease as any of the people she had heard talking as she passed them. War talk – it was dreadful to hear it again, and she felt tired and old. Not that she was all that old, she told herself stoutly as the decrepit lift rattled its way to her flat on the fourth floor. Fifty-five isn't that old – but last time I was young and I could cope. Will it be the same this time? She thought confusedly of bombs and guns and ENSA and shivered. There can't be a war – not again. There can't be. Max must be right.

Max had assured her there wouldn't; he was deeply involved with the crisis, having clients with business interests in Suez, and his calm reassurance should have comforted her. But it didn't, because there was Bessie and her reports of what Alex said. The old man was not quite as active as he had once been in his fund-raising activities for Israel – and at the age of eighty-eight, who could blame him? But he was as passionately interested in Middle Eastern matters as he had ever been, and busied himself with numbers of committees dedicated to Zionist affairs. During her daily visits to him he would talk interminably to Bessie of what was going on – and Bessie would telephone Lexie and report it all, anxiously. She too feared war, and Lexie had to soothe her, over and over again, telling her that it was all right, Max said it would be all right, not to worry – but all the same she worried, and everyone around them worried. London was an uneasy place to be that summer of the Suez crisis.

When she opened the doors and saw the cablegram envelope on the mat she was quite unfussed at first, just picking it up and going to the kitchen to get a glass of iced tonic water before attempting to open it. Not until she was sitting in her big cool living room with the glass, beaded and inviting, in one hand and the cablegram in the other, did she realize that there might be some significance in it.

Max was away for a couple of days, in Paris, where there were complex negotiations going on over his clients' Suez holdings, and as she stared at the flimsy envelope the thought rose in her mind on a wave of cold fear; could Max be in some sort of trouble – ill, perhaps? He'd been looking far from well lately and she'd fretted over that, wanting him to see doctors, but he'd pooh-poohed her anxieties and told her it was just the pressure of work at the moment. As soon as this silly fuss was over they'd go on a little holiday: the Balearics, maybe. He'd never shown her the island of Majorca, and she'd love it – and now she looked at the envelope and, setting down her glass with a little clatter, with shaking fingers she tried to tear it open. He was ill, he had to be. Why else a cable? And then even as her commonsense told her that his clerk, Bill Alderton, who was travelling with him, would have phoned her from Paris if there was anything to worry about, she saw the name at the bottom of the sheet of paper she had managed to pull out of the envelope, and breathed again. Then felt a shock of anxiety tighten in her once more.

'ARRIVING HEATHROW 9 A.M. WEDNESDAY 8 AUGUST STOP CAN YOU MEET STOP MOLLY.'

Molly, coming to London? After all this time? She smoothed the cable on her lap and stared at it as though the intensity of her gaze could uncover more information, but the words just stared back at her, laconic and demanding. Can you meet. Coming to London. Can you meet.

Max won't be back in time, she thought, panic lifting in her. Oh, my God, he won't be back in time. It's tomorrow she's coming, tomorrow morning, and she wants us to meet her and Max isn't here. I'll have to tell her, send a cable, she can't come –

It was absurd to be so alarmed. Deliberately she put the cablegram back in its envelope, pushed it into the pocket of her cotton dress, and leaned back in her armchair to sip at her cold drink. Absurd. Why be so alarmed? She's your daughter, not someone to be afraid of – all right, you haven't seen her for a long time, but she's still your daughter. Older and

384

wiser now. The old sillinesses that used to be between us must have dwindled by now, the old antagonisms surely dusty and dead. If she didn't want to see me, she wouldn't be coming.

It's Max she wants to see, her private voice whispered, and she shook her head irritably. The old habit she'd once had of talking to herself inside her head was something else that should be dead and dusty by now; it was ridiculous to be reacting like this to a promised visit from someone she cared about. Ridiculous. And she went into the spare bedroom to see what would be needed for Molly's arrival. There was no sense in getting agitated, she told herself as she plumped pillows and set towels ready in the bathroom. I'll go tomorrow morning, and when Max gets home on Thursday, he'll be agreeably surprised. We'll all have a cosy weekend talking – and finding out why she's here, the little voice whispered malevolently, and whether she's making some sort of mischief. And again she stifled it, refusing to pay it any attention. But it wasn't easy.


It was almost inevitable, she told herself bitterly, that circumstances should make her be late at the airport. She'd allowed all the time she could possibly have needed, only to find herself in a snarl of rush-hour traffic at Shepherd's Bush that brought her late on to the Great West Road and even later to the terminal building. Parking the car was an agony of frustration as she found herself caught behind a dawdling old Morris which couldn't make up its mind where it was going or how it was to get there, and when at last she did reach the arrival sector for transatlantic flights she was breathless, tight and tremulous as a newly tuned violin. She felt that if anyone touched her she would emit a high-pitched sound, that all round her the very air shook with her tension.

She saw Molly at once, standing beside a trolley on which four handsome matching cases were stacked. She had a flight bag slung easily over one shoulder, and looked as fresh and unruffled as though she had just stepped off a tube train after a ten-minute hop from the West End to Regent's Park. There was a little space around her, in spite of the hubbub of the airport lounge, and people were staring, whispering to each other, clearly recognizing her and yet not certain who she was. Her films, after all, hadn't been particularly good ones, and her parts in them hadn't been all that spectacular, yet she was still a familiar face, and passers by were clearly aware of it.

She was wearing clothes that were clearly not English: exceedingly well-cut yellow cotton trousers and over them a matching shirt and jacket. None of it was creased, and her hair and face were in perfect order. Although Lexie herself had dressed carefully that morning she was suddenly aware that what she was wearing was all wrong: a Mary Bee dress in cream silk, waistless and elegant, and, she had thought, perfect for this heavy August weather, but in comparison with Molly's relaxed chic she felt fussy and overdressed.

Moving a little more slowly now, not wanting to seem agitated, she began to edge through the crowd, and then, suddenly, there was a shrill cry of, 'Ooh, look, Joe – there's that lady from the telly – you know, from that there *The Name of The Game* – what's 'er name – Alexandra Asher – ' And then there was a woman pulling on her arm, asking for her autograph, and she looked down at the scrap of grubby paper that was pushed under her nose and felt a lift of – what? Embarrassment, or triumph? Dealing with being recognized and asked to sign things had been part of her daily life for years now. Her television show got good ratings, and even when it was off the air for the summer, as it now was, people knew her. Usually she found recognition rather tiresome, not wanting to smile and be charming to complete strangers, but now, as she realized that Molly had seen her, the sense of triumph overwhelmed the moment of embarrassment. I mayn't look as relaxed as she does, she thought as she smiled brilliantly at the woman in front of her and signed her scrap of paper with a flourish, but I'm not negligible. This'll show her.

But when at last Lexie reached Molly's side, Molly made no mention of the little episode, only smiling and bending to kiss her cheek. Her own face was cool and she smelled faintly of Joy perfume, expensive and fresh, and she said easily, 'Lexie, my dear – how good of you to come out like this. I guess you had a tough time getting here, hmm? The plane, would you believe, got down on time.'

I won't apologize, Lexie thought furiously. I won't. I'm here – that should be enough – and she smiled at her.

'It's good to see you,' she said. 'Was it a good flight?'

'Not bad at all. Where's Max?'

'In Paris,' Lexie said, and there was a malicious edge in her. I'm glad he's not here, she told herself as she looked round for a porter to take the luggage to the car park. She'll have to put up with me and like it.

Again the familiarity of her face came to her rescue as a porter saw her, and, deliberately ignoring other eager passengers, took the luggage with much jollity and heavy jokes about knowing the name of the game, and at last they were moving out of the mêlée. Still Molly made no mention of the attention Lexie was getting from passers by, and that helped Lexie enormously. She had been thrown off balance by being late, had got off on the wrong foot, but it was getting easier by the moment. I can cope, she told herself as the luggage was loaded into the car and Molly settled herself in the passenger seat and Lexie tipped the porter. I can cope. We'll be all right.

They talked commonplaces most of the way into town, and Lexie was glad of that. She was a regular driver, but London traffic, which seemed to get thicker and more clotted with each day that passed, still alarmed her a little and she needed to concentrate. By the time she at last drew up outside the flat she felt better than ever. She'd slept little last night, worrying about how she and Molly would talk to each other, how they would be together, but it was all right now. They were going to be all right – and she showed Molly to her room as easily and as cheerfully as though they'd seen each other only a few weeks ago, rather than a few years.

'I'll make you some breakfast,' she said, as Molly stood in the middle of the pretty little room, looking round. 'Your bathroom's just through there.' She pointed along the hallway outside. 'You'll find me in the living room there, when you're ready. Make yourself comfortable and – ' She hesitated at the door, wanting to communicate her sense of relief at how easy their meeting had been, in spite of her anxiety, and said diffidently, 'I'm so happy to see you, Molly. It's been much too long. It's all been so silly – it would be lovely if we could be – well, happy together. I hope we can, and I'm so glad you're here – '

Molly looked at her for a moment and then ducked her head in a way that made Lexie feel suddenly odd, for it was one of her own gestures, and she recognized it as such. She'd seen her own programmes on television, knew her own mannerisms all too well, and to see one of them reproduced in this way was extraordinary.

'It's good to be here,' Molly said. 'I've meant to come any time this past six years but somehow – ' She shrugged and turned away to the bed, beginning to take off her jacket. 'You know how it is in this business. You can't always do what you want. If you go too far away from the coast you miss out on what's going on, the parts there are – you know how it is – ' Her voice trailed away and she looked over her shoulder at Lexie and smiled briefly.

'I know,' Lexie said. 'No need to fret about it. I'll make some breakfast – '

'Only coffee and juice, please,' Molly said. 'I couldn't cope with anything else.' Lexie nodded and went away to find Mrs Potter, her daily help, and get her busy squeezing oranges.

Molly took a long time unpacking and Lexie waited in the living room with her head thrown back on her chair, trying to make up her mind about how she had reacted to her overtures of affection. Had she welcomed or dismissed them? It was extraordinary how contained a person she was, how little she communicated even though her face was an open one and her expression animated. She's got a good façade, she thought, staring at the window. A good façade. An actress's façade. Was she acting with me? Dammit, was she acting with me? And some of the unease that had filled her at the airport came creeping back into her.

And with it a little shock of guilt. I was hateful, she told herself, hateful. More concerned with how I looked, with the effect I was having on her, than with seeing her. Why do I do it every time? From the moment she was born I've got it wrong. And I so much want to get it right now. She's a beautiful woman, she's a talented woman, and I want to love her without any complications. I want to love her as a daughter and every time I get it wrong –

Beside her the phone shrilled. She jumped and then picked it up, just as Molly came out of the spare bedroom at last, along the hallway into the living room. Lexie smiled at her, not seeing her very clearly because her eyes, dazzled by the window at which she had been staring, had shaded everything with a blush of green.

'Mrs Cramer?' the phone clattered at her. 'Hello, is that Mrs Cramer?'

'Bill,' she said, and at once the lurch of anxiety was there. 'Bill, where are you? Where's Max?'

'No need to worry, Mrs Cramer.' Bill's voice sounded clipped and very distant and she had to strain to hear him. 'He just felt a bit under the weather, so he's coming home early. I'm staying here to tidy up – he should be with you by about nine tonight. Flying out of Orly as soon as he can get on a plane. He's at the airport now – will you tell him, when you see him, it's all worked out as he wanted? Chesterfields closed at the rate he set, and as long as the bank and Davidson get the figures before business starts in the morning, there'll be no problems. Would you mind repeating that, Mrs Cramer? It's really very important – '

'Chesterfields closed at the rate he set, and the bank and – who was it – Davidson – must get the figures before business starts in the morning. I've got it. Bill, what's the matter? How do you mean, under the weather? What's been – '

'Really, nothing to worry about, Mrs Cramer,' Bill said, and she knew he was lying. 'He'll be with you by nine at the latest, maybe earlier. Be sure he gets the message – it's really vital – ' The phone clicked and the dialling tone buzzed in her ear as she sat and stared at Molly and the greenness in her vision faded, leaving everything looking dull and ominous.

'It's Max,' she said after a moment with as much brightness in her voice as she could put into it, and knowing it sounded false. 'He'll be home earlier than I'd hoped. Tonight instead of tomorrow – '

Molly's face lit up and for the first time the façade slipped, and she looked young and eager. 'Really? That's fantastic! Oh, I am glad – I was real disappointed not to see him there at Heathrow. Does he know I'm here?'

'No,' Lexie said absently, still looking at the phone. 'No. He – that was his clerk in Paris. It'll be a great surprise for him – '

'Oh, yes,' Molly said and lifted both clenched hands in the air in an odd little gesture of jubilation. 'Yes – can we meet him at the airport?'

Lexie shook her head. 'I don't know what time he'll be there. He's got to get a place on a plane. No booking, I gather. So we'll just have to wait – ' She smiled at Molly as gaily as she could. She mustn't know, she was thinking feverishly. She mustn't know Max isn't well, oh God, she mustn't know. And she didn't know why she was so anxious to keep her anxiety about him to herself, or why it was so imperative that Molly shouldn't share her fear. It just was, and somehow she had to contain her feelings for the rest of the day.

She didn't know quite how she was going to do it, because the anxiety was biting very deeply indeed. Max who was never ill, Max who was always so punctilious about business, to come home before a piece of work was finished – it was terrifying.

But Molly solved the problem for her. She drank the orange juice Mrs Potter brought her and then refused the coffee. 'I can't do without some sleep, Lexie,' she said and yawned hugely. 'I thought I could cope with this change in times, but it's knocking me out. Can I go to bed? Would you mind?'

'No, of course not,' Lexie said eagerly, gratitude sharpening her cordiality. 'Of course go to bed. Then when Max gets here you'll be fresh and ready to see him – though he may be a little tired, of course. He's been working rather hard in Paris – ' Oh, please let it be overwork, just overwork, she prayed inside her head. Let it be overwork.

'Great,' Molly yawned again and then, with an air of great casualness, said, 'I have a script with me. It's for a new film – I have to consider it. Would you care to read it while I sleep? I'd be glad of an opinion – '

Lexie nodded uncertainly. 'Well, yes, if you like. Not that I'm any sort of expert. I mean, I've always been a dancer and singer. Not an actress. My television shows – they're just games. I'm not used to scripts really – but if you like – '

'I would like. Let me know specially what you think of the Georgina character. I'd really like to know.' Once again she yawned and stretched and got to her feet. 'I'll go to sleep then. Call me as soon as Max gets here, won't you? I'll fetch the script for you – '

She went and brought the script and dropped it into Lexie's lap, and then left her. And when Mrs Potter too took her leave and the flat lay around her, hot and still in the heavy August afternoon, the only way to control her worry over Max was to read. She might as well read Molly's script as anything else, she told herself. So she opened its green cardboard cover and began.

# 46

By the time she'd finished reading, the noises from the street outside had changed, the afternoon's slow rumble giving way to the shrill din of the rush hour, finally mellowing into the mid-evening purr as people made their way into the West End for theatres, restaurants and cinemas. The only sounds inside the flat were the rustle of the pages as she turned them and the occasional rattle of the refrigerator in the kitchen.

The heaviness that settled on her, she decided, wasn't just her anxiety about Max and the seemingly interminable waiting for him; it was the script. It took her a little while to get into the rhythm of it: the terseness of the dialogue, the camera directions written in language she didn't fully under-stand – what was MCU? she wondered, and then decided it was a medium close-up, and puzzled out that POV was point of view – but slowly the story caught her, and the characters began to prowl around in her mind.

It was a story of two women, a mother and her step-daughter. At first it seemed to be just a sentimental tale of feminine love, but then it changed, became more sinister, as the mother's character, Georgina, showed signs of being first odd, and then, as the tale developed, a person of almost monstrous wickedness – malicious, manipulative and sly. Lexie read on eagerly, needing to know why Georgina was as she was, fascinated by the woman's evil effect, and was almost startled to find how gripped she was as the true depths of the older woman's depravity came out.

But it was the part of the daughter, named Alice, which really haunted her. A marvellous part for an actress, she found herself thinking: a girl who was both vulnerable and tough, eager and yet frightened, bursting with a hunger for sex and unable to recognize what it was that drove her. She and Max had been to see the film *Baby Doll* only last month and, sitting now in her living room in her quiet London flat, Lexie felt the same sense of brooding Southern American

391

angst in this script that she had found in that Tennessee Williams' film, and she actually turned back to the title page to see if this too was his work. But though it wasn't, it had the same power, the same gloomy intensity, and she felt its strength still with her as she closed the last page and leaned back in her armchair.

And was grateful. She wouldn't have believed it possible that she could be distracted from her anxiety about Max, that she could have passed the long afternoon as she had, and she felt a surprising lift of gratitude to Molly for giving her the script to read.

There was a rattle outside the flat as the lift gates clanged, and she jumped to her feet to hurry to open the front door to see if it was Max, but it was only her next-door neighbour coming home and she nodded at him, embarrassed, and went back into her own flat, straight to the kitchen. Whenever he got back, he'd need supper. This would be no night to go out to eat. And there was Molly, too. She raised her head to listen, but all was silent as Molly slept on.

She strung out her supper-making as long as she could, but washing a salad and preparing eggs for a herb omelette couldn't be stretched all that much, and by the time he did at last arrive, at half past eight, she was sitting on the edge of her chair in the living room with her hands tightly clenched on her lap, unable to think clearly at all. She was so absorbed in her own tension that even when he did unlock the front door and come in, dropping his overnight bag beside the table in the hall, she still sat there, unable to run to him.

'Did Bill call you?' he said. Then she did move, hurrying to help him off with his jacket, needing to touch him, to fuss over him as she undid his tie and loosened his collar.

'He called,' she said. 'What is it, Max? You're never ill – what happened?'

'Panic you not,' he said, trying to sound flippant, but she heard the fatigue in him and, tucking her hand in his elbow, she led him to the living room sofa and made him sit down with the cushions in the small of his back with his feet up. 'It's no more than some stupid bug. I must have eaten something. Upset stomach – I flatly refuse to give you all the horrid details. Too distasteful. It couldn't have been worse if I'd eaten a bad oyster – which I hadn't, by the way.'

'Did you see a doctor?'

'A doctor? Because of a bad go of bellyache? Don't be ridiculous, darling! Anyway, you know what French doctors are. He'd have given me something very undignified to use, and the way I feel I could never have managed it!' And he laughed, inviting her to join in, but she couldn't.

That he'd been ill was very clear. His skin had a parchment tone to it, his temples looked sunken and his eyes dull. She put her hand out to touch his face and it was hot. At once she was on her feet.

'I'm calling a doctor,' she said. 'You're feverish –'

'Please, no –' He reached out and caught her skirt. 'Honestly, darling, it's just a bug. If I'm still upchucking and the rest in the morning, fair enough. Right now I need a little peace and quiet, a bath and some sleep. That's all. Any messages from Bill? Did he say anything about Chesterfields?'

She gave him the message, and he nodded, pleased, and got to his feet and went to the phone. 'I'll call Donald. He should be home by now – he can deal with it and then I can take the rest of the week off. It went very well, thank God. This Suez business is going to be all right, you know. There'll be no war. I'd bet on it –' He grinned at her as he dialled and she smiled back, but uncertainly. He did look a little better now, she thought, or was it just that she was getting used to his pallor? She stood there, as he talked to his assistant, trying to decide what to do; to call the doctor in spite of his refusal would annoy him, but what did that matter if he needed treatment? On the other hand, to wait till morning might be wiser, let him have some sleep –

Across the hallway she heard the door click open and turned to see Molly. She was wearing a wide-skirted housecoat in a deep blue and her hair was rumpled and her eyes sleepy. She looked very young and Lexie's spirits lifted at the sight of her. But Molly didn't return her smile. She stood in the doorway looking at Max's back as he stood at the phone.

'That's all right then!' he said with great satisfaction as he cradled the phone at last. 'Donald'll get that sorted out, and everyone will rest better this weekend. A very satisfactory end to a mess – good God! Molly! Where on earth – how – my dear one, how marvellous to see you! I had no idea – why didn't you say you were – oh, this is too much!' He held his

393

arms wide and she walked into them to cling to him as tightly as he hugged her.

Lexie didn't mean it to happen, had schooled herself for this moment, but it made no difference. There it was, the great hot rush of sensation, the anger, the resentment, the whole horrid brew, and she laughed and said brightly, too brightly, 'Darling, I hadn't a chance to tell you – a cable yesterday, here today – all too sudden for words!'

But they were paying her no attention at all, quite absorbed in each other, and after a moment she went out to the kitchen, needing to be busy, not trusting herself to say the right thing, very much afraid she would say the wrong one. And truly not wanting to.

She could hear their voices all the time she made French dressing for the salad and began to cook the omelettes, heard them chattering and laughing, and she felt bleak and alone and suddenly very tired. The day had been an exhausting one and the tides of emotion that had filled it now ebbed leaving her drained. She didn't care about anything much any more. Only about getting the omelettes right.

She was just about to turn the first one out on to its plate when they came into the kitchen. She looked up to see Max grinning at her. His pallor had been replaced by high spots of colour and his eyes were glittering a little.

'Lexie, darling, what are you doing? We ought to celebrate – Molly's first night in London after all these years, and you're cooking? That won't do – come on, best bibs and tuckers, somewhere special –'

'You're not well, Max,' she said flatly, and slid the omelette on to its plate. 'Molly, I hope you like yours baveuse because that's how I always do them. Max likes them that way. The table's set in the dining room. Take this in, and I'll bring ours as soon as it's done. We'll share one as usual, Max, all right?' And she knew she was being absurd to parade their closeness in this way – as if it made a bit of difference to Molly that usually she and Max shared one omelette!

'Lovely,' Molly said and took the plate and smiled at Max, her eyes as bright as his. 'Much nicer to stay here, Max darling. We can be cosy, talk all night –'

'He's tired,' Lexie heard herself saying. 'I don't think he should –'

'Marvellous,' Max said, not seeming to hear her. 'I'll open some wine, then. Lexie, is that bottle of Frascati still in the fridge? Glory, glory, it is. I'd better not have any, not with the way that damned Paris bug's hit me, but watching you enjoy it'll do me a power of good. Come on, Lexie. Scramble 'em for speed, darling. I'll enjoy that – real nursery food, hmm?' He kissed the top of her head as she poured more eggs into the pan, but she knew he was distracted, too filled with delight at seeing Molly to realize how tense she was.

They sat at the table long after their small meal was finished, as Molly chattered with more excitement and glitter than Lexie had ever seen in her, larding her talk of Hollywood doings with household names, making it abundantly clear that, though her own name might not figure as large as she'd like on cinema posters, she was well acquainted with people whose names did, and they sat silently listening and watching her. For her own part, the silence was watchful, but she knew that Max's was full of sheer pleasure. He watched and listened and smiled and his face was so full of delight in her company that Lexie couldn't bear to look at it.

'And then, would you believe, the wretched man went off to that God awful stupid Justice of the Peace and married her! It was asking for trouble – after all, we'd been to the same wretched man – but they'd forgotten and didn't ask us and –'

Max lifted his chin and his expression changed, became concerned. 'What was that?' he said quietly and Molly stopped in mid-flow and looked sideways at him.

'Wow, but you're a noticing kind of a fella, Max,' she said after a moment. 'Really fast on your feet. You lawyers!' She reached into her housecoat pocket, pulled out a pack of cigarettes and lit one. 'Not much I can put over on you, huh?'

'Not a great deal. What did you mean, you'd been to the same wretched man?'

She shrugged. 'I did what they did. Got a bitty happier than I should have done at a party – it was one of the English colony affairs, and to tell the truth, darling, godawful boring – and Laurence had been trying to get me to do it for ever, though God above knows why, so –' Again she shrugged. 'So I just went and did it. And it was the same man, and what we didn't know was he gets paid for every paper he calls with his stories. But no one was as interested in me as they were in Marilyn and her chap of course, so they didn't use the story

395

when it was Laurence and me –'

'It's an appalling system,' Max said with a sudden note of violence in his voice. 'Appalling that people can just marry like that without –'

Lexie's head snapped up. 'What did you say?' She hadn't really been listening, had been trying to push down her resentment of Max's absorption in Molly, but now she was brought back by Max's sharp change of mood.

'She's telling us she's married, Lexie,' he said. 'Just went and got married –'

'Well, maybe it wasn't quite like that,' Molly said and for the first time there was an uneasiness in her. 'I mean, we'd talked about it, done all the preliminary things you know, licences and all that and blood tests. It was just – well, anyway, I married him last fall. Laurence Searle. He's a designer. Very big time –'

'What sort of designer?' Max said. 'And why isn't he here with you, and –'

She shook her head at him and reached for the wine bottle to refill her glass. 'Don't want to talk about it, Max. Don't want to talk, so I won't. You know better than to push, too. You promised me, remember? When you first came to Hollywood, found me? Promised. No questions, only answers when I feel like it. So I don't feel like it.' She emptied her glass at a single draught and Max frowned a little and leaned back in his chair.

But he said no more and Lexie, after opening her mouth to speak, glanced at him and then followed his example. There seemed nothing she could do, because Molly, she now realized, wasn't as controlled as she had been. She glanced at the wine bottle. Max had had none, and she herself had taken only one glass which still stood almost untouched in front of her, yet the bottle was almost empty and she looked again at Molly's slightly sweaty forehead and bit her tongue.

'Talk about the script instead,' Molly said to Lexie, and Lexie realized that this was the first time she'd addressed her directly since Max had come home. 'Did you read it, Lexie?'

'I read it,' Lexie said. 'Very interesting.'

'It's a great part, isn't it? Alice? It's mine. Alice is mine.'

'It should be a very good film,' Lexie said guardedly. 'And yes, it's a very good part, I imagine. I can't really know, of course. I'm not that much of an actress – but with a good

396

director it could do very well.'

'Oh, the director is great.' Molly laughed suddenly. It sounded shrill in the quiet room. 'The best, Laurence says. Absolutely the best. And he should know. He's his friend, after all, isn't he? His *special* friend. His darling Toby. That's why he's using me for the part. He had to.' Again she laughed, and it was a sharp discordant little sound. 'I told him he'd have to. If he wants Laurence to go on the way he does, and me to be a good little wife who doesn't tell tales out of bed, then he's got to.' She looked sideways at Lexie and laughed again.

There was a brief silence then Lexie said, 'Why did you want me to read it, Molly? If you've got the part, and he's a good director – I imagine he knows what he's doing.'

'Georgina,' Molly said impatiently. 'Didn't you read it properly? Georgina's supposed to be English, and you still talk that way, even after all that time on Broadway. There's really no one else they know who could do it, not with a name. None of the big names will, it's such a – well, she's not exactly a sympathetic character, is she? And the big-time ladies don't like playing nasties. So I thought – you're a marquee name in New York, and they know you here, too – maybe if you do it – and it's a great publicity angle, isn't it? Could be time to tell the world, momma and daughter, new film – it's a good angle, eh, Lexie?' She stared at Lexie, who stared back and thought – is she as drunk as she seems? Or is it an act? Am I really hearing this? Is she saying what I think she's saying? About the man she's married, about the reason she's doing this film, about – and suddenly, totally unbidden, an image rose in her mind.

She saw herself in an alleyway outside a stage door and Ambrose standing there, her lips hot and bruised with the kiss she had just given him, looking at her as she stared at him. She saw him pulling his cravat into place and heard him saying to a shadowy young man somewhere in the background, 'My dear, women! Like bitches in heat, some of 'em – for pity's sake get me out of here.'

And she looked at Molly's tight little face and the glitter in her eyes and wanted to reach out and hold her warm and close and tell her it didn't matter, it would be all right one day. That there were tender, loving men as well as men like Ambrose and this Laurence, that she had found Max, and that Molly too could find what she needed.

But she didn't. She just shook her head and said, 'I don't think so, Molly. It's not my sort of –'

'Oh, of course you can!' Molly said loudly. 'Of course you can! You could do it, with Toby to direct you. You could do anything. He could make a horse play Hamlet so's you'd believe it. I may hate the goddammed fag, but he's the best director there is. The script's fantastic – you know it is – and that could be the one that really makes it for me, at last. All those years with that rotten contract and now at last I'm free. I can do what I want and there's this film. And I want you for it. I've got to have you. I could make it work with you. I could get the feeling right – all the bad feeling and the hate and the –'

She stopped suddenly and the silence between them became so heavy it was almost like an actual weight pushing down on her, and then Max said quietly, 'Molly. That was –'

'No,' Lexie said loudly and got to her feet. 'I don't want you to say anything, Max. Do you understand? Not anything. Molly, I'm sorry you feel – I'm sorry if there's bad feelings and hate in you for me. I made some dreadful mistakes with you, but none of them were meant to – well, I made mistakes. But I'm not paying for them in public, you understand me? I'm a performer, I always have been and I'll do a lot for my work. But I don't strip. Do you hear me. *I don't strip*. That's what it would be if I did this with you, and so I won't. Good night, Molly. I'm going to bed. Max?'

He said nothing, looking only at Molly, and the expression on his face made Lexie want to weep. He looked as stricken as if he'd been physically hit. His pallor had returned and he looked ill again. She moved round the table and touched his arm gently.

'Come on, darling,' she said. 'You really must get some rest. You're exhausted.' To her surprise he nodded, and got to his feet and let her tuck her hand into his elbow and lead him towards their bedroom.

He stopped when he got to the door and looked back at Molly who was still sitting at the table, her head bent, so that her hair swung forward to hide her face.

'I hope we can make it better in the morning, Molly,' he said. 'I do love you both so much, you see. We must make it better in the morning.' But she said nothing, and was still sitting there when they went into the bedroom and Lexie closed the door behind them.

# 47

But next morning there were other things to think about, and it wasn't until late the following day that Lexie remembered what had been said, and when she did it was like remembering another life.

It had started at around four in the morning, as the night sky began to thin out beyond their bedroom window, promising dawn. She woke suddenly, to lie staring at the greyish square of uncurtained glass, her heart beating so hard she could feel it thumping on her ribs. It had taken her a long time to doze off and now she felt that she had been sleeping only a few minutes, yet she had woken, and didn't know why.

Then she heard it again, and sat up. Max wasn't beside her. She strained her ears and once more it came, the dreadful choked sound, and she almost tumbled out of bed and out to the bathroom to find him clinging to the wall and retching desperately, almost unable to catch his breath as each wave of nausea hit him. His face was putty-coloured now, his eyes seemed to bulge in his head, and when she touched him he was clammy with cold sweat.

Quite how she understood what to do, she didn't know, but she moved automatically, not thinking. She held him close until at last the retching eased, as it did, slowly, then wrapped him in a blanket from their bed and sat him in the armchair in the living room while she rushed to dress, pulling on a pair of trousers and shirt and pushing her bare feet into sandals. Then she went back to the living room and helped him put on slippers and dressing gown, murmuring encouragement all the time, and, wrapping him again in the blanket, took him to the front door and down in the lift to the car. Getting him in wasn't easy, for he was shaking in the coolness of the early morning air, but at last he was there in the passenger seat and she was beside him and starting the engine, telling him how they'd get him to hospital fast, see a doctor, better than calling the local one out, he needed specialist care, it wouldn't be long now.

All the time she talked she tried not to let the most frightening part enter her mind; the fact that he didn't argue with her, that he just obeyed her directions, let her lead him and push him and do as she chose with him. That wasn't her Max; her Max would pooh pooh her fuss, tell her not to be so daft, would argue with her that he was fine, absolutely fine – but this Max just sat beside her, slumped in his seat, swallowing hard as nausea lifted in him again and again, and sometimes, despite his obvious attempts at self-control, retching dreadfully as he held a towel she had given him to his lips. But clearly there was no need for the towel, because the sound was dry and rasping in his chest and throat.

She decided first to go to the Middlesex Hospital. There might be another one nearer, but it was the one she knew best, and as she drove at full tilt through the dimly lit roads with their scattering of early traffic she found herself remembering the other times she had been there: When Poppy Ganz had been ill, when Barbara – and she changed her mind suddenly, and when she reached Marylebone Road turned left instead of going straight on. St Mary's. She'd go to St Mary's, because taking him to the Middlesex would be like taking him to die.

Praed Street was heavier with traffic as the morning bustle around Paddington Station began, and she swore aloud as a lumbering bus held her up and for the first time he spoke, in a voice husky with the effort. 'It's all right, Lexie. All right – I'm fine. I'll be fine. Just need to get something to stop the pain –'

'Pain?' she said sharply, as at last the bus made way for her and she could squeeze past towards the hospital. 'You didn't say you had a pain –'

'Didn't want to worry you before. But it's worse now – damned bug –' He closed his eyes and began to take deep breaths through his nose again, and she knew the nausea had come back.

Finding a sleepy hospital porter with a wheelchair to come and help Max out of the car and into the casualty department seemed to take an age, and she was white with tension by the time she managed it. She snapped at him loudly, her voice echoing in the big casualty department, and a nurse appeared, putting her head round a screen in the far corner.

At last someone was there to help, for the nurse took one look at her frightened face and came bustling over to harry the porter with his wheelchair out to the car, and supervised Max's transfer to a cubicle in the casualty department. Then there was a doctor, young and tousled in a white coat, sweeping importantly in to examine Max, and she could sit down on one of the benches and wait for – she didn't know what. Her legs were shaking now, and she was cold. She shivered a little in her thin shirt but there was no one to notice or care. She sat and listened to the murmur of the doctor's and nurse's voices as they dealt with Max and felt very alone in the big dim waiting room filled with the smell of yesterday's busyness, yesterday's pain and yesterday's fear.

It seemed to get easier, then, for a while. The young doctor told her with an air of authority that he thought her husband should be admitted for observation, some special investigations. He would see he went up to the ward at once, and when she told him firmly that Max was to be a private patient in a room of his own rather than sent to a public ward his manner changed slightly, became a shade less lordly, and she felt a twinge at that. Had they treated Poppy or Barbara less well than they should have because they didn't have Lexie there to take care of them, to make it clear they were persons of substance? Guilt and distress for them as well as her fear for Max sharpened her tone and made her speak to the young doctor more tartly than she meant to, but though he bridled he said nothing, and arranged for Max's admission to the Lindo Wing for private patients.

It was full morning by the time he was settled in the small green-painted room, and she sat there at his bedside looking at his face as he slept fitfully, relieved of his pain at last by a morphine injection. She listened to the distant sounds of the hospital and smelled its smells, the clatter of trolleys mixed with the scent of breakfast bacon, the clicking of footsteps in the corridors confused with the heavy redolence of carbolic, ether, floor polish, and the voices of nurses, high-pitched and busy, tangled with the smell of illness. It was not that there was an actual odour she could identify: just a mist of uncertainty and fear and doubt. She shivered again in her thin clothes and watched him sleep, trying not to let the fear grow

401

bigger than she could contain.

The sister in charge arrived on duty, and, recognizing Lexie as a television face, immediately made a fuss of her and her new patient, giving her breakfast she didn't want but insisting she eat it, and bringing a comfortable chair into Max's room so that Lexie too could rest. ('You look worn out, my dear, and a little zizz will do you the world of good – I'm afraid Dr Jefferson Lockhart won't be here till this afternoon, so you might just as well, mightn't you?') Lexie had relinquished herself to her care gratefully, and actually did doze off for a while as the morning wore on and Max seemed more comfortable.

It was not until the sister had brought her lunch and Max had another injection of morphine and slipped again into a drugged sleep that she remembered. With a little clatter she put down her coffee cup as the thought came to her, and Max moved uneasily in the narrow white bed. But he didn't wake, and after a moment she got quietly to her feet and went out to the corridor.

Talking to Molly wasn't easy, because sister, with eagerness to be helpful written all over her, had insisted she use her office phone, which meant that she had an audience. But she did her best to explain, standing with her back to sister who sat at her desk with her head bent over some paperwork, ostensibly ignoring the conversation but clearly agog.

'I hope you weren't worried when we weren't there this morning –'

'Not really,' Molly said. 'I thought you'd gone out some place. What's up?'

'Max is ill. In hospital –'. She felt an absurd twinge of triumph. That'll show her – didn't worry, indeed. That'll show her –

'Ill? What is it? He said he had a bug or something, but I didn't think it was bad enough for him to go to the hospital. He was okay last night at supper – you said he was tired, but he seemed okay to me –'

'He was taken ill in the night – we're waiting to see a specialist. I hope Mrs Potter looked after you, made you food and so on – she'll organize something for your supper if you ask her –'

'I told her not to bother. I've checked into a hotel. I've just called a cab to take me. I was going to leave a note for you

402

but you've called, so –'

'You were going to leave without seeing us?' Lexie said sharply.

'I thought it might be better. You were one very angry lady last night, weren't you? You even made Max mad at me so –'

'*I* made Max – what are you talking about? You did it yourself – don't try to suggest that I –'

'Oh, it doesn't matter. You hate me anyway, I know that. You always have. And now you hate me more because Max doesn't. Well, if that's the way it is, I guess that's the way it is. I'll talk to Max myself some other time. Which hospital is he in? Where is it?'

'He's in no condition to be visited,' Lexie said, keeping her voice as steady as possible, although she could feel the anger boiling in her. 'So there's no point in –'

'Hey, now, you tell me where he is!' For the first time Molly sounded as though she cared. Every word she'd uttered so far had been cool, remote, totally controlled. But not now. 'You have no right to keep me away from him –'

'When he's fit for visitors, I'll let you know,' Lexie said. 'Which hotel will you be in?'

'Where the hell is he?' Molly shouted it so loudly that it seemed to Lexie she could be heard in the small room. She glanced swiftly at sister, who still sat with her head down over her work, apparently oblivious. But Lexie knew she hadn't missed a word. 'You have to tell me!' Molly was still shouting. 'I want to come and see him and –'

'As soon as he's a bit better, Molly. If you'll tell me which hotel you'll be in. But really, he can't cope right now –'

She heard Molly take a deep breath before she spoke. 'I'll be at the Cumberland. But call me soon, you hear me? I have to go back to the States Wednesday, and I want to see Max before I go.' There was a brief silence then she said, 'Hell, Lexie, I'm sorry. I guess I was – look, call me, will you? Everything's such a mess it's making me stupid. Making me say things I don't mean. I know you don't hate me, not really. Do you?'

'No,' Lexie said after a moment and felt her face get hot as tears rose in her. Damn it, why did it always happen between them this way? Wanting to be close, always wrenching themselves apart, always tears with Molly, always tears –

'No, I don't. I – ' She became aware again of sister, and bit her lip. 'Look, Molly, let me see how things are with Max. Then I'll call you. I'll come to the hotel, see you, and bring you here to see him. As soon as I know what's happening. I promise.' She hung up the phone and at once sister looked up with practised sympathy and said, 'Are you all right, my dear? Is there anything I can do?'

'I'm fine,' she said and managed to smile. 'Fine. I – will the doctor be long now, do you think?'

'Not long – two o'clock, he said, and he'll be here on time. He always is. Er – is there anyone else you want me to call for you? Any friends or relations or – '

Lexie shook her head and turned to go, then stopped at the office door and looked back at her, frowning a little. 'Is there any reason why I should call anyone else? I mean – what do you think's wrong with my husband?'

Sister stood up, straightening her black belt and smoothing her apron over her hips, and it was as though the real woman had disappeared behind the starched image of the professional. She smiled gravely and shook her head at Lexie.

'I really can't say, my dear. That will be up to doctor. He is, of course, very ill – '

'How ill?'

'Well, he's feverish, his blood pressure is not all it might be, and there's clearly an abdominal problem.' She ushered Lexie out of the office towards Max's room again. 'But until Dr Jefferson Lockhart has seen him and done his examination I really can't say more. He won't be long now, so really, my dear, all we can do is wait for him – '

She knew then. She sat in the armchair looking at the door which sister had closed so gently behind her after bringing her back, and then at Max, asleep on the pillow with a fine line of white showing beneath his half-closed lids. She listened to his uneven breathing and she knew. Whatever the precise diagnosis was, Max had some dreadful illness. It wasn't just a bug, something he'd picked up in Paris, something from which he'd recover and they could both forget. It was part of him now, and therefore part of her. But for how much longer it was impossible to know.

# 48

Late that night, they took him to the operating theatre so rigged with bottles of saline and blood that she felt he was lost somewhere beneath them on the trolley. She stood in the corridor and watched the gowned porter wheel him away, as the nurses behind her prepared the bed to receive him back, feeling certain he never would come back. That wasn't her Max lying there on that narrow metal shelf on wheels; not that faintly yellow-faced creature with closed eyes and tired lines breaking up the parchment skin. He had gone somewhere else, and she wanted to run down the corridor after the trolley and pull him off it so that together they could go and search for the real Max.

'My dear, you look exhausted.' She started at the voice of the night sister behind her. 'Don't you think you should go home now? I dare say he'll be in theatre a long time, you know, and then it will take some time for him to come round from the anaesthetic. Go home, get some sleep. Come back in the morning – '

'No,' Lexie said sharply, and the sister's brows creased slightly.

'Very well,' she said. 'If you want to stay – I'll fix a chair for you in the waiting room and find a dressing gown. Then you can get out of your clothes for a while. That should help, I imagine.'

'What operation are they doing? He told me, that doctor, but I didn't understand. What operation?'

'A laparotomy,' the sister said. She was a small person, young and round and neat, and out of her uniform she would probably have been a pretty girl, but in it she seemed ageless, a sort of all knowing Vestal, and Lexie put out her hand to her, needing her reassurance. But all she did was shake her head. 'I'm afraid it's not very good, my dear. There's a major obstruction, it seems. Probably the head of the pancreas – '

'But what does that *mean*?' Lexie said it almost despairingly. 'I don't understand – '

'It's a form of disease that's very difficult to treat, I'm

afraid. We can only hope an operation is possible. Now, please, my dear, do come and rest. Sit down and sleep a little.' She insisted Lexie change into the dressing gown and settled her in the armchair in the waiting room, then went rustling away to leave her to her terror.

It was easier after they brought him back because at least she was no longer alone. She could sit beside his bed and look at him, could watch every breath, study the nurses as they checked his pulse, took his blood pressure, examined his dressing, trying to find clues to his progress in each of their actions, in the expressions on their faces. But they were impassive, young, smooth-faced creatures doing a technical job. They avoided catching her eye, shutting her terror out of their minds because they couldn't share it, and didn't want to.

The surgeon came to see her, briefly, a tall thin man in a neat dark suit looking like any other businessman at the end of a day's work, a little tired, abstracted even, and when he told her in quiet, conversational tones how sorry he was that Max's cancer was so fast-growing that it was inoperable, how sorry that he was so ill, but glad that at least he had been spared a long drawn out period of pain and distress, she was not surprised. She had known since the afternoon that this was what it was and now she asked, in a voice so controlled that it surprised her, how long it would be before – and then her voice failed and she couldn't get the question out.

'I'm very much afraid it can't be more than a short time,' the surgeon said, more distant than ever now, no emotion in his voice to gild the words with any real humanity. 'I am so sorry, Mrs Cramer. Indeed, for his own sake it would be better if he did not linger too long. A most malignant form of disease, I'm afraid, clearly very fast growing. I am truly sorry.' He touched her hand briefly with fingers as dry as old twigs and went away, leaving her to the nurses and their blood pressure machines, their charts and their blank young faces. And Max's barely breathing body lying in a narrow white bed in a green-painted room, but really long since gone from her. Long since gone.

That day and the next slid past, and she would not move from the room, although the day sister tried to persuade her to go, but she just shook her head numbly. Sister shrugged and let her stay, bringing her tea and toast from time to time, which she tried to swallow just to please her, and found comforting, to her own surprise. She slept occasionally in the high-backed armchair they'd given her, and whenever she woke did so in a great wash of guilt, terrified that something had happened while she slept, that Max had woken, sat up, asked for her and been hurt at her defection into slumber. But he never did. He just lay there, breathing those shallow bubbling breaths, his eyes half closed in the coma into which he'd slipped from the anaesthetic.

There had been one moment, deep in the night, when she thought he'd woken. She had been sleeping herself, deeply, and had woken suddenly in a panic, her heart thumping in her ears and her face wet with tears. She had stared at him and he had seemed to turn his head on the pillow to open his eyes and look at her with one of those familiar old quizzical glances of his, as though to say, 'Isn't this ridiculous? What are we doing here, Lexie, you and I? What has this to do with us?'

And she had got to her feet, clumsy with fatigue, to hurry over to him. But he had lain there, silent, and she couldn't be sure whether it had really happened. It didn't matter, really, because there had been comfort in that moment. Her pulse had slowed, her panic had ebbed, and she had bent and kissed him and felt a moment of peace.

'Please let me call someone for you,' sister said next morning, almost pleading with her, clearly alarmed by the way she sat there so doggedly, so alone in her vigil. 'A relation, a friend perhaps?' And she did think for a while about that. Bessie? How could she call Bessie to sit with her, Bessie now so old and frail? She couldn't, and not only for Bessie's sake. To have her there would mean splitting her concentration; she would have to look after her, show concern for her, and she had none to spare. All her energy was to be used for Max and herself. She had none for anyone else, not even Bessie. So she shook her head.

'A business colleague of your husband, then? Really, my dear, this could go on for several days yet, I'm afraid. A coma like this – it's a blessing in disguise for the poor patient, of course, who feels no pain, and knows nothing of what's happening, but for the relations it's – do, please, try to think of someone we could bring here for you.'

Again she considered that carefully. Peter, Max's partner?

Someone else from the office? But they too would need attention, time that belonged to Max and herself, and again she shook her head.

So when he died she was alone still. Four in the morning it was. The window of the small green-painted room showed a thinner blackness than it had all through the night, and in the street below she could hear the footsteps and shouts of late-night roisterers and she thought – it's Saturday, fun night, party night, people-out-late night – and Max is dead. They've pulled the sheet over his face and what a stupid thing to do, as if it made any difference when he's not been here these past two days, when he's been dead ever since I brought him here, and I was afraid to go to the Middlesex Hospital because I thought he'd die there, and I brought him here and now he's dead, dead, dead – and the word rang in her ears and she shook her head, almost pettishly, to clear it.

They were kind, very kind, turning all their attention to her now they had no need any more to take Max's pulse or blood pressure or fuss over his bed. It was as though she had become an ill person now to replace him in their lives as they took her to an empty room and coaxed her to undress, take a bath, crawl into the bed and sleep.

'Day sister will sort the formalities out for you,' the night staff nurse said, smoothing the sheet as she settled her. 'Just you rest now. That tablet I gave you will help – you'll be able to cope better in the morning.'

And somehow she was. She sat with sister in her office dealing with the papers involved, nodding as she explained about death certificates, about the hospital bill, about arrangements that had to be made for funerals, calm and quiet, tearless and grateful for that. To be so cold inside, so empty – it was a sort of comfort. There was pain lurking somewhere outside her, wanting to pounce, to jump inside her skin and make her shriek with the agony of its presence, but now she was empty and that was something for which to feel real gratitude.

The flat, when she let herself in, was orderly and cool. She stood in the kitchen looking at the note Mrs Potter had left on the table, trying to imagine how it had been when she had written it, trying to remember that Max had been alive then. Or seemed to be alive, breathing shallowly in a narrow white bed with his eyes only half closed.

'I cleaned the spare room,' Mrs Potter had written in her big effortful loops. 'The which it needed badly considering it was only one night it had been used the young lady leaving it considerable disturbed and I will collect my money Monday trusting that will be all right on account I have my gas bill waiting and oblige Yrs Edith Potter, Mrs.'

She put the money ready on the table then and there, not knowing where she would be on Monday, filled with a sudden acute anxiety about Mrs Potter and her gas bill, wondering whether she should drive to her home, give her the money right away, and then quailing at the thought of those eager little staring eyes, wanting news of Max, wanting to exclaim and commiserate, and she couldn't face that. Better to leave it there, till she came as usual on Monday. She could leave the key with the porter downstairs. He'd hold on to it to let Mrs Potter in – and she filled her mind with the minutiae of domestic arrangements as she went to change her clothes, finding herself a fresh cotton dress, putting the shirt and trousers she had lived in ever since the small hours of Thursday morning in the garbage bin. She would never wear those again, not ever, ever, ever –

Call Bessie? Not yet. Not yet, can't call her yet. I need time. It's got to be Molly. Oh, God, it's got to be Molly. And for the first time she let herself think about what she had done. In a fit of jealous pique she had refused to tell Molly where Max was, had refused to allow her to see him and now he was dead and she would never see him again. And surely she would never forgive her for it.

'Any more than I'd forgive her,' she said aloud to the mirror as she brushed her hair. 'Any more than I'd forgive her.'

Being active, moving about, helped. She drove the car through the lunchtime strollers in the warm sunshine towards the West End, concentrating on the traffic, giving way with unusual courtesy to every Sunday driver who dithered on the road in front of her, carefully choosing a place to park, walking the five minutes to the hotel with precise rapid steps, businesslike and purposeful. To be busy helped.

The receptionist bridled with pleasure when he recognized her, and she stared at him, puzzled for a moment, when he greeted her as 'Miss Asher', then managed a thin smile of acknowledgement.

'Is Miss Rowan in her room?' she asked. 'Miss Molly Rowan? If you could find her for me, please. It's – it's rather important.'

He shook his head. 'She's gone, Miss Asher.'

'Gone?' She frowned, uncomprehending. 'You mean she's out? I'll have to wait then, I suppose or – '

'No, I mean she's *gone*. Left the hotel. The gentleman as well – '

Again she stared at him, confused and unable to comprehend. 'Gentleman?'

The receptionist, clearly enjoying himself now, leaned confidentially on the counter. 'Well, yes, Miss Asher. He arrived on – let me see – it must have been Thursday night, around seven. I was on late turn that night – yes, Thursday, not long after she checked in herself, and she was that surprised to see him – well, I can't tell you. Really surprised – ' And he looked at her knowingly and grinned. 'Can't say she was pleased, so much as, well – very, very surprised. He checked into her room, said he was her husband.' And though he didn't smirk, she felt the relish of doubt in him as he said it. 'And then yesterday it was, she left, together with him. Yesterday morning, very early. I was on again, as it happens, I'm on mixed duties this week, so you could say I was here for all of the time she was. A lovely person, isn't she? I saw that film of hers, you remember? *One Night in Pasadena*, it was. She looks lovely. Not unlike yourself, Miss Asher, if I may say so – ' And again she felt the relish in him and smoothed her face, refusing to let him see he had any effect on her.

'I see. She left no messages?'

'Messages? Not to my knowledge. And I was on all the time as I said, but I could check, of course – ' He went bustling away behind the partition that enclosed the desk and she heard his voice, high and self-important as he spoke to someone there.

'Well, there you are then! She did, after all! Left a letter with the chambermaid who brought it down in the afternoon, after I'd gone off duty. For a Mrs Cramer – not for you, I'm afraid – '

'I'm Mrs Cramer,' she said, and held out her hand. 'It's my married name.' He looked at her doubtfully and with a sudden spurt of anger she pulled her purse out of her pocket

410

and rifled in it for her driving licence. 'There,' she said savagely. 'Identification, all right? Now can I have my letter?'

She went to the car to read it, sitting there in Seymour Place for some minutes gazing out at the people passing by before slitting the envelope with her thumb. She was afraid of the letter and didn't know why. But it had to be read, and at last she smoothed the scrawled sheets of paper on her knee and took a sharp little breath before starting.

'I don't know whether to post this, or what to do,' it started, without any address, any preamble at all. 'But then I thought you must contact the hotel, surely, eventually and they'll tell you I left and give you this and that'll be quicker than sending it by post. The thing is, I've got to leave. Laurence got here last night and if I don't go back to the Coast with him now there's no movie, and no marriage either. I happen to want to keep him as much as I want to do the movie, so there it is. And yes, I know I'm a goddammed fool as far as he's concerned but what's that got to do with anything? I hope Max is okay – I'd have come to see him if you'd let me, but I can understand why you didn't. He's yours and you feel the way about him I do about Laurence, and when that bloody Toby starts trying to muscle in, I do what you do. I keep him out any way I can. Now Laurence says we've got to get back or we lose the backing for the movie, so what can I do anyway? I'm sorry about yesterday. I didn't mean to be so horrible. I never do, you know that? I really do want to be comfortable with you, I always have ever since I can remember. You were the greatest thing in my life when I was a kid, you know that? You used to come in so beautiful, so cool, and I used to want to die for you. But there was Barbara to make it better when you weren't there, and so I guess I managed well enough. Until we were packing up the apartment and I found that birth certificate, then I could have killed you. All those years wanting to love you and thinking you couldn't love me because I wasn't yours to love, and then finding out – oh, I was one mad kid, I guess I still am, and I know I'm not explaining well, but I've only got a little while for this letter and I have to get it done – I've still got a lot of packing to do – anyway, listen, I didn't mean to be so horrible about that script. I mean I did a bit, I guess, I did want to get at you, but it's true all the same. I

411

could play Alice marvellously if you were Georgina, because although the way they've written her she's a bad person, she isn't really, she's just a bit mixed up, she had it bad too and together we could have worked it, made people understand about us as well as about Alice and Georgina – anyway, they'll get someone else, and I'll do my best. He's a bastard, Toby, but he's a good director, so you'll be hearing from me. That movie'll be a good one, and you'll be sorry you didn't do it with me. Give my love to Max. I'll write him as soon as I get back to LA.'

And that was all. No signature, just those pages of rapid scrawled handwriting. Very slowly Lexie folded them and put them back in their envelope. Everyone's gone now, she found herself thinking as she stared out of the car window and watched a man walking his small chattering daughter along the street towards an ice cream van at the corner. Everyone's gone. Max and now Molly. It's just me again. And Bessie. There's always Bessie. And she switched on the engine, let in the clutch and set out for Hackney.

# 49

There were children in the park, shouting unintelligibly at each other, repeating over and over again the same high-pitched sound and, irritated, she moved to the window and closed it, in spite of the heat. She'd have to install air conditioning if this weather was going to go on, she thought, and then grimaced at herself. To spend more money on this tired old terraced house would be ridiculous, and after all, Bessie was happy enough with it as it was. She'd lived here for forty years now. She seemed not to notice what the house was like or what the weather was like; hot or cold, cheerful or miserable, there she would sit in her armchair, happy over her sewing, watching her precious television set and seemingly asking little more.

Lexie sat down, picking up the paper and trying to concentrate on the disapproving article she had been reading about the new rock and roll craze that was dominating the dance floors of Britain, but it was almost impossible to take in more than three words at a time. Over and over again she read the same sentence and still didn't know what it said, and she threw the paper down and said abruptly, 'I think I'll go for a walk.'

'Shall I come with you?' Bessie peered at her a little mistily over her glasses, and Lexie shook her head.

'No, it's all right. You watch your programme. I'll be back in an hour or so.'

'It's only some sort of religious discussion,' Bessie said, but she turned back to the set, fascinated as ever by its moving shadows. Lexie went and made sure the back door was locked – the days when they could safely leave the house and not worry about intruders were long since gone, and leaving Bessie alone demanded extra care for security. She even checked the windows before leaving. They'd done a good job eventually of making the house attractive, she told herself as she moved from room to room, through the handsome new kitchen with its American–style work units and special oven with the eye-level grill of which Bessie was so inordinately proud, and the neat bathroom complete with shower, a rare treat for a London establishment. It had been perhaps silly to spend so much money gutting the old house, restoring its two flats to a single home, putting in central heating, but Bessie had been adamant about not moving, and anyway it had given Lexie something to occupy her mind during the long painful months after Max had died. Fighting it out with lazy builders and recalcitrant painters and lackadaisical suppliers of furniture and appliances and cur- tains had drained off her energy, had sent her to bed each night exhausted and therefore able to sleep. So perhaps it had been worth it for that, even if the house did stand out in the middle of what was fast becoming a dilapidated area, like the proverbial peony in a cabbage patch.

Outside the air was hot and exhausted, thick with the smell of diesel and dust and Lexie felt the sweat start to trickle between her breasts and for a moment thought of going back inside, but then, as a child went shrieking past on roller skates, making her dodge, decided she would walk after all. To go back would help nothing.

The park lay before her, dried and brown, the trees drooping sadly in the weary evening air, and as she walked dust spurted up inside her sandals, then into her face, making her nose itch, and she rubbed the back of her hand across it and felt the grittiness. A swim, that's what I need, she told herself, perhaps a swim. But on Sunday the local pool closed early and it was gone seven in the evening now. She walked on, her head down, aware of her physical discomfort but even more of the emotional turmoil that filled her.

Face it, she thought. Face it. You've got to. Next week it'll be a year, and you've known all along that would be the worst time. A year without him, a year of silence from Molly. Not really a year, of course, she told herself then. I've been writing to her, haven't I, even if she hasn't answered? Not a real silence – but what's the use of shouting into blankness? If she never answers me isn't that the same as silence?

But now she has answered, hasn't she? She's answered now, just when it's the anniversary of Max's death. *Almost* answered, and she slid her hand into her dress pocket and felt it there, the sheet of paper that had been in the envelope that had arrived last Wednesday. She had shifted it from pocket to pocket, bag to bag, ever since, telling herself it was because she didn't want to risk leaving it lying around where Bessie might see it, but knowing the truth inside herself; that she didn't want to be parted from it.

Now she took it from her pocket and read it again, still walking slowly along the dusty path. It had been sent by a public relations company in Los Angeles and it was signed by a name totally strange to her, but the message was clear enough.

'Dear Mrs Cramer,' she read. 'I am instructed by my client Miss Molly Rowan to tell you that she will be in London shortly to deal with preliminary publicity for the film, *A Daughter's Story* and that she will be visiting you soon after she reaches London. We cannot at this time say precisely when her visit will take place, since final arrangements have not yet been firmed up, but we would be grateful if you could make yourself available to meet Miss Rowan when she arrives. Her schedule will be an extremely tight one, as we are sure you realize, and there will be little time to spare. Our representative in London will notify you as soon as there is any information on the plans that are being made –'

At first she had been hugely, furiously, angry at the coolness of it, the effrontery of these people. To assume that

414

she would drop everything to be available, that she had no activity of her own, that she would simply open her arms wide and say, 'Wonderful!' – how dare they? she had cried to herself as she had put down the letter the first time she read it, but now, re-reading it for the umpteenth time, she could no longer summon up the same fury. All that she could feel was relief, relief that Molly was coming, that she wanted to see her, and the fact that she had chosen this cavalier way to give her the information didn't matter. All that was important was that Molly was coming, Molly was coming, and if she was lucky, if for once Providence was on her side, she would arrive before the anniversary of Max's death. If she did, then it would be all right. She'd be able to rest again, would be able to remember Max with pleasure instead of this huge consuming guilt that had been with her for every moment of every day for the past long months.

She had become obsessed with that idea, in spite of telling herself furiously that she was being stupid, that she was falling into a state of mindless superstition. She had developed this notion that if Molly were to come and they could be friends again before the year was up, she could go on living, could find a pattern for passing her days and living the life she had left to her. She could maybe go back to work, take on some new television programme (and she shut her mind tightly against the idea that perhaps, after so long away from the screen, after so many refusals of work, no one would want her again because she was forgotten), start to do more than sit with Bessie, visit old Alex Lazar occasionally, and just rot.

Because that's what's happened to me, she told herself as she reached the end of the pathway and turned to make her way back. That's what's happened, isn't it? You're tired and listless and you do nothing. You behave as though you're Bessie's age, rather than twenty years younger, and if you go on like this you might as well be dead.

I wish I were, her little voice whispered at once, but she ignored it. She had to, because it had been saying that to her for far too long. And every time it seemed to be more and more reasonable. Not to be thought of, not to be thought of –

When she got back to the house Bessie was no longer watching her television set, but pottering in the kitchen

415

washing salad for supper, and at once Lexie tried to remonstrate with her, telling her there was no need to do it, *she* would, but Bessie shook her head at her and went on slowly slicing cucumber with her slightly shaky fingers.

'So what's the sense of giving me such a fancy new kitchen if I'm never allowed to do anything in it?' she said. 'A salad is no trouble. If I was trying to roast a chicken for you, I'd agree, but a salad –' She becked her head at Lexie, smiling cheerfully, but there was something worrying her. Lexie could see it at once, for Bessie let her eyes slide away from her gaze, and she sat on the edge of the washing machine and folded her arms and watched her.

'What is it, Bessie?' she said after a while. 'You're bothered about something –'

'Me, bothered about something? Nothing at all, what should be bothering me on a nice Sunday evening? Don't be –'

'Oh, come on, Bessie. This is me, not Alex. You can tell him any lies you like, but not me. So what is it?'

She put down the cucumber knife and stood looking miserably at Lexie. 'Oh, it's such a shame!' she blurted out. 'Such a shame! I don't deny you had your problems, you two, but she doesn't have to be that way! She could have called, written even, said she was coming –'

'Molly?' Lexie stood up straight. 'She's called?'

Bessie shook her head. 'That's the trouble. If she'd called, I'd be so happy, but as it is – she was on this news programme. They did an interview at Heathrow. She's in this daring new film, they said, and there's going to be a special première here. They were talking to her on the news. On my television.' And she shook her head at the enormity of it.

'Where's she staying?' Lexie said and Bessie stared at her, puzzled.

'You don't seem surprised,' she said. 'I thought you'd be surprised, upset maybe and –'

'I knew she was coming. I just didn't know when. No, don't look at me like that. I'd have told you if there'd been any point in it. They just said some time in August. And now she's here –' She lifted her chin exultantly. 'She's here!'

'And you didn't tell me.' Bessie shook her head at her, not sure whether to be hurt by the silence or not, and certainly mystified by Lexie's sudden exhilaration. 'You could have told me – this way I was so upset when I saw her on the television, and –'

'I'm sorry, Bessie darling.' Lexie hugged her. 'I'm truly sorry. But I was in such a state of – well, never mind. Look, we've got to find her. I have to find out where she's staying, talk to her –'

'But you said you knew she was coming. Didn't she tell you? Didn't she say where she'd be?'

Lexie had hurried from the kitchen to the hallway to collect the telephone books from the small table beside the front door. 'No,' she called. 'It was some public relations set-up who wrote from America – look, I'll call all the hotels. All the big ones, Claridge's, the Ritz – I'll find her, one way or another –'

She was sitting on the floor, rifling through the yellow pages, looking for the hotels listing when Bessie came hobbling out to the hallway.

'Don't,' she said gently. 'Lexie, dolly, let her come to you. Don't go running after her this way. It's not –' She stopped. 'It's not right.'

Lexie looked up at her. 'Why not?'

'Because it isn't. I don't know why exactly. I just know if you two are going to get things right she has to come to see you. Like you did when you and I – I expect you've forgotten.'

'Forgotten what?'

'You came to me, wanted me to come on tour with you. When Poppy, God rest her soul, got ill, all those years ago. And I couldn't because of Fanny being so ill and the business and all – I just couldn't. And you were so angry and we –' She shook her head, her voice suddenly lost in tears, and Lexie stared at her and then scrambled to her feet and went and put her arms about her, feeling her thin bones tremble under her hands.

'Bessie, please, don't! Don't upset yourself – I was young and stupid and – I was just thinking of the way things were then, not about – it was all so – please, don't upset yourself.'

Bessie shook her head. 'I'm not, believe me, I'm all right.' She took her handkerchief from her sleeve and blew her nose loudly and peered up at Lexie from beneath slightly puffy eyelids. 'It's just that it's the same now with you and Molly as it was for us then. It had to be you who made it right, and Max helped you to, do you remember? Now it has to be Molly who makes it right, and –' She lifted her chin then, and for a moment she looked as she had when Lexie was a small child, sharp and eager and ready to deal with anything that came her way. '– and me! I'll deal with it, make it easy for you, the way Max made it easy for us. I remember, if you don't. I'll do what Max did –'

'Bessie, I –'

'No.' Bessie said and her voice now was strong again, no longer the voice of a tired old woman, but a fighter's voice, and her eyes glittered a little. 'I've made up my mind. I'll do what Max would do. He'd want me to. So no arguing. Go finish the salad. Cut bread, put out the cheese, make yourself busy. Me, I've got phone calls to make.' She pushed past Lexie and, bending a little stiffly, picked up the telephone book from the floor where Lexie had left it and went to sit on the bottom stair with it.

Lexie stood there for a moment, uncertain and startled, and Bessie grinned at her. 'How often do I have to tell you?' she said. 'Do as you're bid!' And Lexie, hearing the voice of her long ago childhood, blinked and after a moment nodded and went obediently back to the kitchen.

# 50

She actually managed to eat some of the supper they'd prepared, but she tasted none of it, chewing mechanically and watching Bessie, trying to work out what was going on in her mind. But it wasn't possible. Bessie just sat there eating her own meal impassively.

She hadn't been like that when she'd first come back to the kitchen. She had taken herself upstairs to her bedroom to use the extension telephone beside her bed, leaving Lexie to set the table and finish making supper, while counting each ting of the bell that told her Bessie had made another call. But clearly she had found where Molly was staying, because at last she had come downstairs, moving more easily than she usually did, apparently unaware of her arthritic knees and hips in her excitement, to look at Lexie with her face alight with triumph.

'I found her,' she said. 'She's staying at the Savoy. I spoke to her – '

'You spoke – is she well? Is she – '

'She's very well, she said. She sounded well enough. She's coming here.'

'Here?' Lexie put down the teapot with a little clatter. 'When?'

'Tonight. I don't know when exactly, but tonight. As soon as she can get away, she said. She'd got to do an interview and then, as soon as she can get rid of them, she'll come. She said she was glad I called. She's decided not to come, she said, wasn't going to call or anything, but then talking to me – I told you it was right it should be me, didn't I? I told you – '

She was full of suppressed excitement. Lexie could feel it coming from her as though it were actual physical heat, and she was standing more erect than she had for a long time. Over the last year or so Bessie had let her age creep into her, had grumbled over her occasionally painful hips and knees, had begun to stoop and to hobble when she walked. But not now; now she had her head up and seemed unaware of her creaking joints, moving round the kitchen easily as she fetched milk from the refrigerator, then pulled her chair to the table and sat down, and Lexie looked at her and felt a great wave of affection, and leaned over the table and took her hand and squeezed it. Bessie peered up at her almost shyly, went a little pink and ducked her head.

They dragged out supper as long as they could, both sitting with their heads half cocked listening for a car outside, for footsteps on the front path, then washed up with great meticulousness and went to sit in the living room again. It was a measure of Bessie's state of mind that she didn't switch on her television set, and they sat there in the quiet evening trying to read newspapers and magazines and both listening, listening, listening.

At eleven Lexie decided that Molly wasn't coming after all. She contemplated that thought, trying to drum up anger at Molly's cruelty, not so much for herself as for Bessie, but all she could feel was a deep weariness, and she opened her mouth to say that it was late, they might as well go to bed, but Bessie raised her chin and said simply, 'She's here.'

Lexie stared at her and listened too, and then was aware of it. A car had pulled up outside, had switched off its engine and a door had slammed.

'It mightn't be –' she said uncertainly, but Bessie was on her feet, going out to the hallway. 'It's her,' she said confidently and opened the front door, not waiting for a ring. Lexie followed her and then stood very still in the middle of the hallway. She could see her silhouetted against the darkness of the night outside, and was for the first time for many years very aware of the crookedness of her shoulder. She looked like a caricature of herself, a drawing of the Bessie of Lexie's childhood, and she rubbed her face suddenly with both hands, needing to pull herself out of the almost trancelike state into which she had fallen.

When she looked again Molly was there bending over Bessie, hugging her, and then looking at Lexie over Bessie's shoulder. She nodded back, trying to smile but feeling her face stiff and tight.

'Hello, Molly,' she said. 'I – hello.'

'Hello, Lexie. You're looking well.'

'Thank you. You too.'

'I'm fine – fine –' She came into the living room and stood in the middle of it, looking round. She was thinner, and it suited her. Her face had sharper planes now than it had had when she'd been younger, and her body had a boniness about it that made her look eager and intense, as though she was poised for action and would at any moment be up and away, running.

'You've sure changed this place. Didn't this use to be your bedroom, Lexie? When you had the flat down here and Bessie lived upstairs?'

'We've made it into one house again,' Bessie said and bustled about, pulling chairs forward, offering cushions, urging Molly to sit down. 'Lexie put in central heating – no more coal to be carried everywhere, no more soot – and you should see the kitchen – and the bathroom! A real picture, both of them could have come out of magazines. It's lovely – lovely. There! Are you comfortable there? And – what about –' She jerked her head towards the window and Molly looked at her almost warningly and then smiled.

'The driver'll wait there for me,' she said easily. 'They've hired him for me for the whole week I'm here – he knows he has to wait. He's okay –'

'If you're sure,' Bessie said and then, a little uneasily. 'Let me go out, see he's all right, give him a cup of tea, maybe –'

'No,' Molly said sharply and then more gently, 'It's all right, Bessie, it's all right –' After a moment Bessie nodded, sat down on the edge of her chair, and folded her gnarled hands on her lap to sit and gaze at Molly, her face bright with pleasure. Lexie looked from one to the other of them, feeling herself filling with a queasy mixture of puzzlement and anger. It was as though they were having a private conversation, deliberately excluding her.

'What's the matter?' she said and knew her suspicion was in her voice and didn't care. 'Is there something that –'

'It's nothing, Bessie fussing, is all. So, Lexie. You've been busy here. Not as fancy as that apartment in Hanover Gate, though. That was a really great place. Big and cool and the park so near and all – you should have stayed there, you two –'

'We've got a park near here too,' Bessie said loyally, and then laughed. 'Though Regent's Park it isn't. Not so fancy, but still, it's nice. I didn't want to move, you know how I am. I get used to places, like to stay put, so Lexie, bless her, she came to live with me again. She's wonderful, my Lexie. Looks after me like –'

'Yes,' Molly said. She leaned back in her chair and closed her eyes for a moment and they sat and looked at her and said nothing. Lexie couldn't. She had wanted this meeting so much, had pinned so much of her own need to it, but now Molly was here she felt it all coming back again: the doubts and the resentment and the – and she had to face it. The jealousy.

Molly looked marvellous, poised and beautiful, at the height of her perfection. She's gone thirty, Lexie thought. Thirty years old and in all these years I've never been able to get it right with her. Will I ever? Will she ever forgive me for bearing her? Can I ever forgive myself for her life? If only I could start with her again, be back in New York again, having her, keeping her, not letting Barbara love her, not letting her be kept from me – why does she fill me with so much pain when I love her so much? As though she had heard the question Molly opened her eyes and looked directly

421

at her.

'We have to talk, Lexie. I'd made a plan to talk, you know that? I asked my agents to write, tell you I was coming –'

'They wrote.'

'And then decided I wouldn't do it. That I'd manage things my own way, without – and then when Bessie called, it all changed again. It was kind of meant, I guess. Though maybe – anyway we have to talk.'

'Yes,' Lexie said, and then with an enormous effort dredged the words out of herself. 'Molly, I'm sorry. I didn't know he was so ill. If I'd realized what would happen, I'd have told you where we were, you could have seen him –'

Molly closed her eyes again, sharply, as though they were on a spring, and when she spoke her voice was high and thin, not the low agreeable sound it had been. 'That, I don't want to talk about. Not ever. The only thing you can do about that is forget it. I won't talk about it. You hear me?' And now she opened her eyes again to stare at Lexie. 'D'you hear me? I never want you to talk about that again.'

'Oh, God,' Lexie said and took a deep breath and then said it again. 'Oh, God. Are you going to leave me with that for the rest of my life? Can't you forgive me for –'

'Forgiveness doesn't come into it. It's nothing to do with it. I just don't want to talk about it. What happened to Max has nothing to do with how – with the way we were, he and I. Can't you see that? We had a special thing going, and that's what I want to remember. I don't want to think about how it was afterwards. It's like the time before when I didn't know him. He's just gone back there, that's all. I don't have to think about him any other way – just the time he was with me and the time he wasn't. That's all. So don't talk about anything else. There's nothing to forgive because there was nothing that happened.'

Again there was silence and Lexie sat and looked at her, trying to see into her mind. To deny that Max was dead – how could that help her? Yet it was what she was trying to do, and suddenly she was filled with a vast pity for her daughter. To deny that Max had died was almost to deny that he had lived; she had made him into a child's fantasy, a figure who came from nowhere, went back to nowhere, and in between existed only as a phantom, a dream image, and that was infinitely sad. She opened her mouth to say so, to try to tell Molly that she understood, that it was all right, that she would never again ask for forgiveness, would never again invade her dreams with truth, when Molly sat up sharply and began to speak again.

'Listen, Lexie, there are things I have to say and I haven't a lot of time. I have to leave London tonight to – well, never mind. That isn't important. Just listen. I'm on my own. You understand? I'm on my own.'

She held out her hands to show the backs of them to Lexie. 'See? No more wedding ring. I threw it at him –' She stared down at her hands for a long moment and then shoved them deep into her pockets.

'I'm on my own because Laurence has gone. He's gone to his god-dammed Toby and as far as I'm concerned they can both rot. I did all I could to make it right, you know that? I really did. If he said jump, I jumped. If he said crawl, I crawled. I started it to please him, because he said it would keep us together, and I went through with it to please him, not to please me – I knew it'd be impossible, but he insisted. Said I'd have to go through with it, so I went through with it, and they rewrote the script to make it fit into the film and then – after all that, he told me it was no good. That he was going to Toby after all, and that was the end of it. He wants no part of her, none at all. I have to manage on my own, he said. He doesn't give a damn what I do. So I have to – I've nothing left but work, now –'

Lexie was staring at her, shaking her head, totally bewildered by the cascade of words, and she put her hands up and almost shouted, 'Molly, for God's sake stop – I can't keep up with you. What is it you're talking about? Your husband? He's left you?'

'He's left me. Of course he's left me. That's what I've been saying. He made me go through all that and now he says it sickens him. He wants nothing more to –'

'Go through what, for God's sake?' Lexie cried. 'You're not explaining properly. I can't –'

'Molly.' Bessie's voice was quiet and clear and Lexie looked at her, grateful for the calmness in her, and Bessie smiled at her briefly, reassuringly, then looked at Molly again. 'Shall I go out to the car?' she said gently and after a moment Molly nodded.

'Yes. It's – yes, I suppose so,' she said and now she

sounded tired, not angry or confused or anything else but deeply weary.

Bessie got to her feet and went out of the room. Lexie stood up to follow her, but Bessie shook her head and went out, down the dark path to the darker bulk of the car that was parked at the kerbside.

Lexie watched her go and then after a moment returned to Molly, to stand beside her chair and look down at her.

'Have you married again? Is that it? Is that who's in the car?' she said, and when Molly seemed not to hear her reached down and touched her shoulder.

At once Molly shrank back and Lexie felt her face fill with a tide of colour. She went back to her chair, feeling as though she'd been slapped, and Molly seemed to feel her distress as well as some compunction, for she leaned forward and said, 'No, I'm not marrying again. Not ever. It's not something that – there's work, you see. That's all there is. From now on I'm going to work, and it's going to be the best work anyone ever saw. You just wait and see, Lexie. You were a star of a sort, but you can't imagine the huge star I'm going to be. That's all I want, now or ever. Nothing but that. I'm going to be the biggest goddammed star there ever was and I know I can do it. As long as I don't waste my energy on people, on getting married and – who needs it? You didn't either, did you? Not for most of the time. All those years in America and then afterwards – you were on your own, weren't you? And wasn't it the best time, the time you did most in? Wasn't it? That was when you were a star, when you made it happen for you – but once you got all hooked up into people, you ruined it. Well, I'm not going to. That's why I've come, you see. You're going to have to do it for me. It doesn't matter for you any more.'

Behind them the front door slammed and there was a bustle in the hall and Lexie turned and looked to see Bessie standing there. Behind her there was a man in a chauffeur's uniform and Bessie said to him a little breathlessly, 'Just put it all down there, will you? That's it. And then, if you don't mind, wait in the car –'

The man walked over to the sofa and set down his burden. Lexie stared at it and then at Bessie and then, at last, at Molly.

Molly wasn't looking at the man. She was looking at Lexie and then, as Lexie got to her feet, clumsy with amazement,

424

she said, 'You see? I had to come here. Where else could I go? You'll have to take her on just for a while, anyway. Later, maybe, I can try again. Later –' Her voice trailed off and her eyes slipped away from Lexie's face.

Bessie bent over the sofa and very carefully unbuttoned the cover on the carrycot the chauffeur had set down. She reached in and carefully brought out the child who was lying in it.

'Her name's Sophy,' she said breathlessly. 'Molly told me on the phone. Her name's Sophy. She's three months old. Imagine. Three months old –' She held the child out to Lexie and put her in her arms, and Lexie stared at her, feeling her mouth go dry with amazement.

'You knew?' was all she could say, stupidly, looking from the child to Bessie and back again. 'You knew?'

'Only when I phoned,' Bessie said, and laughed and leaned forward to touch the baby's cheek. She was half asleep, her eyes blinking in the brightness of the light, but she roused at Bessie's touch and turned her head towards the finger, the small mouth grimacing and pursing. 'Look, she's hungry –'

'Everything you'll need is in the carrycot – at the bottom there,' Molly said and stood up. She still didn't look at the baby, or at Lexie now, only at Bessie. 'I told the nurse to fix everything you'd need for tomorrow. There's a vacuum flask with the milk – you'll see if you look. I have to go now.'

'*Go?*' Lexie said and twisted her head to stare at her. 'Go? But you've – what about her?' She held the baby close to her with a sudden instinctive movement and the baby whimpered. Without thinking Lexie began to rock her, bouncing her gently in her arms.

'I told you,' Molly said. 'I told you – I'm going to work. It's better that she should be with her own. You and Bessie – better that way, Laurence doesn't care, he'll never care. He'll never go looking for her the way Max – he doesn't care. But you do, don't you? You'll look after her till I can work things out –'

'But –' Lexie said, and then had to swallow to get the words out. 'But you can't just give her to me this way and then go away! You can't!'

'Why not? You gave me to Barbara, didn't you? I know you didn't go away, but it was easier for you. You could work in New York, and you did. You went away to work. It

425

didn't make any difference that you came to the apartment to sleep and eat – you went away to work. It was like you weren't there, I always knew that. It was Barbara who was there, who looked after me. Well, now I have to go and work. And there she is and what do I do with her? Take her away on the road with me, on location, give her to a nurse to look after? I've done that already. Three nurses there've been since she was born. Three – they don't stay. They can't understand about work and they can't keep up with me and they don't stay. I was going to try with them again, see if I could make it work, but I know I can't. And Bessie phoned and I knew that was the way it had to be. You and her. So here she is. And I have to go. I'll come back when I can – whenever I can. I don't know when – there's work – just like there was for you, there's work. I have to go, for Christ's sake!' And she almost shouted it, staring at Lexie with her eyes glittering. 'You hear me? I have to –'

There was a silence that seemed to ring in their ears, and then with a brusque little movement Molly went to the door, where she stopped for a moment. But she came back and this time she did look at the baby in Lexie's arms. She said nothing, just stared down at the small face, and the baby seemed to look gravely at her, her dark blue eyes fixed on her mother's and then she smiled, a wide gummy grimace that creased the round cheeks into little cushions of pleasure. Molly put out her hand as though she were going to touch her and then turned and went. They heard her footsteps as she ran down the path and then the slam of the car door.

After a little while the baby began to cry.

# Epilogue

They were sitting in a row on the wall, eating sweets which Josh had stolen from the shop on the corner. They'd said Sophy could have the same share as Josh, because if she hadn't been so good at pretending that she had something in her eye and crying so dreadfully the shopkeeper would have noticed what Josh was doing behind his back while he bent over her, but she said she didn't want them. It was good being like that, she'd discovered, doing things people didn't expect you to do, and not doing things they did expect you to do. It made them interested in you all the time, and she liked that. People were best when they were interested in you, in what you were doing and saying.

Now she sat and watched them eating the sweets, swinging her legs and liking the feeling of emptiness she had. The sweets would have been good, but the empty feeling was better. It made her feel strong and in charge of herself and the boys too, and that was better than sweets could ever be.

Josh caught her watching him and held out the last piece of chocolate. 'Go on,' he said. 'It's nice,' and again she shook her head.

'I've already said no. You shouldn't keep asking people after they said no. It's stupid.'

'No, it isn't. People change their minds.'

'I don't.'

'Yes, you do,' Daniel said and licked the inside of the paper that had wrapped the chocolate, chasing the last crumbs with his long pointed tongue. 'You said you was goin' to stay out of school and go to the pictures, and you didn't. You went to Madame Tussaud's instead. That was changing your mind.'

'No, it wasn't,' she said witheringly. 'It's having a better idea. That's what I did. I had a better idea, so I went and did that instead. It's easier to get into Madame Tussaud's for nothing when all those stupid tourists are there, and there's a lot there now it's summer, so doing that was a better idea. I have better ideas all the time.'

'So do I,' said Quentin. 'All the time. I've got one now.

Let's go and be Neil Armstrong doing giant steps down at the playground.' He jumped down from the wall and began to walk stiff-leggedly and slowly, in a circle, jerking his arms as he went.

'That's not how spacemen walk!' Sophy said and laughed, a clear ringing sort of laugh, and she listened to it and was pleased. She'd been practising that laugh a long time and now it was sounding good, just as though she hadn't practised it at all.

'I'll show you.' She jumped down from the wall and began to move like the Apollo Eleven spacemen she had seen on television. Her arms moved heavily and slowly and her legs rolled under her as she thought herself into being Neil Armstrong, first man on the moon. She was heavy, heavy, heavy, heavy and there was no air and the whole world was watching her on their televisions, taking giant steps for mankind –

'That's right, that's it!' Josh was crowing. 'Look, Quentin, she makes you look like a caterpillar, *that's* the way it is –' He clapped his hands and jumped down beside her, trying to imitate her, and then Daniel came too as Quentin watched, scowling, and some people walking along the path towards the playground stopped and watched and laughed. It was good, Sophy decided, very good. And time to stop, because if she went on too long they'd stop looking, and she ran back to sit on the wall, while the others went on pretending to be spacemen very badly and the passers by went away, bored. I've got it right again, she thought, and squeezed her arms against her side, feeling good.

Soon Josh came and sat beside her again. She let him sit close enough for his bare arm to touch hers, and she laughed inside herself because she knew he liked her a lot and sitting that way made him feel good. He was twelve and knew about liking girls more than Daniel and Quentin did. They were only ten, as she was, but rather stupid. Girls of ten, especially a girl like Sophy, were much better than boys of that age, she decided. Even twelve-year-olds were a bit dull and, bored suddenly with Josh sitting there beside her and breathing unevenly the way he was, she jumped down.

'I think I'm going home,' she announced, rubbing her dusty hands on the seat of her jeans and then through her hair. She liked to see her curly hair all fluffed up: it made her look more interesting. 'Gran'ma'll be waiting for me.'

'You never care whether she's waiting or not,' Josh said. 'You never do. You said you do what you like, all the time.'

'So I do. Only I have to tell her something –' She nodded mysteriously and then laughed. 'I have to tell her something I want to do. She's going to make a fuss about it, but I'm going to do it. So I better go home now. It'll be easier if I do.'

'Why?'

'Because she gets miserable when I'm out a long time, because my Auntie Bessie died. Ever since then she gets ever so miserable if I'm out.' She lifted her eyebrows at him turning her mouth down expressively. 'What can I do? She *needs* me.'

'My mum says your Auntie Bessie was a hundred years old when she died,' Quentin said suddenly across from the pathway. 'Was she a hundred years old?'

Sophy considered for a moment. Auntie Bessie had been eighty-eight when she'd died. She remembered that because it was such a nice neat number, but it wasn't as interesting a number as a hundred. 'Yes,' she said casually. 'She was a hundred all right. And a bit more.' Again she ran her hands through her hair and turned to go, but Josh jumped down off the wall to join her.

'I'll walk there with you,' he said. 'Go on, you two. I don't want you. Hop it –' Daniel and Quentin looked at him doubtfully for a moment and then made faces, but they stayed where they were as Josh took hold of Sophy's arm and began to walk with her towards the park gates.

'What is it you're going to tell your gran'ma?' he said after a while as she showed no sign of responding to his hand on her arm. 'Is it good or bad?'

'It's good for me, but she won't like it,' Sophy said, and to Josh's delight tightened her arm against her side in a sudden little spurt of excitement, so that his hand was held close against her warm body. 'But all the same, I'm going to do it.'

'Do what?'

'Promise you won't tell?'

'See this wet, see this dry, cut my throat if I tell a lie,' Josh said at once, licking a finger and holding it out to her and then wiping it across his neck. 'Tell us.'

'You know that programme they do on television? On channel nine? The one the children go on and dance and that?

429

And they measure the applause and then they say who's won? And then the winner gets on other television shows? Well, I'm going to do that.'

He stopped still in the middle of the path and pulled on her arm so that she had to stop too.

'You're not!'

'I am,' she said. 'I've decided. I think it's the best idea I've ever had.'

'When are you going on?'

'Oh, I don't know! It isn't fixed up yet. But they'll let me, once they've seen what I can do. First I'll sing, and then I'll do a little dance, and while I'm dancing I'm going to tell funny things. Not jokes, just say things to make them laugh. I've worked it out. It'll be good.'

'Yes,' Josh said after a moment and then followed her as she began to walk again. 'Yes, I expect so. You're ever so good at things like that. How did you fix it? I mean, to be on the television?'

'I haven't yet,' she said. 'But I will, once I've told Gran'ma and she's got used to the idea. She'll have to get used to it. I've made up my mind it's going to happen, so it will. I can always make things happen that way, just making up my mind. You know that, don't you?' And she looked sideways at him and grinned wickedly and he went very red. Indeed she could. She'd made up her mind to it that he would like her best of all the girls who played in the park, long before he'd even noticed her, and she'd made it happen, just the way she wanted to, and now he thought of no one but her, all day long and most of the night too. And she knew it.

'She won't let you,' he said after a moment. 'Will she? My mum wouldn't let me.'

'Because you wouldn't be any good,' Sophy said. 'But I'm very good, and Gran'ma knows it as well as I do.' She laughed then. 'She keeps trying not to know, but she can't help it. She used to be a dancer too, you see. She told me, and I've seen photographs and everything. So she can't stop me. I won't let her.'

They'd reached the park gates now and she stopped and pulled her arm away from his grasp. 'Go away now, Josh. I don't want you to come any further. I have to go home on my own.'

'See you tomorrow, by the swings?' he said hopefully, yet

knowing he was wasting his breath. 'Same time?'

'Maybe,' she said, and began to skip away down the pavement towards her house. 'Maybe. But maybe not. I'll think about it,' and she went, not looking back at him, just dancing along the pavement, her long slender legs in their tight jeans flashing and her dark hair swinging on her shoulders. He watched her all the way, saw her go across the road, dodging the buses and the cars, and into her own gateway, and went on watching for a long time after the front door had closed behind her.

And then, kicking a stone along the road as he went, he made his own moody way home. Maybe she'd come tomorrow, and maybe she wouldn't. No one could guess what Sophy would do. That was the trouble with her; she made you think about her all the time, made you notice her and then drove you mad thinking about her. And once she knew you were thinking about her, she stopped being interested in you. It hurt dreadfully and yet it was the best thing about her.

Sophy, he thought as he pushed open his own gate and went up the path to the front door. Sophy. I wonder what Sophy will do tomorrow?